MIA

MIA

A novel by Joseph Sciuto

IGUANA

Publisher: Meghan Behse
Editor: Lee Parpart
Front cover design: Meghan Behse

ISBN 978-1-77180-401-1 (paperback)
ISBN 978-1-77180-402-8 (epub)
ISBN 978-1-77180-403-5 (Kindle)

This is an original print edition of *Mia*.

The following individuals have provided me with countless knowledgeable and fun-filled hours of enjoyment talking about the wonderful game of baseball:

Carl Rabvosky, forever in my thoughts; Vince O'Donnell; Jay Santiago; Tommy Lombino, the 1986 trip to Anaheim to see Boston and the Angels; James Pileski; Randall Yamanouye; Tom Mankiewicz and his lovely assistant, Annie; Willie, I loved our trips to the Hall of Fame; Cornelius Mohabir; Harry Dillard Hunt, the biggest St. Louis fan I have ever known; James W. Smith Jr.; Bo Queen; and finally, Dr. Ronald Cotliar and his two sons, Jonathan and Steven, our conversations during the Joe Torre era will always bring a smile to my face.

CHAPTER ONE

One of the first memories I have is of sitting in my grandmother's living room in the Bronx watching the great Sandy Koufax striking out one Yankee after another to win Game 4 of the 1963 World Series for the Dodgers, thus completing a sweep of the mighty New York Yankees after the Yankees had won two consecutive World Series titles in '61 and '62.

My parents, aunts and uncles and my grandmother bowed their heads in sorrow and disbelief. It was as though a sacrilegious, blasphemous ritual, one that could be punished only by eternal damnation, had just been witnessed and verified by the Vatican.

The strangest thing about that memory is that I was not yet born.

**

I felt like a character in a Frank Sinatra song: down and out. Life was full of laughter and tears, sadness and hope, but through it all I kept my head held high.

Of course, life could have been a lot worse, but at that moment it felt like Old Blue Eyes was speaking directly to me through my car radio. You see, I had just quit the job I had for the last twenty-five years … the job that I had dreamed of having since I was a little boy growing up in the Bronx. Actually, that's a lie. The job I *really* wanted was playing center field for the New York Yankees, but after a brief, less-than-illustrious career in the majors, playing for a team other than the Yankees, I hung up my glove and switched over to the suit-and-tie end of the business.

It was a natural fit, and since I was one of the few major leaguers with a college degree, it wasn't such a difficult transition. I didn't even have to move; the team that let me go hired me back as a junior executive, and that was that. We were in a rotten market, sandwiched between two established teams with a loyal fan base that went back ten generations. We were lucky to draw a million fans a year at our ballpark, which was a paltry number compared to the three million fans in attendance these two teams pulled in per year at their stadiums. Our TV and cable contracts were a third the size of most major league team contracts, and our salaries were the pits. What the New York Yankees paid for two superstars a year was our entire team's annual budget.

Even so, I had a pretty good career. In two years, I went from junior executive to General Manager of Baseball Operations. In the first year alone, our overall win total jumped an amazing twenty-five games. After three years, we were consistently making the playoffs, and over my entire twenty-three years as GM, we made it to the World Series five times and won the title three times. All of this without ever once having more than a seventy-million-dollar budget to work with. To put that in perspective, the Yankees, Red Sox, Dodgers and Cubs have yearly budgets of more than two hundred million.

I don't know if it was me, divine intervention or our great scouting and farm systems, but in those twenty-three years we put together some terrific teams. We'd start with a bunch of so-called rejects — players let go by other teams — and put them on a field with a bunch of talented newbies, then wait for the magic to happen. More often than not, it did. Everyone just seemed to blend together and give us a winning combination. We had some wonderful managers who really knew how to get the most out of our players. They were able to relate to the players and make them play as a unit.

I was on the cover of *Sports Illustrated* more times than most superstars in all the major sports. It was embarrassing. No matter how many times I told the press that I was a small piece of the puzzle, they insisted I was a genius. A "baseball wizard," they called me. They wrote books about me and even made a movie, which was a total flop. I guess my appeal didn't cross over to the big screen.

For a long time, it was like living a dream. Then one day I woke up and realized that my success, and even my luck, had come at a huge cost. Take my parents, for instance. They were thrilled at my success, but it meant we hardly ever saw each other, and in the end, I wasn't even there to say good-bye to them when they died. Both times, when the players were on winter vacations, I was down in Central America scouting Latino prospects. By the time I got the news, both my parents were on the way to the funeral home where a few friends paid their respects. Then they were on their way to the cemetery. I made it to their gravesides just before their bodies were lowered into the ground. My final farewell to the two people who sacrificed everything for me came as their caskets disappeared into the cold, unforgiving earth.

Friends tried to console me by reminding me how much I did for my parents when they were alive. True, I made sure they never had to worry about money, and I begged them to come live with me in California, but even that was just selfishness on my part. All their friends and the few relatives we had left were all in the Bronx. Having me home for Christmas or their birthdays or their fortieth wedding anniversary would have meant the world to them. They would never admit it, but I could sense it when talking to them over the phone. What I did for my parents was what was expected of any decent son, but when it came to the really important things, I was missing in action. The excuse was always work, and it was a shameful excuse, considering the position I held.

There were other costs too — like never having time to start a family of my own. The few serious relationships I had with women always ended poorly. Work always interfered. When the baseball season ended, my workload only increased … I'd get hung up in negotiations with greedy agents, winter meetings, and the never-ending demands of scouting young talent around the world that we could purchase for cheap. It was one of the only ways we could compete with teams like the Yankees and Cubs.

***

I pulled into the parking lot of the Starlight bar and parked. Despite its bright and shiny name, the Starlight was a bit of a dump, inside and out. But it felt like home, in that it reminded me of a bar right in the Bronx. During the day, it had its regular customers whose average age was "ancient." At night the place transformed into a hip gathering spot for the twenty-something set, with hot girls prancing around and guys playing pool at a lone, beer-stained table. At night, the jukebox blasted loud unnerving music by bands who I'd been reliably told belonged to the Seattle grunge scene, whereas the daytime crowd preferred Nat King Cole.

At fifty years old, I preferred the daytime atmosphere … just like I did at forty and thirty-five. The barmaid was a Californian beauty named Lauren. She had been the daytime bartender for nearly fourteen years. Now, at thirty-five, she was still gorgeous, if you could look past the bruises that occasionally bloomed around her face, courtesy of an abusive husband who she refused to leave. Of course, I'd never learned to ignore them.

There was a time I had a serious crush on her, but after an extended trip out of town, I came back to a jubilant barmaid with a ring on her finger and three months pregnant. She was an aspiring actress and met her future husband in an acting class. Naturally, he never landed a role and had an aversion to any type of work that didn't involve the film industry. He did specialize in one thing, and that was beating the shit out of his lovely wife and occasionally landing a punch or two on the faces of their two children.

Johnny was a real gem and Lauren simply could not leave him. Behind the bar, she was a tough, no-nonsense chick who could exchange barbs with the best of them, but in the grips of her supposed soul mate she was pure mush, despite repeated promises that she had had enough and was going to take the children and leave.

Almost as soon as I sat down at the bar, Lauren plunked an ice-cold Budweiser in front of me. This was before I could comment on the latest bruises on her face, which were so bad that blue-and-red patches shone through what looked like three extra layers of makeup. Catching me staring at her, she raised one finger to her mouth and looked at me as if to say, "Please, don't go there."

When she turned and walked away, I was left admiring the view. What a wonderful view it was. I was pretty sure it was also covered with bruises, but unlike her face, she was able to hide any damage behind a tight-fitting pair of blue jeans.

I had offered to help her many times, but she'd always use the same comeback. Unless I was willing to pay for a divorce, put a ring on her finger and adopt a six- and seven-year-old, she didn't have any real good options. Strange, I saw it from a totally different perspective, but then I wasn't the one married to him.

In the world I grew up in there was nothing more cowardly than a man hitting a woman. My father wouldn't raise a hand to my mother if she were sticking a knife in him.

Even so, domestic violence was nothing new to me, and I did what I could to stop it from creeping onto our teams. Every contract I signed included a clause that plainly stated that if any player of ours was guilty of rape or of hitting a wife, girlfriend or any of their children, their contract would be immediately terminated. I didn't give a shit if they were hitting .350 with 120 RBIs and thirty home runs. They were gone.

I watched Lauren move around the bar. After touching base with some of the regulars and refilling and replacing empty glasses and bottles, she plunked herself onto a stool behind the bar, next to me. She bumped her shoulder into mine like an old pal, then grabbed a peanut from a bowl and started to crush it with her lacquered thumbnail.

"So what brings you in so early?"

"You, of course. What other reason would I have to come into this dump?"

"Surely, you're not that desperate. You know, they just opened a new place not far from where you live, where all the bartenders are hot, barely clad young women. With your resumé, you should have no problem scoring."

"If nothing else, I'm loyal. You should know that about me."

"What, the little guy not working anymore? You know, they have pills for that type of dysfunction."

"Cute! Very cute! Besides, I quit my job today."

"So the Yankees finally called. Please, please, take me to New York with you."

"If I knew that is all it would take to get you away from that piece-of-shit-husband of yours, I would put you and the kids up at the Plaza. And no, the Yankees did not call."

"So you finally went to a team that will pay you the ten million a year you deserve?"

"No, but I am quite sure there are a few offers on my phone. What team would you like to see me go to?"

"One of the two other teams in this town. Surely, you don't think I want to lose the best tipper to come into this bar, even if it is only a few times a month."

"Ah," I said, poking her in the arm. "So it's all about the money? I knew it all along."

I was expecting her to swat at me and laugh, but she went quiet, and when our eyes met, I was sure she was about to cry. She swiveled away and popped off the stool, then stood there, looking down at the half-crushed peanut between her fingers.

"Hey," I said, swiveling to face her. "What'd I say?"

"Nothing," she said, still looking down. Then she tossed the peanut back on the bar, used one finger to poke at my knee and walked away.

"Huh," I said to myself.

As she pushed through the swinging door to get back behind the bar, I could swear I saw tears rolling down her face. But by then she had already picked up a cloth and was wiping off the necks of a row of bottles of Scotch, with her back turned to me. I was trying to enjoy the view again, but she wasn't making it easy. Something was wrong, and her silence was giving off sparks.

I moved down three stools to where she was now scrubbing away at a spot on the mirror behind the bar. I stared at her reflection until she finally saw me. Her hand hung there in mid-mirror. She was caught. Those were tears, all right.

"Lauren," I said. "Get over here."

She dropped her head and her hand, put the cloth next to a bottle of whiskey and wiped her fingers under both eyes before turning to look at me.

I looked up at her and gestured to her battered face.

"That's a pretty good makeup job, but it's not perfect," I said.

She started to turn away again, but I gently caught hold of her elbow.

The pain and hurt in her eyes were terrifying, yet I did not let go and she did not offer any resistance. "It's not too late, Lauren."

Tears rolled down her cheeks and I reached up to wipe them away. She grasped my hands and clasped them inside hers. "You should have let me know."

"I didn't think it was fair to you."

She thought about this quietly for a minute, then walked over to the fridge and came back with another ice-cold Budweiser.

"I'm going away for a long time, and no, it is not to meet with owners from other teams."

"You're always going away, Joe." She looked at the TV and at an ESPN reporter. The reporter was talking about my resignation.

"They already have you going to ten different teams. It must be nice to be so highly regarded and respected."

I reached into my pocket and took out a faded business card with a private phone number written across it. "You can always reach me at this number. The only other people to have that number were my parents." She took the card and placed it inside her pants pocket.

Over the next few hours I had about ten more beers. I had a few minor conversations with some of the other regulars, but mostly I kept my eye on Lauren as she moved around the place, taking care of everyone. At the end of the night, we met at the bar again, and I took out my money clip, which had about two thousand dollars in it, and handed it to her.

"There's enough there for a couple of weeks at a hotel. If you ever need help, and I mean *ever*, I want you to call that number." She looked down at the money and back up at me, her mouth hanging open and her eyes misting up again.

"I don't know what to say."

"Then don't say anything," I said. Then I kissed her on the cheek and whispered, "I love you, Lauren." She looked at me like she'd just been hit, but her expression softened, and she let me go.

I walked out of the bar just as the younger crowd started arriving. It was already dark outside. I decided to walk home and pick up the car in the morning. Suddenly, I heard Lauren's voice calling after me. I turned and looked back at her figure standing in the shadows of the bar. From a distance, she looked no different than the gorgeous young woman I'd met years earlier. She ran toward me and threw her arms around my neck, almost throwing me off balance.

"Please, please, don't go away for very long," she whispered into my ear. She was still holding on to me.

I held her and whispered back, "Just don't lose that phone number and I will never be far away."

When she finally let go, I reached across and ran my hands through her soft blonde hair, then tucked one of her long front locks behind one ear. Then I turned and started to walk home.

CHAPTER TWO

I crossed the street and walked down the side streets of Studio City toward my home. Unlike many of the ballplayers and other sports executives, I decided not to live by the beach or in Beverly Hills or in Bel Air. Studio City was small, and unlike many parts of Los Angeles, it was not pretentious or gaudy. In many respects, it reminded me of Throggs Neck back in the Bronx, where I grew up and where my parents' home still stood, transferred to me in their will. Even though it had been nearly five years since their deaths, I had never even considered selling the home. The pride and care that they put into that home and the love they had for each other and for their only child was a constant reminder of everything good in the world.

Besides, if the Yankees ever called, I would have a lovely home to live in, not far from the stadium.

It was another beautiful Southern California night. The sky was clear, littered with stars, and there was a tinge of a chill in the air. It was the middle of October, and whereas most of the country was getting ready for winter, the citizens of Southern California would be hustling through seventy- and eighty-degree days and an occasional night that might dip below sixty.

Normally, at this time of year, I would be just about ready to pack my bags and head down to scout Latino players playing in the summer leagues in Central America. Then I would take a short break and head back to the States to attend the winter meetings in early December. Those would be held in some ungodly place, like Chicago, where winter begins sometime in September and where, by early December, the whole town is already in a deep freeze.

Depending on the year, I would either have owners and GMs knocking on my door consistently or not at all. In a year when I had a homegrown superstar, the talks would be nonstop. I would have scouted some kid from Panama or Puerto Rico, who I'd been tracking since he was about thirteen years old, or I'd go under the radar and find a young player in Cuba. If they were fresh and eligible for free agency in a year or two, the managers would be circling like piranhas. The other teams knew we were too poor to sign the best young players when the Yankees and Red Sox could offer financial security for the next hundred and fifty-five years. So the teams that felt they were legitimate contenders would offer half their star prospects in their farm systems to get the services of this so-called superstar, who they were certain could help lead them to a title in the next year or two.

This was the hardest part of the job. These kids were like family to me. I'd known them for nearly half their lives and exchanged Christmas gifts with their families. Many of them were living in unimaginable poverty. How could I, in good conscience, try to hold on to them by appealing to their sense of loyalty when we would be woefully underpaying them? And even if I had no conscience, their agents had already brainwashed them with promises of mountains of gold. There was no way I was going to get in the way of their future riches.

We always parted on good terms and with tears in our eyes, and I made an effort to keep in touch with the players and their families.

On the flip side of the coin, I usually ended up with at least two or three top prospects that, in turn, helped to keep us in contention year after year. When that happened, I didn't have to worry about them going anywhere for at least five years.

So in years when I didn't have any homegrown superstars with two years or less on their contracts, I was the one reaching out to other teams as they tried to unload the "deadwood" that was keeping them from a championship. Players who signed extended luxury contracts but who never lived up to expectations had to go somewhere. If these under-performers had two years left on their contracts and were still owed twenty million, I could usually get them for about four million, with the selling team picking up the remaining sixteen million on their contracts. It was like walking into a bookstore, hitting the bargain table and picking up a bunch of classics selling for ninety-nine cents. Occasionally, the classics still had bite in them, even if the average reader wasn't smart enough to appreciate their undying genius.

Quite often a player didn't live up to expectations simply because of the market they were playing in. Playing in New York, Boston or Chicago was quite different than playing for a small market team. In the mega-sports cities, every mistake you made was magnified a thousand times. Many talented ballplayers withered under the pressure and never reached their full potential. Playing for a team like ours and being surrounded by two teams that grabbed all the headlines, there was very little pressure. Some of these same ballplayers who underperformed in bigger markets had their greatest years playing for us. The deadwood once again blazed gloriously under kinder conditions.

I entered my house and marveled, not for the first time, at how uninviting and even unfamiliar it felt. For all its luxury, this house had always felt about as welcoming as a rundown hotel room with dirty bedsheets and no air conditioning. The house itself was quite large, with five bedrooms and six bathrooms. It measured five thousand square feet — or so my real estate agent told me. I never checked. It had a large swimming pool, which I still hadn't used, a basketball court and a batting cage.

Behind the pool sat a guesthouse, with three more bedrooms and two bathrooms. It was the guesthouse that sold me on the entire property. I figured that my parents could always use the excuse that they felt like intruders living in a house with my wife and two children (the family that never materialized), but with a large guesthouse they had less of an argument if they ever needed to come live with us. Of course, once I got them into the guesthouse, I would work on convincing them to move into the big house with all of us. I had the whole thing worked out in my head.

I opened the refrigerator. As always, it was well stocked with beer and also included a few items of processed food that I could throw into the microwave if I got hungry. I decided to skip the food and go with more beer. I cracked open a cold Budweiser, walked into the living room and turned on the TV. It was programmed to ESPN (the worldwide leader in sports news), but I quickly changed the channel and started watching Ingrid Bergman in the George Cukor classic *Gaslight*. Since my teens, I'd had a major crush on Ms. Bergman, and I'd never gotten over it. I had always referred to her simply as "the face." Her oval face was pure perfection, like Ken Griffey's swing.

Out of the corner of my right eye, I could see the flashing red light of my answering machine. I reached over and saw that I had sixty-three unheard messages. Combined with whatever was on my cell phone, which had been turned off all day, I probably had over a hundred messages. I would answer all of them tomorrow morning, and I took comfort in the fact that many of the messages were probably from the same people. Despite my resignation and my passionate, unequivocal statement that I would not be going to work for any other team, that didn't stop the offers from coming in. Baseball types tended to think that if you put enough money on the table you could lure anybody back — even a corpse.

But there was something they didn't know and could never compute. I no longer cared about money. I had enough of the stuff to live three lifetimes, and coming from a middle-class family, I never felt that I lacked for anything that I really needed. I never went hungry, like so many of the Latino ballplayers I scouted over the years. I never had to make a glove out of a Cheerios box. I never had to make a baseball out of discarded yarn.

Ballplayers who came from such wretched backgrounds always feared that one day they might have to return to such conditions. No amount of money was ever enough to subdue that fear. I totally got that.

As I lay there on the couch letting the familiar scenes of *Gaslight* play before my eyes, I began to be aware of a sense of ease that was seeping into my limbs for the first time in years — decades, probably. It felt really good to just lie there, gazing at the beautiful Ms. Bergman while drinking a couple of ice-cold beers and not having to worry about negotiations, statistics, drug tests and traveling to lovely Chicago in a month or so.

CHAPTER THREE

I woke up at around six in the morning, still on the couch, with the TV blaring an infomercial, and surrounded by empty beer cans. I got up and shook off the stiffness from the night before, then hauled myself into the kitchen and made a strong pot of coffee. The first sips of a good dark roast made everything right for the moment. I put on a pair of dungaree cutoffs, a faded Yankees T-Shirt and a pair of running sneakers. I grabbed my headphones, set my device to the twenty-four-hour Beatles station and walked out of the house, where I did a few stretches and set out on my regular morning run.

For a guy who likes to drink my weight in beer, I've managed to stay fit. But that wasn't always the case. After retiring, prematurely, as a player, I started to gain weight at an alarming rate. Suddenly all those beers were catching up with me, especially since I was no longer working out for two or more hours a day.

I don't know how much weight I packed on, but it all came to a head when my lovely mother, who never said an unkind word about anybody, asked me when I went home for Christmas if I planned on playing Santa Claus that year. After realizing what she had said, she blushed like a little girl and started apologizing. I hugged her tightly and said, "Maybe this year, but not next year or any year after that." As she walked away, I realized more than ever why my father was so madly in love with her. She was undeniably beautiful — an olive-skinned Italian stunner with large expressive brown eyes — but it was her kindness and compassion and her unconditional love for family and friends that endeared her to everyone and inspired such fierce loyalty from me and my father.

After that, I got serious about my fitness. As soon as I got back home after visiting my parents that Christmas, I started running every morning, regardless of where I was or what the weather was doing. I could be in Central America, Chicago or New York, and it could be raining, snowing or boiling hot, and I'd still be out there, putting in my miles. I never had much of a choice in the matter. I wasn't going to give up beer, so I became an obsessive runner and, truth be told, I liked running, especially once I finished.

As I put my headphones down over my ears, the Beatles' "I'm Only Sleeping" came on, and I ran into the early Southern California sunshine, past the sign for Universal Studios, past the CBS lot, onto Moorpark and up toward the Starlight bar. I stopped in the parking lot, got into my car and drove back home.

Once I got there, I pulled my SUV out of the garage and parked my car in its place. I took a shower and took about an hour to answer all of the phone messages with more or less the same message: "I appreciate your interest in my services, but right now I just have to figure out what I want to do with the rest of my life. I will be gone for a while, but once I get back, I hope we can keep in touch. Grateful as always, Joe."

An agent usually handled this type of stuff, but after my playing days were over, I dropped the agent who was representing me, and I handled my own contract negotiations and all business related to me personally. My life was already filled with complaints and maneuvering from greedy agents representing the players. I didn't need one representing me. Even so, I always gave good recommendations to honest agents and steered them in the direction of our young players. I was always on the lookout for agents who would put the players' interests ahead of their own.

After showering and grabbing a suitcase from my bedroom, I placed the bag in the back of my SUV and pulled out of the driveway. The one good thing about traveling so much was that I always kept a spare suitcase fully packed with everything I needed so I could leave town on a moment's notice without the hassle of packing or the worry that I might leave anything behind.

CHAPTER FOUR

I stopped at Du-par's Restaurant and Bakery, a diner not far from where I live, to have breakfast. The early morning crowd had already scattered, and there were only a few customers in the place. I looked at the menu, decided on what I was going to have, and before I looked up, the waitress, Martha, was standing beside me ready to take my order. She was in her late thirties or early forties and slightly overweight but with an appealing and pleasant face. She spoke softly, which was unusual for a waitress at a busy diner, and she had a lovely smile. She took my order, and as she was walking away, she turned and asked, "Are you the general manager of—"

"Yes, that's me."

"Sorry, but I should have said former general manager. Is it really true?"

"Yes, I most definitely resigned."

"My son and I are big fans. I try to take him to as many games as possible but sometimes it's hard. We do watch all the games on TV. All day yesterday, he kept on telling me what a disaster it was going to be this year without you."

"Well you tell him not to worry because there are some really talented people left behind and I expect them to do a better job than I ever did. The team is going to do well next year. How old is your son?"

"He's nine," she said. "He's a really good kid. A sweet kid."

"And does he play little league?"

"He used to," she said, looking down and not moving.

"What happened?"

She paused, as if she was unsure how much to share. Finally, she said, "Last year he was diagnosed with a fairly serious disease, so he was forced to sit out a year."

"I'm so sorry to hear that."

"Thank you," she said, then visibly pushed herself into a brighter mood. "But he's a strong kid and he promises me that he will be back next year."

"Of course he will," I said.

She was trying not to cry and in a barely audible voice said, "I'm sorry. I'll put your order in right away and come back with your coffee."

I took out a pad and a pen that I always carried with me in the case that held my laptop. Martha came back with my coffee and I asked, "What's your son's name?"

"Stevie," she replied.

"Short for Stephen?"

"Exactly."

"That was my father's name," I told her. "He and mother were my good-luck charms." I wrote *Stevie* on my pad and Martha went off to get my breakfast. I wrote the child a letter, short on sentiment but loaded with inspiration and the positive outlook I forecasted for the team next season. I finished the letter by quoting the famous Hall of Famer and all-around wonderful person, Ernie Banks, who said, "Never stop dreaming, because when you stop dreaming you stop living." Then I wrote, "I expect to see you playing Little League next year. All my best, Joe."

Martha came back with my breakfast and a fresh cup of coffee. I handed her the letter for Stevie and, like a concerned mother, she asked if she could read it before giving it to her son.

I replied, "I would expect nothing less from a loving mother."

She walked away and after about five minutes she came back to check if everything was good with my breakfast. I told her everything was great, and she affectionately squeezed my arm and said, "Thank you!"

I finished my breakfast and reached back into my pack and pulled out three thousand dollars. Martha cleaned off the table and came back with the bill. She told me I had to pay at the front of the restaurant and thanked me once again for the letter. I stood up and took her hand and placed the three thousand dollars into her palm and closed her fingers around the money. "That's for you and your son." She looked at me and didn't say a word as I collected all my belongings, paid the bill and walked out of the diner and toward my SUV.

A few moments later Martha came running up to me in the parking lot and said, "I can't take all this money."

I smiled and told her the negotiations were final and there was no going back.

"Why?" she asked pathetically.

"Because every kid deserves a chance to pursue his dreams, especially a fan of our team."

I got into my vehicle as I watched Martha stand there, staring, with her hands by her sides. Eventually she turned slowly and walked back into the diner, looking over her shoulder twice as she did. Suddenly, I became deaf and blind to all outside stimuli as a clamor of indistinguishable voices inside my head battered my ears and a parade of distorted images seemed to pass before my eyes. I shuddered terribly as I grasped the steering wheel tightly, and like a horrifying dream, it all disappeared as the sun's glare touched my face like the gentle touch of a mother's hand.

I drove out of the parking lot and made my way to the bank a few blocks away. Between Lauren and Martha, I had given away all my cash. It was easy to be generous when you had so much money. It was much more difficult to be charitable with your time and your presence. I took out five thousand dollars and, without thinking, asked for the money in all hundred-dollar bills.

I got back into my SUV and drove off to destinations unknown. I passed by the lovely North Hollywood Park and its well-manicured baseball fields. Occasionally, during the off-season, when I wasn't off in Central America scouting, I would go and watch my friend's children play little league baseball. He was a wonderful relief pitcher and an even better human being, and I cherished his company.

As the bright green of the field practically leaped out to greet me, I thought about that one pitch, that one stinking pitch that ruined his life. It was perfectly placed on the outside corner of the plate. It was Game 7 of the playoffs, and we were ahead by a run in the bottom of the ninth, with two men out and a man on first. The batter swung late but was able to get enough wood on the ball to send it 310 feet down the line and into the stands in left field. With that, we lost an opportunity to go to the World Series.

In the end, this meant shit, but my friend took it hard. No amount of consoling seemed to help. I went so far as to extend his contract by two years. It was an easy case to make. He was, after all, our best reliever. But this vote of confidence did nothing to help; he spiraled into a deep depression and there was no coming back for him. A couple days before Christmas of that year, he put a gun to his head and killed himself. He killed himself over a stinking pitch — a perfectly placed pitch that the batter was lucky to get wood on. I insisted that his newly signed contract be honored, for his family, and the owner of the team agreed. It was a small victory.

CHAPTER FIVE

I put on Bob Seger's "Roll Me Away" and headed south on the 101 Freeway. I flew like an eagle, still unsure where I was headed, and drove a whole five miles over the speed limit while the rest of the cars on the highway sped past at twenty miles over the limit. What can I say; I was a child from the Bronx and always would be. Cars weren't an essential part of our lives, like they were for teenagers who grew up in the suburbs. Besides, I flew almost everywhere I went. I was more comfortable in a plane going through extreme turbulence than I was in a car going ten miles over the limit.

I might not have known where I was going, but I sure as hell didn't see myself heading north, especially in November. So I stayed south and crossed over into Arizona, and for countless hours, all I encountered was barren, lifeless desert. Instead of feeling like a soaring eagle, all I could imagine were scavengers circling my gas-guzzling truck, waiting for it to break down so they could have me for dinner.

Suddenly, I spotted a sign for a town called Salvation. It was five miles ahead, and as I got closer and turned off the highway and headed into the town, there was another sign welcoming me: Salvation (Gateway to Heaven), Population 550.

I must admit, it was kind of eerie, but after spending so much time in Central America, I was used to towns being named after saints, angels and books from the Bible. The Catholic Church had tremendous influence down there, and despite the poverty, you could always count on a lovely church standing tall and proud amid the dilapidation.

The town looked deserted. As I drove past the first few rundown houses, I noticed tumbleweed blowing past my slow-moving truck —

the type you see in old western films. In the distance, a church steeple towered over the one-storey town. Thankfully, I spotted a bar and grill with its neon sign half lit up. Appropriately enough, it was called Tumbleweeds. I parked and thought to myself that if Lauren ever really wanted to get away from her piece-of-crap husband, she might apply for a job at this off-the-road establishment.

I pulled the door open and entered the bar and grill. The first thought that crossed my mind was that going north might not have been such a bad idea. Being holed up in a ski resort in Colorado with a nice warm fire crackling away and pretty waitresses serving you drinks would have seemed like heaven at this moment in time.

This fine establishment made the Starlight look like a cocktail lounge at the Plaza Hotel in Midtown Manhattan. Tables were scattered randomly across the dining area, and the few tables that were occupied held a class of human beings that looked like they were straight out of central casting for a movie about the Dark Ages, or maybe a zombie flick. The men were all old and haggard and had long uneven beards and greasy hair. The women were not much better; they had less facial hair, it was true, but their dirty, downtrodden looks reminded me of those black-and-white photographs of desperate Americans living in the Dust Bowl during the Great Depression. These people were all drinking, but no one was talking.

Fluorescent lighting made the place feel like a coroner's laboratory, and the customers were about as lively as a bunch of cadavers. I was so shocked at the appearance of the place that I almost turned around and walked out, but I needed a beer, so I pushed past my reluctance, stepped up to the empty bar and sat down at one of the six stools. The bartender greeted me with a friendly, "What can I get you?" without taking his eyes off the TV. He was engrossed in the TV western *Bonanza*, from the 1960s, and occasionally laughed out loud at the most unusual scenes, usually when someone had just been killed.

"A beer," I replied, and without asking what type, he pulled out of the refrigerator an ice-cold Budweiser, which he placed down in front of me. "Wow! What a coincidence. That's just what I was going to order."

He ignored me and continued staring at the TV. I dropped a hundred-dollar bill onto the bar. This caught his attention.

"Surely, you don't think I have change for that?"

"Well I was planning on having a few."

"Well you better plan on having quite a few, or else you will be leaving me an awfully big tip."

I finished my beer in two big gulps. Without taking his eyes off the TV, the man reached over and grabbed me another beer. I must admit, that first beer went down nice, as did the second and the third. My mouth felt scorched — or maybe it was just my imagination after driving through the desert for half a day.

The show ended, and while waiting for the next episode, the bartender reached over and grabbed me another beer, then pushed the three empties farther down the bar. I remarked, "You can just throw them in the garbage if you like."

"And then how would I know how many to charge you for?"

I decided not to reply and simply to enjoy the cold, refreshing taste of the beer. It's strange how after a few beers even a weird, smelly, moldy establishment like this can start to feel comfortable. I started to watch *Bonanza* and found myself engrossed in the trials and moral predicaments of the Cartwright family. I doubt I had seen this show twice in my whole life. I doubt my parents even watched it, yet here I was, fifty years old, a former GM of a Major League Baseball team, watching this show from the 1960s with a grumpy old bartender and what looked like a room full of extras from *The Walking Dead*.

During a commercial, I turned and nearly jumped off my stool. Sitting on the stool right beside me was what I suspected was a girl, dressed in a dirty waitress's uniform, staring directly at me. She — it, whatever — looked extremely grungy, and besides the fact that she was wearing a dress, the only clues to her being female were her long curly blonde hair and lack of facial hair.

She continued to stare at me without blinking until the bartender screamed, "What did I tell you about staring at people, Mia? Stop it! Now go clean the windows before I whip your little ass." He took a bottle of Windex from under the bar and threw it at her, along with a dirty rag.

She gathered the bottle and rag and started to walk toward the front windows, occasionally looking back at me. I shook my head as I turned my attention back to the TV and *Bonanza*. The beers kept flowing and my comfort level rose. The customers behind me barely spoke a word, and except for the fact that they had this habit of slamming down their drinks after taking a sip, I would not have known most of them were even there.

I started to get hungry. Whereas when I first walked into this establishment I couldn't imagine eating anything they might cook, now that I had some liquid courage inside me, I was suddenly more open to the idea. *What's the worst that can happen?* I thought. I asked the bartender for a menu and he screamed, "Mia, show this customer a menu."

Mia grabbed a menu — a ratty, plastic-covered affair that couldn't have been cleaned more than once or twice in a dozen years — and handed it to me. As I looked down at the menu, she stood right beside me. She was so close that I could smell her breath, and let me tell you, it was about as fragrant as a latrine. I tried to inch away from her, but with each move backward, she countered with a move forward. I was practically falling off the stool when I cut bait and asked, "Can I please have a burger with fries?"

She scribbled the order on a pad and handed the slip to the bartender. "Is that a good choice?" I asked hesitantly.

"Yes, very nice," she replied, in a very meek and surprisingly soothing tone. She took the menu from me and started to walk away as I called after her and said, "Thank you." She turned and smiled and suddenly I saw the human being behind the mask.

The bartender, who by now I understood was also the owner, shuffled off to the kitchen. Within seconds, I heard him screaming at what I could only imagine was the cook. "You stupid son of a bitch — how many times do I have tell you, east is *that* way. You're facing north. Mecca is east. If you are going to spend your time praying, at least pray in the right direction. Here, you got an order."

The owner stomped out of the kitchen, muttering under his breath. "If they ever find out about him, he won't have to worry about east, west, north or south," I heard him say. "They'll be burying his ass in the direction of hell."

He handed me another beer as he edged the empties a little farther down the bar. *Bonanza* went off the air and I gingerly asked, "So what are we going to watch now?"

"*Gunsmoke*! Unless, you have a better idea?"

"No! That sounds great."

Within about ten minutes, Mia returned with a burger and fries, a bottle of ketchup and a paper napkin. I did not look too closely at the food. I was starving, so I just closed my eyes and bit into the burger. I was surprised to discover that it wasn't half bad — certainly no worse than the garbage they sold at the games.

After I'd finished, Mia picked up my plate, and out of habit, I reached into my pocket and grabbed a hundred-dollar bill and handed it to her. She looked at me and the bill in her hand as though she was hypnotized. "That's your tip. Thank you very much."

In truth, I usually carried around loose twenties, but I wasn't about to ask her for change. Besides, if anyone in this establishment could use the money, I figured it was her. She said, "Thank you," and bashfully ran away with the dirty plate and the bottle of ketchup.

"I see you already ordered dessert," the owner remarked. "Just be sure to sprinkle plenty of holy water down there." He laughed and laughed as I finished off another beer.

CHAPTER SIX

I knew before I even asked the bartender the question that it might be the stupidest question I could ask, but I did anyway. "Does this town have a motel?" He laughed and nodded in the direction of Mia and remarked, "No! But lucky for you, you already have a room reserved."

"No!"

"Well then, you can sleep on a cot in the back with the cook, but that will cost you. Or you can just do what all our other customers do and put your head down and fall asleep." I turned around and to my amazement all the customers at the tables were asleep.

"Don't you ever close?"

"No! Why would I do that? Like them, I sleep here too, and why not make an extra dollar or two when one of them wakes up and needs a drink. Don't you worry, she doesn't sleep here and will be getting off in a few minutes." Naturally, this disgusting excuse for a human being was talking about Mia, who was staring at me as though she expected me to follow her out of this shithole and into whatever makeshift shack she was living in tonight.

The choice was obvious. I followed Mia out of the shithole.

About a half a block down from the bar, my SUV came into view. I was greatly relieved to see it still in the same spot where I had parked it and looking undamaged. The thought ran through my mind that maybe the safest choice would have been to sleep in the car. It would not have been the first time I had done that, but now it was too late. I didn't want to offend Mia, even though we had barely spoken two sentences to each other by this point. How bizarre was that? For all I knew, she might have been an ax murderer or intending to use me in some kind of religious ritual.

We entered what appeared to be a dilapidated building, without any lights or obvious signs of life, except for what I thought might be the rattle and feasting of rats. We climbed a quivering wooden staircase, which I didn't think could hold the weight of two people. It probably wouldn't have held both of us except for the fact that Mia likely weighed about sixty pounds — and that included the dirt she was carrying.

We opened the door to what appeared to be an apartment. It was dark inside, except for one small lamp that was turned on and an open window directly across from the door, which allowed some light to filter in from the street. I must admit it was not nearly as bad as I would have thought. There wasn't much furniture around, and those few pieces I saw were pretty battered, but it was all neatly organized, and the apartment didn't smell like there were any decaying corpses hanging around.

Mia led me over to a couch and gestured for me to take a seat. When I did, she walked into a small alcove, opened a refrigerator and took out a Budweiser. To my surprise, she put a coaster down on a table beside the couch and placed the beer on top of that. She sat down on the other side of the couch and for a long, uncomfortable moment, she simply stared at me.

"I do not want anything from you, Mia. I'm just thankful that you are allowing me to sleep here."

She smiled and said, "I know." She then reached over and turned on an old black-and-white TV. It was small, probably no more than eighteen inches, and the same type my parents bought for me to have in my room when I was growing up.

Gunsmoke came on the screen. What a surprise! But after a moment, Mia changed the channel and put on an episode of *I Love Lucy*. She laughed like a child as she watched the crazy antics of Lucy and her neighbors. That is the last thing I remember that night.

The next morning I woke up early, just as the sun was coming up outside Mia's window. She was asleep on the other side of the couch. The TV was off, and it was quite apparent to me that Mia had changed out of her waitress outfit and put on a more comfortable, ill-fitting, ragged outfit.

The way the sun struck her hair was uncanny. It was as though Leonardo da Vinci himself had painted Mia's long golden curls. In my whole life I don't think I have ever seen hair so mesmerizing yet so natural, like the movement of a river over a bed of rocks.

I stood up and stretched as quietly as possible. In truth, I just wanted to get the hell out of there and back on the road to Los Angeles, but I was drawn to the window and the field outside. The field was naturally unkempt with knee-high weeds covering the entire area, but among those weeds I could swear I saw crosses, like one might see in a cemetery. I suddenly felt a presence next to me, turned, and there was Mia standing right beside me. So much for a quick and quiet getaway!

I asked, "Are there pets buried out there?"

"No," she replied.

"Surely, there can't be humans buried out there?"

"Yes, the evil ones."

I looked at her, half expecting her to say, "I'm joking," but then I realized where I was and who I was talking to, and it suddenly seemed oh so very normal.

"Hopefully, no one close to you?"

"No one close to me," she replied.

"Are your parents still alive?"

"No, they're buried out there."

I stepped away from the window and sat back down on the couch. She continued to stare out the window as I seriously contemplated the idea that this was all one big LSD flashback.

"Are *your* parents alive?" she asked as she turned from the window and looked directly at me.

"No, they passed away a few years ago."

"I'm sorry. Were they nice?"

"They were perfect."

"Do you miss them a lot?"

"Yes," I replied. "I was very fortunate to have such loving parents." She lowered her eyes and then walked quickly over to the refrigerator and took out a beer. She placed the beer on the table before me, but I waved her off and said, "No! No, Mia. It's too early."

She left the beer on table. I picked it up and handed it back to her and said, "I'll have it later." She smiled as she put the beer back in the refrigerator.

I decided to go for my run. I couldn't just leave. It didn't feel right. I took my suitcase out of the truck and changed into my running outfit. I figured that by the time I came back, she might have left for work and I would simply leave her a note and a bunch of money. Yes, money would make everything okay.

I told her I was going for a run, and I left my suitcase behind so she wouldn't think I was just skipping town. I opened the door and started walking down the rickety staircase. As I did, she followed me.

I pointed to the church steeple at the end of the town. It was about a mile and a half away, and I told her I would be back in about half an hour. I started to run, assuming she would stay put, but instead she started running alongside me and quickly matched me stride for stride. I figured it wouldn't be long until she got tired out, but as I watched her breathing, I realized that it was as steady as mine, as though she had been running her whole life.

Suddenly, after about a mile, she simply stopped as though frozen in time — as though she'd run into a brick wall. By this point I realized that her breathing was even more perfect than mine. There was no struggle, no gasping for air, not a single sign of fatigue. I was actually getting kind of jealous. I slowed down and walked back a few steps and asked, "Are you okay?"

She nodded, but as she did so, she stepped back and hovered there. It was as though she was scared to cross some type of imaginary line — that if she passed it, she would turn into a pumpkin. I couldn't understand why. There was nothing obviously different about this location compared to all the others that we had just trespassed over without incident.

Across the street, there was a small convenience store, a sort of grocery store that looked as dilapidated as every other store we had passed, except that it appeared open.

"We can walk if you like," I offered.

"No! I'll wait for you here," she replied, looking suspiciously around as though someone might be watching her.

"I'll be back shortly," I said as I continued to run toward the church, occasionally looking back at the solitary figure simply standing there.

As I approached the church, I saw a gathering of people on the steps and a hearse parked nearby. I stopped running and stood a safe distance away. Mia's behavior had me a little concerned, and I wasn't sure if I wanted anyone to be able to identify me if I came across them again later. The longer I stood there, the more I began to think that the sun was playing tricks on my eyes. Two things seemed especially odd. From what I could tell, the crowd was separated into two groups, all male and all female, their ages ranging from very young — two or three years old — to very old. That was unusual enough. More disturbing was the fact that something about their coloring and possibly even their movements made the people in the church look more like specters than flesh-and-blood human beings. This I couldn't explain very easily, though I thought it might have something to do with the changing angle of the sun and the way the light was striking the structure, creating shadows and beams of bright light. The whole scene looked surreal and cryptic, like something from a horror film rather than anything you would see in real life.

Four men walked over to the hearse and removed a coffin, then held it steadily at the stairs of the church. Then the driver's-side door of the hearse opened and out stepped a character who looked remarkably like Jesus Christ. He wore a ragged robe on his thin frame and a crown of thorns around his head, and even from a distance, I could see that he was bleeding from the side of his head. Another man entered the scene, dressed like a Roman soldier. He walked over to the Jesus figure, handed him a crucifix, then started whipping him repeatedly. The flogging continued as Jesus — or the man playing Jesus — suffered silently, like in the movie versions shown on Good Friday. After a few minutes of this, the four men started walking the coffin up the steps of the church, and Jesus followed behind. The parishioners formed two lines, one male and one female, and fell to their knees mourning and crying as the person playing Christ passed before them.

I turned around and ran back toward Mia, who was standing exactly where I left her. I suddenly realized that I was extremely thirsty. I crossed the imaginary line, grabbed her hand and walked across the street in the direction of the convenience store.

When she saw where I was headed, Mia stopped abruptly again and refused to go into the building with me. I was in no mood to argue. I left her there, walked into the store and looked at the man behind the counter. I smiled at him as I thought to myself that he looked like one of Jesus's disciples. If I were in a better mood, I would have jokingly told him that the Passion play at the church was just getting started and they were missing a few apostles.

I opened the refrigerator at the back of the store and grabbed a large bottle of water and a couple of sodas for Mia. As I walked toward the counter, I grabbed two large bags of chips and placed everything on the counter.

The missing disciple looked at me and said, "You're not from around here, are you? You some type of heathen, hanging around the devil's daughter?"

"No," I said. "I'm Catholic, and the girl you are referring to is not the devil's daughter." As soon as I said the words, I regretted falling into his twisted logic.

"You lie, you filthy disgusting Judas."

"Whatever," I said, trying to disengage. "Can I just pay and be on my way?"

He looked at me as I reached into my pocket and grabbed a hundred-dollar bill and placed it on the counter. It seemed unlikely that he would be able to make change, but I soon realized that that was the least of my problems. He looked down at the money and said, "Twelve pieces of gold. You Jew! You traitor!"

He reached beneath the counter and pulled out a rifle, but before he had time to take aim, I grabbed the gun and slammed the butt into his stomach. He staggered backward into the window display, knocking over a dusty postcard rack and falling backward onto the floor. I grabbed my merchandise, left the hundred on the counter, flung the gun down the aisle toward the refrigerator and ran the hell out of there. I grabbed the devil's daughter's hand and we ran hard all the way back to her apartment. As I doubled over in her foyer and grabbed both knees with my hands, I noticed once again that she was not even winded.

CHAPTER SEVEN

I stared out the back window of Mia's apartment, at the graves of her parents and the other evil ones that were supposedly buried there. I was in a partial state of shock, and if it wasn't for the fact that I had every intention of escaping this godforsaken place as quickly as possible, I would have had a few beers. Mia had already placed a beer in my hand, but I couldn't risk it.

I had to admit, Mia was a very attentive host. As I stared out the window, I couldn't help feeling guilty about abandoning her here. It would be like signing her death warrant. It would be only a matter of time before her corpse would be buried out there — or worse, left to rot and be ravaged by whatever wild animals haunted this place.

This was one of those rare and tragic moments when money offered no solution. Conscientious action was required. I would need to turn to the principles of my religion and the morals that my parents raised me to live by. I turned to Mia, who was as usual, standing right beside me, and said, "I will be leaving in a few minutes, and I think you need to come with me."

"Okay," she replied.

"You want to come with me?" I asked.

"Yes." Her voice was flat, resolute.

"Okay, gather up whatever you want to take with you because we are not coming back here. Identification — do you have a social security card or anything that confirms who you are?"

"Yes," she said, before dropping to her knees, reaching under the couch and retrieving a small metal box with a key attached to it. She handed me the box, and I opened it. Inside I found a pile of papers, including death certificates, birth certificates and Mia's social security card.

Mia left my side for a few moments, then reappeared holding a yellow plastic shopping bag.

"Is that all you're bringing?" I asked. She nodded and just stood looking up at me with those unblinking eyes. I zipped up my suitcase, handed Mia the metal box and we left the apartment.

As we walked toward my truck, I had an overwhelming feeling that it was not going to start. It had never once not started for me, but then there is always a first time, and I thought what a fitting climax that would be to this nightmare, stranded here in the town of Salvation, surrounded by uninhabited desert and unfriendly evangelicals.

I opened the passenger's-side door for Mia and then went around and got in on the driver's side. I put the key in the ignition, said a Hail Mary, touched the small statue of Saint Jude on my dashboard, turned the key and, what do you know, it started right up like usual. I reached over and put Mia's seat belt on, since she didn't seem to be doing it herself. As I leaned back and got ready to pull out of the spot, I glanced in the rearview mirror and saw Jesus and the disciple from the convenience store walking toward us. Jesus was holding his cross and I could tell they were starting to skip, picking up speed. I hit the gas and peeled the hell out of there as the disciple took aim with his rifle. I could swear I heard gunfire, but then it could have all been in my imagination.

CHAPTER EIGHT

I should have known that once I left my comfort zone — the baseball diamond and the world of statistics, on-base percentages and contract negotiations — at least a little hell would rain down upon me. But I never guessed that it would come down upon me like a biblical plague. Thankfully, I made it out alive … and yet here I was with the devil's child riding shotgun in my SUV, and my God, did she smell.

I wasn't sure if holy water would do the trick, but I was tempted to stop at the first hotel outside of Salvation and throw her ass into a shower.

I still wasn't sure if she was a ten-year-old girl, a teenager of either sex, a woman of thirty, an androgyne or an alien. The one thing I was sure of was that she was a pitiful little thing and, like I said, my Catholic God … not to mention my parents … would never have forgiven me if I left her behind to face the wrath of those insane Passion players.

I had about a thousand questions I wanted to ask her. Despite all the time I spent in zealously religious regions of Central America, I had never come upon a place like the town of Salvation. It was hard to believe that such a place even existed in America. I was curious to know how Mia had survived until now, with her family gone and the townsfolk convinced that she was Satan's spawn. I occasionally glanced across at Mia, but every time I was about to say something, I choked, literally and figuratively. I wasn't sure where to start or whether she would have any answers. Then there was the fact that my mouth felt as parched as the desert that was whipping past us as we headed back to civilization.

Finally, I managed to ask, "How old are you, Mia?"

She kept silent and continued staring out the window. I repeated the question, and again, she ignored me.

At this point I concluded that she must be a woman because only a woman would refuse to respond to such an impertinent question. I felt ashamed until suddenly she turned to me and said, "I'm sorry, did you ask me a question?"

I looked at her, stupefied, and said, "Yes, but don't worry about that now. Is everything okay?"

"Yes, thank you," she replied. Her voice was as gentle and as soothing as a cool breeze on a hot summer night. It made for a striking contrast: Here she was, this foul-smelling urchin, and yet her voice could have belonged to an angel.

I reached over and turned on the radio. I had it tuned to the twenty-four-hour Beatles channel. They were playing early Beatles classics, and after a few moments, I could see a dimpled smile cross the pale, sunken countenance of my passenger.

CHAPTER NINE

With a great sigh of relief, I crossed into the lovely state of California, and in another hour and a half, we were in the beautiful city of San Diego. I pulled into the parking lot of a luxury hotel overlooking the Pacific Ocean. It was a hotel I knew well, having stayed there plenty of times when I traveled with the team to play against San Diego.

I had called in advance from the truck and was lucky enough to get a suite with a breathtaking view. I checked in at the front desk and immediately noticed all the guests looking with disgust at the dirty, smelly little girl standing directly behind me. I pulled her closer and stared down those uncharitable jerks, even though I understood their curiosity and even, to some extent, their involuntary disgust. She did smell, and she was a sight to behold with her ratty hair, dirt on her face and body, and her unkempt clothes. But I was brought up to respect all human beings and especially to defend the honor and dignity of women. None of these assholes had any idea what this girl had been through. I didn't have the full story either, but I was beginning to suspect that she had been through a lot. In fact, I had little doubt that if any of these posh idiots were forced to live her life, they wouldn't have lasted a week.

Mia herself appeared oblivious to the stares and judging looks. She stood there, transfixed on the ornate fountains and the colorful murals that decorated the hotel lobby, not noticing a pair of teenage girls watching her and whispering.

I hustled her away from them and we made our way to the suite. As I swiped the card and pushed open the door, Mia gasped. It was the largest suite in the hotel and consisted of a spacious living-room area and two separate bedrooms with attached bathrooms. From where we stood, we could see a pair of L-shaped couches and a set of sliding glass doors that led to a terrace. The doors were open a crack to let in the fresh air, and a pair of long white curtains billowed into the room.

Mia asked, "Is this your home?"

"No, sweetheart, this is a hotel, a place people stay for short periods of time while on vacation or away on business. My home is about three hours from here and it definitely does not have this view."

We walked over to the balcony and looked out at the ocean. "Have you ever seen an ocean?"

"Only on TV," she said, continuing to stare through the window at the glistening water. She pointed down at the surf, where some medium-size whitecaps were picking up momentum.

"What causes the waves?" she asked with a childlike curiosity.

"The wind."

"Is that all?"

"Yes."

"It seems like there should be something else. They're so beautiful."

I opened the balcony door and she stepped outside right away. She leaned against the railing and watched the power of the waves crashing against the beach. The smell of the ocean was reinvigorating, and yet not even that powerful aroma could mask the unpleasant smell emanating from Mia.

In as subtle and delicate a manner as I could manage, I told her she needed to take a shower. I led her into the bedroom with the view of the ocean and into the bathroom. I opened up the shower door and explained to her how the hot and cold water worked and pointed out the shampoo and conditioner. I grabbed a bag from the closet and told her to put her dirty clothes into the bag. Then I told her that once she was finished showering and felt clean, she should dry herself off and put on the robe provided by the hotel, which was hanging across from the shower door.

I told her I was going to the store to pick up some things and that I would be back in about half an hour. She seemed alarmed but I reassured her that I was coming back and that there was no reason to worry. She nodded as I gently touched her chin and looked into her pale-blue eyes. "No one will hurt you again. I promise."

I left the suite and went down to the lobby. I was dying for a cold beer and stopped off at the bar. I looked up at the TV as the bartender put an ice-cold Budweiser in front of me. ESPN was on and there was a picture of me on the screen, with some commentators speculating on what team I was going to. I had thought by now that I would be old news and then I realized it was only two days ago that I resigned. It seemed like an eternity. I downed the beer quickly and ordered another. My mind was in a state of confusion and I didn't even notice any of the customers sitting at the bar.

A very attractive lady in her mid-thirties with long, straight blonde hair and deep-blue eyes turned to me and said, "It's like paradise down here." Her stylish dress and jewelry suggested that she was used to such surroundings.

"Yes, it is quite lovely."

"Certainly beats the everyday toil of Los Angeles. The type of place one could very happily call home."

"Yes, it is much more relaxing, no denying that," I said as I looked very closely at her. "I get the feeling that we have met before. Am I wrong?"

"No, Mr. Ciotola, you're not wrong," she said. "We have…"

"At the winter baseball meetings about ten years ago. You were just a child. Your father is Walter Baker?"

"Your memory is almost as remarkable as your baseball acumen. I wasn't quite a child, unless you consider twenty-six still a child. I'm Catherine." She held out her hand and we shook.

"And how is your father doing?"

"He's well. A little exasperated and annoyed. After all, we haven't won a World Series in over fifty years. Losing all the time can be tiresome, especially as you get older."

"I have always had great respect for your father. Even though baseball might be his passion, his one true love has always been his family."

"Whenever your name comes up, he never fails to mention the beautiful and touching letters you sent to him after my mother died. I think those letters are the only things he kept from that terrible time."

"Is he grooming you to take over the team?"

"I think so, but I still think he has some reservations about me, especially because of my age and because he will forever see me as his little girl." She paused and looked at me with hope in her eyes. "I think if I could just arrange a meeting with you, it would really help my cause and alleviate his worries."

"I am not the type of person who feels comfortable misleading friends and sowing hope where there is none. Despite the news reports, my resignation is very real, at least for this year. And if I ever do decide to come back, it will be with the team that I have been with my whole career."

"Unless the Yankees call?"

"Yes, unless the Yankees call, but they already have a great GM. Sometimes it is hard to beat back childhood dreams. I grew up cheering for the Yankees, and some of my fondest memories are watching games with my parents and occasionally going to the stadium. The stadium was only a twenty-minute drive from where we lived in the Bronx."

"The boy from the Bronx going home to run baseball operations for his favorite boyhood team. It would make a wonderful Hollywood movie."

"Yes, indeed it would, if only my parents were still alive. Sharing one's good fortune with the people you love and cherish is what really makes it special."

"Yes, Mr. Ciotola, that is so true. So should I simply give up all hope of ever hiring you?"

"No, because if I ever do decide to go back and the team I have spent my career with decides they don't want me anymore, well, then there is hope. You have my phone number?"

"You mean, the number I have called at least fifty times in the last two days and each time it went straight to voice mail?"

I wrote down my private number, which only my parents and now Lauren had ever had, and I handed it to her.

"You understand that number is very private and only one other person has it. Please don't pass it along to anyone."

"Surely, Mr. Ciotola, you don't think I would ever compromise your privacy?"

"I wouldn't think so, especially since your father is a person I hold in such high regard."

"So tell me, what brings you down to beautiful San Diego?"

"An unexpected twist in my travel plans."

It was no coincidence that I met the lovely Miss Baker at this hotel bar. I was quite sure an employee from the hotel called her the moment I stepped foot in the place, and like a good businesswoman, she hurried on down here. If she wasn't fortunate enough to meet me at the bar, she would have made sure she introduced herself to me in some other, inconspicuous manner. I admired her determination and I also knew that whoever her contact at the hotel was, he or she had already told her about the grubby and disheveled little girl I was with. I needed to clear up that mystery and so I told her the true story about Mia and the town of Salvation. She listened intently and I could see that she was genuinely moved.

I paid both our bills, shook her hand and walked toward the lobby door. Just as I opened the door, she came running toward me and said, "I know of a place where you can get everything a young lady needs. Would you mind if I came along with you? I would love to help."

"It's as though you read my mind, Catherine. I would greatly appreciate it. I know nothing about buying clothes and necessities for women."

We took her car and drove to an eclectic-looking boutique a short distance away. I tried my best to give Catherine an estimate of Mia's measurements. She was about five foot one and probably weighed no more than ninety pounds. Her foot size was about that of a ten-year-old girl. Catherine assured me that there was nothing to worry about, and within half an hour, she had picked out blouses, pants, underwear, sandals, sneakers and some simple accessories, including a sky-blue scarf and a thin metallic belt. The only thing I added to the haul was a pair of pajamas with pictures of Charlie Brown and Snoopy playing baseball. After that we went to a drugstore where we picked up an assortment of hair products, some makeup and a few other toiletries, which Catherine assured me were essential.

Catherine dropped me back at the hotel and told me she would be in touch. She also said not to worry, that baseball was off the table and that Mia's welfare was paramount.

CHAPTER TEN

I had been gone for nearly two hours, and when I walked into the suite, I couldn't see Mia. I called out to her from the living room, but she did not answer. I walked toward her room and could easily hear the water in the shower running. Surely, she couldn't still be in the shower? I entered the bedroom, opened the bathroom door a crack and peeked inside. I could see her silhouette behind the shower door. I shook my head and wondered at my stupidity. Of course she could still be in the shower. It was Mia. If I were gone for ten hours she would still be in the shower.

I knocked gently on the side of the shower, turning my head in the other direction, and in a reassuring and gentle voice I told her that I was back and that if she stayed in the shower any longer her skin was going to start peeling off. I stepped out of the bathroom as I heard the water turn off. A few minutes later, Mia walked into the living room wearing the robe, which was about ten times too big for her. I looked at her face and must have let out a sound of shock because she looked back at me, surprised.

"Mia, your face…" I said, unable to finish.

She held her skinny fingers up to her cheek and looked back at me, uncomprehending.

What I saw was nothing short of horrifying. She looked like a concentration camp victim. Her cheeks were hollow and her eye sockets were buried in deep shadow. She was emaciated and as pale as a corpse, and for a moment I almost wished she hadn't cleaned up. The dirt and grime had been providing a good cover for this poor little creature's sickly complexion and sunken features. The only thing that gave me hope was the glimmer in her pale-blue eyes and the shine and luster reflecting off the golden curls of her shoulder-length hair.

It took me a long moment to adjust, and once I did, I started to show her all the new clothing and accessories and supplies that Catherine and I bought for her. Her eyes grew wide with delight, and then just as quickly clouded over with worry. She opened the metal box with her identification inside and took out all the money I imagine she had in the whole world, including the hundred dollars I left her as a tip. She tried to hand it all to me, about $118.00, and I explained to her that I didn't want her money and that everything she saw was a gift from me. I tried to explain that I never wanted any money from her. I had her put her money back in the box, took her hand and showed her the Charlie Brown and Snoopy pajamas I'd bought for her.

"You like Charlie Brown?"

"Yes," she replied. "He likes baseball."

"Yes, he does. Do you like baseball?"

"Yes, I love baseball."

She held the pajamas in her hands and stared down at the pictures of Charlie Brown and Snoopy on the pajamas and I could see a glimmer of a smile cross her lips.

I suggested she go back into the bathroom and put on the pajamas, and she did. A few minutes later, she came back out and stood in the middle of the living room, beaming. With both hands on her tiny torso, she smoothed over a section of the light flannel pajamas to show off an image of Charlie Brown wearing his trademark smile. As she stood there, the image of the emaciated girl gave way to one of hope, encouragement and joy. Chuck had that effect on children and adults.

"Those look very nice on you," I said.

"Thank you," she said.

"Are you hungry?" I asked.

"Starving," she said.

"That I can believe."

I found two dinner menus on a desk in the living room and started going through the menu. I asked Mia what she liked to eat and without hesitation she replied, "Chocolate!"

I ordered steak and vegetables for both of us and a large piece of chocolate cake for Mia. I said she could have it if she ate enough of her dinner first. I had to be careful not to let her eat too much; if she was nearly as starved as she looked, a big meal taken in all at once would make her sick. Her body had to get accustomed to eating normally after being malnourished for so long.

I cut her steak into small pieces and told her she needed to eat it slowly, along with the vegetables. She did exactly as I said, all the time eyeing that beautiful piece of chocolate cake.

She ate about half the steak and all the vegetables. I cut the chocolate cake in half and put half in front of her and the other half into the refrigerator. I told her she could have the other half tomorrow. When she shot me a look of disappointment, I immediately felt guilty, like a parent, but I knew it was for her own good.

I had to remind her over and over again to eat the cake slowly. She was going at it like a hungry tiger. The problem with Mia was that I knew so little about her and I felt embarrassed to ask her questions that I would never dream of asking another girl. When she showed me the box with her identification, I was in such a rush to get the hell out of that town that I forgot to look at her date of birth. In the car when I asked her about her age, twice, she either didn't hear me or pretended not to hear. After she finished her cake, I asked her if I could look inside her box and check her identification, in case we went to a place that asked for proof of age. I had to know her age. It was very important for several reasons.

She picked up her box and, without flinching, handed it to me. I opened it, picked up her social security card, looked at the date of birth, closed the box and handed it back to her. "Great," I remarked with a smile.

Mia was ten years old. I couldn't help but draw the comparison between Catherine Baker at ten and Mia at ten. Catherine at ten probably looked like a Disney princess. Mia at ten was looking like a creature described in the pages of Grimms' Fairy Tales.

Catherine at ten was probably already preparing to take her SATs in the hope of getting into Yale — an easy enough feat, since her father was an alumnus and had donated millions of dollars to the university. Mia, on the other hand ... well, I wasn't even sure if she could read and write.

It was all so insane. Ten! For God's sake, she just turned ten! She couldn't have been seventeen or eighteen, or even better, twenty-five. No, she had to be ten. I don't know why that age terrified me. I had spent plenty of time with kids just a little older than her, tutoring twelve-year-old ballplayers in Central America. I had always had their well-being first and foremost in my mind, and baseball second, always building strong relationships, not only with the young boys but also with their families.

And there it was in a nutshell. It wasn't so much that she was ten but that she was a girl. A girl who had been abused and who was severely malnourished, without family or, seemingly, friends to help her survive. A ten-year-old girl working in a bar! How was that possible? She had even been denied the one thing that gave many of my Central American friends hope: religion, and belief in a loving God. No, for reasons I couldn't even begin to understand, Mia had been cast off as an evil creature who could never have any share in her community's religious life. The more I thought about it, the more I realized that it wasn't she who was like a creature out of Grimms' Fairy Tales, but me — Joe Ciotola, the baseball guru, the most sought after GM in the game.

I stood up and walked over to the bar. I grabbed myself a cold Budweiser and looked across at Mia, who was leaning against the railing of the balcony, watching the sun set over the beautiful Pacific. I picked up the phone and called the lobby. I told them I would be staying for a week. There was no rush to get home. It was here in paradise that I would undertake the most important and worthy challenge of my life.

I walked out onto the balcony and leaned against the railing beside Mia. "We're going to be staying here for a whole week. Does that sound good to you?" She looked at me with the same enthusiastic expression she had when she first saw the chocolate cake. "Yes, yes, thank you so much," she said. Then she threw her arms around my waist and hugged me tightly. I wasn't expecting that and was slow to respond, but when I finally hugged her back and kissed her on her head, the clean, fresh smell of her hair was even more refreshing than the glorious ocean air.

CHAPTER ELEVEN

I took a long, refreshing shower, changed into a pair of sweatpants and a T-shirt, grabbed a beer and watched TV with Mia. Actually, it was more like I watched Mia change channels every few minutes. She seemed exceptionally excited about the vast variety of channels and the clarity and brightness of the picture.

And by the way, Mia was able to read and write. I found this out when I asked her to sit beside me while I pulled up an article on my laptop explaining the reason and the cause of waves in the ocean. It was a good piece that detailed how ocean tides were affected by the gravitational pull from the moon and sun. She read the whole thing out loud, while occasionally writing down points of interest on a pad I handed to her. It was like she read my mind and was showing me what I wanted to see — that she had managed to get some basic schooling under her belt in her short and brutal life so far. I felt guilty for having tricked her into this test. Actually, I felt like a little boy caught with my pants down, running through a crowded schoolyard with no place to hide. But she was sweet about it and really just seemed to want to prove herself to me. It occurred to me that we were already starting to resemble a father and daughter.

I had a few more beers while watching a few hundred channels flash by, then I went off to bed. I was exhausted and quickly fell asleep. I don't know how many hours passed, but I suddenly felt a presence beside my bed. It was still dark out, but a single shaft of light was streaming in from the next room over. I struggled to open my eyes, and when I was finally able to focus, I saw Mia standing there in the light. She was wringing her tiny hands together.

"Mia! Is there something wrong?" I asked anxiously.

"I ate the rest of the chocolate cake. I'm sorry, but I couldn't help it."

I laughed as I sat up in bed and turned on the light. That's when I saw the bits of chocolate around her mouth. She hadn't even tried to hide the evidence. I patted the duvet cover and she sat down next to me. I looked at her and said, "Chocolate has been known to have that type of effect on people. Forcing them to eat it, regardless of how much they fight the urge."

"Are you very mad?" she asked.

"No, sweetheart, I'm not mad," I said, and I explained the reason why I didn't want her to eat too much. I asked her if she felt sick at all and she replied, "No! Chocolate makes me feel good."

I promised her that once her system got used to eating regularly and she was at a proper weight, she could have as much chocolate as she wanted, within reason. I grabbed a tissue off the nightstand and wiped clean the crumbs and frosting from around her mouth. I then told her to brush her teeth and go to bed. She lingered beside the bed for a little longer and then started walking out of the room. I stopped her, gently turned her around and kissed her on the top of her head. "You're a really great kid. Do you know that?"

She hugged me and smiled up at me bashfully before running off to her room. As I lay back down on the bed, a feeling of paternal warmth blissfully overwhelmed all my senses, and all the fears and anxieties I'd felt just a short time ago seemed to evaporate all at once. I fell back to sleep and woke up at five in the morning. I walked out of my room and into the living room. The balcony door was open and the smell of the ocean filled the air. I looked into Mia's room and she was sleeping as peacefully as a little kitten.

I changed into my running gear, wrote Mia a note telling her I was going for a run, and left it beside her pillow. I took the elevator down to the lobby and found it empty except for the night manager. I walked down to the water. It was still quite dark outside and the sky was full of stars, and the moon, descending into the ocean, sent a mysterious and glorious glow across the surface of the water. I started to run along the beach, and found to my surprise that I was able to lope along as effortlessly and gracefully as a colt. It was low tide and occasionally I splashed through rivulets of water left behind by the receding tide. In the distance, I could see the lights inside the houses atop the overhanging cliffs. The squawking of seagulls cut through the tranquil hum of the ocean as the blanket of stars above disappeared and the moon sank into the bottomless abyss of the Pacific.

CHAPTER TWELVE

It was after seven when I opened the door to our hotel suite. I could hear the shower running in Mia's bathroom, and as I walked toward her room, I heard the water shut off and I stepped back. I picked up the breakfast menu and smiled as I looked down at the choices. This week as a special they were offering chocolate chocolate-chip pancakes.

Mia walked into the living room dressed in a bright yellow blouse and dark jeans. Her hair was dripping wet, and her face was still as gaunt and pale as it had been the day before, yet her demeanor was changed. She no longer looked like the poster child for lost causes but more like the hopeful seedling of a soon-to-be-lovely flower.

"I'm all clean," she said proudly.

"Yes you are, and you look adorable," I said, causing her to smile shyly. She was not used to compliments and didn't respond. I walked over to her and cut the price tags off her blouse and jeans. I wondered if she ever had clothes that were new, apart from the pajamas she'd worn the night before.

I showed her what was on the breakfast menu and her eyes lit up. I ordered her the chocolate chocolate-chip pancakes with scrambled eggs and bacon and had to remind her repeatedly to eat slowly.

My private cell phone rang — the number that only my parents had before I gave it to Lauren and Catherine. For a moment I thought it was my mother calling. She was the last one I'd ever talked to on that phone, and that was a number of years ago. I picked the phone up with trembling hands and listened to the sound of Catherine's voice. Her voice was pleasant, soothing, with an unmistakable tinge of caring and concern, which I had only previously heard in the voice of my blessed mother.

Catherine had called thinking that we were leaving today and wanted to tell us to have a safe trip back to Los Angeles. She was overjoyed to hear that we were going to stay for a week. She was busy preparing for the winter meetings. Her father wasn't going, leaving her as the chief representative of the team — the "acting general manager," she said with a laugh. She asked if she could come over and meet Mia. We agreed that today was as good as ever. She would be joining us for lunch.

She hung up, yet her voice kept ringing in my ear like the calm and loving chirping of a mother bird singing to her newborns. I looked across at Mia and told her we were having a guest over for lunch. She seemed a little nervous and I reassured her that I was quite certain that she would like her, that she was the lady who had picked out all her nice new clothes and was the daughter of a very old and dear friend of mine.

I turned on my laptop computer and pulled up the current roster on Catherine's team. Their third-place hitter and left fielder had just been named the National League's MVP. He had put up monster numbers. It was his fourth year in the majors and he had improved steadily each year. He was still under contract with the team for another three years and was still being paid the league minimum for fourth-year players who were still playing for the same team that they came up with as a rookie. He would be an unrestricted free agent in three years, and if he kept up the type of production he was putting up, he would be cashing in big-time with a long-term contract probably worth a quarter of a billion dollars. There was no way a small market team like Catherine's would have the money to re-sign him.

The team had stayed competitive for most of last year but faded badly toward the end and finished four games out of the playoffs. They had talent but were definitely a few players away from being a truly competitive, championship-caliber team. I had a few ideas, but before sharing them, I had to be sure of a few things. I had to be certain that the daughter had the same impeccable character as her father.

CHAPTER THIRTEEN

Catherine entered the suite with a bouquet of flowers and a bag of children's vitamins. After exchanging pleasantries with me, she walked over to Mia, who was standing by the couch. Catherine handed her the flowers and said, "And these are for the beautiful young lady and the wonderful addition to the Joseph Ciotola household." Mia accepted the flowers and graciously thanked Catherine in a barely audible voice. She seemed a little puzzled and then I realized she didn't know my full name. Before I could explain, Catherine gently took her hand and held on to it as they both sat down on the couch. Catherine's compliments and the ease with which she took Mia into her confidence were quite amazing.

Catherine never once exhibited the least bit of shock or uneasiness at the sickly and pallid complexion of the child. Instead, she ran her hands gently through Mia's curly golden hair — asking and being granted permission first — and admired it like it was a precious jewel.

We ate lunch, and except for the word or two I was able to squeeze in, I was left out of the conversation. Before it was all over, Catherine had arranged a girls-only day for Mia and herself: pedicures, manicures, massages, facials — the works. It was like Catherine had cast a miraculous spell over the child. The type of spell that only a mother or someone who really cared could effect.

I escorted Catherine to the elevator, and she remarked, "You are going to have your hands full."

"You think so," I replied, surprised at the remark.

"Yes, because once that young lady is healthy and fit, she is going to be a knockout, and believe me, she is going to have a regiment of boys knocking at your door begging to see her. Think you're ready for that, Joe?"

I laughed with relief and said, "I haven't thought that far in advance. You must remember, I'm new to all this. I cannot tell you how much I appreciate all that you have done." She laughed and said, "It's not very often I meet a man as good and caring as my father. There are not many individuals who would have taken that poor child with them, especially knowing so little about her. You saved a life, and that outshines all your baseball accomplishments."

The elevator door opened and Catherine walked inside and pressed the lobby button. The doors started to close, and I suddenly stopped their movement with my hands. I asked her if she could step out and she readily did.

"I looked over your team's roster this morning and I came up with a few ideas."

"I thought you were through with baseball for at least a year."

"I guess it's not such an easy thing to just step away," I said. "It was more out of habit. If you like, you can come by tomorrow and we could talk."

"I appreciate the kind offer, Joe, but I am going to have to decline."

I was surprised by her initial response and said, "Can I ask why?"

"Of course," she said. "It's simple. I want to keep things clear between us. If I was in your position, the first thing I would think is that I was being played. All the kindness and help with Mia would seem like a trick to get you to work for our team. I don't work like that and after talking to my father last night and telling him how I found out you were staying at this hotel, he reminded me in no uncertain terms that we as an organization do not play by the dirty rules other teams resort to. He said, 'That Mr. Ciotola must have had a good laugh' at the amateurish way I pretended to just run into you."

"He's right," I said, laughing. "You didn't fool me. But I didn't think it was amateurish at all. You were acting in the interest of the team, your father's team, and it's not like your intent was to hurt or undermine me."

"Thank you for saying that, but the answer is still no."

She pressed the button for the elevator as I suddenly said, "But now you are acting in your own interest, stroking your own ego." She turned and looked at me with anguish in her eyes. I continued to try and explain. "Do you think for a minute I would be so ready to offer my support if I thought you had played me? It's just the opposite. And it's not you I would most like to help by sharing my thoughts about the team, but your father."

Her eyes softened as she looked dismally down. I continued, saying, "He hasn't been feeling well, has he? Is that the reason he's not going to the winter meetings?"

"He'll be fine. He just doesn't get around very well anymore, but he's as sharp as ever."

"I'm sure he is," I said as I lifted her head up and looked directly into her eyes, which were swimming with unexpressed emotion. "You're lucky to have such a wonderful father, and he's lucky to have you. Less than twenty-four hours ago, you were ready to hire me as your GM, and now you don't even want to hear a few suggestions I have to offer — suggestions that, for all I know, you might seriously hate."

"I would love to hear your suggestions," she said. "Only a fool would not listen to what you have to say. It would be like an aspiring writer refusing to hear advice from Shakespeare. Or at least Hemingway ... maybe Stephen King."

That cut the tension, and we both laughed.

"I seem to be depreciating by the minute, or at least jumping from sonnets to horror," I said, still laughing, while also impressed that Catherine seemed to know books as well as baseball. "Anyway, I appreciate the compliment, but I have to ask you to please stop putting me on a pedestal. It makes me feel uncomfortable and it is totally unfounded. I am also currently under no legal obligations to my former team, so whatever suggestions or opinions I might offer you are totally above board and do not in any way represent a conflict of interest. Besides, I left my team in good shape for at least a couple of years. I doubt they will even send any top-level representatives to the meetings."

"According to news reports, they are not even looking for a GM. I guess they expect you back sooner than you think."

"They will eventually need a GM, and hopefully they will hire one of the many wonderful and talented people that worked for me all these years. If you would be so kind as to send over your team's updated roster, including the farm system, and all the finances related to the team's operations, I would love to sit down with you tomorrow afternoon and go over some possibilities."

"I would be honored, and I will send all that information over to you once I get back to the office."

Catherine took the elevator down and I walked back into the suite and looked across at Mia, who was admiring her beautiful bouquet of flowers. She asked softly, "Is Catherine your girlfriend?"

I replied with a laugh, "No sweetheart, I'm probably old enough to be her father."

"She is very beautiful and sweet."

"You like her a lot?" I asked.

"Yes, a whole lot."

"Well she thinks you're wonderful. So already you have made yourself a friend and I think that's great."

CHAPTER FOURTEEN

After Catherine left, Mia and I kept being drawn outside to enjoy the gorgeous sunshine and the stunning coastline. It was the kind of balmy, cloudless day that made it feel like a crime to stay indoors.

For our first outing we took a long walk along the concrete boardwalk that began at the hotel and stretched into a nearby residential area. It hugged the coast for almost a mile, meandering through tall grasses and beach roses and areas shaded with palms.

We'd been walking for a while when I told Mia that if she behaved, I would buy her a chocolate ice cream cone on the way back. I said it like that — "if you behave" — which was a phrase I remembered hearing from my mother and father quite often when I was much younger. Mia looked at me, obviously puzzled and concerned, and asked, "Have I not been behaving?"

"Oh no, honey, of course you've been behaving. That's just an innocent phrase that people use. You have been nothing short of perfect."

I could see in her eyes that she was still uncertain. It bothered me to see her even slightly upset, but I thought it wise to let the matter go; otherwise I might confuse her even more.

We walked in silence for a while, until we came across a lookout that jutted out over a small cliff. We stopped and looked at the ocean, and I plugged a quarter into the machine so Mia could see longer distances. She was sure she saw a shark's fin at nine o'clock and a whale spout at twelve o'clock, and I tried to find them, but even with magnification, my 50-year-old eyes weren't up to the task.

We walked back to the hotel and stopped for ice cream, as promised, and Mia ordered chocolate with chocolate sprinkles. By the time we got to the hotel, the pointy end of her sugar cone was leaking melted chocolate onto the parking lot between her feet. She laughed as she popped the rest of the cone in her mouth and used a leftover napkin to clean the worst of the mess off her sticky hands. We then went up to our suite, where we spent a couple of hours reading and watching TV. I took a brief nap, and when I woke up the sun was low on the horizon, but still about half an hour from setting.

Mia wanted to go down to the beach to squeeze a little more fun out of the day, so I rubbed the sleep out of my eyes and we headed down the path to the water. There weren't many people around. Mia's eyes were transfixed on the ocean and on the flock of seagulls flying above and walking beside us, squawking and searching for food. It was a beautiful, cloudless evening and I asked Mia if she wanted to get her feet wet. She took her scandals off and I bent down and rolled her jeans up to just above her ankles. She stepped gingerly into the water and giggled as the surf lapped at her toes.

I started looking around for a skipping rock, and as I was doing that, Mia walked farther out into the water. I stood up and called to her not to go too far out. She didn't hear me, and kept walking. Just as I was heading toward her, yelling at the top of my lungs for her to come back, a large wave came crashing down onto the beach and Mia disappeared beneath the water. I went rushing out to the spot that I last saw her, and amazingly, I was able to see her right away, even though she was fully under water in her clothes. I plunged my arm into the surf and grabbed her hand just as the undertow was starting to take her farther out. The pull was incredibly strong, and I was thankful that I'd spent the last thirty years running and staying fit. I held on to Mia's arm and she grasped mine, and after a struggle, the ocean released her. I picked her up, turned and started walking quickly back to the shore, but not before another large wave came crashing down upon us, nearly taking us both down.

Finally, we made it back to shore, with me still holding Mia in my arms. I gently set her down on the sand and hunched over her, trying to regain my composure. That was when I heard the oddest sound —

odd, that is, for a moment of such heightened drama. Instead of crying or whimpering or even shouting with relief, Mia was laughing as she looked up at the sky. Just as I was about to scold her for what seemed like her completely inappropriate response to almost drowning, she surprised me again by asking, "Joseph, why is the sky blue?" I looked at her soaking wet hair and at the wonder and excitement in her eyes and shook my head. "I don't know," I said. Fifty years on this planet and I don't think I'd ever asked myself that question — even though I'd spent my whole career looking up at the sky, following the arc of a baseball off the bat of a ballplayer.

We started walking back to the hotel, dripping wet, and she asked, "Are you going to buy me a chocolate ice cream cone?" How could I possibly say no? We made a detour from the hotel and walked up to an ice cream stand. I bought her a chocolate cone dipped in chocolate sprinkles — her second dose of chocolate for the day — and I had a vanilla cone dipped in multicolored sprinkles.

CHAPTER FIFTEEN

I was looking over the email that Catherine sent me concerning the team's current roster and its finances. Mia was taking a shower and was probably thinking of that big piece of chocolate cake she would have me order her for dessert after finishing dinner. The child was addicted to chocolate, which was fine with me. It certainly beat a lot of other things that children her age were getting hooked on these days.

Catherine's team's payroll and budget were just above a hundred million dollars, which was slightly below the average for major league teams. Their attendance was not very good, especially considering the brand-new ballpark they were playing in and the beautiful weather they had year round. They were averaging just about twenty-five thousand spectators per game, yet for the first three months of the season, while they were competitive and in first place for a few weeks, that number jumped nearly seven thousand, to a respectable thirty-two thousand ticket holders per game. The team made a profit, thanks mainly to their cable and TV contracts, but all that profit went straight back into improving the team.

Suddenly Mia appeared out of nowhere and proclaimed happily, "I'm all clean!" I looked at her, after getting over the shock of her materializing out of nowhere without making a sound, and remarked, "And don't you look marvelous." She smiled shyly as she looked down at the computer screen and asked, "Did you find out why the sky is blue?"

"No. I was waiting for you," I said. I closed the documents Catherine had sent over and sat her down in front of the computer. I guided her to a search engine and had her type in "Why is the sky blue?" It took her a few minutes because she didn't know how to type, but once it was all there, I had her press the "enter" button and a whole bunch of articles showed up on the screen.

She opened an article that had been posted by NASA and she read it to me slowly, pausing for long moments to look at the pictures and graphics. Her eyes seemed to expand like a batter's eyes when a pitcher is unfortunate enough to send a ball straight down the middle of the plate.

The article explained that even though light from the sun looks white, it is really made up of all the colors of the rainbow. When light shines through a specially shaped crystal called a prism, the prism separates the light into all its different colors. The article talked about the way light beams around the universe, traveling in waves, the way water does when energy passes through the ocean. Mia pointed at the screen and kept reading. "It says 'some light travels in short, "choppy" waves,' while 'other light travels in long, lazy waves.' And it says that blue light waves are different because they're shorter than red light waves."

I was beginning to see how Mia had managed to survive in Salvation. This kid was obviously bright.

"Oh!" she exclaimed, looking at me, then back at the computer. "I found the answer! Here's why the sky is blue! It's because when sunlight reaches Earth's atmosphere and is 'scattered in all directions by the gases and particles in the air ... blue light is scattered more than the other colors because it travels as shorter, smaller waves.' This is why we normally see the sky as blue. It's because blue waves are smaller and more common than waves of other colors!"

Finally, after fifty years, I had the answer to a question that I'd never thought to ask. Mia and I shared a high five, and I left her at the computer watching videos posted by NASA, explaining phenomena we see every day of our lives, usually without asking the question *why*.

I lay down on the couch, closed my eyes and immediately fell asleep, for the second time that day. I dreamed that I was walking with Mia along the beach, listening happily as she explained the reason why the sky was blue. I had no problem hearing her low, soft voice, even with the sound of crashing waves ringing in my ears. The sky never looked more beautiful. Suddenly, I couldn't hear Mia's voice anymore. I looked beside me and she was gone. I looked all around and yelled, "Mia! Mia! Mia!" but the only answer I got was the sound of the crashing surf.

I looked over the vast ocean. In the distance, I saw Mia struggling, her arms flailing hopelessly against the immense power of the ocean as her head disappeared below the surface. I ran into the water, and just as I was about to dive in and swim to her, a colossal wave crashed directly into me, sending me reeling backward. I woke up in a cold sweat and looked up at Mia, who was standing over me.

"You were having a bad dream," she said anxiously.

"Yes," I said, "but now that I'm looking at your beautiful face, everything is perfect."

She smiled faintly as she went back to the computer and I got up and walked over to the bar. I remembered what Catherine had asked me: Was I prepared to handle a beautiful ten-year-old girl and the attention she would begin attracting as time went on?

There was no doubt that I was woefully ill-prepared for this and every other aspect of caring for a ten-year-old girl, but that wouldn't stop me from being the best father I could be.

I was confident, for example, that I had a handle on the simple things, like making sure Mia had good, healthy food to go along with her steady diet of chocolate. When I was fully awake and had recovered from my dream, I called room service and ordered dinner. I had the chicken cacciatore, and I ordered Mia a rib-eye steak with vegetables and the large piece of chocolate cake for dessert. Like the woefully ill-prepared father I was, I gave in to her craving for chocolate and let her eat the entire piece right then and there.

After dinner, we sat on the balcony and watched the sun set over the ocean and turn the whole sky red. Mia flipped through a notebook and read out loud from the notes she had taken from the NASA site about why the sky is blue.

"As the sun gets lower in the sky, its light is passing through more of the atmosphere to reach you," she said. "Even more of the blue light is scattered, allowing the reds and yellows to pass straight through to your eyes.

"'Sometimes the whole western sky seems to glow. The sky appears red because small particles of dust, pollution or other aerosols also scatter blue light, leaving more purely red and yellow light to go through the atmosphere.' Wow."

I had seen many sunsets in my life, but none quite as beautiful as the one I was currently looking at, accompanied by the soothing and musical narration of the enthusiastic ten-year-old sitting beside me on the balcony.

"Look at that," she said, pointing. "The sun looks like it's waving."

It was only a few days earlier that I'd set my eyes on what I thought was the most pathetic sight I had ever seen — an urchin of indeterminate age or gender, dressed in a dirt-encrusted waitress uniform. I remembered wondering if she was even able to read or write. Now that pathetic sight was not so pathetic as she explained the Earth's atmosphere and the wondrous sights our planet had to offer each and every day.

Before going to bed, I wrote down instructions for Mia on how to turn the computer on and off, how to get on to the internet, how to search for things that might interest her and how to save information. After one trial run, she had it down like a professional.

I didn't even bother to ask her if she was going to bed. After all the chocolate she'd consumed throughout the day, I did not expect her to fall asleep anytime soon.

CHAPTER SIXTEEN

I woke up at my usual time of 5:00 a.m., changed into my running outfit and walked into the living room where I found Mia sitting at the computer, dressed in shorts, a T-shirt and sneakers. She was watching a video about oceans and was so absorbed that she did not hear me enter. I called her name and she turned and looked at me.

"Have you been up all night?" I asked.

"No," she replied softly and defensively. "I got up a little while ago so I could go running with you. I like to run."

She bookmarked what she was watching and turned the computer off. I had her put on a sweatshirt because I knew it would be very cool by the water this early in the morning.

We walked down to the ocean and I placed her on the outside, away from the ocean, and told her under no circumstances was she to run ahead, cut across and run on the inside along the water. The episode from yesterday and the nightmare were still very fresh in my mind.

At exactly one o'clock, after Mia and I had both showered and changed and had a light snack and some more time looking at NASA videos together, Catherine knocked on the door of the suite. She was holding a briefcase, with a laptop computer and paper files neatly assembled in separate compartments of the briefcase. After she put down her things, she kissed and hugged Mia as though they had known each other for ten years.

The reciprocal ease and comfort that Catherine and Mia displayed toward each other made me feel even more inept at parenting. Mia seemed to glow whenever she was near Catherine. The only time I got that response from her for an extended period was when I put a big piece of chocolate cake in front of her.

Catherine was beautiful and smart, carefree and classy. She was the lady who walked into a crowded room and caused every head in the place to turn. Men and women took notice of her wherever she went.

We ordered room service and ate lunch sitting on the sofa, then moved to a table to talk baseball. Catherine took Mia by the hand and sat her down right beside her. "My father never excluded me from casual meetings about the game and I think it would be a good precedent to include your daughter in all such meetings." She looked at me and smiled. "After all, she might one day take on the burden of carrying on your legacy. Isn't that so, sweetheart?"

"Yes," Mia replied softly as Catherine gently squeezed her hand. Catherine turned her laptop on, then opened her briefcase and took out a paper file. Catherine knew the ins and outs of her father's team and seldom looked down at the charts, graphs and notes she had before her. In a sense, she reminded me of myself when I became the GM of my team. Her options were limited because of payroll restrictions. I listened carefully to everything she had to say and how she intended to improve the team. Her ideas were sound, and most baseball people would have agreed with her plans, but her team wouldn't be any closer to making the playoffs, never mind winning a championship, than they had been the previous year.

She stopped talking and said, "Please feel free to speak up anytime you like. I'm all ears, Joe."

"Well," I said, "the Cardinals are looking for a big bat."

"You think so?" she asked. "I mean, are you sure that's their biggest priority right now?"

"Absolutely," I said. "As you know, they lost the series this past year because they couldn't score any runs. But consider the fact that their starting rotation is the best in the game. It's so good that they have two pitching phenoms that any other team would have brought up last year. They both have one more year left on their minor league contracts."

"Wish our team had that problem," Catherine said. "It was our third and fourth starters this year that cost us a chance at the playoffs."

"You have what the Cardinals want."

Catherine thought for a minute, then said, "The MVP of the league, who still has three years left on his rookie contract."

"That's right. Those two pitchers won't come cheap, and the Cardinals will be very reluctant to give up both. They'll offer one and probably twenty million in cash. You insist on both and ten million."

"You want us to give up the *MVP*?" she asked incredulously.

"He's not taking you to the playoffs. At least, not with the current pitching staff you have."

"He kept us competitive for a good part of the year and he's a fan favorite."

"Is he clean?" I asked, and she hesitated just long enough to confirm my suspicions. The league had done a lot to control steroid use after allowing it to infest the game during the 1990s and early into 2000, but there were always new products on the market that masked the use of the power-enhancing, illegal substances.

"His urine tests have all come back clean," Catherine belatedly replied.

"That's good," I said with little enthusiasm as she lowered her eyes and ran her hand through Mia's golden hair. "Having fun?" she asked, and Mia nodded eagerly.

Catherine turned back and looked directly at me. "And how do you propose I make up for lost production?"

"That's where the ten million comes into play. The Phillies are trying to get rid of their on-again, off-again centerfielder, who they only play against left-handed pitchers. They've destroyed the kid's confidence. I scouted him for years in the Dominican Republic and he had no problem hitting lefties or righties. He's not going to give you the production that your MVP has delivered, but he's a great fielder and has amazing speed. Given the opportunity he could easily steal between thirty and forty bases. He has always had a wonderful on-base percentage, and playing full time he could easily hit twenty or more home runs a year, and he seldom strikes out. The Phillies will gladly unload him and the three years remaining on his six-million-a-year contract."

Catherine looked down at her notes, and before she had time to say anything, I finished my presentation by adding, "The Red Sox's wonderful pitching coach is retiring this year so he can be closer to his family down here in beautiful San Diego. I think if you reached out to him, he would welcome the opportunity to help bring along such highly touted pitching prospects."

Catherine and I talked for a while longer and then she closed the baseball discussion by saying, "There's a lot to think about and naturally I will have to discuss all this with my father and our team personnel."

She was obviously skeptical about my proposals, and in a way I was relieved. I really didn't want to feel any responsibility if she followed my advice, made the deals and everything went sour. She reminded Mia about their planned girls' day out the next day and thanked me profusely for my advice.

I walked Catherine to the elevator and as I watched the doors close I couldn't help feeling sorry for her. Yes, Catherine was beautiful, young, intelligent and very rich. But she had taken on the burden of helping her aging father win a championship, and in the world of sports, that was not something I would wish on any child.

I walked back into the suite and looked across at Mia, who had moved over two seats and was sitting in front of my computer. I stepped behind her and looked down at the screen, which displayed the statistics and data on Catherine's team. She looked up and asked, "Maybe I could help you with your team like Catherine helps her father?"

I smiled and replied, "That would be great, but for now how about we go take a nice long walk along the beach and on the way back we can stop off at the ice cream parlor and get you a double scoop of chocolate chocolate-chip ice cream with chocolate sprinkles." I was quite certain that, at least for the moment, that took her mind off baseball and coming to work for me.

CHAPTER SEVENTEEN

Catherine picked Mia up at around ten in the morning and told me not to expect them back until early evening, at the earliest. Catherine did not mention anything about our little baseball talk the day before. I walked them to the elevator and then went back into the suite. I dialed my lawyer's number and gave him the lowdown on Mia. I made it perfectly clear that I wanted to adopt the child and that I wanted it to be as easy as possible on her. She had already been through enough, and I would not put up with a parade of social workers and judges questioning her like she was some sort of criminal. This was not such an unusual case for him. He had represented numerous ballplayers from Central America and was able to relocate their families and, on occasion, their friends to the United States so that they could be together.

He did not think it would be very difficult for me to adopt Mia, especially since she was an American citizen and both her parents were dead. The only problem that could arise was if she had other relatives. I sent him copies of Mia's birth certificate and her parents' death certificates. He said he would get right on it.

Hours later, Catherine opened the door to the suite with the extra passkey I gave her. If such a thing was possible, she looked even more radiant. She hid Mia from me and told me to close my eyes. When I opened my eyes, I was speechless. Mia looked angelic; her face was glowing and her pale-blue eyes sparkled like aquamarines. Her golden glimmering locks of hair softly caressed her face and now she truly looked like an angel in a da Vinci painting come to life. She smiled and her dimples further illuminated the heavenly aura about her. Her face was still sunken but far less than just a few days earlier. I guessed that the ten pounds of chocolate she'd devoured over the last three days was having a beneficial effect.

Catherine's warning kept running through my mind. "Once Mia is healthy and fit, she's going to have a regiment of boys knocking at her door. Are you ready for that, Joe?" Was I ready? Was I ready? It played like an annoying refrain from a poorly written song and I was having trouble drowning it out.

I finally snapped out of it as Catherine started recapping their girls' day out. I poured her a glass of white wine, gave Mia a soda and opened an ice-cold beer for myself. Catherine asked Mia to finish telling me about their wonderful day. Mia picked up right where Catherine left off, with a story about how their pedicures were interrupted by a fire alarm and they all wound up on the sidewalk wearing little foam toe separators on their bare feet until they were let back in the building. We laughed and laughed at that, and Mia went on to describe their very fancy lunch at a nearby French bistro, which included her first ever chocolate eclair. Regardless of what she was talking about, Mia delivered the information in her soft, melodic voice, which was difficult to hear but was as pleasant and soothing as the early morning chirping of birds that reaches your ears just before you open your eyes to the promise of a new and wonderful day.

When they had finished regaling me with stories, Catherine got up to go and I walked her to the elevator. As I was telling her how much I appreciated all she was doing for Mia, she turned and looked at me with a blistering intensity that caused me to take a step back. "What do you know about the scars that run up and down that beautiful child's back? Scars caused by some sort of medieval whipping device."

I looked at her, bewildered, and then it all came rushing back to me like a tidal wave. The religious lunatics back in God's country, the obviously misnamed town of Salvation, where the so-called devil's child was begotten and roamed before I helped her escape.

"I've never seen her back without clothes on. I had no idea."

"Well something needs to be done about this. The authorities need to be notified."

"No! Mia's been through enough. I didn't see any other signs of children being mistreated. If you go to the authorities, the only one you will be hurting is Mia."

"How can you be sure there aren't other children being used as whipping posts?"

"Drop it, Catherine. Please, just drop it."

"Will you at least ask her how she got those scars?"

"I will … when I feel the time is appropriate."

After seeing Catherine off at the elevator I walked back into the suite and found Mia looking into a small makeup mirror Catherine had bought for her. "I don't know about you, but I don't think any mirror has seen such a pretty face as yours."

She blushed as she put the mirror down and ran into my arms. She held on tightly as I felt her warm tears pass through my shirt. I could easily have looked down and seen the scars on her back covered only by the loose-fitting blouse she wore. Instead, I closed my eyes, placed my hand behind her head and kept her face pressed softly against my chest.

CHAPTER EIGHTEEN

Since I had not seen Mia all day, we decided to take a long walk along the beach with the promise of a double scoop of chocolate chocolate-chip ice cream at the end. It was a clear, chilly night. Mia was appropriately bundled up in the new clothes that Catherine had bought for her during their girls' day out. I could not even imagine how much she had spent on Mia since they met, but it was an awful amount and she refused to take any money. Catherine had expensive and exquisite taste and Mia was being showered with her generosity.

As usual, my lovely Mia made me feel like an idiot — not purposely, but nevertheless like an idiot. The child asked a thousand questions. Her curiosity was limitless. "Where does sand come from? What is it made of? What makes the moon glow full and brilliantly some nights and not so brilliantly other nights? Where do the seagulls go at night?" Questions I don't ever remember asking at her age or at any age.

Waiting in line at the ice cream parlor, I looked across at Mia. She was sitting at our table writing in her little notepad, which she carried in her coat pocket. When I returned to the table with our ice cream cones, she put her pen down and took her cone out of my hand, smiling as she did.

"What'cha writing?" I asked.

"Just reminding myself of the things I want to look up on the computer when we get back to the hotel."

I glanced at the open notebook and saw a list of questions ending with "Where do seagulls sleep?"

"Ah-ha," I said. "I see you've made a long list of all the questions that I couldn't answer during our walk."

Mia looked up at me and smiled. "Yes, but that's okay. We can look them up together."

Back at the suite, with our bellies full of ice cream, we left the door to the balcony open, and even though it was chilly outside, Mia and I were comfortable enough inside the hotel room. I sat on the couch with a cold Budweiser in my hand as I listened to her explain the different geological components of sand and its composition in different parts of the world.

Who would have thought that there were so many different types of sand and so many different uses for the stuff? It was even used on the infields, pitching mounds and warning tracks of baseball fields. It helped with draining problems caused by rain during the games and especially during long rain delays. Mia put added emphasis on the use of sand on baseball fields, repeating what she read out loud a couple of times and jotting down notes in her notepad.

As I watched her flip through her notebook and listened to her hold forth on the latest object of her fascination, I couldn't help marveling at the transformation that was taking place before my eyes. The change from just a few days ago was simply amazing. Who would have thought that in the town of Salvation, a place specializing in ignorance, I would stumble upon a waif who would blossom into a living wonder.

CHAPTER NINETEEN

The following morning, after Mia and I came back from our run, Catherine called. She had made an appointment with her doctor for Mia. She thought it was very important that Mia have a complete checkup. I agreed and told her that I knew she was busy and that I could take her. It was at that moment that Catherine snapped and literally yelled, "No, I'll take her. It's not like you know anything about females and what questions to ask the doctor."

"I need to learn. How about if I just come along and listen?"

"No! It will only make her feel more uncomfortable if you come along. Please, let me talk to her."

I handed the phone to Mia as I fought back the urge to rip into Catherine, but then I thought better of it. I needed Catherine and there was no denying it. She was a godsend, and hopefully whatever was irritating her would have calmed down by the time she came to pick Mia up.

After a short phone conversation with Catherine, in which she mostly nodded and indicated her agreement, Mia went into her bathroom and took a shower. I walked out onto the balcony and looked out at the beautiful Pacific and breathed in the remedial power of the ocean air.

Catherine arrived shortly after noon, leaving plenty of time to get Mia to her one o'clock appointment. Catherine was all smiles, but the only time any of those smiles seemed genuine was when she was talking to Mia. I walked the girls to the elevator and got a hug from Mia and a fake smile and wave good-bye from Catherine. Apparently, whatever was stuck up her butt was not fully removed.

I walked back into the suite and sat down on the couch and that's when the craziness took hold of me. Could Catherine be making a play to take Mia away from me? In all truth, she had as much right to the child as I did, and she also had the money to fight me in court and she would almost definitely win. Maybe she was the flip side of the religious zealots in the town of Salvation — one of those people who is never happy unless she's fighting a crusade to rid the world of some evil. She was so angry about the scars on Mia's back and the possibility of other children suffering the same fate that I wouldn't have been a bit surprised if she was planning some avenging strike against the town. I could see the whole scene unfolding, complete with the Archangel Michael disguised as Catherine.

Deep down I knew that Catherine was better equipped than I was to raise a ten-year-old girl. If this had been the option I was given on the day I took her away from that town (a town that not even Rod Serling could have imagined) I would gladly have handed Mia over to that spoiled, rich, pompous, crusading daughter of a billionaire. But things were different now that I had gotten to know the little squirt. After washing off layers of dirt, she turned out to be a little gem ... a precious one, encased in a nugget of gold, in fact. Who the hell would of thought that? It was like picking Mike Piazza at 256 in the draft, expecting nothing and getting the best hitting catcher since Yogi Berra.

I sat there staring at the wall until I realized something amazing: I had learned more about our universe in the last few days than I had gleaned in the last fifty years. It was not like I ever asked myself, "Why is the sky blue?" And why was that? Was I not curious? I hoped that wasn't true. As I thought about it some more, it seemed more likely that any lack of curiosity I might have exhibited had more to do with being alone. I suddenly wished I had someone there to play catch with ... back and forth, back and forth, like I had done a million times before. Instead, I just stood up and walked to the refrigerator and took out an ice-cold beer. I took a long, refreshing sip and tried to think rationally.

Maybe all of this was … was some type of midlife crisis? After all, I had just turned fifty and just quit a job that I loved. Sure I had missed some huge moments, like being at my parents' bedsides when they passed away — after they had sacrificed everything for me — but I was sure they understood. I was rich, famous, sought after by every team in the major leagues, excluding the Yankees, and yet I had *nothing*, or rather, *no one*. No one to share my life with, no one to tuck in at night and talk to about things totally unrelated to baseball, no family like I was brought up in, no wife, not even a dog or cat.

Screw it all. That crusading, entitled blonde-haired beauty was not taking Mia away from me. I called Catherine on the phone and it went straight to her message. I didn't panic and simply and rationally drank a few more beers. I had dealt with stress my whole life. Sure it wasn't the same type of stress as this, but I had dealt with young ballplayers from Central America not much older than Mia, and I always put the ballplayer's safety and health above all else, and I was quite certain that I wasn't using Mia as a crutch to make up for my own shortcomings. I would be the best father possible, even if I had to read a thousand self-help books on how a father should properly parent a soon-to-be-teenage girl.

After a few more hours passed, I called Catherine again, and once again, it went straight to message. Previously, I had not left a message, but this time I did. Before I started to speak, I made sure I was fully composed. It took a lot of self-control, but I put on my calmest voice and simply said, "Catherine, it's Joe. Just wondering how everything is going. Please give me a call when you have a chance."

I sat down on the couch, had a few more beers and turned the TV, but I couldn't concentrate. I kept spinning these wild scenarios around in my head. None of them were really crazy or dangerous, but for a guy like me, they were a little bizarre. Even I had to admit that.

Half an hour later I called Catherine again, and naturally it went straight to message. Still sounding composed, I said, "Catherine, I am starting to worry. Please call me."

Amazing, I thought. *This young woman wants to be the GM of a Major League Baseball team, and yet she can't take a moment to listen to her messages. Doesn't she realize that responding to a message from a GM like me could spell the difference between making a deal that brings you a championship or finishing dead last in your division?* Apparently not! A daughter of privilege; what else would one expect? If she had to spend one day like poor Mia had to live, she would be destroyed for life.

I walked out onto the balcony and suddenly the sight of the ocean, the smell of the air, the squawking of the seagulls and the sight of beautiful women walking along the beach in bikinis was making me feel nauseated. So I went back inside and had another beer as the overwhelming thought that I was no longer the GM of any baseball team struck me like a Nolan Ryan fastball to the head. Now I really needed Mia in my life; otherwise my brain might simply deteriorate from lack of use.

Finally, at seven o'clock, the privileged princess decided to return my many calls. I took a deep breath before I answered, "Hello!"

"Hi Joe, it's Catherine."

"Catherine, where the hell have you been? I've been trying to get in touch with you all day."

"I'm sorry if I worried you. I shut off my phone when we went into the doctor's office and forgot to turn it back on."

"What did the doctor say?"

"Well our little girl seems to be in excellent shape considering all that she has been through. Her heart and lungs are strong, and all her limbs seem to be nimble and flexible like an athlete. Her reflexes are excellent. She's about twenty pounds underweight, but with all the chocolate she's been eating recently that shouldn't be a problem for too long. The doctor took blood and urine tests and we should get back the results in a few days, but he didn't think there was any need to worry."

"How about the scars?"

"They're all healed and don't seem to be causing her any pain. He thought they were most likely inflicted by some sort of whip."

"Wielded by a bunch of nut jobs. Where are you two?"

"Down at the bar. I desperately needed a glass of wine and Mia wanted a chocolate shake. It has been such a rough day, Joe. I'm sorry if I was curt with you this morning, but my father is starting to worry me more and more. I know he doesn't feel very well, and he's been forgetting things that he never would have forgotten even six months ago, but he's also refusing to go see a doctor. He snapped at me at least three times this morning, which is three times more than I remember him snapping at me during my entire life. He said not to worry, that the best thing that could happen was for him to simply die and be back with his wife. He said at least that way I would be free to live my own life and not be tied to an invalid."

I could hear her choking back tears. As I listened to her, I was overtaken by guilt after all the terrible things I had allowed myself to think about this amazing young lady.

Finally, she paused and said, "We'll be up in a few minutes," and I said, "Take all the time you need."

A few minutes later, Catherine and Mia entered the suite. For the first time all day, I wished they would have stayed away longer. Suddenly, I had a difficult time looking at Catherine, embarrassed about thoughts I had never vocalized — unfair thoughts about her being a spoiled little rich girl.

Mia hugged me as Catherine threw herself down on the couch. As I returned Mia's hug, I tried to contain the emotions that were flooding my body and mind after this strange day of worry and paranoia. "I heard the doctor gave you a clean bill of health."

"Yes," she said in her soft, melodic voice. "And now, I don't have to worry about eating too much chocolate."

"Is that what the doctor said?"

She lowered her eyes as Catherine turned her head toward the two of us and remarked, "Sort of, but not exactly. Isn't that so, Mia?"

"Yes, sort of," Mia replied as she blushed.

"I think I might have heard him say that you should also eat more vegetables, fruits and fish … along with a healthy dose of chocolate."

"That sounds a little more likely," I said. Then I kissed Mia on the head and asked Catherine if she wanted a glass of wine.

"Yes, please. A very big glass." I walked over to the bar as Mia sat down next to Catherine. Moments later, I handed Catherine a very large glass of white wine and opened a beer for myself. I looked at Mia and asked, "And for you, young lady? A whiskey, bourbon or maybe a nice martini?"

Mia smiled and shook her head as Catherine hugged her tightly and remarked, "Her chocolate shake was extra large with three generous scoops of ice cream."

I laughed as I looked at the two of them and couldn't help feeling that in a few weeks, after Mia put on a little more weight, she would easily be able to pass for Catherine's daughter.

Catherine picked up the remote control to the TV and turned it on. She flipped through the channels as she drank her wine rapidly. Suddenly, she stopped on a channel showing the movie, *The Bells of St. Mary's*, starring the beautiful Ingrid Bergman playing a nun (never in all my years of Catholic school did I ever see a nun that even came close to such heavenly beauty as Ms. Bergman) and Bing Crosby playing a priest.

Catherine said, "Oh, I love this movie." She hugged Mia tightly as Mia looked across at the screen. In the movie, Ms. Bergman and Mr. Crosby were walking through a church, and there were repeated scenes of Christ on the Cross. In a heartbeat, Mia broke away from Catherine and ran into her bedroom.

"My God, I guess that shake really went through her … poor baby," Catherine said. As I looked back at the movie — at the church, the crucifix, Ms. Bergman and the stations of the cross — it all hit me like a thunderbolt from heaven.

"It's not that; it's the movie and the relics in the church. It represents the hell that poor child had to live through. The whippings. The scars."

"My God, I didn't even think of that," Catherine said, quickly shutting off the TV. I looked across at the blank screen and for the first time in my life I wished I had nothing to do with being a Catholic, or even a Christian. I would have preferred being an atheist, agnostic, a Hindu or a Buddhist.

Catherine started toward Mia's bedroom and I stopped her. "It's better if I take care of this." She sat back down, and I walked toward Mia's bedroom, feeling like a defrocked priest confessing to a mistreated child and hoping for penance and forgiveness.

I entered her room and saw a noticeable lump of blankets stacked in the middle of the bed. I sat on the edge of the mattress and gently poked the lump and said, "I could be wrong, but I'll bet there is a beautiful little girl under all those blankets. A beautiful, intelligent, caring little girl named Mia, but I could be wrong." I poked the lump once again and asked, "Is that you under there, Mia?"

She giggled and I continued, "You know, when I was your age I used to play hide-and-seek with my beautiful mommy. And when it was my time to hide, I always used to hide under my bed and my mommy would pretend she couldn't find me, and when she would pass by my bed she would ask, 'I wonder where my little Joey could be?' and I would always giggle, and then she would reach under the bed and pull me out and hug me, and she used to laugh and pinch my nose and say that I could never really hide from her because she loved me way too much and that she would always be there to protect me. And you know what? I will always be there to protect you because I love you so much."

She lifted the blankets and I hugged her like my mother used to hug me, and then I pinched her cute little nose and kissed her on the top of her head and reminded her that I would always be there to protect her and that no one would ever harm her, ever again.

CHAPTER TWENTY

We ate dinner in the suite, and despite the fact that Mia had just wolfed down a large chocolate shake a little earlier, she had no problem eating a large piece of chocolate cake, along with a few morsels of vegetables and a piece of fish. Catherine's dinner consisted mainly of several glasses of white wine and a few bits of steak.

Catherine was getting sloppy, and despite every effort to disguise the fact, her speech was starting to slur, and no amount of laughing and joking could hide the pain she was feeling. She was a glass or two away from a meltdown, and when I told her she needed to slow down and refused to refill her glass, she got up off the couch and stumbled toward the bar. "I'm not that little girl you remember at the winter meetings. You don't tell me what I should or shouldn't do."

I had been through this drill many times with drunken ballplayers, both rookies and veterans, commiserating over slumps, contracts, girlfriends, wives, deaths of a child or a parent. I didn't reply to Catherine's remark and instead looked at Mia, who looked at Catherine with eyes wide and forehead creased with anxiety.

Catherine grabbed the bottle of white wine and attempted to refill her glass, spilling wine all over the bar. She turned from the bar, stumbled and dropped the glass. As she fell toward the floor, I reached out and caught her. She laughed as I raised her to her feet and held on to her tightly, but these brittle little sounds of false mirth were quickly followed by a flood of tears.

"He can't do his job anymore," she sobbed into my shirt. "He's trying so hard, but he can't do it."

I held on to her and let her talk, patting her back and stroking her hair. Although I could make out only one in every few words, it was clear that she was worried sick about her father. I realized then that watching him decline was going to be incredibly sad — much like watching an aging ballplayer who had been idolized throughout his career then suddenly slowed down, his bat speed diminished and his skills all faltering at once. His greatness and durability, a thing of the past; and while the memories were immortalized in old TV footage and barroom discussions, he'd never again hear applause from the stands after a great catch or a game-winning hit. Catherine's father was at that age where the past still shone like a bright star but the future was no longer his to grasp. It was his daughter's time to fulfill his dreams and her own.

When Catherine stopped speaking and slumped against my shoulder, I picked her up and carried her into Mia's room, then waited a moment as Mia rearranged the rumpled bedsheets. I then laid Catherine down. She was completely passed out, and I asked Mia to make her as comfortable as possible. She quickly set to work covering Catherine with a spare blanket and arranging her head on the pillow. As I was about to leave the room, I remembered to ask Mia to turn Catherine on her side — the safest position for someone who had been drinking too much and gone unconscious. I would have done all of this myself, but I thought it was better to enlist Mia's help than to risk laying hands on Catherine without her permission.

I walked out of the room, grabbed a beer and went out on the balcony. It was a beautiful, clear night, and as I leaned up against the railing and looked out at the ocean, I reflected on the final words in F. Scott Fitzgerald's *The Great Gatsby*. The exact quote eluded me, but I remembered Fitzgerald's line about all of us being "boats against the current." No matter how much we struggled to move ahead and look toward the future, we always seemed to be pushing up against our past.

Mia walked out onto the balcony and wrapped her little hand around my hand and she held on tightly.

"Catherine is worried about her father," she said. "She's afraid that he wants to die and be with her mother."

"Is that what she told you?"

"Yes. She was sad all day. She tried to hide it, but I could tell. I feel very sorry for her. Catherine is so nice."

I looked down at Mia and at that moment, with the moon shining brightly and a blanket of stars covering the sky, she reminded me of a child who belonged to the sea ... not a fictional mermaid but a muse who understood the deep, dark and beautiful universe that existed beneath the surface.

I gently ran my hand across the top of her hair and looked into her eyes and they seemed to have lost the fear they exhibited just a short time ago when she ran and hid under the bedsheets. I could not even begin to imagine what went on inside her head or what she dreamed of when she closed her eyes and fell asleep. She seemed to adapt to her new environment very quickly, which made me hope that some part of her early childhood was normal. Her curiosity was insatiable, and she not only asked a lot of questions but also wasn't content until she found the answers, even if it meant staying up all night and searching the internet.

"Would you like to live here?" I asked.

"Yes. It's very beautiful," she said. "And I found out today that they have a zoo where you can go visit all the animals from around the world, and another place where you can see whales, dolphins, sharks and penguins."

Her eyes grew wide when she mentioned penguins. I told her the name of the place was SeaWorld, but I could tell that she already knew that.

"Catherine said if she has the time she'll take me before we leave."

"Even if she doesn't have the time, I will take you. Maybe all three of us can go. I think that would be really nice."

"Yes, it would be really nice," she repeated in her low, melodic voice that seemed to travel effortlessly on the sea breeze like an angelic melody, soothing and peaceful.

"It's a date," I said as she looked into the suite and in the direction of her room.

"You love Catherine?" I asked.

"Yes," she replied, hesitating a little as she squeezed my hand tightly. "But I don't love anyone more than I love you."

She wrapped her arms around my waist as I fought back tears. I lowered my head and kissed her several times on the top of her head and said, "And I don't love anyone more than I love you."

***

Mia took the laptop and went into her bedroom to keep an eye on Catherine. I sat down on the couch, opened a beer and turned on ESPN. I figured that more than a week had passed since my resignation shocked the baseball world, and that by now, I was old, forgotten news. I was right. Thankfully, there was not a word about me on any of the channels. The basketball season was just beginning, and the sportscasters and analysts were making their predictions. It had been years since I had followed any other sport very closely, but I was well aware that my favorite basketball team, the New York Knicks, were going through an unprecedented losing streak, and according to all the talking heads on the TV, that streak was not in any jeopardy of being broken.

Catherine's phone had been ringing repeatedly from where she'd left it on the coffee table. At first, I just ignored the calls, but after the fifth call I decided that I'd better look and make sure it wasn't an emergency. I picked up her phone and looked at the calls and they were all from her father.

I couldn't just wake Catherine. Personally, I didn't think that was even possible. She was so drunk, and it had been only an hour since she lost consciousness, so I was left with the uncomfortable responsibility of calling her father and explaining the situation. "Hi, Mr. Baker — sorry, your daughter can't answer her phone because she is passed out cold, drunk, on the bed of my soon-to-be-adopted daughter, in the hotel suite where we are staying." Yeah, that sounded reasonable enough … so reasonable that I opened another beer and downed it as I tried to think of another excuse. The truth was that I didn't have another reasonable excuse. I thought of having Mia make the call, but in the end I just picked up my phone and dialed Mr. Baker's number, hoping and praying he wouldn't answer and that I would be able to leave a message. Naturally, he picked up on the first ring.

"Hello, Mr. Baker. Joe Ciotola calling."

"Hello, Joseph. How are you?" Mr. Baker sounded wonderful and personable like I always remembered him. In all my years as a GM, I never heard any baseball person say a negative thing about Walter Baker, and that was because he was a truly great guy, never one to stab a competitor in the back, always straightforward and honest … a real gem in what was a cutthroat business at the best of times.

"I imagine you are calling me about my daughter. She called me earlier from the bar at the hotel where she told me she was watching your newly adopted daughter put down a large chocolate shake. Catherine sounded quite drunk then and my guess is that she is passed out in your suite."

"Yes, she's passed out on my newly adopted daughter's bed. I'm sorry."

"Don't worry about a thing. If she was going to be passed out anywhere but home, I could only hope and pray that it would be in the presence of a gentleman like you."

"Sir, I don't need to tell you what a blessing and a help Catherine has been to me and Mia. You raised a perfect child and I can only hope Mia turns out just like her."

"I have no doubt that with a father like you that is exactly how little Mia is going to turn out. Please tell my daughter that I am sorry for the way I behaved earlier, and that I don't want her driving home until she is sober, and that I love her so very much." I could hear Mr. Baker trying not to choke up.

"I will definitely tell her that," I said. "And how about we all go out to dinner before I leave."

"I would love nothing more, and I can't wait to meet Mia. Thank you, Joseph."

"Thank you, sir."

I sat down on the couch, full of relief, and opened another beer. This time I drank it slowly as I watched ESPN with the sound turned off. Mr. Baker loved his family, and the few times I'd met his wife, I never doubted for a minute how much the two of them were in love. Even after twenty-five years of marriage, they had looked at each other as though they were still newlyweds.

I left the balcony door slightly ajar. The breeze was refreshing, and the bouquet of oceanic currents was hypnotic and life-affirming, like the smell of freshly cut grass at the ballpark. I had been a resident of Southern California for more than half my life and yet I had probably visited its lovely beaches less than ten times. I had never been to Santa Barbara or Laguna Beach, and the six times a year my team visited down here I usually stayed at this hotel, yet it seemed like I didn't have any recollection of the surrounding beauty. How could that be? Suddenly, at age fifty, wealthy beyond my wildest dreams and relatively healthy, it was as though I had lived my life with eyes half closed.

I picked up a writing pad off the table and wrote Catherine a note saying that I had talked to her father and that he said to tell her that he loved and adored her and that he was sorry for any misunderstanding they might have had the day before. I placed the note under her phone and got up off the couch and glanced into Mia's room. Catherine was still passed out, and Mia was lying across from her, staring intently at the laptop screen.

I walked into my bedroom and went to sleep.

CHAPTER TWENTY-ONE

The following morning, I got up at my usual time, put on my running gear and walked out of my bedroom. It was still dark outside, and Mia and Catherine were sitting at the table. Mia was reading to Catherine from the laptop. To my surprise, Catherine didn't look one bit the worse for wear after her drunken debacle. Either that or I just wasn't used to waking up and walking out of my bedroom and into the presence of such a beautiful lady.

"Wow! If I didn't know better, I would think I was still asleep and dreaming. The sight of two such beautiful women before sunrise."

"Well if that's what you're seeing, you better go back to sleep because you're apparently not fully conscious. One gorgeous lady, yes," Catherine replied as she pointed to Mia and then continued, "but two, no way."

"Don't sell yourself short," I said. "You're breathtaking at any time of the day or night."

"Unless you're planning on asking me out on a date, there's no need for the flattery."

"Mia, what do you think?" I asked.

"She's the most beautiful girl in the whole wide world."

Catherine turned to Mia and jokingly replied, "Okay, enough from you. I already promised to take you to SeaWorld and the zoo."

I sat down at the table and looked at Catherine and asked, "You feeling okay?"

"Yes, it's amazing what getting disgustingly drunk and passing out for ten hours will do for a girl's health. If I said anything stupid or behaved recklessly, I apologize."

"That's the problem — you didn't say anything. You just passed out on the couch. And after numerous attempts to revive you, we transported you to bed. Isn't that so, Mia?"

"Yes," she replied as she looked back down at her computer.

"Thanks for getting in touch with my dad."

"It's no problem at all," I said. "He's such a wonderful gentleman. It's always a pleasure talking to him. I told him that before we depart, we all need to get together and go out for dinner."

"That would be great. I know he wants to meet Mia. I have talked so much about her."

I looked across at Mia, who was still dressed in her pajamas and asked, "Are you going to go running with me this morning?"

"Yes," she replied as she looked up from the laptop.

"Well then, I think you better go change, unless you plan on running in your pajamas."

She got up and walked into her bedroom as Catherine looked at me and said, "When I woke up this morning, hung over and feeling lousy, I turned over and saw Mia sleeping next to me with her head on top on the computer, and suddenly everything seemed wonderful and good. Have you started the adoption process?"

"Yes, my lawyer is looking into it as we speak. Mia will never be taken away from us." As the words came out of my mouth, I realized that by saying *us*, I automatically included Catherine, and that I didn't feel at all threatened by her, like I had the day before when my imagination went off the deep end.

"I need to ask you something, and please don't take it the wrong way," I said. "Do you honestly, deep down, really want to be the GM of your father's team?"

"Yes," she replied immediately and almost as quickly added, "unless you have changed your mind and want the job. Then I will gladly take the position as president of the team."

"I'm sorry, Catherine, but that is just not going to happen, at least not this year. Even before Mia, I had firmly decided that I needed time away from the game, and now that dirty little girl who I met in that crazy town of Salvation has become my top priority, and I plan on giving her my full attention."

"I understand. She is a lucky little girl to have found you."

"And to have found you. And so, back to the original question."

"Yes, deep down, I want to be the GM."

"Great! I think if you let your father know that *deep down* it is a dream of yours to be GM of the team, whatever misunderstandings you are having with him at the moment will clear up rather nicely."

Mia walked back into the room dressed in her running gear, and announced that she was all ready to go for our run. We took the elevator down, walked Catherine to her car and watched her drive off. I took Mia's hand and we walked down to the beach.

"I lied," Mia said.

"I know, and so did I, but we did it not to hurt Catherine's feelings … so it's okay."

"Okay," Mia repeated as I stopped, bent down and looked at her. "I won't tell her any of the things she said about her dad."

"I think that's best," I said. "She would be embarrassed to find out she'd said anything about him. We don't want that."

"No," Mia said. "We don't want that."

"I never asked, how did you like the doctor?"

"He was very nice."

"And he didn't make you feel uncomfortable?"

"No, he was very nice and very smart."

"Would you like him to be your primary doctor?"

"Why? Am I sick?"

"No, angel, you're perfect, and that's the way we want you to stay. Catherine and I have primary-care doctors who we usually visit once or twice a year and they perform routine examinations to make sure everything is working fine. It's quite normal, and nothing to worry about."

It was clear that my question made her nervous, even though I was quite certain Catherine had explained all this to her. It wasn't Mia's body, despite the scars, that worried me. After all, the child could outrun me. Her stamina was unbelievable. It was her psychological makeup and the trauma that she had been through that worried me. If the proverbial dam was ever to burst, it was the mental overload I could see fracturing and overwhelming her entire being.

We started running, and then I suddenly stopped and put a restraining hand on Mia. She looked up at me, puzzled, and I bent down and said, "I have an idea. How about if we go to SeaWorld today? I don't know about you, but I would love to see some penguins."

Mia's eyes grew wide and I could see that the idea of seeing penguins completely erased any anxiety she might have had about the doctor.

"What about Catherine?"

"I have a feeling that Catherine might not be quite up to it today, but we will call her and ask. I'm fairly certain she has been to SeaWorld quite a few times and won't mind a bit if we go without her."

"Really?" she asked.

"Really," I said. "I have no doubt she'll understand our need to visit the penguins and dolphins."

We started running again and I was quite certain she wasn't thinking about any doctor, but about seeing the penguins and all the fish at the theme park, and maybe a chocolate cake or two.

CHAPTER TWENTY-TWO

The first thing Mia did when we got back to our suite was turn on the computer and search for information on SeaWorld. Usually, the first thing she did was to go take a shower, put on clean clothes and walk out of her bedroom and proclaim that she was "all clean!" So it worked … I finally outsmarted the child … I took her mind off the doctor and placed it squarely on the penguins.

The speed with which Mia was able to learn how to use the laptop computer was simply astonishing, which once again left me wondering more and more about her past. What had she been like three or four years ago, before her parents died and left her an orphan, a child forced to work at that crazy, surreal restaurant and bar, eating scraps of leftover food and living in that depressing apartment? She had apparently had some type of formal education for at least a year or two before she became an outcast, pegged as the devil's child by the town's religious crazies. Her curiosity was limitless, but then it wasn't so unusual for children her age to be very curious. Nevertheless, it was her ability to grasp complexities and to process information that was unusual for any age. I had so many questions! I hoped to get the answers to them all, but I had to be careful. I was worried I would upset the balance between us and the rapport we had developed by asking even the most common sort of question, like, Did you ever attend a real school with an actual teacher and fellow classmates?

I thought about this conundrum in relation to baseball. The game of baseball was one big question, and the only honest, unequivocal answer I could truthfully offer was that after nine innings, the team that was ahead was the winner. Moreover, if it went into extra innings, the team that went ahead and held its opponent scoreless or scoring fewer runs in their half inning was the winner. There were so many variables that the most one could ever do was to theorize. Baseball was not a science, despite what the great hitter Ted Williams might want one to believe in his best-selling book, *The Science of Hitting*. Baseball, at the major league level, was a game that required great skill. It was no myth that the hardest thing in all of sports was hitting a baseball coming at you, curving and sinking, at ninety-five miles an hour. Yet on any given weekend, the worst team in baseball could sweep the best team in the game, whereas the odds of the worst team in football or basketball beating the best team were minimal.

I had no doubt that it was going to take nine innings or more to get answers to the many questions I had about Mia, but like I said, I was in no rush. The best thing I could do for this child, at this moment in time, was provide her with peace of mind, a sense of security and an abundance of love.

SeaWorld opened at ten thirty and it just so happened that they had a behind-the-scenes Penguin Encounter, where, for an additional charge, you got to meet a penguin up close and personal. These encounters were usually sold out way in advance, but since it was the off-season, they had openings for both the 11:30 a.m. tours and the 1:30 p.m. tours. Since Mia's enthusiasm was spiking at unseen levels, I booked the earlier tour.

Mia took a shower, changed into a hip pair of dungarees and a T-shirt and proclaimed herself "all clean," all before I had a chance to order breakfast or take a shower. I reminded her that it was only 7:30 a.m. and that the park was only a fifteen-minute drive from the hotel. She looked at me slightly dumbfounded and disappointed, but once I told her that chocolate chocolate-chip pancakes were still available, she immediately cheered up. I ordered breakfast, took a shower and changed into clean clothes — not nearly as hip as the outfit Catherine had bought for Mia, but good enough for a dad and quite comfortable.

Just as I walked back out, a kitchen assistant knocked on the door and delivered our breakfast. I tipped the young man and sat down at the table with Mia, who had a difficult time choosing between looking at penguin videos on the computer and eating. I made it easy for her and reached over and closed the laptop and placed it to the side. I pointed at her plate and said, "Please eat your breakfast before it gets cold." It was my first disciplinary act of parenting since taking custody of Mia.

At first it felt good, and then it suddenly didn't feel so good. Mia lowered her head and cut into her pancakes but without the zeal she usually displayed when anything with chocolate was put before her. I reached over and touched her hand and said, "You can watch all the videos you like. I just want to make sure you don't forget to eat." I opened the laptop and pushed it back beside her. She looked up and said, "Thank you," in her soft, melodic voice.

"You're welcome, honey."

It was with her mouth full of chocolate chocolate-chip pancake that Mia suddenly looked at me, smiling and chewing, and said "I love you so much." I could see a flash of chocolate and pancake as she spoke, but she closed her mouth and swallowed the bite.

I could feel myself beaming and almost blushing as I said, "And I love you so much."

I couldn't help seeing the irony. Here I was, the supposed guru of baseball GMs, a tough negotiator who didn't blink at the outrageous demands and threats from agents or the oversized egos of ballplayers, and yet before this child I was putty. Even though I had dealt with thirteen-, fourteen- and fifteen-year-old kids, all boys, for nearly twenty-five years down in Central America and throughout the States, it felt totally different with Mia. I had no doubt that a large part of it was because she was a girl, but I also knew that a large part of it was because she was my responsibility, my child, and I was already thinking that one day she would grow up to be a famous scientist, doctor, movie director or quite possibly an influential environmentalist who would help save the planet. I already knew I would be the proudest father in the world.

Before leaving for the park, I called Catherine and told her of our plans and asked her if she wanted to come along. She was too busy, but she wanted to know all the details when we got back. We got to the park a few minutes before it opened, and we parked as close as possible to the entrance. As soon as we got there, Mia flung off her seat belt and jumped out of the car, waiting with barely concealed impatience while I gathered up a few things and joined her for the walk to the front entrance.

I had Mia take a coat with her because the temperature was kept at thirty-two degrees at the Penguin Encounter. (Can't have the stars of the show being uncomfortable.) I also carried a coat. At the entrance to the park, I gave my name and we received our day passes to the park, along with separate tickets for the tour. We were also given pamphlets, which included a map of the park and all its attractions and restaurants, and a brief history of SeaWorld and the millions of guests that visit each year.

Mia searched the map for the penguin exhibit, and once she found it, she took my hand and led us directly to the tuxedo-clad birds. Before passing through the gates of SeaWorld, the closest I had ever come to a real live penguin was talking with former Dodger third baseman Ron Cey, who was nicknamed "The Penguin" because of the way he walked. After being kindly escorted out of the park at closing, I knew more about penguins than I ever thought possible.

Before entering the exhibit, we were told that when it was time for the behind-the-scenes tour to begin, an announcement would be made and a guide would escort us to our destination. In the meantime, Mia and I walked into a giant arena where we were treated to an amazing sight — an island oasis with hundreds of penguins huddling behind a giant protective glass partition. The whole thing was almost the size of a football field. We watched, fascinated, as they waddled around, diving into pools of water, conversing and eating a healthy diet of fish.

The scene mesmerized me, but after a few minutes I snapped out of it. As for Mia, she literally looked possessed, and if it wasn't for the partition, I swear she would have jumped in and tried to join the colony. I jokingly waved my hands in front of her face and asked, "Do you have a favorite?"

She blinked back into the moment and smiled at me, saying, "I love them all." I chuckled and said, "Good."

A guide announced the start of the Behind-the-Scenes Close Encounter Tour, and all those who had signed up were ushered down a hall decorated with pictures of penguins, scenes of aquarium personnel taking care of the birds, and visitors mingling with the penguins. We entered a room where the guide showed us a pictorial of all the different species of penguin — eighteen at last count, including some who lived in warm climates. Who would have thought? All I had ever seen were penguins waddling around in snow and ice, and diving into bone-chilling water. Mia and I were both fascinated to learn that there were penguin species living in South Africa, Australia and on the coasts of Peru and Chile.

Besides Mia and I, there were only six others on the tour: an attractive young lady, who I imagined to be a teacher, and five of her students, all of whom seemed to be around Mia's age. The guide cautioned the group that we should bundle up because we would shortly be entering an area that was significantly colder. Mia had her head buried in a penguin pictorial and didn't hear this advice, so like a good daddy, I put her jacket on her and buttoned it up.

We followed the guide over to a restaurant-style refrigerator door. He opened it, sending a cold breeze pouring out into the waiting area. We walked into a new room, and suddenly we were standing on the other side of the glass partition, on the edge of the frozen rotunda, with hundreds of penguins waddling right past us, just a few feet away from our eager faces. All that separated us from the penguins was a two-foot chain-link fence that opened onto the rotunda. Mia stepped forward and leaned over the fence and was about to pet one of the penguins when I grabbed her. "What are you doing?" I screamed at her. "You can't just reach out and touch them."

"I just wanted to say hi," the startled child pleaded. I was quite certain she was going to start crying, and here I was, standing there, feeling like an abusive idiot, with the critical eyes of the teacher, the students and the guide pinned on me. Even the penguins seemed to be judging me.

"Oh it's okay," the guide remarked in a matter-of-fact tone. "The penguins won't hurt her. They're so used to humans that they hardly notice us — although some of them are a little more sociable." At that, he reached over, opened the fence and let out a single whistle, then called out the name "Rex." At this invitation, a handsome three-foot-tall penguin broke from his group and waddled over to ours. "Good boy," the guide said, before bending down and rewarding the potbellied star with a small fish from a pouch around his waist.

Naturally, my daughter was the first to step forward and start petting Rex. The one thing my child did not lack was initiative, but then living and surviving among the religious crazies in the town of Salvation was like going through boot camp — if you survived that, you were ready for anything. The only problem was that she would not stop petting Rex, and all the other children were being deprived of their moment in the sun with the star. But this time I did not raise my voice and simply bent down and gently nudged Mia along. At the same time I did this, Rex decided to display his vocal abilities with a piercing scream. Our guide had already told us that this was quite natural for penguins, but when you are not expecting such a lovely, penetrating sound, it can throw you off and possibly leave you deaf for life. Mia's hands flew to her ears, but she giggled and giggled as the other children and the teacher got to pet Rex.

Then after everyone had had their turn, Mia went back in for a hug. The guide said it was perfectly okay, and Rex seemed to be totally enjoying it, but Mia wouldn't let go, and finally the guide had to intervene and separate them, but not before Mia kissed the bird on the side of the face a number of times.

Just as I thought I was free and we were walking out of the penguin exhibit, I asked Mia which exhibit she would like to go to next. (I had already ruled out the shark exhibit because the last thing I needed was for her to try and hug a man-eater). Mia replied that there was one more behind-the-scenes Penguin Encounter, and if we could go to that, she would love it.

"They might be sold out," I cautioned, knowing damn well that I had no such luck. "I thought you wanted to see the dolphins."

"I'd rather visit the penguins," she said. I looked at her and realized that there wasn't any way I could say no. So I took her hand and up we walked to the booth, where I asked if there were any more tickets available for the 2:30 p.m. behind-the-scenes tour, and of course there were.

The second tour was exactly the same as the first, except my lovely Mia's enthusiasm was even higher, especially since there were only two other people on this tour — both senior citizens who seemed a little squeamish about petting and hugging Rex. Fortunately for everyone, Mia's affection for the bird easily made up for their lack of intimacy. Once again, the guide had to peel her arms from around Rex, who seemed a little peeved by the guide's action. He gave the guide the evil eye and wobbled off as Mia waved good-bye.

We walked into a gift shop that featured a vast array of plush toys and stuffed animals, or should I say stuffed fish and birds. Mia immediately became transfixed on the stuffed penguins that most resembled Rex in size, color and shape. I asked if she would like one and she said yes. I handed her a Rex lookalike that was nearly as big as her. Naturally, she named him Rex.

It was nearly 4:30 p.m., and we had not eaten since breakfast. We walked into an ice cream parlor and I ordered two extra-large chocolate sundaes with extra chocolate syrup. After all, this was Mia's day, and as I looked across at her sitting at a table with Rex, I was reminded that she was still a child. This was something I seemed to forget at times, probably because it seemed like she was the one tutoring and teaching me new things every day. She was ten years old, at times exhibiting the intellectual abilities of a college student, and at other times, like today, behaving like a seven- or eight-year-old ... not that I knew much about how seven- or eight-year-olds behaved.

Mia ate her sundae with gusto, and when I was unable to finish my extra-large sundae, I slid the remaining half over to her and she finished it off like a true champion. I then reached over, like my mother used to do with me, and wiped her chocolate-smudged face clean. I didn't want her to accidently kiss Rex and stain the life-size penguin, even though I saw that as a real possibility in the future.

After one last visit to the penguin exhibit to say good-bye to all the penguins, we left the park at exactly 6:30 p.m., one hour past the park's closing time. Mia sat Rex in the backseat of the car, buckled him in and then sat up front with me. I drove off as the evening darkness descended around us, leaving Mia, Rex and me in a protective cocoon, separate from the rest of the world.

"And did you have a good time?" I asked.

"Yes, the best time ever. Thank you so much," she replied as a long pause followed and I could sense that something was bothering her.

"The guide asked me if you were my daddy," she continued, "and I said yes, he is my daddy. Is that okay?"

I came to a stop at a red light and looked across at her and replied, "Of course that's okay. People have asked me if you were my daughter and I have told them all that you were and that I am so proud of you. Is that okay?"

She looked at me and her eyes sparkled. She smiled and her dimples gave off a glow that seemed to blot out the surrounding darkness.

Back at the hotel suite, my phone rang and it was Catherine. She wanted to know if we were available tomorrow night to have dinner with her and her father. He so wanted to meet Mia and, of course, to see me. We agreed to meet at seven o'clock and have dinner at the hotel restaurant.

Catherine wanted to talk to Mia, and I handed the phone to her. Mia's face lit up as she told Catherine all about her day visiting the penguins and getting to hug the real-life Rex on two occasions. She was standing a few feet away from me and yet I could only make out a few words. She spoke softly, yet her voice had a musical quality to it, like singing. I wondered if her voice would change as she got older. I hoped not, even though it would be helpful if her voice went down an octave and achieved a little more volume, especially since I already saw her as a professor, a doctor, a famous scientist giving speeches to distinguished guests and dignitaries. Strange, the one thing I did not want for her was to follow in my footsteps and decide to go into the world of sports. I had no doubt she would make a great GM, manager or scout ... actually, I could see her playing on a professional baseball team, she had such great stamina and agility. I had long felt that it was only a matter of time before a woman broke into the big leagues. A .300 batting average with an on-base percentage over .400, and fans and executives could gradually become blind to gender.

I turned to Mia as she handed me back my phone and said, "Catherine sounded great."

"Yes — she was so excited when I told her about the penguins."

"I think penguins are universally loved."

"Yes," she replied as her face glowed, and once again, I was reminded that she was a child ... a gifted, beautiful child ... but still a child. "Yes, they're wonderful."

CHAPTER TWENTY-THREE

Mia and I arrived early at the restaurant the next night and were seated in a semi-private section of the eatery. Catherine made the reservation and I had no doubt that she asked to be seated in this section. The waiter, Fernando, greeted us and took our drink order. I handed him a hundred dollars, along with my credit card, and told him to charge the bill on the card and add an additional thirty-five percent tip. It's easy to be generous with money when you have plenty.

Mia ordered a chocolate shake, which I was surprised they even served, and Fernando was quick to ask, "Are you the pretty little girl who has been ordering all our chocolate dishes?"

Mia, taken aback by the question, looked at Fernando and nodded.

"Yes, she's the pretty little girl ordering all your chocolate dishes. She's addicted," I remarked.

"Well the good news is that we have a whole bunch of chocolate back there, so you can order all the chocolate you want."

"Thank you," Mia replied as Fernando smiled and walked off to get our drinks.

Walter Baker and Catherine walked into the restaurant and were escorted to our table by the maître d'. I stood up and greeted Mr. Baker with a handshake and a hug. Catherine introduced Mia to her father, and he reached out and gently cupped her little hand between his hands, smiled and said, "It's a pleasure to meet you, young lady. You're all my daughter talks about."

"Thank you," Mia said. "It's very nice to meet you."

Catherine hugged Mia. "Isn't she a little doll? I've already warned Joe that in another five years he's going to have his hands full with all the boys knocking at his door and begging to see her." Catherine pulled Mia's chair close to her and Mr. Baker sat down next to me.

"So, Joseph, how is retirement treating you?" Mr. Baker asked.

"It's been eventful, and unexpectedly gratifying," I said, then looked across at Mia and smiled. "It's unbelievably beautiful down here."

"Beats spending your winter vacations down in Central America scouting young prospects?"

Suddenly, the image of hundreds of young Latin ballplayers and their families, mostly dirt poor, passed before my eyes. I had made a number of their dreams come true, and in turn, they reinforced in me the importance of family and taught me that being humble was not a weakness but a strength.

Fernando brought our drinks, and Mr. Baker ordered a scotch neat, while Catherine asked for a glass of white wine. Catherine had recovered quite nicely from her overindulgence of a couple of nights ago, and she looked stunning in her light-blue wrap dress and low heels. I had the feeling she would look good in anything.

Fernando handed out menus, and Catherine, like an attentive mother, reminded Mia that the doctor wanted her to eat more protein and vegetables. The girls split a New York steak and a plate of steamed mixed vegetables. Mia's reward was a specially prepared chocolate cake, served heated, with chocolate sprinkles and whipped cream, which Catherine had ordered when she made the reservation.

Catherine helped Mia eat a little bit of the cake — not that she needed any help. The girls then excused themselves and went off to the bathroom to freshen up. Mr. Baker and I ordered after-dinner cognacs and espressos. I turned to him and said, "You have raised an amazing daughter."

"Yes, she never stops amazing me," he said. He picked up his snifter and twirled the cognac around. "Since my wife died, I have leaned on her so heavily that I can't help feeling guilty. I don't want her involved with the team. I don't want her involved in anything to do with the game. Actually, I had plans to put the team up for sale, but she insisted that I give her a chance, and after all she has sacrificed for me, how could I say no? She's convinced that I want a championship more than anything in this world, when all I really want is for her to be happy. She's so beautiful, and I don't remember the last time she went on a date."

"I think she has real potential to be a wonderful GM," I said. He looked at me and smiled.

"She doesn't have the instincts. After talking to you, she came to me with the ideas you proposed and said she just didn't see the logic in it, trading the newly crowned MVP for two minor league pitchers. I looked at her and said, 'This is the man you made a fool of yourself in front of in the hope he would take the GM job and now you don't see the logic in his proposals. If he had accepted the job would you be so quick to shoot down his ideas?' I pointed out that with a budget one-fourth the amount of the Yankees and the Red Sox, you have delivered three world championships, and every year you've been there, you have put a competitive team on the field that has made the playoffs over eighty percent of the time."

"Thank you for that generous summary of my career," I said. "Coming from you, those are incredible compliments. But I have to say, I think you're being really hard on her."

"No, I'm just being realistic and a loving father. She will be named the permanent GM in the next few days, and if we have a really good year and she insists on keeping the team, I will have only you to blame."

"And why is that?" I asked.

"Because after some soul-searching, she came to the right decision and decided that your proposals give us a much better chance of having a winning season this year and into the future. She's already negotiating with St. Louis."

"And how is that going?"

"The proposal at first took them by surprise, and they asked her if she had my support. I got on the phone and told them it was her team and that she would be named the permanent GM in a few days and that I was stepping aside and taking on the role of a de facto fan and the title of president. They're not stupid. You don't build a team like they have in St. Louis and a farm system that's second to none without really good baseball people on your payroll. She asked for thirty million and they're about ready to settle on eighteen million."

I laughed and said, "I told her to ask for twenty million and hope for ten."

"I never said she wasn't smart. She sensed their interest and she took advantage. It's not like they don't have the money."

"I call that instinct," I said with a laugh and a sip of my cognac.

"And maybe with a little more tutelage from you, she might turn into a female version of you?"

"She doesn't need me. She can get all the tutelage and advice she will ever need from her father."

He looked at me and smiled. "I would love to have met your parents," he said.

"I'm sure they would love to have met you," I said. "But why?"

"Because not only are you the best GM, scout and miracle worker in the game but you are a perfect gentleman ... conscientious and caring ... in an otherwise cutthroat business where your competitors rejoice over your grief. To be able to maintain your high moral standards, it only makes sense that your parents must have been righteous, good and loving people."

"Yes, they were, sir, and thank you for saying that."

"Any other person in your position would have left that little girl in that godforsaken town, or at the very most, would have dropped her off at an orphanage."

"And if it wasn't for your daughter, I don't know what I would have done. It's not like I know anything about ten-year-old girls."

"Yes, Catherine has a bit of a crusader in her. If she sees a wrong, she tries to change it, and if she sees someone suffering, she tries to help. She's undeniably the team's Florence Nightingale, and I am prouder of her charitable work with the hospitals, the homeless and the shelters for abused women than I am of any positive results she might get out of our team on the field."

Mr. Baker picked up his snifter and once again swirled the cognac around and then took another sip. "She's falling in love with Mia and, if I'm not mistaken, with you. Besides me, she says you are the best man she has ever met."

"She's still very young and I have no doubt she will meet plenty of eligible men a lot better than me, and a lot closer in age."

"You know, when I married my wife, I was thirty-eight and she was only twenty-four. If you had asked me on my wedding day what was the one positive I knew I was going to get out of our marriage, it was that I was sure I was going to die first. I loved her so much that the idea of living without her was too much for me even to imagine. Sitting beside her on her death bed, I prayed to God … begged him … to take me right then and there, moments before her."

"He couldn't do that. You still had Catherine to raise."

"Yes, Catherine, my beautiful, caring and loving daughter who has shackled herself to an albatross that she doesn't have the strength to break free from, nor the willpower."

"I don't see that at all. I don't see her love for you as a weakness, but a strength. A reflection on how wonderful a father you have been."

He looked across at Catherine and Mia walking back toward the table. His undeniable love and caring for his lovely daughter were expressed in every wrinkle on his face and in the unblemished pride reflected in his eyes. The ladies sat back down and Catherine pointed at the snifter in her father's hands and said, "Wow! I don't remember the last time I saw you drinking a cognac."

"Would you like some?" He handed her the snifter and, like her father, she twirled the cognac around and took the smallest of sips.

"It tastes wonderful," Catherine remarked as she handed her dad back the cognac.

"Would you like one?"

"I would love one, but someone has to drive. Maybe when we get back home."

"And you, Miss Mia, would you like another dessert?"

Mia's eyes lit up, but Catherine, being the ever-dutiful mommy, replied, "I'm sure she would love another dessert, but that will have to wait until tomorrow. Isn't that so, sweetheart?"

"Yes," Mia said, unconvincingly, in a voice that was even lower than usual.

Fernando brought the credit card voucher with my card, and I signed it. I put the receipt and card in my wallet as I listened to Catherine complain about having invited us and that she should be the one paying.

We walked them to their car and watched as Mr. Baker got into the passenger's-side seat and Catherine walked around to the driver's side, and then out of the blue, she turned back around, walked toward me and threw her arms around my neck and whispered, "Please, don't leave."

"How long would you like us to stay?" I asked, not having fully absorbed the shock of having this lovely lady all over me with her father staring at us through the passenger's-side window of the car.

"Forever!" she replied.

"That's a long time."

"Yes, it's a lifetime and I will make it worth your while. Am I clear?"

"I think so, but do you think we can carry on this conversation tomorrow when your father is not looking directly at us and Mia is not a foot away?"

"Of course," she replied as she stepped back, looked me in the eyes and kissed me on the lips as though we had been a couple for years. She then bent down and hugged Mia and finally got into the car and drove away. I was so embarrassed I couldn't even wave good-bye to Mr. Baker.

I took Mia's hand and walked to the front desk and asked the attendant if it would be too much trouble if I booked the suite we were staying in for another two weeks. He laughed and said Miss Baker had already taken care of that and had paid for the suite for the next two weeks and however much longer I planned on staying.

I replied, "Of course she has. Is there any chance you can erase her payment and put the charge under my credit card?"

"I'm sorry, sir, but she warned me that you would try such a thing and threatened me with severe consequences if I did so. Miss Baker is royalty — you do understand?"

"Of course," I said as I looked down at my little daughter, who I was quite certain knew a lot more than she was letting on. I would interrogate the little miscreant once we were back in the suite.

The attendant called after us just as we were ready to get into the elevator, "And Miss Baker wanted to assure Mia that the hotel has ordered a bunch more chocolate delights and there is no chance of us running out."

Back in the suite, I cornered my lovely daughter and asked, "When you and Catherine went to the restroom to freshen up, did you happen to discuss anything in particular?"

"Yes, we discussed how wonderful you are, and Catherine said that she was in love with you and if everything turned out the way she planned, she would be my adopted mommy."

I tried to contain the wild emotions and inner turmoil that were suddenly swirling inside of me, and I spoke to Mia in as soothing and casual a tone as I could manage. "And is that all you discussed?" I did not want her to feel at all interrogated or pressured. Anything of that kind would seem cruel.

"Well…" she said, nervously. "I told her I thought you were in love with her too. Did I lie?" She said this in the softest and most pathetic voice one could imagine, full of worry at having done the wrong thing.

"No, angel, you did not lie." I kissed her on the forehead and said, "You should know by now that you are just perfect."

"Thank you," she said as she hugged me tightly around the waist. From a corner of the sofa, Rex was sitting upright in his tuxedo and appeared to be watching us. This made Mia giggle, and she ran over to pick him up, then took him into the bedroom to tuck him in for the night. I walked over to the refrigerator and took out a cold beer.

In my long career in the game of baseball I had seen many star ballplayers unsuspectingly kissed by beautiful women who seemed to jump out of nowhere, but it had never happened to me. I guess GMs are just not sexy enough, but what happened tonight was both disconcerting and flattering. I would be lying if I said I did not find Catherine Baker exceptionally attractive, smart and caring, and if I was ten years younger, I'm sure I would have allowed myself to at least dream of going out with her. But that wasn't the case, and her behavior, right in front of her father, and the things she said, just didn't fit the profile of the woman I knew and the one her father described to me. I tried not to dwell on it, but it was all I could think about.

I tossed and turned all night, and when I did manage to get some sleep, I had this terrifying nightmare that Mia had decided to go live with the penguins at SeaWorld, and the only way I could see her was by going to SeaWorld and communicating with her through the large glass partition, in some ancient sort of sign language. Except for her lovely face, she had taken on all the physical characteristics of the other penguins, and if that wasn't bad enough, I was banned from going on the Behind-the-Scenes Close Encounter Tour, so I couldn't even get a hug from my sweet little daughter. I woke up in a cold sweat — and I mean a cold sweat — and since it was just about my usual time to get up and go for a run, I decided to simply get up.

I changed into my running gear and walked out of my bedroom to find Mia sitting at the table, working on the computer. She was dressed in her running gear, and in the chair next to her was Rex. I asked her what she was reading and she didn't respond … or if she did, I didn't hear her, which was always a possibility. I looked over her shoulder at the computer screen and in big bold flowery lettering the headline read, "Responsibilities of a Maid of Honor." I didn't even ask. I figured the less I knew the better chance I had of not dropping dead of a heart attack while running.

I took my daughter's hand, patted Rex on the head, and together we walked out of the suite and onto the elevator. "Did you sleep well?" I asked.

"Yes, wonderfully," she replied.

"And Rex?"

She looked up at me as though I was insane, and in all honesty, I was starting to feel insane. Here I was, a fifty-year-old man, a respected, albeit recently retired GM, having trouble conversing with a ten-year-old whose IQ seemed to be increasing tenfold by the day. She looked back down and said, "He slept wonderfully too. Thank you."

"That's good," I said, smiling.

Without warning she turned to me and hugged me tightly, and I hugged her right back. Thankfully, I didn't notice any downward change in her body temperature. That nightmare was a little too real, despite also being completely off-the-charts silly. That part — the silliness factor — was even more worrisome than the dream itself had been. What was happening to me? I had heard that all new parents felt at some point like they were falling to pieces, and I wondered if it was already my turn, so soon after becoming a father. I resolved to take things one step at a time, starting with today's workout.

We started running, and at the eight-mile mark, which was usually my limit, I continued running and so did Mia. A couple of extra miles were like nothing for her. Never in my life — a life spent around some of the best-conditioned athletes in the world — had I ever seen a better, more graceful athlete. If she were a racehorse, I would be a billionaire.

At about the eleven-mile mark I finally had to stop. She could have gone on forever, or until the urge for a three-thousand-calorie chocolate cake set in and she couldn't resist.

We walked back to the hotel and I was tempted to ask what she wanted to do today, thereby possibly getting a hint into Catherine's plans, but then I decided once again that maybe it was better that I didn't know. We entered the suite and she ran into her bedroom and into the shower and fifteen minutes later re-emerged and proclaimed, "I'm all clean."

I was just about ready to order breakfast when there was a knock on the door. It was the kitchen attendant with our breakfast.

Apparently Catherine had taken the liberty of ordering that for us too. Mia had her usual chocolate chocolate-chip pancakes with the addition of a fruit bowl and scrambled eggs and a note that read, "You promised. Enjoy! Love you."

"What did you promise?" I asked.

"That with each meal I would also eat healthy foods along with my chocolate dishes."

"I think that is a very wise decision."

"Yes, for Catherine I will do anything. She said that once we're all living together she won't have to write me reminder notes. But I love her notes, and I told her if she wanted she could still write me notes once we were all living together."

I took the top off my breakfast tray and besides the sausages and scrambled eggs there was also a note, which read, "I love you." Mia asked what my note said, and figuring that she already knew, I just handed it to her.

"Very nice," she said and continued, "I read that in a relationship it is very important for the boy and girl to tell each other as frequently as possible how much they love each other."

"Is that so," I replied lamely.

"Yes, so please remember to tell Catherine how much you love her. If you like, I can remind you."

"I think I can remember that."

"I would think it would be very easy to remember because Catherine is so beautiful, kind and smart."

"Yes, she is definitely all those things," I remarked, and thought to myself, *and quite possibly insane.*

After we finished breakfast, I jumped into the shower, closed my eyes and stood there for a long time, letting the water splash against my face. This was not how I pictured retirement. I was not complaining, but nothing — literally nothing — that had happened since I abruptly quit my job had been what I expected. Was I dreaming? Or had I accidently jumped into an alternate universe that was very similar in appearance to the one I had been in for the first fifty years of my life but decidedly different when it came to the people? Or had I entered the *Twilight Zone*, and would I, at any moment, hear the voice of Rod Serling saying, "And here we have Joe Ciotola, successful and beloved baseball executive, who sacrificed everything for the game … never having made time for a family … too busy even to be at the bedside of his dying parents … left with a bundle of cash, regrets and not even a plaque in the Baseball Hall of Fame in Cooperstown. After all, fans don't care about the behind-the-scenes expertise of GMs who couldn't make it on the field of glory and so had no other choice but to become suit-and-tie executives." I stepped away from the running water, opened my eyes, shook my head and repeated, "Think rationally, Joe, rationally, rationally, rationally…"

I shampooed my hair, ran a soapy washcloth across my entire body twice, rinsed off and dried myself with a towel. I stood before the bathroom mirror and thought to myself, "Not bad for a fifty-year-old guy; not bad at all." I got dressed and walked out of the bedroom. My phone rang and I picked it up and it was the lovely Catherine — and I was immediately flung back into that alternate universe.

"I have great news," she said. "Mia's blood work and urine sample all came back normal, except for a little iron deficiency, which we will correct with a few more changes to her diet."

Mia was standing beside me, and I repeated the good news to her. She in turn wrote me a quick note, which read, "Don't forget to tell her you love her."

I turned my back on my nosy daughter, and before I could say a word to Catherine, she said, "I'm sorry if I came on a little strong last night, but don't think for a moment I didn't mean every word I said."

"But did you have to do it in front of your father?"

"Yes!"

"Wow! You didn't even have to think that one over."

"I've told my father how I feel about you, and last night I simply presented him with the proof. He's so concerned that the team is an obstacle to my happiness and that the team is stopping me from having a meaningful relationship, that last night I showed him how well I can multitask, especially when it comes to someone I really want and love. My father adores you, Joe, and last night he told me that I couldn't have picked a better guy and that he couldn't be happier. I don't want to guilt you into loving me, and if you really don't feel the way I do, I will respect your feelings and back off. I am not the child you used to see at the winter meetings."

"That's quite obvious, and I would be lying if I said I didn't feel the same way about you, but…"

"The fourteen-year difference," she said, correctly reading my only objection. "How about if I promise you that when you get too old and cranky, I will take you out back and shoot you."

"You promise?"

"Yes, I promise. And just for the record, I am a very good shot."

"Just my luck," I said.

While she was laughing at that, I walked out onto the balcony and shut the door. Mia might talk softly but she seemed to have wonderful hearing.

"I want to ask you one more thing," I said.

"What's that?"

"How much does your falling in love with me have to do with Mia?"

"I love Mia with all my heart, and she certainly has stirred maternal feelings in me, but in many respects, Mia has simply confirmed all the wonderful things I've always heard about you, not only from my daddy but from all the players and executives throughout the game. My father has always been the most perfect man I have ever known, and you are the only man who I can honestly say has shown the same integrity and caring as my dad."

"That's mighty high praise. I don't know if I can live up to it and I would hate to let you down."

"If I had any doubts, I wouldn't be throwing myself at you and making myself out to be the biggest loser in the world."

Everything was happening so quickly that it was difficult for me to process. Despite all the wonderful things Catherine was saying about me, I found it hard to believe that a young lady so attractive, smart and compassionate could not find a guy closer to her age, with the same qualities. I knew ballplayers whose charitable contributions off the field went far beyond anything I had ever done. Players and executives far better looking, honest and empathetic, who I knew Catherine also had to know because a few were on her team. I leaned against the railing and looked out at the beautiful ocean and asked the lovely lady, "And where do you suggest we live?"

"To be honest, I haven't thought about that…"

"Surely, close to your father?" I asked.

"Most definitely next to my father," she replied without hesitation. "I have no doubt you would never think otherwise."

"Surely not, and in another year if I decide to go back to my team, you don't think that might present a problem?"

"Why? You already said that if you went back it would be on a reduced timetable, with no traveling and fewer visits to the ballpark. And it's not as if your team's stadium is a much farther drive from here than where you presently live."

I imagined, like any sensible baseball person, that she didn't think there was any possibility that the Yankees were calling, and so I asked, "And if the Yankees come calling?"

"Oh please, don't even mention that team. I hate everything about them, and where I can understand that they were your favorite team growing up, it's time to let go of that dream and concentrate on Mia and me and possibly other additions to our family. Surely, if you truly love me as you say you do, you will forgo any idea of working for that despicable organization."

"Are you sure you're not a closet Red Sox fan?"

"Oh please, they're almost as bad as the Yankees. So if it was between me and the Yankees, who would you choose?"

"Well, whereas working for the Yankees has always been a dream, marrying you is like a fantasy come true. You easily win out."

"Spoken like a true gentleman, and a man of integrity. And now you know why I love you so."

"You do realize that we have not even been on a date, and yet we are talking about getting married."

"Dates are overrated. Besides, it's not like we don't know each other."

She might have known me, but to say that I knew her was seriously going out on a limb. Less than a day earlier, I could truthfully say I had never even thought about taking her on a date ... at least one not chaperoned by "our" ten-year-old daughter ... never mind having her propose to me (talk about crazy) and then us having a discussion about our future together and the possible addition of other children.

I had to admit, retirement had not been boring. First there was my eventful visit to the town of Salvation, where I walked away with a dirty urchin — who at first sight might have been a boy or girl, ten years old or thirty, illiterate or not — only to find out after a couple of days that she was smarter than me and playing matchmaker. Now without even knowing about it, I was engaged to a bombshell blonde fourteen years younger than me. As a successful GM, there were times when I simply went with my gut instinct, and lucky for me, my gut turned out to be correct the vast majority of the time. And as I stood there on our hotel balcony trying to make sense of it all, my gut was sending me one simple message: *Don't be an idiot — just marry her. Just marry her. It's not like a better offer is going to come your way, and besides, be honest with yourself. You've been in love with her from the moment you started talking to her at the bar that first day. It's one of the main reasons you're still down here in lovely San Diego. You might not know everything about her but that didn't stop you from falling in love with her.*

At this point, I turned and looked into the suite at Mia, who was sitting on the couch looking out at me. Still on the phone with Catherine, I said, "How are the negotiations going with St. Louis?"

"Please don't go there; it's insulting. If you think I am throwing myself at you to get at your baseball acumen, you are dead wrong."

"I did not think that, Catherine. Yes, I was stalling, but then it's not every day that I receive the most flattering proposal one could ever imagine."

"And you accepted the proposal, and I know your word is as good as gold."

"Oh, I'm not backing down. I just want to be sure that you're certain about all this."

"I've never been more certain. Would you like me to go over all the reasons once again?"

"No, I've never been very comfortable with receiving too much praise."

"Not even from your future wife?"

"Especially not from my future wife," I replied as I could hear her laughing.

"Well just for the record, I can't get enough praise ... so at any time, please feel free to lavish it on me."

I laughed as I looked at Mia, who was holding up the note reminding me, "Don't forget to tell her you love her." I gave her a thumbs up and said to Catherine, "Your lovely daughter is holding up a sign reminding me to tell you that I love you."

"And is there a reason why you're not obeying her?"

"I love you," I said, amazing myself as I did, and feeling the shocking truth of the words like a hammer in my chest. "I love you and I love you even more."

"Continue please."

"And I love you, love you, and I feel like the luckiest guy in the world to be marrying such a perfect, beautiful, caring and intelligent woman."

"Not a bad beginning, but I expect you can do a lot better."

"I caught our daughter reading an article titled, 'Responsibilities of a Maid of Honor.' Should I assume that she is going to be your maid of honor?"

"Of course; who else would I pick? If not for her, you never would have come to San Diego and we wouldn't be on the verge of getting married. And if not for her reassuring opinion that you love me as much as I love you, I might never have been so bold and forthright last night. She's adorable and wise beyond her years and we're going to be the happiest family."

I looked at Mia and couldn't help thinking that my little pint-size daughter was full of surprises, yet after a moment's reflection, it suddenly wasn't so amazing at all that she had helped engineer this strange but highly desirable scenario. She had an aura of innocence and vulnerability that would never make one suspect her of any selfish motives. Mia had a daddy, but like any child her age, she also desired a mommy.

Of course, it was totally absurd to attribute any selfish and conniving motives to daddy's little girl. All I had to do was remember the way she acted at SeaWorld with Rex, the real-life penguin, to know that this little girl had a heart the size of San Diego.

I turned back toward the ocean and said, "And now there is the legal question about Mia. I have already been in touch with my lawyer, whose preliminary searches have come up empty, which is good. Mia is literally an orphan. Her parents were her only living relatives and they're both dead. That's confirmed. He doesn't see any major obstacles getting in the way of me adopting her. Of course that was all before I knew we were getting married."

"I also want custody of her," Catherine said suddenly, and a little more forcefully than I expected. I was starting to understand that when my lovely Catherine wanted something, she made it crystal clear.

"Of course you do," I replied and continued, "Well if you want custody from the very start, we are going to have to get married very soon."

"I have no problem with that," she said. "The sooner the better."

"I will get back in touch with my lawyer and tell him to hold off on submitting the paperwork to the courts for a couple of weeks, but no longer. I want this child in my custody as soon as possible."

"In *our* custody," she snapped.

"Yes, Catherine, in our custody, which means that I wouldn't waste much time planning a wedding or looking for a dress. Once we're married, I will have my lawyer submit the adoption papers under both our names, as husband and wife. That should make the adoption process even easier."

"As far as I'm concerned, we can get married tomorrow. I don't care about any church wedding."

"I hope not, because if you truly want Mia as your maid of honor, there will be no religious service. I will not traumatize that child any more than she already has been."

"Oh my God, I forgot all about that. I'd like to kill those bastards for what they did to that poor child."

"Of course you would."

"Stop making fun of me."

"But you make it so easy, Catherine. Let us not forget that humor in a marriage is one of the keys to success. My parents joked with each other all the time and they were married for over forty years. And I would bet that your mom and dad joked with each other all the time too."

"Yes, they were constantly teasing each other," she said, before going quiet. Suddenly I could hear her choking up and crying.

"I'm sorry, I didn't mean to make you sad."

"Just give me a moment and I'll be all right." I turned and looked back into the suite at Mia, who was holding up her reminder sign.

"If it helps, your soon-to-be daughter just held up her sign, once again reminding me to tell you that I love you."

I could hear Catherine suddenly laughing in the background. "And once again, I don't hear you following that wonderful advice."

"I love you, Catherine, and have since I first saw you downstairs at the bar."

"You're definitely getting better at this, and I'm sure that with enough practice you'll be perfect."

"It's not easy to live up to your expectations. You know, Catherine, before we get married, it might be a good idea to write down some guidelines. If you really don't want me sticking my head into your team's business, I won't. I will be overjoyed spending the next year taking care of Mia and being the best possible husband to you. My original plan was to get as far away from baseball as I could. Never in my wildest dreams, when I resigned less than a month ago, did I imagine that I would be adopting a ten-year-old girl and marrying a girl who was both *in* the league and *way out* of my league."

"Ha ha, good one," Catherine said. "Amazing the luck some men have."

"Yes, I have hit the lottery. I like to think that my parents are shining a guiding light down upon me."

"I have no doubt about that, and for the record, the negotiations with St. Louis are going great. I expect an agreement to be signed in the next few days ... all that is left is the physicals ... so please say a prayer and keep your fingers crossed."

"Have you talked to the pitching coach from the Red Sox?"

"Yes and he said he would be extremely interested in bringing along the two young pitchers, as long as the only traveling he had to do was during spring training. He seemed a bit surprised that St. Louis was willing to trade both of them."

"He's a pitching coach and he has been in the game over forty years. He's won a few championships, and he knows that never would have happened without superb pitching. I imagine he knows that at the very least, one of those two pitchers, barring injuries, is going to have a wonderful career, and with a little luck, both will. And if that happens, they could provide a one-two punch the likes of Koufax and Drysdale, who swept that despicable team I won't mention in the 1963 World Series with very little hitting."

"Wow! Wouldn't that be nice?"

"Yes, it would be wonderful. If I may, can I make one more suggestion without you breaking off our engagement?"

"Don't be such a wiseass. Yes, go right ahead."

"If everything goes as planned, I wouldn't attend the winter meetings. Let St. Louis shine. Besides, you are going to be bombarded with enough criticism right here in your own town. Why let every sportswriter across the nation also pour it on?"

"Don't think I have the backbone?"

"Oh, I have no doubt you have the backbone, but why not let the action on the field speak for itself?"

"Be honest, you just don't want me gone during what should be honeymoon bliss time."

"I would have to be a fool and a liar if I said otherwise. That being said, I think it would be a good idea to stay away."

"Don't you think that would make me seem weak?"

"Not after trading away the league's MVP for two highly respected pitching prospects and eighteen million. Weak, no; crazy, yes."

She laughed and said, "Wow! That makes me feel so much better."

"If it helps, I was called crazy quite a number of times during my tenure as GM."

"And now all those naysayers would do anything to hire you."

"I don't know about that. After all, they were entitled to their opinions and I try never to hold grudges. Baseball can be a very petty business, with a lot of oversized egos involved. You never know when one of those egos will throw a deal your way even though they have a better one on the table ... simply because the other guy made some unflattering remarks about that person ten years ago."

"I'm going to have to go. I have meetings scheduled throughout the day. How about we have dinner tonight?"

"With or without the child?"

"Don't be foolish ... of course with the child. She's my maid of honor and we have quite a bit to discuss. I love you, Joseph."

"I love you, Catherine. I'm just waiting to wake up from this fantastic dream I am having."

"It's no dream. Working for the Yankees was a dream, but the two of us becoming husband and wife is the real thing."

I opened the sliding door and walked back into the suite. I looked across at Mia, who was sitting cross-legged on the couch with Rex in her lap. She was staring at me with a smile on her face.

"So?" she said.

I smiled back and said, "So what?"

"*Dad!*"

Hearing that one little word melted me and I quickly told her everything — that I had followed her instructions and told Catherine I loved her, repeatedly, and that we were going to get married very soon. "She can't wait to become your official mommy and then we will be one happy family."

She jumped off the couch, still holding on to Rex's left wing, and she and the bird hugged me. I kissed her head and gave Rex a pat and then sat them back down on the couch beside me. Whereas I was dreading what came next, I had to find out some answers because at some time I was expecting some type of blowback, and I wanted to be prepared.

"I would like to ask you a few questions. If you don't feel comfortable answering them, just tell me so and I will stop. And nothing you say will change a thing. Catherine and I are your parents, regardless of what you say, and nothing is going to change that. Nothing!" She looked so nervous and I knew this was going to cost me one very large piece of chocolate cake.

"How did your biological parents die?"

"They drank poison," she said in her typically low voice as she lowered her eyes.

"So they committed suicide?"

"Yes. The preacher told them that it was the only way to expel the devil from their bodies and go to heaven. They wanted me to drink it too but I ran away and hid."

"And do you know who discovered their bodies once they were dead?"

"The preacher came with a doctor and they took them away in an ambulance."

"Did they search for you?"

"I don't know, because I hid on the other side of town."

"Where we first met?"

"Yes. They don't go to that side, because that is where the devil lives."

"How is it that your parents got buried on the devil's side of town if he was expelled from them?"

"Because the devil was inside me, and as long as I refused to drink the poison, my parents could not go to heaven, because I was their child and I had to be destroyed before God would let them in."

"Wow," I said, taking a moment to absorb this twisted information. "Mia, honey, I hope you know that that's just not true. That's insane, actually. Totally crazy." She lowered her head and her eyes searched the floor as though she expected at any moment that the devil was going to reach up from hell and grab her. I reached under her chin and tilted up her head. "You're the most perfect and loving little girl I have ever known. If I'm sure of anything it is that when God looks down upon you, he sees an angel. The most beautiful and perfect child he has ever created."

I could tell from her downcast expression that my little speech wasn't having much effect. Mia was traumatized, that much was certain, but one thing she had working for her was her intelligence. She was extremely inquisitive, and I had no doubt that, with time, she would see the absurdity of all those unfounded beliefs. It might take twenty years of therapy, but someday she would be free of the lunacy that had taken her parents from her and stolen her childhood.

It was very hard on me, but I had to continue. I had opened this can of worms and now I was the one searching for answers, regardless of how painful they might be.

"How did you get hold of your parents' death certificates?"

"After they were buried, the doctor attached the certificates to the crosses over their graves. I waited for a long time and then I took them off."

"Did you love your parents, Mia?"

"I wanted to…"

"But you couldn't?"

Mia looked up at me, placed Rex gently off to the side and turned her back to me. She lifted up her shirt to reveal a chaotic tangle of scars of all different sizes and shades of red and white. I knew enough from watching baseball injuries heal to know what this meant. Mia had been tortured over a period of years.

"They did this to you?"

Mia nodded and looked down at her feet.

I couldn't speak. I looked at her back for a long and disturbing moment. It was like something out of the Dark Ages. I knew then that her parents deserved to be dead, and that all those brainwashed idiots living on God's side of the hideously misnamed town of Salvation deserved to be shot. They were dangerous — as dangerous as the religious zealots infiltrating our government and the courts, their ideologies based on twisted interpretations of obscure passages from the Bible. These people wielded religion as a weapon, and they did real harm. I was seeing the effects up close, and I thought my brain was going to explode from agony and disbelief. How anyone could torture this perfect child — or any child — was something that would not compute.

Mia turned back to face me and found my arms open and tears streaming down my face. She sank into my chest and let herself be wrapped in a silent hug. It was at least a few minutes before I could collect myself enough to ask my next question. When I finally did, I held her hands in mine and smiled as I spoke, trying to pull us both out of this spiral.

"Mia, how did you become so smart? Did you at one time go to school?"

"Yes, before we moved to that town. First and second grade."

"Do you remember that other town?"

"Yes, it was far away but it was very nice. I had a lot of friends and we used to play all the time. I was happy and then those people from the town of Salvation visited my parents and that's when they decided to move."

"Were they relatives, aunts or uncles or cousins?"

"No! I had never seen them before."

"When you moved to the town of Salvation, did the people who visited your parents also live there?"

"Yes, but they came and went. They always brought back new people I had never met before. New followers."

"With new followers?" I repeated.

"Yes, they were the disciples. There were twelve of them and they were all men, and they brought back new followers."

So they were a traveling band of religious lunatics. That was certainly a comfort to know. I had witnessed a lot of religious fervor down in Central America, but what I was hearing from Mia and what I had seen with my own eyes simply took the cake. The people in Central America looked upon their God as I had looked upon my own — as all-forgiving and loving ... not like the vengeful God of the Old Testament, but the God who preached the Sermon on the Mount — a guide to a moral, loving and forgiving way to live one's life.

"Did you attend school in the town of Salvation?"

"Yes, but only for a short time. It wasn't like my old school. They taught us passages from the Bible, which we had to memorize and recite each day."

"And what made them believe that the devil possessed your parents?"

"The elders discovered dirty magazines, books and videos that they said belonged to my parents. They had a trial and they were found guilty. The disciples performed rituals to expel the devil but they could not get rid of him, only the poison could expel him from my parents' bodies and from my body."

I wish I could say that this reminded me of an Edgar Allan Poe short story, or an episode from the *Twilight Zone* or *Night Gallery*, or a horror film about the Salem Witch Trials, but it didn't. This was real, and as I looked at my daughter, I fully realized that the ultimate victim at the heart of this insanity was my lovely Mia. Mia, who was now looking at me worriedly while wringing her small hands in her lap.

"Mia, what's wrong?" I asked, though the question itself seemed insane, given everything she had been through. How could anything be right? How was she as healthy and happy as she seemed to be?

"I was just wondering ... did I do something wrong? Do you ... do you still love me?"

I reached out and hugged her again and heard her sob quietly, once. "Mia, I love you more than anyone in this whole wide world," I said. I held on to her tightly and kissed the top of her head.

"But not more than Catherine?"

"More than anyone," I repeated.

"But you can't tell her that, because that would hurt her. You're supposed to love her the most."

"It will be our secret. Is that okay?"

She nodded and wiped away a tear as I continued, "And what would my beautiful daughter like to do today?"

She lowered her eyes and asked in her typical low voice, "Can we go visit Rex?"

"At SeaWorld?"

She nodded.

"Of course, honey."

I called SeaWorld to see if there were any available openings for the behind-the-scenes tour. Naturally, there were, and I asked if there was any chance that Rex could make a guest appearance. The lady I was talking to started to laugh and said she would get in touch with the guide and tell him that there was an urgent request to see Rex.

Suddenly, the idea of seeing Mr. Rex once again seemed like the most normal thing in the world to do. I still hadn't gotten over the shock that Catherine and I were getting married, but at least that was great news for all those involved. As for the town of Salvation, it would take more than an exorcism to rid my mind of that place, and I also knew that I was going to have to tell Catherine everything Mia had told me. She deserved to know. My worry was that my crusader wife-to-be might decide to rid the world of that town.

CHAPTER TWENTY-FOUR

We got into my car and drove to SeaWorld. Naturally, Mia wanted to get there as soon as it opened so that she could take in the full exhibit and see all the penguins that lived behind the glass partition. She wanted to invite Catherine, but I told her that her soon-to-be mommy was busy running her baseball team. She seemed to take that news with a grain of suspicion, and then I told her that we were going to have dinner with Catherine and that she wanted to discuss all the things that she had learned about being a maid of honor.

Mia suddenly remarked, "I will always love you more than anybody, but I don't think we should tell Catherine, because it might hurt her feelings."

I assured the lovely child that we could keep both secrets: that I loved her more than anybody and that she loved me more than anybody. After all, we didn't want to hurt Catherine's feelings. I could sense that the question-and-answer session we had at the hotel was still bothering the child. Thankfully, visiting Mr. Rex seemed to take her mind off that. Unlike the other children and adults on the tour, who seemed hesitant to hug the handsome bird, my fearless and loving daughter had no problem hugging Rex for a prolonged period of time. And if I was not mistaken, I was pretty sure Rex enjoyed being hugged by Mia, who he seemed to remember quite well. Two more spots came open on the second tour, as if by divine intervention, and so Rex got an extra, extra dose of loving.

Driving back toward the hotel, I turned on ESPN radio and the lead headline had to do with the trade of the current MVP of the National League for two top pitching prospects and an undisclosed amount of money. The experts immediately started in on Catherine, saying it was apparent that "Mr. Baker's daughter had no right being the GM of a minor league team, never mind a major league team." Trading the current MVP, who still had three years left on his rookie status, made no sense. If rumors were correct, and the team would soon be up for sale, its value just dropped drastically. One wag offered that "When St. Louis lifts up the World Series trophy next year, they should send out a loud thank you to Miss Baker, who made it all possible."

I turned the radio off and Mia asked, "Is that the trade you and Catherine talked about?"

"Yes, but don't pay attention to the men on the radio. They don't know what they're talking about and please don't say anything to Catherine about what you just heard."

Mia nodded as I pulled into a parking space at the hotel. We took the elevator up to the suite and I could easily detect that what Mia heard on the radio was bothering her. Inside the suite, I tried to explain to her that I had heard the same type of criticism about some of the baseball trades I made, but in the end I had the last laugh because, by the close of the season, the same people who were criticizing the trades I had made at the beginning were forced to eat their words after my team won the World Series.

"Is Catherine's team going to win the World Series?" Mia asked.

"I don't know, but we are going to be rooting really hard for them and that will definitely help."

"And what about your team?"

"I resigned from my team. Hopefully, they'll do really well, but this year I want Catherine's team to win the World Series."

"Me too."

Mia and I both smelled like fish. Visiting Rex was fun and seemingly therapeutic for Mia, but it definitely required a shower afterward. I walked into the shower and turned on the water. I was still thinking about what those so-called baseball experts had to say about Catherine and realized that their words had really stung me. It was quite disturbing. After nearly thirty years in the game, I had learned how to tune out the nonsense that I heard on the sports channels. I focused exclusively on the team I had on the field and how I might improve their chances of winning. Naturally, as I put together one winning team after another with a limited payroll, I didn't have to worry about much criticism. Winning has a way of quieting the skeptics. Yet disparaging criticism, second-guessing and analysis was simply part of every sport. In a sense it drove the money train; it was free advertising, even if it was hard to listen to.

The difference now was that I had a different horse in the game … someone I had become amazingly attached to and who would soon be my wife. Strange … the idea that I was marrying this beautiful woman still didn't seem real to me. Maybe once I put a ring on her finger, heard those magic words — "You may kiss the bride" — and dare I say, made love to her, that would all change … or maybe once I actually kissed her? I wouldn't have called the previous night's kiss, with her father looking on, a real kiss. It was more like a surprise attack and I wasn't even sure I had kissed her back.

Strange … but I felt like I had to protect her in a different way than I had to protect Mia. With Mia it was like I had to protect her from the very God I prayed to, from all the evil perpetrated in his and his son's name, from the misinformation and distortions inherent in ideological readings of the Bible. Mia was a child, and an amazingly resilient and resourceful one, who had survived for nearly two years under some of the worst conditions imaginable. Yet she was still a child, and as her father, it was my responsibility to defend and shield her from all evil, including physical and mental trauma. It was my responsibility to hopefully re-educate her, undo the damage and provide all of the resources that she would need to reach her full potential, and above all, be happy.

Catherine was a mature, intelligent highly educated woman who was born with the proverbial silver spoon in her mouth. In fact it was probably me who would have to sign a prenuptial agreement. I had no doubt that Catherine had hundreds of millions of dollars set aside in trusts for her. Still there was a vulnerability about her, which I had witnessed in some of the most highly paid and talented ballplayers I had been around. It was like they always had something to prove, and it was difficult for them to handle any sort of criticism. I had counseled a number of great ballplayers on the need to dial back their defensiveness, block out the criticism and concentrate on the big picture. They needed to learn how to ignore the minor hiccups that were guaranteed to pop up here and there during any baseball season. A few listened, but most didn't. Hopefully, I would be able to get through to my fiancée, but I would have to tread carefully.

My first instinct was to tell her to block out all the criticism. In a sense, she was a veteran and had been around the game her whole life, but she had never been in a position to take the heat that was going to be thrown at her for the next four weeks, and once the season began, every time the team went into a long losing streak. Her father had built a reputation, and deservedly so, of being a really good guy, both on and off the field. His name and the team's logo were plastered everywhere around this town, sponsoring and financing a wide variety of charitable causes. Entire wings of hospitals were named after him, shelters for battered women, baseball leagues for disabled and disadvantaged children, and food banks to feed the homeless. He gave back to the community in a way that few if any other owners of sports franchises gave back. The press, understandably, went relatively easy on him and his team. They loved the man, but that love did not necessarily get passed down to his daughter.

Catherine was on the board of all her father's charities, and even though she was seriously involved in all the major decisions and spent countless hours helping out at the grassroots level, she was nevertheless looked upon by the press as a privileged, rich and spoiled child. And it didn't help that she was drop-dead gorgeous.

I got out of the shower, dried myself off and put on a nice pair of slacks, a dress shirt and a pair of Salvatore Ferragamo shoes. I walked out of my room and hung my one and only Armani sports coat on a chair beside the table. Mia proclaimed that she was "all clean," and as

I looked at her, I couldn't help thinking that it hadn't taken her long to become a little fashionista. She was dressed in a black Balmain dress, laced with silver diamonds that ran directly below her neckline, black socks that came up to her ankles and a pair of black Mary Jane glitter flats. She looked like a princess, and all I could think about at that moment was Catherine's warning about all the boys that would be knocking down the door to see her. It wasn't like I knew anything about fashion, but I did notice that Mia had forgotten to take off the price tags and the attached designer labels.

The phone rang and it was Catherine. She asked if we could just stay in and order out. She was exhausted. She would be over shortly and would be spending the night if that was okay with Mia and me.

"Of course," I replied, and couldn't help thinking that this girl worked fast ... almost too fast...

And then, as if reading my thoughts, she said, "Don't get too excited. I will be sleeping with Mia."

"Mia and Rex," I added, and I could hear her laughing.

"Of course, Mia and Rex. And how was the real-life Rex today?"

"Wonderful! I see the real and promising possibility of a long-term loving relationship between the two of them."

"I'm sure you do, but don't get your hopes up too high, because I see an army of human, teenage suitors bombarding us with requests to see our daughter in just a few years."

"Well thank God you have a lot of experience dealing with such situations."

"Excuse me!"

"Don't play coy. I can't even begin to imagine how many teenage boys were knocking at your door."

"Yeah, and they were all greeted by my mommy, and when it came to protecting her little girl, she didn't give the little rascals an inch. She could be as stern and uncompromising as a drill sergeant."

"Great, because that's exactly how I want you to behave when the time comes for us to protect our little girl from those teenage miscreants."

She laughed and said, "I'll be over shortly."

I looked across at Mia, and as much as it hurt — she looked so adorable — I told her to go change because Catherine wanted to eat in and I didn't want her to think that she had ruined our plans to eat out. She understood and changed into her Charlie Brown pajamas, and I changed into a sweatshirt, dungarees and sneakers.

It was better this way because, after the trade announcement earlier that day, sportswriters and camera crews would be searching every restaurant and bar in town, hoping to get a glance and comment from Ms. Baker. And all they had to do was see me dining with her and all hell would break out ... a hell and clamor I'm quite sure Catherine was aware of and something that we needed to discuss.

Catherine walked into the suite holding a suitcase, which immediately told me that she planned on staying for more than one night. She wrapped her arms around me and we kissed, and unlike last night, I was quite certain that I kissed back. Life, for the moment, was grand.

She hugged and kissed Mia as I poured her a large glass of white wine. We ordered dinner and sat down to chat, with the conversation mainly centering on the real-life Rex. Catherine listened, enthralled, and made approving sounds in all the right places as Mia described in great detail how we had gone to see Rex and how he had seemed to recognize her and had waddled right over to her for his hug. I listened and watched the two of them like a spectator at Wimbledon. I couldn't believe my good fortune, having these two amazing young women so solidly in my corner and in my life. There was no doubt that Mia had become immeasurably important to Catherine ... a sort of elixir it seemed ... confirming a maternal inclination that was life-affirming and beautiful to see. Throughout the meal and afterward, while the ladies sat on the couch discussing the impending wedding, Catherine ran her fingers through Mia's curly locks of hair at least three dozen times. The subject of baseball had not come up once, even though its presence was as real as if we were sitting on second base.

Baseball is a business, plain and simple. The Dodgers left Brooklyn because the city refused to build them a new stadium. The die-hard Brooklyn fans were left weeping and felt betrayed, yet in the history of the game, the Dodgers' move to Los Angeles was a financial bonanza. Their attendance had always been among the highest in the league — topping four million at times, and never below three million. In contrast, my team barely touched two million in attendance in each of the three years we won the World Series, and the two other years we went to the series and lost. All the other years we were significantly below two million. In the celebratory chaos of the clubhouse, while raising the World Series trophy above my head, I was already thinking about next year — realizing, as I scanned the players that helped us win it all that year, that at least a third of them, if not half, would be playing for other teams next year.

It was a struggle, each and every year, just to stay competitive, and without the brilliant staff and scouts I had working for me, it would never have been possible. Yes, we were making more money because of TV rights and some semblance of profit sharing, but teams like the Dodgers were making three times as much because their product, even when it was significantly deficient to ours, was always in greater demand.

My dream was always to play in the big leagues, and my love for the game of baseball had never diminished, yet once I signed my first minor league contract, the childlike joy I felt playing the game was greatly lessened by the business side of it all. A ballplayer is an asset as long as he produces, and once that player's production wanes, he is tossed aside like a useless piece of machinery. But unlike a normal older worker in the everyday world, the ballplayer at least retires with a great pension, and if he is wise, a nest egg so large that a nurse, a soldier or a person doing life-saving cancer research would find it unfathomable.

Catherine had already finished an entire bottle of white wine and was almost halfway through her second bottle. Even though she seemed to be handling it quite well, I was preparing myself for another meltdown, like a few days ago. When she put out her hand to show me a ring she had been wearing since I met her, I thought we were just about at that point. She was struggling to say whatever was on her mind and she started to cry, and then she asked, "Would you be greatly insulted if I moved this ring over one finger and used it as my wedding ring? It was my mother's wedding ring and I think it would mean so much to her and it would make Daddy really happy."

"I think that would be wonderful," I replied as I reached over with a tissue and wiped away some of the tears from her cheeks. She then turned to Mia and said, "See how simple that was? One big thing already out of the way."

Mia hugged Catherine and nestled her head against her breast. Catherine hugged her back and they remained embraced in each other's arms for what seemed like an eternity. If a word was spoken between them, I did not hear it.

Catherine finally decided that it was time for bed. She had a very big day tomorrow and she needed to be at her best. I didn't dare ask her what was on the calendar. Once again, she unexpectedly threw her arms around me and kissed me passionately. Not one to disappoint, I naturally kissed her back — the whole time praying that she didn't vomit in my mouth. She walked into Mia's bedroom and closed the door behind her.

I sat down beside Mia and said, "Catherine is having a difficult time."

"I know, and I feel so sorry for her. I wish I could help."

"Believe me, sweetheart, just you being beside her is probably the best help and support she could ever hope for. She loves you so much," I said as I ran my hand gently through her hair. "I just wouldn't bring up baseball," I cautiously added as she looked down at her pajamas and the images of Charlie Brown and Snoopy playing baseball.

"Should I change my pajamas?" she asked anxiously as I laughed.

"There is never a situation where Chuck and Snoopy need to be removed from the scenery. Never!" And with that statement, baseball, for the moment, was once again a game — not a business — but a game played by millions of children across the country.

CHAPTER TWENTY-FIVE

I tossed and turned all night long, and when I did manage to fall asleep, I had a recurring nightmare. I was standing in the batting box, looking across at the great Sandy Koufax on the mound. Then, in slow motion, he went into his high-kicking windup, concealing the ball for a second and then coming over the top and throwing a hundred-mile-an-hour fastball directly at my head. I tried to duck, to hit the dirt, but it was like I was frozen in time, paralyzed, and a tenth of a second later the ball collided with my head, shattering my batting helmet, and all went dark, except for the voices of concerned teammates and the muffled sighs of apprehensive fans.

My feelings toward Catherine were sincere, but to say that I didn't have my doubts would be a lie. It all seemed so sudden, like a plan put into motion without taking into account any of the numerous consequences. She was understandably on edge. Trading away the current MVP, who still had three more years left on his rookie contract and who was not eligible to file for free agency until the expiration of that contract, was a big deal, but it wasn't the end of the world. All his drug tests had come back clean, but I had my suspicions. The speed with which his home runs left the park was awe-inspiring. In fact, they were so astonishing that they were gone in a blink of the eye and they were no doubters. No long, high drives that might or might not go out and that have the fans standing up and looking anxiously at the flight of the ball and where it lands. His were solid line drives that probably never went higher than fifteen feet off the ground. The only other ballplayer I saw consistently hit home runs like that was Barry Bonds.

Every day, in every sport, there were unscrupulous entrepreneurs coming up with new ways to beat the drug tests and manufacturing new performance-enhancing steroids that went undetected. Ballplayers were easy targets. The difference between a steroid-using ballplayer averaging forty home runs a year and driving in over a hundred runs, and a clean player averaging twenty home runs a year and driving in seventy-five runs was usually, when it came time to negotiate contracts, the difference between signing a seven-year deal worth over two hundred million and a three-year deal worth forty million. In short, between players' egos and the huge payoffs, it wasn't all that hard to flip some players … most were eventually caught and suspended and their careers cut short, but not before cashing in big-time.

After turning a blind eye to steroid use for nearly two decades — more home runs and once-untouchable records falling by the wayside meant more ticket sales and higher TV ratings — baseball was finally doing a good job cracking down on steroid use … yet I had very little doubt that between ten and fifteen percent of the players were still using.

The polished, self-assured and charming Catherine I met at the bar that very first day, whose star kept shining brighter and brighter, was finally starting to lose some of her luster. She needed to take a step back, take some time off and simply relax, but instead she kept adding to the turmoil. I needed Catherine, and Mia needed Catherine, and I also knew that Catherine needed both of us. If I wanted this to work, I needed to attack the problem head-on before it blew up in all our faces. If that happened, it would be Mia who would turn out to be the real victim — and I was not about to let that happen.

Before I got up out of bed to go for my run, I made a solemn pledge that sometime that day I would have a serious talk with Catherine about the rapidly flowing barrage of events that had taken place in just the last few days … not least of all, my unexpected engagement to this beautiful lady and the fallout that was soon to follow as it became public.

When I resigned my post as GM, I had every intention of staying away from the game for at least a year. I had traveled the world and yet I had seen nothing. The game of baseball had become an all-consuming obsession, and like all obsessions, it had narrowed my world. I scouted young talent in Japan, Korea, Central America, Canada and South America, and unless it had to do with baseball, I ignored it. I had learned very little about these amazing countries, their cultures and their histories.

Now with Mia in my life, I was enjoying learning for its own sake, for the first time since college. I could feel my mind opening up to all of the wonders of the universe beyond baseball. I had learned about all the different species of penguins and how they likely evolved from the dinosaurs, why the sky was blue and how waves formed in the ocean. I had also been shown in vivid detail how dangerous religion could be when it was distorted and used to divide people instead of creating harmony. I was starting to think that religion used for these purposes was as dangerous and deadly as automatic weapons. At the age of fifty, I was enjoying the tutelage of a ten-year-old girl with a second-grade education and the curiosity of Leonardo da Vinci, and I didn't want to give any of it up.

I got up from the bed, put on my running gear and walked out of the bedroom to find Mia and Rex sitting at the table. Mia was reading articles about the responsibilities of a maid of honor and jotting down notes on her pad. Rex was staring off into space but, all the same, looking like quite the handsome penguin.

"And so, did everyone sleep well?" I asked.

"Yes. Catherine is still asleep."

"I figured she might be," I said. That's when I noticed the worried expression on Mia's face. "Is everything okay?" I asked as Mia looked toward her bedroom. At that point, I wasn't sure I wanted to know. I knew I had made a solemn pledge to get to the bottom of all the turmoil, which seemed to be swirling around like a tornado, but it was way too early, and I couldn't even buttress my courage with a few beers.

Mia stood up and walked over to me. I bent down because she wanted to whisper something in my ear, even though her normal speaking voice was unlikely to carry much farther than the table.

"I don't think I can be Catherine's maid of honor," she said.

"And why is that?"

"Because I don't have the money to do the things that a good maid of honor is supposed to do, and I don't want to hurt Catherine's feelings."

"I see, but I wouldn't worry about that," I said. "Catherine and I are going to have a very simple wedding, with very few people, and your only responsibility will be to stand by Catherine and look real pretty while we recite our wedding vows."

"Are you sure? What about the bridal shower?"

"There's not going to be any bridal shower. And it's Catherine's responsibility to buy her maid of honor a beautiful new dress for the wedding."

"Can you ask Catherine for me and make sure that's all she wants me to do?"

"Yes, I can definitely ask her. But I don't want you worrying about any of this. If you ever need money to buy something, all you have to do is ask me."

"You already buy me everything."

"Do you remember the conversation we had a few days ago in the car coming home from visiting Rex?" She nodded, and I couldn't help feeling that her innocence was the most precious gift I had ever received. I continued, "Well that is what daddies do for their children. That's what my daddy did for me and that's what my daddy would want me to do for you — because you, my beautiful little daughter, make me so happy."

We hugged and that worried expression on her face disappeared.

After our run, we took the elevator back to the suite. I opened the door, and to my surprise, Catherine was awake, fully dressed in a black business suit with a pencil skirt and heels, and pacing back and forth while talking on her phone. She winked at Mia and me, and a section of her long blonde hair fell endearingly in front of her other eye as she leaned into her call. I had to admit that she did not look at all like a lady who had, just the night before, drunk a bottle and half of white wine and stumbled off to bed. She looked amazing — classy, sexy, in control and ready for anything that might be tossed at her.

She stopped before me, lowered the phone for a moment and kissed me while whispering, "Love you." She turned back around, putting the phone back up to her ear, and with every measured step she took, I felt the resolve I'd possessed while lying in bed that morning dissipate, like a helpless whiff at a hundred-mile-an-hour fastball.

She turned back toward us, lowered the phone and this time she gave Mia a kiss and whispered, "Love you." A few moments later she hung up the phone and asked, "And how are my two marathoners?"

"Wonderful," we replied in unison.

"Great! I have a favor to ask of both of you — or actually, the three of you." She nodded toward Rex, who was still sitting at the table beside the computer. "At ten o'clock I will be holding a press conference and I would love for the three of you to watch. "Can you do that for me?"

"Yes," we replied, though I was pretty sure Rex just mumbled his assent.

"Wonderful," she said. "And now I have to run." She picked up her briefcase, kissed both of us, patted Rex on the head and walked out of the suite. Mia and I looked at each other and nodded, and then she ran off into her room to take a shower. I tried not to even speculate about the press conference. I simply tried to hold on to the image of that beautiful woman — that loving, caring and in-control person — in her dark business suit, walking back and forth and into our lives.

CHAPTER TWENTY-SIX

Mia turned on the TV an hour before the press conference was to begin, so for forty-five minutes we both got caught up on all the relevant news going on in the world of sports. At that time of the year, the middle of November, it was mostly football and basketball, with a little hockey thrown into the mix. Rex sat next to Mia and I sat next to my daughter on the other side of the couch. About fifteen minutes before the press conference was set to begin, a couple of baseball analysts were going over what they expected to be covered, most notably the big trade of the current MVP for a couple of number-one pitching prospects and eighteen million in cash.

At ten o'clock, Mr. Baker stepped up to the podium. Behind him, next to a banner with his team's logo, stood Catherine, a few top executives and the manager of the team. Mr. Baker warmly greeted the press and went on to say, "I am here today to officially announce that Catherine Baker, my lovely daughter, will be our new general manager. As you are all aware, Catherine has been by my side since she was just a toddler, and she has participated in the daily operations of the team since she graduated from college some fifteen years ago. I cannot think of a more dedicated, loyal and fervent fan of our team than Catherine, and I have total faith and confidence in her judgment and her ability to hopefully lead our team to a championship that our lovely city and its wonderful fans so richly deserve. I will remain president of the team, but my involvement in its daily operations will be significantly reduced, and I will be more of a cheerleader and fan than a hands-on leader. I'm confident that Catherine, our wonderful manager, players, coaches and scouts will do an outstanding job."

He turned toward Catherine and continued, "And now I give you our new general manager, Catherine Baker." They hugged, and Catherine walked to podium and, like her father, warmly greeted the press. She looked amazing, even more so than when she'd left the hotel, if that was possible, and I couldn't help feeling that the male members of the press might be so captivated with her beauty that they might not hear what she had to say ... but then who was I kidding? These were the same journalists I had dealt with throughout my career. They were like sharks circling a capsized ship, sniffing for blood. Sharks don't care about a pretty face.

Catherine started by saying how honored she felt that her father had the confidence to name her GM, and by promising to work as hard as ever to lead this team to a championship for the fans, the city and especially her father. The team's commitment to winning a championship was not put on hold by the recent trade, but hopefully accelerated by addressing a key concern, and that was pitching. With the acquisition of these two highly regarded prospects, the return of their three starting pitchers from last year, and a healthy bullpen, the team would be starting next year with one of the best pitching staffs in all of baseball. Yes, it was a difficult decision trading the current MVP, but it wasn't like St. Louis was going to let these prospects go for anything less than a superb hitter, which definitely addressed one of their key concerns.

She said that to help bring along and tutor the two highly regarded prospects, the team had just hired former Boston Red Sox pitching coach, Vince Castello. He had retired at the end of the year to be closer to his family here in San Diego, and she said she felt fortunate to be able to work out a deal that would benefit both her team and still give Mr. Castello more time to spend with his family than he was getting back out east. She pointed out that Mr. Castello's job would require no traveling apart from the first month of spring training, and his focus and expertise would be concentrated solely on the two prospects. It was not easy talking him out of retirement, but the idea of having to work with such young talent was enough to convince him to jump on board, and for that they were greatly appreciative.

She went on to talk about the possibility of other trades and the signing of free agents — and then came the shocker that almost had me running for a beer, but since it was only 10:15 a.m., I thought better of it.

Catherine paused and took a deep breath before she continued, saying, "And now I would like to address a few rumors. Yes, the team's first choice for the GM position was Joe Ciotola, which shouldn't come as any great surprise to anyone, because I am quite certain he was probably the first choice for many teams. Very rarely does such a baseball wizard like Joe become available. I met with Joe, and he repeated what he has told the press, that he means to stay retired, and that if he ever goes back to the game it will almost definitely be with the team he has been with his whole career if they still want him back.

"I have known Joe for a long time. We originally met at the winter meetings years ago when I was still in ponytails, and over the years our relationship has matured and changed. Recently, it has undergone even bigger changes, and in fact, it has moved to a new level. Joe Ciotola is the only man I have known who possesses all the wonderful and admirable qualities that my loving father possesses: honesty, integrity and generosity. He is a loving and caring person — a man without malice — and he is man who I can easily and honestly admit I had no problem falling head over heels in love with. To my astonishment, he is also in love with me. We are currently engaged, and we plan on getting married shortly, in what will be a private and very simple ceremony."

I could literally hear a collective sigh in the pressroom, and if I'd been drinking a beer, I would have spit it up all over myself. I could even hear Mia letting out a sigh, and considering that I could barely hear her when she was speaking at normal volume, that was really saying something. Yes, it was all true, or should I say partially true, but I wasn't expecting it to be announced to the world — even though it did let me off the hook in a really good way.

Suddenly, I could hear sportswriters screaming out Catherine's name in the hope of asking her questions, and I must admit that my beautiful fiancée handled it all quite well. She joked with the journalists as she looked out over the pressroom and all the raised hands waving in unison, and said, "Wow! Is it that hard to believe that a man could fall in love with me?" This generated a fair bit of laughter, and then came the questions...

The first sportswriter she called on was a tall, gruff gentleman who had been covering Southern California sports for over thirty years, for a number of different newspapers. He asked quite sharply, "Was Joe the person behind this trade?"

"And why would you ask that?" Catherine replied.

"Because it has his fingerprints all over it."

"Well I don't know much about fingerprint analysis, but I can guarantee you that Joe's fingerprints are nowhere to be found on this deal. Joe and I have had a long-standing policy not to discuss anything to do with either of our teams before the information has been made public. Joe found out about this trade at the same time the rest of you did."

The journalist was having none of this. "Surely, Ms. Baker, you don't expect any of us to believe that," he shot back. "You're engaged to the guy, and for the record, he resigned from his job just over a month ago, so there would be no conflict of interest if he had anything to do with the trade."

"Okay, I admit it. I might have dropped Joe a hint yesterday morning that something big might be coming down, and being the baseball wizard that he is, he probably figured it all out before it was announced. I'll try to remember to ask him about that later today when I talk to him."

Mia looked at me and asked, "Why is Catherine lying?"

"Oh, sweetheart," I said, and I immediately knew that I was going to have a hard time explaining this charade. "She's just trying to protect us, in case there is any fallout from the trade. It's an unfortunate side of the business of baseball."

I could sense that Mia didn't quite understand what I meant, or she simply did not buy my explanation. After all, here was a child who, for the last two years, had to hide and crawl and scramble for leftover food, just to survive, all because of a bunch of fanatics who preached a bunch of lies. Sadly, there was no easy way for me to redeem this spectacle in Mia's eyes. The business of baseball — the story of baseball — was a swamp filled with lies and dirty secrets, which would take the greatest historians a hundred years from now to unearth. I knew why Catherine felt the need to lie, but I couldn't explain it to Mia in terms that would make sense to a child who had seen what she had seen and been so harmed by the lies of other adults. I couldn't defend the institutions of baseball that had forced Catherine into this dishonest stance.

Mia, since leaving the town of Salvation, had mostly been in contact with only two people: Catherine and me. She had put her trust in us, and in us she saw truth, honesty and love. She had never seen the business side of the game, and suddenly she was witnessing a side of professional sport, and of baseball in particular, that the average fan knew very little about. It was a far cry from watching Charlie Brown and the Peanuts gang play the game for the love of the sport … even if they had a difficult time catching the ball.

The second sportswriter Catherine called on was a young woman who at least had the courtesy to first congratulate Catherine on her engagement and impending marriage before asking the question, "Can you tell me if St. Louis was aware, at any time during your trade negotiations, of your relationship with Mr. Ciotola?"

"That I wouldn't know; you would have to ask them. But if you are insinuating what I think you are insinuating — that they would have approached this trade differently if they knew the relationship I had with Joe — let me just remind everyone that St. Louis was looking to acquire a power hitter, and whether it was Joe or I who proposed the trade, I don't see why that would matter. Unless you think that with them knowing that Joe and I were engaged they would have made a better offer, like throwing in a third prospect and maybe an extra five million as a sort of a wedding gift, I really don't see how my relationship with Joe is relevant here."

There was laughter among the reporters as Catherine called on another reporter, who asked, "Is it too much to assume that, now that your fiancé is no longer employed by another team, that you will be turning to him for advice and his opinion on matters concerning your team?"

"Now that my fiancé is unemployed and I am the only breadwinner in the family, you can rest assured I will ask him for his opinions and listen to whatever advice he might have to offer on certain matters related to my team. After all, if I was an aspiring painter and had Leonardo da Vinci at my disposal, you can bet I would listen very carefully to whatever he had to say; or if I was an aspiring writer and had Shakespeare at my disposal, I would have to be a real fool not to seek and follow his advice. Yet let me state once again that Joe is not a member of our team, and to think that any future moves we make are going to be contingent on his approval or based on his suggestions would be dead wrong."

Another reporter jumped in with another question. "Will you be attending the winter meetings this year?"

"No," she said. "I expect to be on my honeymoon, and hopefully, the wonderful game of baseball will take a backseat for a short time and we can find other fun-filled activities to keep us busy. But we will be sending representatives to the winter meetings and I'm sure that if any promising possibilities arise, my father will stay abreast of them and act accordingly. After all, it is his team."

The news conference went on for about another fifteen minutes and I could see on her father's face how proud he was of her. Just before leaving the podium, Catherine looked into the camera and said, "Hi, Mia. I love you so much, and in just a few minutes, I'm fairly certain a lovely chocolate dish will be coming your way." She blew her a kiss, and Mia, uncertain at first how to respond, blew a kiss back at her. Catherine left the podium and the stage before any more questions could be thrown at her.

***

Back in the studio, baseball commentators who just one day earlier were calling the trade one of the worst moves by a team in years, suddenly had a change of mind and began pointing out the many positive aspects of the trade for both sides ... with one commentator actually saying that St. Louis might have been duped and would eventually regret ever making the trade.

And why this change of heart? Simply because of my intimate connection with Catherine, and the power and respect I had accumulated over the years. And how did this make me feel? It made me feel like shit. My fiancée performed brilliantly at the news conference, but the only story that was going to come out of that conference was that Joe the wizard was engaged to the daughter's owner, who had just been made GM, and that I was the real one behind the blockbuster trade.

The more I thought about this, the more it seemed connected to other problems in the sport. The game of baseball was slow to evolve ... one could say it moved at a snail's pace. It took forever to allow black ballplayers into the game, even though scouts throughout the leagues were well aware of the prodigious talent in the Negro leagues. Satchel Paige was a showman and a legend throughout the Negro leagues. He would tell his infielders and outfielders to sit down as he went about striking out one player after another. He finally got his chance to pitch in the big leagues when he was in his forties — some will say he was actually in his fifties — and still he was a dominant pitcher at that age. If he'd been allowed to pitch in the major leagues at thirty, forget about twenty, his career statistics would have been as great as Walter Johnson, Cy Young, Bob Feller, Dizzy Dean or Whitey Ford. And he was just one of many brilliant black players who were robbed of their chance to play in the big leagues until Jackie Robinson finally broke the color barrier in 1947. So much talent left to languish on the sidelines. So many players denied the recognition — and the money — that they deserved, simply because of the color of their skin. Other sports were also slow to integrate, but baseball was especially slow.

Just four years after Jackie Robinson joined the majors in 1951, the New York Giants signed another black ballplayer by the name of Willie Mays. In my thirty or so years in Major League Baseball, I had the unique pleasure to talk to many old timers. Almost to a man, they said that Willie Mays was the greatest ballplayer they ever saw. My own father, a die-hard Yankee fan, said that Willie Mays was the best player he had ever seen. Joe DiMaggio insisted on being called the "Greatest Living Ballplayer," but according to the men and women who saw both of them play, it was Willie Mays who deserved that honor.

As a general manager, I stressed to each young ballplayer I signed the importance of knowing the history of the game. How many listened, I don't know, but while attending an All-Star game a number of years back, a black GM and close friend of mine told me he had never been so disappointed as when he approached young black stars, some of them making tens of millions of dollars, and asked them about men like Jackie Robinson, Larry Doby, Satchel Paige, Buck O'Neil or Josh Gibson and found out that they had no idea who these pioneers were ... these men who paved the way for them to be successful and prosperous, to share and develop their talent, not just in front of black audiences but audiences of all races, creeds and religions.

As I sat there reflecting on all of this history and thinking about how the reporters had just treated Catherine, I couldn't help drawing a line between the racism that had marred the sport of baseball for decades and the not-so-subtle prejudice of those reporters who refused to believe that a female GM could have made this trade without help from a man.

As I watched Catherine's press conference, it was apparent from the very beginning, when her father announced that she was the permanent GM, that the reporters (male and female) went after her in an almost condescending manner, and that when my name came up, there was no doubt in their minds that this beautiful, spoiled, rich child was nothing more than a mouthpiece. It didn't matter that since she was a toddler she had been around the game of baseball, or that by the time she was thirty she'd already negotiated contracts, helped with player relations, written detailed analyses of each and every player, and become the person responsible for drafting their former MVP. Whether women would ever be able to play in the major leagues, I wasn't sure. I had always believed that it might happen, and that it should someday be possible. But for anyone to suggest that women could not do as good a job as men working in the front office as GMs, coaches, public relations personnel and scouts was inane.

I had a number of women working on my staff and they worked as well and as hard as the men. Before resigning as GM, I made a list of the people working for me that I thought would make wonderful replacements for me as general manager. A number of those potential replacements were women, yet I was fairly certain that if the owners ever did get around to replacing me, it would be with a man. Baseball was in many ways an exclusive men's club, and whereas there have been a few female owners, teams have usually followed the tradition of hiring men for the top administrative jobs.

I looked across at Mia sitting on the couch next to Rex, and I was pretty sure she was thinking about that chocolate surprise that Catherine mentioned at the end of the press conference. Oh, if only she could always live in a world where her biggest concern was whether or how soon she would get her next piece of chocolate cake! As I sat there gazing at her, I wished that for her, even as I knew that this was wishing for a life of nothingness, devoid of the conflict and complexity that inevitably comes with growth. All I knew at that moment was that I did not want my little girl to follow in the footsteps of her adopted mother and father. She had been through an awful hell, which would most likely haunt her forever, but her future was filled with promise, and the financial cushion that Catherine and I were able to provide for her could certainly help make her dreams come true, whatever those dreams might be.

There was a knock on the door, and the delivery my little girl was waiting for arrived: a large piece of chocolate cake, topped with chocolate sprinkles, syrup and a large red cherry. There were two forks. I put the plate down in front of Mia and asked, "Do you plan on sharing it with Rex?"

She looked at me, slightly confused, and then lowered her eyes and replied, "He likes fish." She was a quick learner, but she still had trouble differentiating between the modulations and pitch in one's voice and whether one was joking or being serious. Either that, or she just didn't want to hurt my feelings and reply, "That's an awfully stupid question. Can't you see he's a stuffed animal?"

I sat next to Mia as she ate her cake and talked to her gently. "Remember when you asked me why Catherine was lying, and I said it was because she was trying to protect us?"

She looked up from her cake, her lips stained with chocolate, and said, "Yes."

"Well what I meant by that is that Catherine was trying to protect us from all the chaos you witnessed at her press conference: reporters yelling and screaming, waving their hands and asking her all kinds of questions. She simply wants us to be a happy family and not have to deal with all that commotion, and one way to accomplish that is by separating us from her team. If she said I was involved with the trade and with her team, it would only cause more commotion, and we don't want that. I quit my job because that was one of the things I did not want to deal with anymore."

"I don't understand," Mia said. "Everyone loves you and they all say that you are a genius and that you're very nice."

I laughed at that and realized that I should have known my little Sherlock would already have looked me up on the computer and read everything written about me. I was ready to lie and tell her that she shouldn't believe everything she reads on the internet, but I just couldn't. I had spent a lifetime treating everybody respectfully ... reporters, fans, ballplayers, the janitor who cleaned my office, the hardworking people working the concession stands ... even the agents. It was simply the way I was raised. As for being a genius, I could strongly argue against that, but what I could not argue against was the hard work and the time that I had put into my job, and my ability to put together a staff and a group of scouts who worked as hard and were as dedicated to the job as I was.

I grabbed a tissue from a nearby box and wiped Mia's lips, even though I knew that in less than a second they would be all smudged with chocolate again. "I just want you to know that everything Catherine said and did today, she did because she loves the both of us so much."

"I know," she said. "I love Catherine so much and I would never say anything to her that would make her feel sad."

"Thank you, Mia," I said as she went back to eating her cake.

I stood up as my phone rang, and it was Catherine. Just from the sound of her voice, I could sense that my old Catherine was back. The one I met at the bar, who unselfishly helped me navigate my initial uncertainties surrounding Mia. The *girl* stuff, as I liked to describe it. She asked me how I liked the press conference. I told her that if they gave Academy Awards out for best performance at a news conference, she would win hands down. She laughed and then asked if I was okay with her making our relationship public.

I replied, "You took a load off my mind and I can't tell you how grateful I am to you for doing that. It's a lot better than some nosey reporter sneaking around and then letting the world know about it before we had a chance to respond. You were quite proactive, and I like that. Also, you were the most beautiful sight I have ever seen on a TV screen."

"Oh really," she said, laughing. "I see you were actually listening when I said I could never get enough praise ... unlike you."

"It's praise that's well deserved, and both our daughter and I agree heartily."

"Wow! I like the direction of this conversation. Praise from my fiancé and my maid of honor, not to mention my daddy, who already gave his approval. Is our daughter currently too busy eating her chocolate dish to talk to me? I have the rest of the day off and I think it's time for a little family outing, but I'd like to check with her first."

I looked at Mia and smiled as I motioned to her to wipe the chocolate off her face, and as she did, I handed her the phone. A few moments later her face lit up, and soon after that, they were talking about Rex, and I was fairly certain that we weren't referring to the stuffed version sitting at the table. Mia handed me the phone, and Catherine said, "I just feel like it's my responsibility to meet Rex. I've heard so much about him — I feel as though he's part of our family. Is it okay if we all go?"

"Of course, as long as I get to hold your hand and you promise not to fall in love with Mr. Rex. He's quite good-looking and he has a lovely singing voice."

"I'll try my hardest but I'm sure it won't be easy."

The sound of Catherine's voice, so soothing and loving, suddenly filled me with nostalgia. It was like the first time I talked to Catherine on my private phone, when I had thought for a moment that I was talking to my mother. I laughed as I looked across at Mia and said, "Yes, we're going to visit Rex."

She hugged me and then ran off to change her outfit. After all, seeing Rex was no small thing and one should be dressed appropriately. Given the hour, we knew that the first behind-the-scenes tour had already been concluded, and so we would get to see Rex only once, but that was certainly better than not seeing him at all.

CHAPTER TWENTY-SEVEN

Mia and I took the elevator downstairs, and as we stepped into the lobby, we were met by a group of photographers and sportswriters waving their hands and yelling out questions. Mia hid behind my leg. It wasn't like I wasn't expecting this to eventually happen, and so I did what I'd always done for the last thirty years when I was assaulted by the press: I patiently and politely answered all their questions, which was made all the easier because my lovely fiancée provided me with all the answers at her earlier news conference.

The press had always been exceptionally nice to me, especially as my legend grew. I understood that they had a job to do, and I understood that part of being a GM was dealing with the press. I considered a number of sportswriters and sportscasters my friends, and over the years, I spent many hours at bars having drinks with them or sitting down and enjoying dinner over a couple of bottles of expensive wine. The press was not the enemy of the athlete or the GM or the manager or the owner. In many respects, the press, if correctly courted, could provide a financial bonanza for a team. And the best sportswriters played another role too. Their love of the game and their skill with language had helped to elevate baseball from a game to a great cultural pastime. I had great respect for the best of them.

I tried to stress, especially to the younger ballplayers, that they should treat the press with the same respect and dignity that they wanted, and if possible, a notch above because it was a lot better to have the press on your side than to have them against you, especially while going through a slump or contract negotiations. Sure, they made mistakes and often misquoted ballplayers, but such errors could usually be corrected by sending a polite email or a short note or by making a phone call and pointing out the mistake. It might not always work, but most sportswriters would find a way to put the correction into his or her next story.

It would always bother me when I would hear a superstar athlete or a movie star complaining about how the press was infringing upon their personal space while all they wanted to do was play ball or act without having to deal with these miscreants. If that was all they wanted to do, no one was stopping them from joining a theatre company in Nebraska or playing ball down in Central America. Surely, no one would be bothering them in either place ... certainly none of the miscreants ... but then they wouldn't be making the big bucks or have their names in lights or make a few extra million at autograph signings or conventions. No, I was secure in the knowledge that dealing with the press was just part of the job, even if it was technically no longer my actual job to speak for any team.

I answered all the questions tossed at me and shook hands and exchanged pleasantries with a number of the writers I personally knew, and then I took Mia's hand and walked toward the front entrance. The best thing about living in this age, with all the media outlets, the internet and the social networking, was that almost any sports story — especially one like Catherine's and mine — had a shelf life of maybe a day before it was old news. This was especially true during the time of year when both college and pro football dominated the sports world.

Catherine was waiting for us in her car a short distance from the front entrance. She apologized for unknowingly leading the press right to us, and I told her it was for the best that both of us addressed the press and got it out of the way. I reassured her that by tomorrow we would be old news. She laughed as she drove to SeaWorld, where for the third time in a week, I got to see Mr. Rex. Naturally, Catherine embraced the handsome bird with almost as much enthusiasm as Mia, and I was left in charge of taking pictures with Catherine's phone.

CHAPTER TWENTY-EIGHT

We were escorted out of SeaWorld an hour after it closed. By now, Mia and I knew the security guards by name, and I was almost tempted to invite them out to dinner. Instead, I tried to hand the guards fifty dollars apiece, but they said they weren't allowed to take money, so I simply dropped two fifties on the ground and we walked away as Mia looked back to make sure the guards picked up the money, which they did.

Catherine suggested we eat at a quaint Italian restaurant that she swore had the best Italian food in all of San Diego. Mia ordered noodles with butter, a safe choice for a child who probably never had real Italian food before. Catherine and I ordered spaghetti with a wonderful Bolognese sauce. We had Mia taste it, but from the expression on her face, it was quite obvious that she didn't think it was all that amazing. She did, however, go a bit nuts for the chocolate-flavored cannoli that we ordered for her dessert, so we ordered a half dozen cannoli to go.

Back at the hotel, I poured Catherine a well-deserved glass of white wine, and on instinct alone, I opened the box of cannoli and put one in front of Mia with a glass of chocolate milk. I knew there was no way that child was content with just the one cannoli she had at the restaurant.

Catherine taught Mia how to transfer the pictures I took of Rex and the girls onto my computer, and she picked it up easily. It was astonishing how quickly this child learned complex tasks ... or tasks that seemed complex to me. I had been working with computers for most of my life and I still had trouble transferring pictures from my phone to my computer. Mia was doing it all by herself after about five minutes.

It was apparent to me from the beginning that Catherine's rapport with Mia was really special, and as I looked at the girls laughing and complimenting that handsome devil Rex, it became even more obvious to me how indispensable Catherine's presence was in Mia's life, and in my life.

***

Catherine and I had a lot to talk about, but it was difficult because so much of what we needed to discuss had to do with Mia. Since the child and I escaped from the town of Salvation, there had been only a few times that Mia had not been in the presence of either Catherine or me. It wasn't like we could just tell Mia to go to her room because we needed to talk about adult matters. Despite the child's amazing assimilation into our world, it didn't take Sigmund Freud to realize that deep down she still had suspicions about her future and our intentions. Asking her to go take a walk by the beach or go to her room and look at TV would only add to her anxiety. We could tell her twenty times a day how much we loved her and bestow gift after gift and chocolate dish after chocolate dish, yet the only thing that would cement the idea that she was in our lives to stay was time. And on this particular day, in which my future wife took the lead and put to rest so many issues concerning the game and our relationship, I decided the Mia questions could wait for another day. It was too perfect a day to mess around with, and I was sure that Catherine's resolutions to some of Mia's potential problems were different from mine.

Mia was the link that fostered the relationship between Catherine and me, and it didn't hurt that she had played the part of a little matchmaker, for which I was eternally grateful. Meeting her also forced me, for the first time in my life, to question the existence of God, along with the validity of my Christian faith and my Catholic upbringing. Even though I had spent so much time in poverty-stricken parts of Central America, South America and Mexico, where Christianity was dominant, I never once asked myself, *If there really is a God, a merciful and loving God, how could he allow such suffering to take place?*

Despite all the immoral and corrupt behavior of the Catholic Church, I had never before questioned the tenets it preached ... even if many of the messengers of those beliefs needed to be castrated or, at the very least, jailed for their actions. It was not until my visit to Salvation, where I came face to face with Mia and her tormentors, that I began to ask myself that question ... over and over again.

Granted, the town of Salvation offered an extreme example, but the poverty in all the other places I visited was a sad and disturbing reality. The Christian religion and the solace and comfort I found in its teachings was quickly dissipating as I began to take precautions to shield Mia from the symbols of my religion. This was difficult because, as I quickly discovered, religious imagery tended to pop up everywhere, especially here in San Diego, where there seemed to be a Catholic church on every other block.

The truth of the matter was that I could protect her for only so long before she had to face her fears and overcome the trauma that nearly killed her. She was a little Leonardo da Vinci ... at least that was the way I liked to see her. Her curiosity was unlimited, and because of that, there was no way for her to avoid the religious symbols, which for her, represented danger and death.

It seemed odd to me at first, but the more I thought about my religious upbringing and the more I questioned the traditions I was taught to uphold, the more critical I was becoming of that other American church, baseball. Baseball and religion were becoming linked in my mind, and I was starting to think of them as twin orthodoxies whose fundaments needed to be approached with skepticism and caution.

Baseball was often referred to as America's favorite pastime, even though football generated five to six times more revenue than baseball. Baseball traditionalists would argue that the game as it stood into the early 1960s should never have been tampered with, that it was sacrilegious to change the rules, yet if baseball hadn't changed and introduced a long-overdue playoff system, half the teams that existed at the time would have gone defunct.

Back in the good old days, before a playoff system was developed, the first-place teams in the American and National leagues went straight to the World Series, which meant that the fans of at least seventy-five percent of the teams had no hope that their team had any chance of finishing first and going to the World Series. In most cases, before the All-Star break, most of those teams were already thinking about next year as they watched a steady decline in their attendance ... unless they were fortunate enough to have great home-run hitters like Ernie Banks or Ralph Kiner, or an amazing pitcher like Bob Feller, who might throw a no-hitter at any time. Baseball's obsession with statistics and records kept many teams afloat long after they had any reasonable chance of going to the World Series.

Since retiring as a player nearly twenty-five years ago, and entering the business side of the game, I have thought long and hard about improving the game and keeping fans, especially younger fans, interested throughout the entire season and hopefully making them lifetime fans like my parents and grandparents.

Today, baseball has an expanded playoff system with three separate divisions in each league and inter-league play. Instead of seventy-five percent of the teams having no hope of going to the World Series with still two and a half months left in the season, now the percentage has dropped to about twenty-five.

Tradition can be detrimental and can veil a conspiracy of immoral and corrupt behavior. When traditionalists start tossing around words like *sacrilegious* and *blasphemous*, it is time to take a closer look at the institutions they are so fervently trying to preserve. This is true of all traditions, whether in sport, religious life or anywhere else. There was a time, not all that long ago, that if a child accused a priest of touching them inappropriately, the parents would have told the child that they were imagining the whole thing. And there was a time when baseball owners colluded, arguing against racial integration, because it would somehow sully the image of the game, and far too many fans bought that garbage.

When institutions take words written by human beings too literally, it creates a culture that brands innocent children, like my beautiful Mia, with labels such as the *devil's child*, and that is just plain wrong.

***

Catherine and Mia went to bed early. They already had tomorrow all planned out. The first half of the day would be spent beautifying themselves in preparation for the wedding: pedicures, manicures, facials and massages. Personally, I thought they looked flawless and couldn't see any room for improvement, but then I could be accused of a certain bias.

Afterward, they would go pick out a dress for the maid of honor. Catherine had already decided to wear her mother's wedding dress. I would then be accorded the honor of taking the two of them out to lunch, and if I so desired, I could go shopping with them for a cell phone and a computer for our little Leonardo. Catherine insisted that Mia carry her cell phone with her whenever she went out … whether she was with us or by herself. Already, she was showing signs of being an overprotective mommy.

Some big questions about our impending wedding and marriage were still to be resolved. We had not talked about when or where we would be getting married, or whether there would be a honeymoon. Nor had we figured out where we would live. I assumed that the marriage would be taking place relatively soon, considering all the preparation that was about to get underway, but then what did I know? The day and night had been so perfect, like I said earlier, that I didn't want to toss any type of fission into the loveliness of it all. I figured Catherine had it all sorted out. After all, I hadn't even known I was getting married until Catherine told me, and who was I to complain?

I opened a beer and sat down on the couch. I turned on ESPN, and as I had assumed previously, there wasn't even any mention of Catherine's news conference. All the talk was of the upcoming college football games on Saturday and the professional games on Sunday and Monday night. That didn't mean the local sports stations weren't still discussing the news conference, but considering all the professional football teams playing in the Southern California area and all the big college teams, I guessed that by midmorning all the talk would be about football.

I turned the TV off, grabbed another beer and sat down at the table in front of my laptop. I turned the computer on and hit the icon for pictures. Instead of pictures of Rex popping up, as I had assumed, I was suddenly faced with a picture of my mother and father on their wedding day, walking down the center aisle in Blessed Sacrament Church. It was part of a collection of pictures of my parents I had uploaded. My mom was a real Italian beauty, with that perfectly glistening olive skin, big brown eyes and long lashes. My father always said he got the better end of the deal when he married her, and it was hard to disagree, looking at her and remembering how wonderful and loving she was ... but then my father wasn't too shabby either.

I could feel tears rolling down my face, and then I suddenly felt a little hand touching me on the back and it was Mia. I went to shut the computer off ... fully conscious of how upset she got around religious symbols ... but she stopped me and asked, "Is that your mommy?"

"Yes," I replied as I struggled to get control over my emotions.

"She's so beautiful."

"So beautiful and kind and loving and always smiling."

"And your daddy loved her a whole bunch?"

"Yes, they loved each other a whole bunch and I miss them so very much."

She hugged me tightly and asked, "Can I see more pictures?"

I had not even asked her what she was doing up in the wee hours of the morning. I was too focused on wanting to spare her any contact with religious symbols, which were all over these pictures of my parents' church wedding. "You don't have to look at them, sweetheart," I said. "I know how much it upsets you."

Mia thought about that before calmly telling me something that really surprised me. "I'm not afraid anymore," she said, in a tone that made me believe her. "I understand the difference between gods, even if they look alike. Your mommy and daddy's God would never hurt anyone."

"You're absolutely right," I said, "but how did you figure that out?"

"Because you and Catherine would never hurt anyone and you both believe in the same God as your mommy and daddy."

"Wow," I said, gazing at her in amazement. "You really are smart."

Mia smiled proudly as I obeyed her request and started clicking through the other pictures in the folder. We hovered over the next one, which showed my parents standing outside the church with the priest who performed the ceremony, surrounded by smiling friends and family.

"That's a good one," Mia said, again sounding genuinely interested. "I like looking at pictures where everybody is happy." I clicked on another picture of my parents walking down the steps of the church toward a limousine, while the guests threw rice at them.

"Why do they throw things at the bride and groom?" Mia asked.

"Oh, that's one I actually know," I said, pleased to not have to look something up for once after being asked a question. "In the context of a wedding, rice is considered a symbol of rain, which is said to be a sign of prosperity and good fortune."

"Oh," Mia said. "I like that."

I clicked on more pictures of the happy bride and groom at the reception, where the guests could be seen dancing, drinking, dining and having a wonderful time. Mia looked so intently at the pictures. It was as though she had transported herself to that moment in time. Occasionally, I would notice a smile light up her face and eyes, reflecting the happiness so beautifully rendered in the pictures.

We finished looking at all the wedding pictures and then I told Mia that she should go to bed because she had a big day ahead of her.

She took a few steps toward her bedroom and then stopped and looked at me. Dressed in her Charlie Brown and Snoopy pajamas, with her long, soft locks of hair caressing her face, she stood there like a pint-size professor contemplating the "theory of everything," or in her case, the dimensions of a large piece of chocolate cake.

I could see her eyes tear up as she said, "I'm so sorry that your mommy and daddy are no longer here. They looked so happy ... but you have the pictures, so I guess they will always be here and that should make you happy."

I reached out and took her by the hands and softly said, "You know what makes me happy? Having you here. That's what makes me happy, and I'm quite certain that my mommy and daddy had something to do with you being here. I like to think that you are a gift from them, because all they ever wanted for me was to be happy."

She threw her arms around me and hugged me as I reached down and kissed her head. Sometimes the most precious gifts needed to be cleaned and scrubbed and nourished before their life-saving values were truly realized. Between all the showers and the chocolate and the love she was receiving, Mia was starting to seem pretty well-adjusted, and I was already at a point where I couldn't imagine life without her.

After Mia went to bed, I went into my own room and lay down. As I started to drift off to sleep, my mind began to drift aimlessly between thoughts of baseball and my new life with Mia and Catherine. I thought about how long the baseball season was — how it started in the middle of February, as pitchers and catchers reported to spring training, and ended as late as the first day of November, depending on circumstances, such as rainouts and national emergencies, as in 2001, when the aftermath of the September 11 terrorist attacks pushed the World Series into early November. *No wonder I had no life as a GM*, I briefly thought; ten months out of the year, I was on high alert, and the rest of the time I was scouting.

Then I thought about Einstein — yes, Einstein — and about how time is relative, depending on your position and your perspective. I could remember being conscious of that fact depending on what type of year our team was having. The years my team won the World Series seemed to fly by, and the down years, which were luckily few in number, seemed like they would never end. Then there was the matter of timing within the game itself. Bat speed, speed on the bases, the rotation and movement of a fastball coming at a batter at a hundred miles an hour — all of these calculations were part of my job for thirty years, and my evaluations were all based on my perception of time. Two fastballs clocked at a hundred miles an hour, one moving in a straight line toward home plate and the other spinning and dipping, often made the difference between a batter hitting a home run or a batter swinging helplessly as the ball landed in the catcher's glove.

Time had been a crucial part of my career in baseball, and yet I felt like I had lost so much of it. As I laid my head down on my pillow and looked up at the ceiling, I felt my parents' presence all about me; their faces were as clear to me as if they were sitting across from me on the bed, their words of encouragement and love ringing in my ears. The haunting question of whether there was a God or not had been erased from my consciousness, as though a magician had waved his wand and cleared all thoughts of blasphemy from my mind. I had thought it would take many years for Mia to adjust to her surroundings and learn not to fear the religious symbols all around her, but once again, she'd surprised me with her speed and her ability to adapt. *Yes*, I thought, getting sleepier by the moment, *time really is relative*. Depending on your physical position, your perception of a particular event — such as a train speeding along — would be different than another person's perception, even though you were watching the same train at the same time speeding toward the same platform.

I closed my eyes and fell asleep for six uninterrupted, restful hours. I woke up, put on my running gear and walked out of my bedroom. Sitting at the table was Mia, with Rex sitting in a chair next to her. She was looking contentedly at the wedding pictures of my parents. She smiled as I took her hand, and we walked down to the beach. We started to run, unsaddled and graceful, like two horses running free toward a rising sun and the dawn of a new day.

CHAPTER TWENTY-NINE

When we got back to the suite, Catherine was already up, dressed and looking especially beautiful. The thought of waking up beside this celestial creature, day after day, was enough to make me as tickled as a toddler waking up on Christmas morning. Mia ran off to take a shower, which gave Catherine and me a few minutes alone. My fiancée was all lovey-dovey and didn't seem to mind that I was all sweaty as we kissed passionately and rolled around on the couch and onto the floor. Luckily, it did not have a chance to go any further than kissing and grabbing, because — speaking of time being relative — Mia's soft proclamation that she was "all clean" rang like a fire alarm. Catherine and I looked at each other and then Catherine replied, "That's great, honey. I just dropped my ring and your daddy was helping me find it." She stood up as she brushed off her outfit and fixed her hair.

"Did you find it?" Mia asked as she moved closer to the couch.

"Yes, angel. You see?" she replied as she showed Mia her mother's ring on her finger. I got up off the floor and didn't bother brushing myself off, because I was already a sweaty mess from running.

"It was way under the couch," I said, like a real idiot — like I was going to fool my little Leonardo.

"Thank you, sweetheart," Catherine remarked as she kissed me and whispered into my ear, "We need to get married, like, today."

"Yes, we do," I whispered back and then watched her walk into the bedroom to clean up.

The girls left shortly thereafter for their manicures, pedicures, massages and dress shopping, but not before Catherine remarked, "I think we should go down to city hall before lunch and apply for our marriage license. What do you say, honey?"

"I say, that is a wonderful idea."

"Great. Then we can have a real celebratory lunch."

CHAPTER THIRTY

I met the girls at the courthouse, and to say that they looked even more beautiful than they had earlier that morning might have seemed like an exaggeration, but they did. They simply sparkled, and that dirty, smelly, emaciated child who I'd met just over a month ago had been replaced by one who would surely, as Catherine predicted, inspire lineups of young male suitors in only a few years. All I could do was thank God that I had Catherine to take care of that army of dirty-minded boys trying to get at our daughter. Italian men — and I was one hundred percent Italian — were fiercely protective of their daughters and were known to exact revenge on boys who were even suspected of making advances. Yes, thank *God* I had Catherine.

Catherine and I found the right place at city hall and applied for our marriage license, and afterward Mia studied the receipt and license like a lawyer studying a contract. When her curiosity had finally been satisfied, we went to eat lunch at a restaurant overlooking the ocean. To start our celebrations, we ordered a bottle of Dom Pérignon, vintage 1998, and a chocolate shake for the child. While looking over the lunch menus, Catherine asked, "So where would you like to get married, honey?"

"SeaWorld, of course. I need a best man, and who better than Rex," I replied as my fiancée nearly spit up her champagne, and Mia's face lit up like a Christmas tree. Catherine quickly killed the child's enthusiasm and remarked, "No, sweetheart, we will not be getting married at SeaWorld. I'm fairly certain Rex is busy that day with more pressing issues."

Mia went back to drinking her shake and Catherine asked, "How about my father's house in three days?"

"In three days," I repeated simply. "Okay, that would be great."

"You sure now?"

"Yes, I'm sure."

"Because if you were planning on having a bachelor party, we could always move the date further back."

"The quicker I rid myself of the title *bachelor*, the happier I'll be. In fact, I'd marry you right now."

Catherine blushed and reached over and kissed me. She then looked at Mia and asked, "Isn't he the best?"

"He is definitely the best," Mia replied.

"So how many guests do you expect?" I asked.

"Just a few. My daddy, my lovely maid of honor, and the entire house staff, who will be given the day off."

"How about your siblings?"

"No, unless my father insists. I love my brother and sister and their families, but I really want to keep it small. They'll understand. And of course, anyone you would like to invite."

"I have no one," I said. "Simple and small suits me perfectly."

"I have one more suggestion," Catherine said. "How would the two of you feel if, after the wedding, we move into my father's house? At least, until we get a place of our own."

I looked at Catherine and then across at Mia, who lowered her eyes as she sucked up the remaining part of her shake. "Are you suggesting that we move out of the hotel that we have come to love, with the amazing view of the ocean, and room service twenty-four seven?"

"I know it's a lot to ask, but once you see my daddy's home, I think you will quickly get over your hotel blues."

"Is that so? And what makes your daddy's home so special, besides you and your wise and charming father living there?"

"Well after we finish shopping, why don't we go pay him a visit? Then the two of you can decide if you think you'll be comfortable living there."

"That sounds reasonable," I said as I looked intently across at my fiancée with what I suspected was an obvious smirk.

"What's wrong?" she asked.

"Not a thing. Despite all the success and good fortune that I have been the lucky recipient of, none of it compares to the overwhelming luck and good fortune I feel to be marrying a beautiful and marvelous lady such as you, and to be the father of such a special and lovely child. And to be marrying into the family of a man I so greatly admire."

I reached over with my napkin and dabbed at the tears rolling down the cheeks of this amazing and independent lady, and then we ordered lunch.

After enjoying a delicious tray of surf and turf selections that included Mia's first-ever taste of shrimp scampi, we waddled out of the restaurant, a little too full, and drove to a nearby mall to buy a cell phone and a new computer for our daughter.

Naturally, Catherine had to buy the child the very best of both. I could see Mia's eyes open wide when she looked at the price tags attached to the displays. My little Leonardo went from a pauper to a princess overnight, and she deserved it all.

As we drove out of the parking lot, I looked at Mia in the rearview mirror of Catherine's car. She was holding the bag with the phone on her lap and resting one elbow on the computer box next to her as she smiled out the window.

"What'cha thinking about?" I asked her.

Mia seemed to snap out of a daydream and carefully listed the first five topics she planned to research as soon as her new computer was set up: sound waves; rainbows; clouds; Saturn's rings; and the Milky Way. Catherine and I looked at each other across the front seats, and I swear you could have seen our proud-parent smiles from the moon.

CHAPTER THIRTY-ONE

As we drove toward Mr. Baker's house, I began to feel a little nervous. As much as I loved Catherine, I had my reservations about moving into her family home. Not only was I marrying Mr. Baker's daughter, which still seemed a little unbelievable to me, but now I would be living under the same roof with the man I had viewed as an elder statesman, a mentor, and at times a business rival, during my whole career. All of it seemed to be stretching reality. But then, maybe this was my new reality.

Catherine turned off the highway that ran along the water and drove a few minutes until we came to a large decorative iron gate. She waved to an on-duty security guard and he pressed a button that caused the two glossy black halves of the gate to part automatically. Waving her thanks, Catherine drove up a hill that suddenly flattened out at the top to reveal an expanse of lush gardens, with greenery and blooming trees and perennials that seemed to go on forever in both directions.

As she pulled up in front of the house, I gradually realized that it rivaled the size of the entire hotel we were staying at. This was no mansion; this was a slightly smaller version of Buckingham Palace. Moreover, it was tasteful. Unlike the gaudy monstrosities that I'd seen so many ballplayers build over the years, this one was more like a Victorian-style palace that one might find in the French or English countryside. I turned to her and jokingly said, "I didn't know that you and your dad lived in a hotel."

She smiled and asked, "Would you prefer we live in a hotel?"

"I'll let you know once our daughter and I inspect the inside."

"I don't think we can wait that long. It's twenty-five thousand square feet."

"So it's the size of the new Yankee Stadium."

"Maybe a little smaller, but I like to think it has a lot more class."

We entered the house through a pair of massive front doors and ended up in a gleaming statue-filled foyer that was the size of most houses. I looked at Mia, who had not said a word since we pulled off the highway, and could see that she was totally awestruck. She looked like the cutest little peanut, lost in a heavenly labyrinth. She took my hand as she gaped up at the vaulted ceiling that seemed to touch the sky.

As we stood there staring up, a distinguished-looking gentleman, casually dressed and about the same age as Mr. Baker, emerged from a side room to greet us.

"Henry!" Catherine exclaimed happily as they shared a hug. "Henry, I'd like you to meet Joe Ciotola and Mia. Joe and Mia, this is Henry, my father's right-hand man."

As we all chatted for a few minutes, it became clear that Henry knew more about what was going on with Catherine, Mia and me than I did. I would later find out that he had been Mr. Baker's butler for over fifty years. Besides Catherine and her daddy, Henry was the only other person living in the house.

As I would learn over the next half hour, the other house staff consisted of six individuals working in the kitchen, two maids and a gardener. They all lived in an adjacent house, a mere eight thousand square-foot home, which Mr. Baker had built for them and given to them as a present, along with the land that it sat on. To put it into perspective, their house was double the size of my house in Studio City.

They all came out to greet us, and like Henry, unless you were told they were employees, you might never have guessed. To say that the workplace had an informal atmosphere about it would be an understatement. They all seemed jovial and content and they all fussed over Mia like grandparents over a grandchild.

After everyone else had said their hellos, Mr. Baker emerged from a side room that was also his study. He was dressed in a polo shirt, jeans and a pair of Avery Island causal shoes, and he smiled and nodded to Henry and the rest of his staff as he approached us with arms open. Catherine hugged her father and proudly held up a sheet of paper, which he gradually came to realize was the receipt for our marriage license. I shook Mr. Baker's hand, but I must admit, I felt uncomfortable. The whole idea that I was marrying his daughter in a few days, and that she had been staying at the hotel with Mia and me these last few nights had, for me at least, thrown our relationship into a bizarre and different orbit. What had been a friendly, business-oriented relationship had suddenly become a family affair, and it didn't help that I was fourteen years older than my future wife.

Catherine did not seem one bit bothered by the changing circumstances, possibly because she had put the whole thing into motion. Since the news conference, she'd been riding a natural high and had not mentioned baseball once. As she stood next to her father, she glowed with warmth and affection, and it was at that moment that I knew for sure that marrying Catherine meant, in no uncertain terms, that her father would never be too far removed from either of our lives … in fact, never more than a few football fields away.

Catherine took us on an abridged tour of the house, which included a spiral staircase that led to the east and west wings where most of the home's twenty-five bedrooms were located. If you weren't in the mood to walk up the stairs, you could take an elevator, which had been installed after Catherine's mother got sick and lost some of her mobility. Catherine said she never took the elevator — there were too many sad memories attached to it — but she had no problem if we wanted to use it.

We toured the east wing, where Catherine showed us our future bedroom and an adjoining one that would be given to Mia. Ours was the size of a small apartment and included a generously proportioned seating area and a large TV. Mia's room was a little smaller than ours, and her bed, which must have been some sort of custom-made creation, was big enough to accommodate her and Rex and most of the real Rex's relatives, should they ever come to visit.

Catherine was completely at ease in this setting. This was no surprise, given that she'd lived here her whole life, apart from those few years when she was away at college. As for me, I couldn't quite relax. The house really did feel like a hotel and like the antithesis of everything a real home was for me. I grew up in a small house with three bedrooms and two bathrooms, and it was probably no more than seventeen hundred square feet in total. My mother and father and I were probably never more than a few hundred feet away from each other when we were all at home. My house in Studio City was about five thousand square feet, and that felt like a mansion. There were times when the loneliness and emptiness I felt in that house were overwhelming, so I was already predicting that I would have trouble adapting to living in a place almost ten times bigger. But if living in this cathedral was what it took to have Catherine and Mia in my life, I would just have to suck it up, and I did. When Catherine asked me what I thought about living there with her father, I enthusiastically replied, "I can't wait for us to move in. It is simply amazing."

Mia agreed, even though she, too, seemed overwhelmed by the size of the place. She was especially sensitive to Catherine's wishes and went out of her way to appease, please and comfort her soon-to-be mommy. I could not even fathom what was going on in that child's mind. If there were different degrees of culture shock, her level had to be off the charts. She was special, and as someone who had spent a good part of my life elevating ballplayers and helping them realize their full potential, I could sense that this little soft-spoken, chocolate-loving girl had the potential to be remarkable. The longevity of a ballplayer depended on his ability to adapt as his skills diminished. My little Leonardo had already proven her ability to adapt and survive, and her career — if one could call it that — was just getting underway.

Mr. Baker took a fancy to Mia even before they met. Catherine, like a great scout, had reported back to her father everything she knew and surmised about the child, and in that report, she did not fail to highlight Mia's limitless curiosity, intelligence and creativity. Already, he had decided tonight to teach her chess, giving Catherine and me an opportunity to go out on our first real date.

Mia and Mr. Baker were comfortably seated in a couple of big leather chairs in his book-lined study, next to a massive fireplace, when Catherine and I poked our heads in to say goodbye. Mia was setting up queens and kings and rooks on the chess board between them, with the help of a diagram given to her by Mr. Baker.

"Don't worry about us!" Mr. Baker called. "You kids have fun. Mia and I have a full evening of activities planned, starting with this match."

"Take it easy on my daddy," Catherine said to Mia, and gave her a wink.

"No!" Mr. Baker protested. "No special treatment allowed. This is a serious match between two serious players, and we'll just have to see who emerges victorious."

Mia giggled as she put the last rook on the board and looked up to give us a quick wave goodbye.

CHAPTER THIRTY-TWO

I breathed a sigh of relief as we walked out the front door and got into Catherine's car. It wasn't the house so much and certainly not the staff or Henry, the butler, but the changed relationship with Mr. Baker that was making me uncomfortable. It was good to be escaping it, if only for an evening. Suddenly, our shared business interests had become a family affair of the most intimate kind. I was marrying his daughter, and it was obvious that there was nothing more important to him than her. After his wife died, his two other children, who had families of their own, continued with their lives, whereas Catherine became his caretaker. Not only had she taken on many of the responsibilities that her mother had held but she also helped run the team. The last thing I wanted was for Mr. Baker to think that I was stealing his daughter away. I had no evidence that he did think that, but I guess I wanted to prove myself to him.

All of this probably had to do with the fact that I knew Mr. Baker's story — how he had pulled himself up by his bootstraps and created every bit of wealth and position he now enjoyed. The way I'd always heard it told, he was a scrappy young kid from a small town in Texas who started working on oil rigs out in the Gulf of Mexico at seventeen. He learned the business and got a hungry group of investors together, whose sole concern was making money, and bought out a near-bankrupt oil company, which he turned into one of the largest independent companies in the country. He bought out his investors and became the principal owner. During the Middle East oil embargo in the early to mid-1970s, he made a fortune. With demand for oil in the US at record levels and supply so limited, his company tripled its output and, in so doing, recorded record profits that made him one of the richest men in America, according to *Forbes* magazine. Shortly before the embargo ended, he sold his company to one of the Big Five oil companies, increasing his already immense wealth.

His first love as a child was baseball, and when the team in San Diego became available, he bought it. They had been a losing franchise for years before he took them over, and since then, they had many solid years but never made it to the World Series. Across the semi-scrupulous world of pro baseball, Mr. Baker was known for his meticulously above-board management of the team's finances. Whatever profit the team made went directly back into the team and its farm system. He never dipped into his personal fortune to go after high-priced free agents, but every penny of extra revenue that came about because of the team — such as revenue from profit sharing, TV contracts and marketing — was money to be used by the team and nothing else.

A good percentage of his personal fortune was distributed to numerous charities throughout the community, and both Catherine and her father sat on the boards of at least a dozen charitable, non-profit organizations. When asked why he didn't dip into his personal fortune to go after high-priced free agents, he replied that he would rather donate that money to battling childhood cancer, "so that those children might one day have a chance to play baseball and pursue their dreams."

It was a position that not even die-hard fans of the team could argue against. The sportswriters and the press loved him. In all his years as an oilman and then as a baseball owner, his financial records and tax returns were never flagged for irregularities or criminality. When Catherine said at her press conference that she had never met a better man than her father, she was speaking the truth.

That momentary relief I felt when we walked out of the house was suddenly replaced with the realization that, except for the time we first met, I had never been totally alone with Catherine for an extended period. As we drove in silence along the water, Catherine must have sensed my discomfort because she asked, "What's wrong, Joe?"

"Why would anything be wrong?"

"That's what I'm trying to figure out," she said. "I'm not sure if you know this, but your future bride has very good instincts."

"Spidey sense activating?"

"I'd say so."

She was a genius at these interrogations, and her first move was to say nothing, leaving the question on the table, as it were, until I cracked.

"I don't know," I said. "For some reason I feel awkward. We have a thousand things to talk about and yet..."

She stopped at a red light, reached over and kissed me on the mouth. It was a quick kiss — a red-light's-about-to-change-to-green-length kiss — but she made it count. "Does that help?" she asked.

"Mmm," I said. "I don't know. We might need to try again."

She laughed and went in for another.

"Yes," I said. "Definitely yes. That helps."

"Great, because there is going to be a lot more of that in our future."

"I look forward to that," I said, and I really did.

"Good. But you're right that we have a lot of things to talk about. Where do you want to start? With Mia?"

"She is definitely a priority."

"She sure is," Catherine said. "My father has taken a real fancy to her. She's simply irresistible."

"The best prospect I have laid eyes on in years, but once we are married and I get all the paperwork to the lawyer and she is officially ours, we have some tough decisions to make, especially about her education."

"I've thought about that. I think the first couple of years, before she starts high school, that she should be homeschooled. I don't think she's ready to be in an environment with a lot of other children."

"You know, she's only finished the second grade..."

"I know, but I think she will easily qualify as a seventh grader and have no problems passing the qualifying exams. If I weren't going to be so busy, I would love to be her teacher. I already have all the qualifications, but I just don't have the time that's needed to teach her correctly."

"Well I have the time," I said. She looked at me and started to laugh. I continued, "You know, I do have a college degree and it's not in physical education."

"I know, but you would have to take a bunch of qualifying tests. Are you prepared to do the studying?"

"Honestly, yes, but I would much rather hire a seasoned professional and make sure that our little Leonardo is properly educated."

"Leonardo?"

"Yes. I started calling her that in my head, and I guess I didn't share that with you. Don't you think it fits? She's so curious and she has so many interests. And I feel like she's going to burst forth with a bunch of different talents the minute she has a little bit of actual training. She's practically taught herself everything she knows. Imagine what she'll do with a bit of guidance."

"You're so right," Catherine said. "How long do you think it will take before our little Leonardo switches places with the seasoned professional and becomes the teacher?"

"Not long," I said. "She already knows more about computers than I do."

"And penguins," Catherine said.

"Without a doubt, penguins," I laughed.

Catherine paused before turning to a more difficult and delicate subject, one that we had had no chance to consider. "What about therapy? She has been severely traumatized, both physically and emotionally, and it's not like the scars are just going to go away or her mind be miraculously erased of the horrific memories."

I looked out the passenger's-side window at the vast and mighty ocean and thought about the hypnotic and relaxing effect it had on so many individuals ... it was so mesmerizing that people were willing to build homes as close to the water's edge as possible, despite the unpredictability and the raging turbulence beneath the surface.

I looked back at Catherine and told her about Mia coming up behind me when I was looking at pictures of my parents' church wedding. I told her about the priest and the large crucifix that was hanging above the altar and how, when I went to click the pictures off, she stopped me and said that she wasn't afraid anymore. "She said she knew that the God that you and I worship is kind and loving because we are so kind and loving."

Catherine smiled and said, "Well that's a hopeful sign."

"Yes, it is a hopeful sign, and the next morning when I woke up, I found her at the computer again, looking at the same pictures of my parents' wedding. She talked about how happy and beautiful my mother looked."

"She's so sweet, but..."

"I think we should hold off on her seeing a therapist. She's doing so well now, and I don't want to throw a wrench into her progress. I don't want her to think that we suspect that something is wrong with her."

Catherine looked at me suspiciously and replied, "The intense trauma that Mia experienced is not going to resolve itself over time. Yes, it's great she was able to look at religious symbols and not totally freak out and run off and hide, but that's still a small step forward. The longer her terrible experiences are left to fester deep inside that wonderful little brain, the harder her recovery is going to be. I've dealt with traumatized children, a lot less traumatized than Mia, and it takes many, many baby steps before a resolution is even in sight."

I looked across at the ocean again and noticed it was at low tide ... meaning that the gravitational pull of the moon was weak and the waves looked less powerful from the shoreline. I learned that from Mia, and as I looked back at Catherine, my instinct regarding that child, not unlike my instinct when scouting young ballplayers, was to lay off ... not to push too hard ... to remain cognizant but not intrusive.

"I saw what that child went through, Catherine, and I don't want her revisiting that insanity on a therapist's coach until the situation warrants it. It's too soon."

Catherine nodded and replied, "Okay."

I thought I detected a note of passive aggression in her reply, and this irritated me, but before I said anything I was going to regret, I paused and reflected on the generous and loving nature of the lady beside me and said, "I know you care about Mia as much as I do, and you're probably right about the therapy, but at this moment I cannot bear to put that child through the pain of reliving those terrible experiences. I know the time will come, and I'm worried I'm being selfish and cowardly, but…"

She interrupted me with a shake of her head and a soft and consoling rebuttal. "No! There is nothing cowardly or selfish about it. You're a wonderful parent, and you're just waiting for the right time. I get it. You love her so much that you can't stand the idea of causing her a moment's pain. It's one of the many reasons it was so easy to fall in love with you."

I took her right hand, which was not on the steering wheel at that moment, and gave it a gentle, thankful squeeze.

We stopped at another red light and once again Catherine reached over and we kissed passionately. We were getting so good at this that we naturally started to take turns closing our eyes and then casting one eye up at the traffic light in mid-kiss, so as not to get caught for too long after it turned to green. I joked that never in my life had I looked so forward to stopping at red lights and said I felt like one of Pavlov's dogs, salivating and puckering up at the sight of a yellow light turning to red. Catherine laughed at this, and the whole world seemed like a benevolent, beautiful place.

We pulled into the driveway of a small mom-and-pop seafood restaurant called The Clipper. Catherine explained that she had been coming to this restaurant since she was a child, and sure enough, she was greeted at the door like she was a member of the family. She knew all the waiters and the busboys, the bartender and the owners, Frank and Mary. Catherine was very comfortable in this type of setting, and if it wasn't for her blonde hair, blue eyes, fair skin and California accent, she could easily have passed for an Italian, back in the old Bronx. She was what one might call a real hugger. If she knew you, like she knew the staff at the restaurant, you were most likely going to be greeted with a hug, not a handshake.

We were seated at a semi-private table with a wonderful view of the ocean and were immediately presented, compliments of the house, with two plates of fresh lump crabmeat served with cocktail sauce, crackers and horseradish on the side, and a bottle of white wine.

"I so love it here," Catherine said as she reached across the table and took hold of my hand. She continued, "I imagine they had a lot of mom-and-pop-type restaurants back in the Bronx, in the neighborhood that you grew up in."

"Yes, they did. One, sometimes two, on every block ... but not so much anymore."

"Do you still own the house you grew up in?"

"Yes, I have never had the heart to sell it. I've kept it exactly the same as when my parents were alive. Even the notes they left for each other on the refrigerator door, I have never been able to take down. Mrs. Bruno, our neighbor to the right, looks after the house for me."

"When is the last time you were in it?"

"It's been a long time," I said, trying to remember the last time I was there. "Too long."

"Is that the house you would live in if the Yankees called?"

"Yes, but I don't plan on working for the Yankees this upcoming year, next year or thirty years from now. And you know why — because they can't offer me a better view or deal than what I am looking at right now." Catherine's bottom lip started to quiver, and then the tears suddenly started streaming down her cheeks. I stood up, came around the table, squeezed into the booth next to her and wrapped my arms around her shoulders.

"Hey, hey!" I said. "I didn't mean to make you cry."

"It's okay! It's okay," she said, between a couple of short gasps. "I'm crying because I'm happy. And when I'm not being a tough GM, I can cry pretty easily, so you'd better get used to it."

"I can already tell I'm going to have the best time getting to know everything there is to know about you," I said, and I meant it.

She shook off her tears and hugged me back, and as she pulled away and picked up the menu, she shot me a big mischievous smile.

"Let's break the bank and get lobster," she said.

It would have taken more than a couple of steamed three-pound lobsters to break the bank, but it still felt like an extravagance. Three pounds might seem like a lot, but one three-pounder translated into about ten ounces of meat. Lobster was mostly shell. It was delicious, if somewhat messy to eat. We cracked open the claws and tails and dragged the speckled chunks of meat through our little pots of melted butter, moaning just a little as we touched the dripping delicacy to our lips. I fed some to her and she fed some to me and we didn't care who might be watching.

Even as we were enjoying our feast, I was thinking a little bit about business and realizing that this was probably the next item we needed to discuss. I was still uncertain about the role I was going to play, if any, in my future wife's business. I approached the subject gingerly, quite happy to play no role whatsoever in any affairs concerning her team or baseball in general. I had already made enough suggestions, which she followed through on. She had traded her superstar MVP for the two promising pitchers, signed the former Red Sox's pitching coach to help bring along the two pitchers and paid the Philadelphia Phillies five million in cash for their platooned centerfielder, picking up the remaining two years on his six-million-a-year contract. I had no doubt that even in the best-case scenario, in which the pitchers turned out to have really good years and the centerfielder lived up to his potential and the team remained highly competitive throughout the year, other trades would certainly have to be made if they wanted to go far into the playoffs and compete for a championship.

In all the years with my team, there was never a year in which one of my star players didn't go down for an extended period of time, and that was one of the main reasons I always had to remain vigilant of other teams' rosters and who they might be willing to trade. Injuries were contagious and it always seemed like once one key player went down, the dominos started to fall, and suddenly three or four players seemed to follow that one player onto the injury reserve list.

Unlike the Yankees and St. Louis, or for that matter, my former team, Catherine's team did not have a deep bench, and their farm system was not replete with many star prospects. In fact, if I was still employed, I would not have been sitting there with this beautiful lady, eating lobster, but would have already packed my bags and headed south to scout fifteen- and sixteen-year-old players, who I might eventually sign and move up into our farm system. It was imperative that I had a strong farm system because my team, like Catherine's team, did not have the big money to sign star players to huge contracts. In fact, for fifteen straight years, my team had more homegrown talent straight out of our farm system on our opening-day roster than any of the other teams. We also had a high rate of players over thirty-five, who other teams had given up on and who I thought still had at least one or two productive years left.

The baseball season was very long, with very few days off, and you always had to prepare for the worst-case scenarios, and so I asked the lovely lady across from me, who had melted butter running down her mouth, "And so where do I stand in relation to your team ... should I offer advice that I might think helpful? Or should I keep my mouth shut and if you want any advice you will simply ask me? It really doesn't matter to me."

"You were listening to my highly praised press conference?"

"Yes and no. It wasn't so easy to listen while my eyes were trained on the glamorous young lady standing at the podium."

She laughed as she wiped her mouth with a napkin and said, "If I didn't know better, I might think that, with all these compliments you are handing out, you might be expecting some pre-honeymoon bliss after we wrap up dinner. After all, your hotel suite is empty, and while I might be a traditionalist when it comes to certain things, I can assure you I'm not when it comes to that."

"Wow! That is the best offer I have ever received that I am going to have to turn down. I would rather wait the three days, as hard as that is going to be, and have an old-time, traditional and blissful honeymoon."

"I can respect that, as hard as that is going to be on me," she said with a laugh.

"So, my beautiful and loving fiancée, the time has come for us to talk baseball."

"It has?"

"Yes," I said. "I'm going to need you to set some rules. Please lay out the parameters that you would like me to stick to when it comes to your team. And don't worry about making me feel bad. After all, I walked away from the game. If you don't want to hear anything at all from me about your team, I am perfectly fine with that. Just know that I am always in your corner as long as what we discuss stays between us and my name is left out of discussions with the press and the people in your organization."

"You really weren't listening to what I said at the press conference?" she asked jokingly.

"It's like I said, I might not have been listening, but I was looking."

"If you honestly believe I would marry the game's best GM and never draw on his expertise, you're deluded! I made of fool of myself trying to recruit you as general manager, as my father likes to remind me, and now that I am going to have that genius sleeping in the same bed with me, you'd better believe I am going to take advantage of your know-how."

"So you *are* marrying me for my baseball prowess?"

"Oh gosh, no! I could have got that out of you with a wink and a smile."

"Wow! Talk about over-confidence … a simple wink and smile is all it would take?"

"Well look how much I got out of you without using any weapons in my arsenal of seductive powers."

I reached over with my napkin and wiped a last bit of melted butter away from her chin. I looked up into her sparkling eyes and somewhere deep inside I felt she might be right. She had me spellbound. She continued, "I'm marrying you because you are the best man I know besides my daddy, and that has nothing to do with the game of baseball."

"But it does have something to do with our little Leonardo?"

"I'd be lying if I said she didn't sweeten the pie. She was a major asset in your favor. That chocolate-loving child has a way of casting a spell over you. She probably already has my daddy eating out of her hands, and the kitchen staff was already concocting chocolate delights for her before we even left."

"I think she might be playing us," I jokingly remarked.

"Of course she's playing us. Have you denied her one thing since you rescued her from that crazy town?"

"No, but then she hasn't asked for anything. It's you who has done most of the spoiling. A new computer, an expensive phone, a wardrobe the envy of every ten-year-old, constantly enabling her chocolate addiction, pedicures, manicures, massages…"

"She's been a gold mine of useful information. How else would I have known for sure that you were madly in love with me, if it wasn't for her confirming the fact."

"Madly in love — is that what the little matchmaker confirmed?"

"Yes, and all I had to dish out for that information was a chocolate sundae."

"She is a conniving little critter, isn't she? Reminding me over and over again to tell you how much I love you. I finally see all the pieces falling into place. Quite an impressive scheme our little Leonardo cooked up."

Catherine reached over and held my hand. "If you do nothing else in your life, rescuing that child from the hell she was enduring would be enough to get you into heaven."

"Believe me, Catherine, I might have rescued her, but she's the one who saved me. She has given my life new meaning and a higher purpose."

"You didn't feel like you had a purpose? I know a few sportswriters and quite a few baseball players and owners who would say that you had a purpose and that you fulfilled it beautifully."

"Don't get me wrong. Baseball has treated me exceptionally well," I said. "It has made this boy from the Bronx rich beyond anything I could have imagined. It has glorified my accomplishments, and to my dismay, it has not given enough credit to my wonderful and talented staff. I could only hope that they get a chance at being GMs. My resignation wasn't a spur-of-the-moment decision. I had to remove myself from the game if I ever wanted some semblance of redemption."

"Redemption?" Catherine seemed genuinely confused. "What could you possibly be guilty of?"

"Overwork ... to the point of missing life!" I said. "I allowed my job to take complete control over my life, even after I was so well established and could have easily taken a few steps back and eased up. That empty house in the Bronx is a reminder of what I allowed the game and business of baseball to take away from me. It wasn't forced upon me. I willfully and totally consented to it all and that is a sin I will have to live with forever."

Catherine played with my hand, pretending to read my palm, and said, "But now you have me and Mia, Daddy and our entire staff that we consider our family."

"You forgot Rex."

"And of course, Rex. A terrible oversight on my part." She laughed as we went back to eating our lobster.

For dessert we split a wonderful piece of tiramisu, two cognacs and a cappuccino each. We discussed our finances, and she assured me that, as we were eating our dessert, lawyers were writing up a prenuptial agreement, which assured her family that on the off chance of a divorce, I would be entitled to nothing ... not the team, any property, bank accounts, stocks or Mia.

"The last part is a joke, right?"

"Yes, Joe, the last part is a joke. In the unlikely chance of a divorce, we will split Mia in half. I'll get the top part and you the bottom part."

"No way, I get the top half and you get the bottom half, and that is non-negotiable."

"Just like a man. Always quick to just jump right in there and get whatever he wants," she jokingly said and continued, "and by the way, I will bring those papers by for you to sign tomorrow."

"Of course you will."

"And if I was you, I would have your lawyer write up a prenuptial for me to sign. A slighted woman's fury has no bounds."

"Is that a warning?"

"Yes, that's a warning, and you would be wise to heed it," she said, smiling. She scooped up the last piece of tiramisu and said with a grin, "Simply delicious."

CHAPTER THIRTY-THREE

We pulled out of the parking lot of the restaurant and drove back down to the highway and toward the house. Catherine was a lot of fun at dinner and for the first time I felt really confident in her presence. She was so beautiful that it was easy just to fall in love with her because of her looks, but tonight I got a look at the whole package ... the funny, loving and relaxed side of this amazing lady ... and it only made her that much more irresistible.

We passed by the hotel I was staying at and she asked, "Are you sure you don't want to take advantage of that empty suite and do a practice run before the big event?"

"I'm sure, but I appreciate the offer."

"You're such a gentleman, Joe. Oh, I so love it."

We pulled into the driveway of the estate and parked. She turned to me and asked, "Are you sure you are okay with living here once we are married?"

"I'm positive, and in an ideal world where my parents were still alive, I would have asked you if they could move in too."

"That would have been so nice, and if my mommy was..." She bowed her head and then looked across at the house and continued, "We do have so much in common ... love of family, baseball, Mia..."

I took her hand and lifted her head, and said, "And most importantly, we love each other." I reached over and tenderly kissed her.

We entered the house and there was an eerie quiet about it. Catherine said, "They must still be in the study." She took my hand and we pushed open the tall door and found Mia sitting there across from Mr. Baker with her chin in her hands, contemplating a move. Henry, the butler, was sipping a cognac as he looked on from a small sofa next to the fireplace. Mr. Baker looked up at us and asked, "Ah, there you are! Welcome back. Did you two have a lovely time?"

"Yes, we did," Catherine replied as she snuggled up close to me. "Who's winning?"

Mr. Baker looked at me and asked, "Tell the truth, Joe. You've been giving Mia chess lessons from the minute you found each other, right?"

I laughed at the suggestion and said, "No, I haven't played in years." I looked at Mia and asked, "Have you played chess before, sweetheart?"

"No, Mr. Baker taught me. I like it. It's fun." She was so focused on the board that it was as though she was hypnotized. I also realized as I looked across at the board that if I didn't intervene, this game had the potential to go on a long time. I held out my hand to hers and started to lift her out of her chair. "You can finish this game tomorrow," I said. "It's getting late."

She looked up at me and then back at the board, obviously disappointed to have to stop. I said, "Now thank Mr. Baker."

She walked over to Mr. Baker, who stood up, and hugged him tightly and said in her soft voice, "Thank you for teaching me how to play, and for feeding me, and for being so nice."

Mr. Baker reached down and kissed her on the head and looked across at Catherine and me. "You two have got yourselves a little genius," he said.

"We all have ourselves a little genius, Daddy."

Catherine didn't want to leave her father, so Mia and I borrowed her car to get back to the hotel. As I turned onto the highway, Mia asked, "Did you tell Catherine that you loved her a lot?"

"Yes, sweetheart, I told her a whole bunch."

"Good, because that is very important."

I looked across at her as she pensively looked out the front window, and she asked, "Are we still going to go for our runs in the morning when we move into Catherine's house?"

"Of course, we are. We might have to drive down to the beach but that will only take a minute. We're always going to go for our runs. That will never change."

"Good," she said.

I looked at her and it still baffled me, and probably would until the day I died, how much she had physically changed, but what I couldn't help wondering about was simply what was going on in that active little brain of this beautiful child.

We walked through the lobby of the hotel and as we waited for the elevator, I asked Mia, "Think you're going to miss it here?"

"Yes," she replied as she lowered her head and looked down at the floor.

"You know, it's not like we still can't come here and have breakfast or dinner in the restaurant, or just dessert."

"That would be nice," she said.

I put my hand under her chin and lifted her head up. In all the time we had been together, I had never seen her cry, and she wasn't crying now, but she was obviously in some distress. I figured that she had used up all her tears running and hiding, searching for food and working in that nightmare of a bar where reruns of *Gunsmoke* and *Bonanza* played continually and where the regulars looked like extras from *The Walking Dead*.

As we entered the suite, I felt the odd sensation of being back home. After living half my adult life on the road, staying one, two, three nights at a time at different hotels throughout the country and the world, I could never imagine any hotel feeling like home. But after a month and a half here, with Mia and Catherine, it actually felt more like a home than my real home in Studio City. Oddly, it felt more like the home I was raised in with my parents back in the Bronx, where everybody was always within earshot of each other.

I sat down on the couch and turned on ESPN. A couple of sportscasters were talking incessantly about the NFL, college football and the start of the NBA season. Mia sat down beside me and without saying a word she rested her head against my shoulder and after a few minutes she fell asleep.

CHAPTER THIRTY-FOUR

My head hit the pillow, and instead of feeling happy about the wonderful night I'd had with my beautiful fiancée, I felt anxious. A few months earlier, when I had decided to resign as GM, my plan, if one wants to go so far as to say I had a plan, was to stay away from baseball. Turning fifty had a strange effect on me. Instead of concentrating on all that I had and all that I'd accomplished, I went in a totally different direction and became fixated on everything the game had taken away from me ... or everything that I *let* the game take from me.

Taking Mia away from that town and seeing her morph into a kind, caring and lovely child, with an intellect far superior to mine at her age, filled a vacancy in my life that I hadn't even known was there. Even though I had mentored and cared for many young prospects and their families, mostly from Latin America, they were never truly mine, except during the off-season hiatus when I visited them for a few months and reported on their progress first hand. Even then, they belonged to their families and their teams, not to me. The ones who eventually signed with the major league team were usually gone in five years or less because of free-agency rules, and when that happened, my guidance and counseling was handed off to their agents and their new teams. I kept in touch with many of them, but never again on the same personal level we had established when they were dirt-poor kids playing the game of baseball for fun.

After my initial hesitation and anxiety about raising a ten-year-old girl, I suddenly found myself feeling connected to her in a way only a parent could feel. For maybe the first time in my life, I looked upon a child not through the prism of baseball, but through the limitless possibilities she possessed in a multitude of different areas. I saw my little Leonardo as a great scientist, engineer, artist, writer, humanitarian, Supreme Court justice and even as president of the United States. What I did not want for her was anything to do with the business of baseball or any other professional sport.

At dinner with Catherine, at first I'd been happy that she felt comfortable asking for my advice on baseball matters, but after lying in bed for a while, staring at the ceiling, it occurred to me that advising her on matters concerning her team could only lead to discord in our marriage, which would adversely affect Mia. The advice I'd given her before she decided we needed to get married was enough to sow discord in our relationship, and that could severely hurt all of us. She wanted a championship for her father, but even in the best-case scenario, that was a long shot, and if these two pitching prospects turned out to be a bust, her team was more likely to finish last in their division. Despite what Catherine might preach, it was apparent that her father meant the world to her, and that her mission was to deliver a championship to him.

It was one thing to be hired as a GM to run a team, but it was a totally different thing to be married to a GM whose father owned the team, and whose relationship was as close as Catherine's relationship was with her father. As a hired hand, the team could just fire me if they were unhappy with my performance, but as an advisor and husband to the GM, it could seriously cause problems at home. If I had known how easy it would be to fall in love with Catherine and that this beautiful woman would actually fall for me, I never would have given her my advice on how to improve her team ... advice she followed, after consulting with her father, as though it was gospel.

I closed my eyes and tried to concentrate on all the positive things that were happening in my life, such as adopting Mia, a girl whose potential and loving personality could brighten any day, and the fact that I was about to marry a beautiful, loving woman who cared as much about Mia as I did.

I fell asleep, and suddenly there I was standing in the batter's box, the crowd roaring as I looked across at the great Sandy Koufax on the mound. He went into his windup, and just as his arm was going over the top, my phone rang and I woke up. It was the phone that only a few people had the number to. I picked it up and it was Lauren, the bartender from the Starlight bar in Studio City. She was inebriated and must have just finished her shift at the bar. She was calling to congratulate me on my impending marriage, but I could tell from her choked-up slur that this was more than a congratulatory call. I asked, "What's wrong, Lauren?"

"Oh, the usual," she said, feigning casualness. "My husband beats me, and I have two children I have to raise on my own with no support from the wife beater. The usual shit, Joe, with no one to blame but my stupid self." She started to cry. I wasn't sure if it had anything to do with the fact that I had just woken up, but my heart leaped out to her immediately. It was an understatement to say that I cared about Lauren. I had been in love with this girl before she'd picked up and married that loser while I was away scouting prospects. When she'd told me the news, my heart had sunk, but I'd pretended to be happy for her.

"I just need to know," she continued, "if I didn't marry that loser, did we have a future together?"

"Yes, but I always hesitated because I didn't think it was fair to you that I would always be away."

"And what am I now, Joe? A hostage to a loser, with two young children."

"You're in a bad situation, that's for sure. And you need to extricate yourself and your children from it. I can help you, Lauren, but you are going to have to follow my rules."

"And what rules are those?"

"First I am going to have my lawyer get in touch with you and you are going to divorce this bastard, but before you do that, you need to move out and relocate."

"To where?"

"You can move down here, to where I am, in San Diego. I'll pay for everything, get you an apartment, help you get a bartending job in an upscale restaurant and pay all your living expenses until you are settled in and back on your feet."

"You would do that?"

"Yes, but first you are going to have to promise me that you are not driving tonight, that you are going to go back in the bar and call a taxi. And when you get back home, you are going to call me and let me know that you have arrived. Don't let this opportunity pass you by. I am giving you a chance to start over and raise your children properly and in a safe environment."

"I love you, Joe."

"Don't forget, I'll be expecting your call within the hour."

I walked out of the bedroom, holding the phone, and peeked in on Mia, who was asleep, hugging Rex. I opened the sliding door and walked out onto the balcony. It was chilly outside, and the sky was draped with stars, and yet as I looked out over the ocean, I could not see the horizon — the boundary where the sky and earth appear to merge. I could see the surface of the water as clear as day, but no dividing line … no reference point … a sailor's nightmare.

The phone rang and it was Lauren telling me she'd arrived home. To confirm that fact, she sent me a picture of the cab next to the building she lived in. The time displayed on the picture was the same time displayed on my phone clock. I reminded her to call me in the morning, after she'd had her cup of coffee and was thinking straight. I was hoping I could get her a speedy divorce with a fifty-thousand-dollar payment to the deadbeat daddy. Enough money to keep him preoccupied for a while. Long enough for his wife and children to disappear and start over.

Domestic violence was nothing new to me. In the world of baseball, and in every other sport, it had always been a problem. It was usually handled behind closed doors, but with the growth of social media and everyone walking around with a cell phone that was also a camera, it was nearly impossible for abusers to hide anymore.

Ballplayers going through a prolonged slump or juiced up on steroids or simply drunk would go home and take it out on their wives or helpless children. I had it written into each contract that if a player was found guilty of domestic violence it was grounds for immediate dismissal, but the players' union was so strong that they were always able to appeal the dismissal on the grounds that the player would seek supervised counseling and deserved a second chance. They almost always won, and the victims were usually always forgiving because in most cases they didn't have much of a choice … they were dependent on their spouses … their identities, self-worth and financial security were linked and tied to the player. The player was a lifeline, a lifeboat that they clung to, but occasionally that boat sprang a leak too large to patch and everyone drowned.

Mia came up from behind and hugged me. I looked down at her, dressed in her Charlie Brown and Snoopy pajamas, and asked, "What are you doing up?"

"I heard you talking on the phone," she said as she hung on tightly. At times, it was like the child sensed that I was drifting away, and this was her way to bring me back to the here and now. I asked, "Can you see the horizon from here?"

She looked out over the vast ocean and replied, "Yes." I did not look but simply kept my eyes focused on her. She then looked up at the sky and readily pointed out the Orion constellation of stars. I looked up as she desperately tried to direct me to the constellation, but all I could see was a large blanket of stars. She remarked that the constellation was named after a hunter in Greek mythology and if one looked closely one could see the shape of a sword.

We walked back inside, and I closed the sliding door behind us. She went back to bed and I went back into my bedroom and lay down, staring up at the ceiling, until I finally closed my eyes and fell back to sleep, and there I was again, standing in the batter's box, looking across at the great Sandy Koufax as he released a scorching, out-of-control fastball that came straight at my unprotected head. I tried to move but was hopelessly stuck, as though paralyzed. The ball crashed into my head and I fell backward in what appeared to be slow motion, and then everything went dark as I hit the ground, and all I could hear was the collective sigh of the crowd.

CHAPTER THIRTY-FIVE

I was greatly surprised to hear from Lauren at nine in the morning. She had been quite drunk the night before, and I figured that after taking the kids to school earlier in the morning, she would have gone right back to bed. She immediately apologized for calling so late the night before and for being drunk out of her mind. I told her not to worry about any of it and said I was glad she called. There was a long pause on her end and then she asked, "Did you mean what you said last night?"

"Every last word," I assured her.

"I'm really afraid, Joe," she said. "It's bad enough that he hurts me. I'm worried about him seriously hurting the children."

"Where is he now?"

"He left early. He got a part as an extra on a new TV show they are shooting. He will be gone for most of the day."

"Great! I am going to have my lawyer call you shortly. I want you to tell him everything, and then I want you to follow his instructions as though they were given to you by God. Do you understand me, Lauren?"

"Yes," she replied as she started to cry.

"If he tells you not to go to work today and to pull your children out of school, you simply do it. No arguments! You follow his instructions. He's familiar with cases like yours. Do what he tells you and today will be the beginning of the end of this insanity. I will be talking to him throughout the day. Please don't let me down. If for no one else, do it for the safety of your children."

"Thank you, Joe. I can't tell—"

"Everything is going to be okay. I will talk to you later."

I looked across at Mia, who I knew was listening intently to the conversation as she pretended to be working on the computer. I had decided early on that I would tell Catherine everything about the situation ... knowing full well that she would pretend to be supportive but would nevertheless pump Mia for every extra ounce of information. Lauren, beaten and bruised, was still very attractive. Take away the bruises, and one could easily consider her gorgeous. The situation had the potential to get ugly, and I had every intention of not letting that happen. I was undeniably in love with Catherine. She was gorgeous, intelligent, creative and resourceful, and she was going to be a great mother to our little Leonardo, and most importantly, she was a stable and loving influence.

I called my lawyer and told him the entire situation. He was quite familiar, as I was, with these types of situations. When a domestic-abuse allegation was raised against one of our players, I always reached out to the victim and offered whatever help and assistance I could provide. I had very little sympathy for a player who hit his wife or girlfriend, or endangered the lives of his children. It was simply cowardly, and I didn't give a damn how important or great the player was to the team.

My lawyer assured me that he would get right on it. It was essential that there was no delay and that the victims, Lauren and the children, be removed entirely from the situation. She would have to quit her job immediately and the children would have to be pulled out of school that very day. He would check her into an upscale hotel in the Pacific Palisades, under a different name, and have all her necessary belongings put into storage until we found her a place to live. He would have her disconnect her cell phone and would give her a new phone with a different number that could not be traced by the average person. She would be told repeatedly not to get in touch with her husband under any circumstances and not to disclose her location or discuss her situation with anyone, including her parents and closest friends. The lawyer would handle all communications with the husband and would file a restraining order against the cowardly bastard.

I sat in a chair beside Mia. She was playing a game of chess against the computer. I asked, "So who's winning?"

"The computer," she replied softly as she struggled to make eye contact with me.

"And before last night, you never played chess?"

She shook her head and said, "Mr. Baker taught me last night. It took me a long time to learn and I had to write everything down."

"But now you understand how to play?"

"Yes, but I'm not very good. I have a lot to learn." She hesitated as she looked at the chessboard on the screen and then she asked, "Is your friend okay?"

"She will be," I replied.

"Can I help?"

I ran my hand through her lovely locks of hair and couldn't help but marvel at this magnificent little creature beside me. "You help just by being here. Would you like to play a game of chess with me? I have not played in a long time and I'm not very good."

"That's not what Mr. Baker says. He says that he has never met a person who could move players around a baseball field better than you, and that anyone that good at moving players and building such great teams is by nature a great chess player."

She cleared the computer screen and uploaded a new game. It was the baseball wizard against my little Leonardo, and who do you think won?

CHAPTER THIRTY-SIX

Catherine called a little before noon to say that Henry was dropping her off at the hotel. She had a bunch of papers for me to sign and she recommended that I have my lawyer look them over. I told her that my lawyer already had his hands full with other matters. I told her about Lauren and tried to leave nothing of importance out because I knew she would be fact-checking with her soon-to-be daughter. Catherine listened closely and said very little until I had relayed the whole story. Then she insisted on helping. After all, she had volunteered at a shelter for abused women, many of whom were married and had children, just like Lauren. I told her I appreciated the offer but that my lawyer was an old hand at this and that he already had things moving along quite rapidly.

Fifteen minutes later, Catherine entered the suite with the extra key card I'd given her. She didn't bother knocking. She greeted me with a series of passionate kisses — so passionate that I had to remind her that Mia was looking right at us. That did not seem to register, and she continued her assault. Finally, I managed to put a little distance between us and she then handed me a manila envelope with the bunch of papers I needed to sign. Again, she recommended that I have a lawyer look them over, and I reminded her that once upon a time I was a GM of a professional baseball team and was familiar with contracts.

"But not prenuptials," she said as she turned to Mia and hugged the confused child for even longer than usual. Catherine said, "My daddy is so in love with you, and he can't wait for you to move in permanently. In just two days, sweetheart, we are going to be one big happy family."

Catherine turned back toward me and asked, "So what have you two been doing all morning ... besides talking to your lawyer about that poor abused mother and her children?"

"We went for our run and we played chess," Mia quickly replied.

"And who won?"

"Who do you think won?" I asked.

"Sweetheart, did you beat your daddy?"

Mia didn't reply as she looked across at me like a lost little puppy. I replied, "I'm rusty and I haven't played in a long time."

"She just learned how to play yesterday," Catherine playfully remarked.

"Okay, wise butt, why don't you play her?"

"I would love to, but my brain at the moment is fried. I've been busy all morning, making final arrangements for our wedding in a few days. Surely, you didn't forget that little detail, unless of course you have changed your mind."

"Not a chance. I know when God has sent me gift, and whereas I might be unworthy of it, I have no intention of sending it back."

Catherine blushed and remarked, "That's so sweet."

I walked over to Catherine and lifted her up and into my arms and said, "I don't know what is going on in that wonderful brain of yours, but the only thing that could be better than marrying you in a few days would be marrying you right now."

"Are you intentionally trying to make me cry?"

"No, but I am intentionally trying to make you understand that the two best things that have ever entered into my life are standing just a few feet away from me, and unlike the many baseball players I've recruited over the years, I have absolutely no intention of losing either one to free agency."

I sat on the couch and read over the prenuptial papers Catherine had given to me. The girls sat at the table and chatted away. It had been apparent since the first time they met that Mia felt very comfortable in Catherine's presence. She talked more, even if it was mostly to agree with Catherine, and she laughed and giggled like a child unburdened by the harsh realities of life. She behaved like the ten-year-old child that she was. Her cautious and guarded demeanor — the protective shield she had erected against a cruel and dangerous enemy — was lifted, and her merriment, like her soft and melodic voice, was soothing like a healing ointment applied to a pitcher's blistered hand.

There were many different sides to Catherine, and depending on the situation, the contrast could appear quite startling. She could be quite calculating and commanding, like she'd been at the press conference, but she could also be flirtatious, like she was at the bar when we first met. She could also be maternal and caring, like my mother, when talking to Mia or in the presence of her father.

Even though she looked nothing like my mother, who was undeniably of Mediterranean origin with her golden skin, dark hair, long lashes and bright brown eyes, Catherine possessed, like my mom, that unique and protective tenor that could make the most frightened child feel safe ... that could wipe away a child's nighttime nightmares like an avenging angel. My mom had always spoken with a distinctive Bronx dialect, and Catherine spoke with a distinctly Southern California accent. The two dialects couldn't be more different, yet they both elicited the same soothing and loving effect that made everything seem wonderful.

In the dead of the night, tossing restlessly in bed, thinking about an impending trade or tomorrow's starting pitcher, I would hear my mother's voice, and see my reflection in her eyes — eyes that were like a mirror into a pure and untarnished soul — and then I would fall peacefully asleep wrapped in the protective arms of an angel.

The prenup was fairly standard. Even though I had never been privy to one, as a lifelong bachelor, I had been around enough lawyers and heard enough ballplayers and agents complain about the conditions, that I had a fairly good grasp of what to expect. In essence, I relinquished all claims to any property, businesses, bank accounts, stocks, bonds or other assets that Catherine and her family jointly owned or controlled. I wasn't interested in Catherine's family's fortune, and I certainly had no designs on it. I was quite satisfied with my own nest egg, but I had to admit that her family's fortune was impressive. They weren't part of the one percent that politicians were always attacking for not paying their fair share of taxes, but part of that 0.001 percent that truly ran the economy, and before whom politicians kneeled to beg for contributions.

In turn, Catherine agreed to relinquish all claims to the fortune that I had earned before we were to be married, in the off chance of a future divorce. This seemed more than fair. The last appendix to the document was truly the only one I was interested in, and that was the one that had to do with Mia. In short, and it was short, it read that upon the future adoption of the child both of her adopted parents would retain full custody of the child and would always see and contribute jointly to her welfare and safety until the age of twenty-one and beyond.

In reality, it was a moot question because neither Catherine nor I had legal custody of the child. Mia could, for all practical purposes, still be classified as a ward of the state. I could have been well on the way to adopting the child if it wasn't for my impending marriage to the beautiful and loving heiress. Before the honeymoon would even begin, I would have all the documents my lawyer requested from Catherine, including our marriage certificate, in his hands, which at the moment were quite full handling the problems of the abused barmaid and her children. I signed the prenuptial and slid the document back into the envelope. I walked over to Catherine, put the document on the table before her and wrapped my hands around her waist.

"All signed," I remarked as I winked at Mia.

"No questions, no concerns ... just like that?" Catherine asked.

"Just like that. I know a great deal when I see it. After all, you're the one with the butler and a job."

She laughed as she stood up and said, "I love you so much."

"And I love you so much." We kissed with a little less passion than before, conscious of the child sitting just a few feet away.

We stayed in the suite for most of the day, except for a walk along the beach. Having a very small wedding was certainly making getting married a lot less stressful. When I asked Catherine if we were going on a honeymoon, she said that she preferred not to go right now, but that certainly in the near future we could plan a nice romantic getaway. That was code for saying that she wasn't comfortable leaving Mia behind just yet, unless we wanted to take Mia with us, which would most likely cut down on the romance. I agreed to the delay.

My phone rang as we were all sitting around the table eating dinner. It was my lawyer, and my first instinct was to get up and talk to him in private, but then I thought better of it. Why rock the boat while it was sailing along so gracefully after Catherine's earlier display of jealousy? So I sat right there and talked to him as both the ladies in my life continued to eat dinner and pretended not to be listening.

My lawyer apprised me of the situation with Lauren. With very little resistance, he had been able to convince Lauren to quit her job, pull the children from the school they were attending and pack and move out of her apartment, and at the moment, she and the children were staying at a hotel in the Pacific Palisades. He had Lauren file a restraining order against her husband and at the same time file for divorce.

He had talked to the husband, who naturally feigned shock and denied all the allegations against him, saying he would never grant her a divorce or custody of his children, who were the love of his life, and that he only hit them, like any good parent, to teach them important lessons that one day they would be happy to have learned.

His resistance and apparent love seemed to dissolve when my lawyer offered him twenty-five thousand dollars in exchange for a simple, no-contest divorce. At fifty thousand and no child-support payments he totally caved and was ready to sign the divorce papers whenever they were drawn up. His final remarks to my lawyer were, "What's the use of fighting it? Everybody knows that the judge is always going to side with the bitch and give her full custody." And besides, he said he didn't want the children to be put through that hell — as though he hadn't already taken care of that every day of their young lives so far. He then asked if he could have the money in cash, to which my lawyer replied, "Of course, but you would still have to sign a document attesting to the fact that you received the money." He was perfectly okay with that, and the transaction was completed by the end of the day.

My lawyer put Lauren on the phone and she thanked me over and over again, saying she didn't know how she could ever repay me. I told her she could repay me by listening to everything my lawyer told her and by simply following his instructions to the letter. I warned her that she was not to get in touch with her husband under any circumstances, and not to give her number or location out to anyone, including her best friends, sisters or her parents. All her living expenses would be taken care of until she was back on her feet. She needed to concentrate on her children and on her own well-being.

My lawyer got back on the phone and he assured me that everything was going as well as one could expect. I thanked him and laid my phone back down on the table. Catherine asked, "Is she going to be okay?"

"She'll be fine," I replied as I looked at Catherine and Mia and sighed.

"What's wrong?" Catherine asked.

"Just remembering something my father used to say, that only a coward hits a woman. It's sad just how many cowards I have known."

CHAPTER THIRTY-SEVEN

Mia and I walked Catherine back to her car. She wanted to spend the last two nights before getting married at home, like a properly raised daughter. She had totally recovered from her little episode of jealousy, and I didn't tell her that I was kind of flattered that such a beautiful and intelligent woman, who could get any man she wanted, could be so in love with me that she would actually feel threatened by a young woman who she had never met.

Before getting into her car, Catherine asked Mia if she was carrying her cell phone with her. Mia nodded and produced the phone from her jacket pocket. Catherine had impressed upon Mia the importance of carrying that phone with her at all times, even when outside and together with her soon-to-be parents. In case we ever got separated, the phone was the quickest way for us to get back in touch with each other. My fiancée downloaded every conceivable contact Mia needed into her phone, just in case our daughter found herself lost or in trouble. Naturally, there were our numbers, Catherine's father's number, the numbers of every single member of the kitchen staff and of Henry, the butler, as well as the CIA, FBI, and National Security Agency (NSA), and the desk phone and cell phone numbers for the San Diego chief of police, who happened to be a Baker family associate. She was more like an Italian mother than my own mom, which was just a reason to love her even more.

As she was getting ready to leave, Catherine kissed me, then Mia, then kissed me again and Mia again, and finally pulled herself away from us, got into her car and drove off. Mia and I just stood there waving, and when I finally looked down, I noticed that one of Mia's sneaker laces had come undone. I reached down and tied her shoelace, zipped up her jacket and took her hand. We walked down to the beach and ambled along the shoreline. It was chilly and the night sky was clear. I listened to Mia re-educate me on all that I had forgotten about the constellations, the sand and the ratio of salt to water in the ocean. Mia talked so softly and the pitch of her voice was so low that at times, in the quiet of the hotel room, it was hard to hear her, but walking along the beach with waves crashing against the shore, every word she uttered miraculously came through as clearly and perfectly as the voice of Sir Lawrence Olivier on the Broadway stage. It was as though the child, being part nature in its most untarnished and unsullied state, spoke most audibly through ocean mists.

Back at the hotel suite, we sat on the couch as I flipped through the TV channels. I stopped at a movie channel that was just getting ready to show the baseball classic *Field Of Dreams*, adapted from the novel *Shoeless Joe* by W.P. Kinsella. It starred Kevin Costner, Amy Madigan, James Earl Jones and a young Ray Liotta as Shoeless Joe Jackson, the legendary baseball player banned from the game because of his involvement in the 1919 Black Sox Scandal in which the Chicago White Sox's best players were paid by a group of gamblers to throw the 1919 World Series against the Cincinnati Reds.

Since the time of Joe Jackson's banishment, baseball historians, fans, sportswriters and the Baseball Hall of Fame have argued about his complicity in throwing the World Series. He batted an astonishing .375 for the series, the highest of any player on either team, racked up twelve hits ... a record that stood for over forty years ... and did not commit a single error. If he was in on the fix, he did a terrible job at helping it succeed. Following a jury trial in 1921, the players were acquitted, but the new commissioner at the time, Judge Kenesaw Mountain Landis, barred them all for life.

The seven other players in on the fix all said that Shoeless Joe never attended a meeting related to the scheme. Shoeless Joe claimed that he was manipulated by a team lawyer into signing a document stating that he received five of the twenty thousand dollars he was promised, and that he didn't know what he was signing. Joe Jackson never learned how to read or write.

If not for this scandal, Shoeless Joe was a shoo-in for the Hall of Fame. His lifetime batting average was an amazing .356. After the ban, his love for the game didn't diminish and he played in "outlaw leagues" under an assumed name. He made various attempts to get reinstated, but to no avail. He retired to his home in South Carolina, and in 1951, he passed away.

Baseball will tolerate players using steroids, but gambling is a different story. It's considered an affront to the integrity of the sport, and fans won't put up with it. Pete Rose tried to make the case that he never bet on his team, but his intimate knowledge of players on other teams amounted to inside information. He would surmise that a scheduled number-one starting pitcher coming off a rough night of drinking would most likely not be at his best the next night, then he would bet huge amounts of money against that team and their ace pitcher. By doing so, he was telling his bookie and other bookies that something was up. He was complicit in what amounted to providing illegal insider information affecting odds as far away as Vegas. He also left a long paper trail of his bets, which was enough to bury any hope or chance of his making the Hall of Fame.

In my judgment, Shoeless Joe Jackson should have been in the Hall of Fame and his banishment from the game was an injustice that should have been rectified years ago. His stellar statistics and play during the World Series were undeniable, and his teammates attested to his innocence. A jury found them innocent, and Judge Landis's decision was a political calculation and one not based on the facts but on his own ambitions.

I had seen *Field of Dreams* a bunch of times, but I was really excited to watch it with Mia, since I knew I would see it through her eyes as though seeing it for the first time again. I always connected to the movie's fantasy elements and got chills during the scenes when Ray, an Iowa farmer, hears a recurring voice as he walks through his cornfield, telling him, "If you build it, they will come." It takes him some time to figure out what this phrase means, and when he finally comes to a decision, he is convinced that the voice is telling him to build a baseball field in the middle of his cornfield. He builds the field with the support of his wife, Annie, and their young daughter, Karin, to the disbelief of fellow farmers and the bank that loaned him the money to buy the farm.

As he builds the ball field, he tells his daughter the story of the 1919 Black Sox Scandal. Ray still feels guilty about an argument he had with his deceased father that was never reconciled and that caused a rift between them that was never healed. His father, a former ballplayer, believed that Shoeless Joe Jackson was innocent, and his son believed he was guilty.

Months pass after he has built the field, and still no one has come. The voice in his head begins to seem like a hallucination. Then one day while walking around the field, he sees a man dressed in an old Chicago White Sox uniform, holding an old-time baseball glove. As he does so, he passes through the remaining cornfield that serves as the outfield wall. The man is none other than the legendary Shoeless Joe as a young ballplayer. Joe tells Ray that there are other players on the other side of the cornfield, his former teammates, and they would love nothing more than to be able to just play again. Ray tells Joe to tell them to all come out and play. After all, that is why he built the field. Slowly, they pass through the cornfield, the entire team that was banished from the game they loved, and they start to practice ... pitching, hitting, fielding and running the bases.

Eventually, another team joins them, and they start playing actual games ... not for money or prestige, but more like young children, simply for the love of this beautiful game. At the end of the movie, Ray looks across at a young catcher as he collects his equipment and is getting ready to pass back through the cornfield. It's Ray's father, and as they look across at each other they feel the connection. His father puts down his equipment and picks up his glove and asks Ray if he would like to have a catch. Ray puts on his glove and they play catch ... throwing the ball to each other ... and at the same time mending the rift that separated them.

I saw that movie by myself while I was still down in the minor leagues, praying and hoping that one day I would make it up to the big leagues. My love for the game back then was still genuine and untarnished. I stayed seated in the theater long after the credits were over, and I cried. When I finally got up and walked into the lobby of the theater, I entered an old-time phone booth and sat down and closed the door. I put all the change I had into the machine and called my parents. I told them about the movie and said once I got a chance to get back home, we all had to go see the movie together. When we were finished talking, my father said, "I love you, son. God Bless." I replied, "I love you too, Dad. God Bless." Then my mother remarked, "I love and miss you so much, Joey. I pray for you every day. God Bless." And I replied, "I love and miss you, Mom. God Bless."

I stayed seated in the phone booth for a long time after we were finished talking. Then I opened the door, went back to the ticket counter, bought another ticket and watched the movie for a second time.

***

Mia sat on the couch next to me and rested her head against my shoulder. We watched the movie together and occasionally I glanced down at her and expected her to be asleep, but she was wide awake throughout the whole movie. At the end of the movie, when Ray is playing catch with his dad, I started to cry and turned my head away from Mia long enough to regain my composure. When I looked down at the child, she was crying. It was the first time I had ever seen her cry. One would not expect a child her age to understand the meaning of a movie steeped so deeply in symbolism, but then again, she was no ordinary ten-year-old kid. She was my little Leonardo.

She asked, "Did you play catch with your daddy?"

"Yes, with my daddy … and mommy. She had quite the arm. I sometimes wonder if I got my playing ability as much from her as from him. Would you like to play catch someday with me?"

"Yes," she replied in her soft, melodic voice, filled with emotion as she wrapped her arms around me. "Yes, I would love to play catch with my daddy."

"Then it's a date. You and me and Mommy."

She kept her arms wrapped around me as she closed her eyes and fell asleep. I didn't know if I would ever have the heart to tell her that the beauty and love of the game disappeared when the business side took center stage. That it was better never to meet your heroes because they were so often very flawed. That Catherine and her father were the exceptions, but then I had no doubt that she would figure it all out on her own.

I would nevertheless shield this child from the fate that Catherine inherited. Chasing her father's dream was not something I would bequeath to any child. Baseball made me rich, and the championships made me famous, and yet at fifty years old I found myself alone searching for a renewed meaning, separate from the fame and fortune — something more purposeful than chasing championships.

I picked Mia up and carried the child into her bedroom and tucked her into the bed beside Rex. I looked down at her, peacefully asleep, and an illuminating feeling akin to a spiritual enlightenment gripped my entire being. I closed my eyes and saw an image of my mother, young, beautiful and glowing, looking down at me … a young boy no older than Mia … sleeping serenely. My mom's protective gaze, like a breastplate of fortified armor, seemed capable of warding off any cruel or evil intentions that might be headed in my direction.

I opened my eyes and walked out of the bedroom and opened an ice-cold bottle of beer. I took a long swig as I looked around the suite. Once again I marveled at how strange it was that in the last month and a half this hotel suite had begun to feel more like a real home to me than any place I had lived since growing up in my parents' house. I doubted since buying my home in Studio City over twenty years earlier that I ever spent more than an entire month at a time there, and apart from my parents coming to visit, I had very few guests.

I doubt if my mother and father spent one night apart during their entire marriage, and the two nights he spent in the hospital before dying, she had a cot rolled into his room and slept beside him. Meanwhile, I showed up when his casket was being lowered into the ground.

I spent two weeks with my mother after my dad passed away. She pleaded with me to go back to work, and against my better judgment, I listened to her and departed for Central America. Two weeks later, a neighbor found her dead on the floor of her beloved kitchen. I could rationalize her death every which way to Sunday: She couldn't stand being away from my father, and my dad couldn't stand being apart from her, and he begged God to bring her back to him. But in all honesty, I never should have left her. I should have stayed with her for at least six months. It wasn't like my job was in any type of jeopardy. And then, after six months, I should have packed up her house and had her move out to Los Angeles to live with me.

The guilt never subsided, and there was no amount of penance or therapy that would help alleviate that feeling. My parents' love for me was all-consuming, and because of that, I knew that even in death they had not forsaken me. I heard my mother's voice all the time. When I had doubts about taking Mia away from that town, it was my mother's voice telling me that if I did not take the child — feed and nourish, shelter and educate her — that it would be an unpardonable sin. She seemed to be telling me that there was nothing more depraved and wicked than *to be able to help and to do nothing*. This time I heard, and this time I obeyed.

I opened another beer and walked over to the sliding door and opened it a crack. It was chilly and windy outside, so I didn't step out onto the balcony, but I wanted to fully inhale the ocean air and so I stood by the opening and took deep breaths, and for a moment, my body felt cleansed and refreshed.

I finished the beer, closed the door and went to bed. I woke up at my usual time, put on my running gear and walked out of the bedroom to find Mia sitting at the table next to Rex, looking at the computer. I smiled as I looked over her shoulder at the article she was reading about Shoeless Joe Jackson. I had her put on a jacket with a hood and then we left the suite. She talked about Shoeless Joe and how she thought it was so unfair how they treated him, and that he should be in the Hall of Fame. Just before walking out the lobby door, I bent down and pulled the hood of her jacket up over her head and retied the laces on her sneakers that were coming loose.

We stepped outside and walked down to the beach. It was windy and chilly like last night. We ran into the wind, alongside crashing waves and the sound of squawking seagulls, and into a new chapter in our lives.

CHAPTER THIRTY-EIGHT

When it feels like a fairytale or a dream, but it isn't: That's when you know life is grand, like winning a championship when at the beginning of the year you had been picked to finish last, or even better, when the priest says you may kiss the bride and you touch the lips of the most beautiful, caring and loving woman in the world ... that's when you know that God has reached down and blessed you.

Catherine was dressed in a simple but elegant floor-length white dress, with her hair pinned back and a little spray of white flowers surrounding her hair where it was gathered into a loose bun. She glowed like the Southern California sun. The guests applauded as she turned from me and hugged her father as tears of joy rolled down her cheeks. She then went down the line of guests, the entire kitchen and house staff and Henry, the butler, and hugged them all ... like I said, she was a real hugger.

I reached over and shook Mr. Baker's hand and he warmly embraced me and whispered into my ear, "Please, never stop loving her."

"Never, sir, and that's a promise," I replied as I looked across at the priest who was talking to the lovely maid of honor, who sparkled like her adopted mother.

Maybe, just maybe, I thought, *the healing that seemed to start as she looked at the wedding pictures of my parents is for real and my little Leonardo can now distinguish the loving and kind God that Catherine and I believe in and pray to from the distorted and angry version depicted in the town of Salvation.*

***

For lack of a better description, the reception and dinner were held in a four-thousand-square-foot ballroom … just another room in this elaborate and sprawling mansion. A bandstand was set up in the far corner of the room and a four-member band, dressed in Beatles attire, blasted away. They donned four mop-top wigs and played a string of Beatles songs, along with more traditional wedding music and Spanish classics. Catherine, knowing I loved the Beatles, could not resist hiring the band, and they were excellent.

The band started playing the Beatles' "I Need You," and that was when I took my bride by the hand and went out onto the dance floor for the traditional first dance. I wasn't much of a dancer, but holding Catherine in my arms and looking into her eyes made me forget my lack of skills and float on air like Astaire. As I listened to the lyrics, I had to agree with the Fab Four that once people got stuck on each other, they tended to stay that way. After a month and a half together, I knew I could never live without Catherine and Mia.

I kissed my bride and then handed her off to her father for the second dance while most of the other guests also walked out onto to the dance floor and started dancing. I reached out and asked the most beautiful child in the room if I could have this dance. She smiled and I spun the lovely maid of honor around like a ballerina, and I remembered her smiling for the first time when I played the Beatles on the car radio as we exited that godforsaken town.

I spun her round and round and she laughed and laughed. Yes, she had come a long way since that fateful day, and thankfully she took me along for the ride of my lifetime.

After the last song was played and all the guests had departed, Catherine and I got down to the most serious business of the day: faxing my lawyer all the requested documents he needed from Catherine and a copy of our marriage license to proceed with the legal adoption of our little Leonardo.

CHAPTER THIRTY-NINE

The winter meetings came and went with no big trades or free-agency signings. The St. Louis Cardinals had their moment in the sun as most of the discussion was about them acquiring the league's MVP. Catherine's team acquiring two celebrated prospects was hardly mentioned in the press releases, which was kind of strange because representatives from all the major league teams and about 160 minor league affiliates were present. Surely, there was plenty of talk about the two prospects, but without name recognition the press was reluctant to even bring them up. Catherine was on her phone, texting and emailing with team executives throughout the four days of meetings. She didn't mention anything to me, and I didn't ask. Even though she'd said that she would gladly seek out my counsel and welcome any advice I had to offer, I was hoping against all hope that she would leave me out of any decision-making or team-related business.

I was already too deeply involved, having suggested all the moves she had made so far. The baseball season was very long, and patience was, at times, the strongest virtue you could possess. Catherine's team was not the 1927 New York Yankees, and so to expect miraculous results starting on opening day would be highly unrealistic and could be fatal. Naturally, I would keep up with her team and watch all the games, and it would be the first year in over twenty that I would be rooting for a team other than the team that employed me. I had already made it perfectly clear that I would not be attending any games, and Catherine said that made two of us. As she so happily remarked, it wasn't like she could do anything once the game started, so why not watch it at home with her adorable husband, beautiful child and her daddy? I took that sentiment with a grain of salt, as they used to say.

***

Lauren was already settled into a big two-bedroom apartment about forty miles up the coast from us. I paid the first year of rent on the apartment and put a substantial amount of money into a private bank account in her name and mine. I made sure that Catherine was well aware of all this and kept abreast of all dealings related to Lauren. Her children were enrolled in a new school and they loved living by the beach. She got a job at a high-end steakhouse just a few blocks from her apartment and was making good money. When I talked to her she couldn't thank me enough and she sounded so relieved and happy, like when I first met her, before she'd married that son of a bitch. Her divorce had already gone through. Amazing how quickly a divorce could move through the court system when it was uncontested.

I had hoped that members of the house staff had some children around Mia's age, but that wasn't the case. They had children, but they were already away at college or living in Seattle, Washington, working at one of the big tech firms and making plenty of money. Mr. Baker treated his staff like family, paid for their children's education and allowed everyone to use all the amenities inside and outside the mansion. Of course, he also gave them tickets to any game they wanted to attend. Naturally, the staff loved Mia, and whenever I couldn't find the little genius, I would walk into the kitchen and there she would be conversing with members of the staff, learning how to speak Spanish.

She was especially close to María, a very attractive middle-aged lady who spoke both perfect English and Spanish. She was Mr. Baker's longest-serving employee and had come to work for him when she was just eighteen years old. She eventually married another employee who was hired a few years later. Sadly, her husband died of a rare bone disease at the young age of thirty-five. They had two children, a boy and a girl. The boy, the older of the two, was working at a tech firm in Silicon Valley. The girl was in her final year at MIT, where she was getting ready to graduate with a degree in biophysics, and she had already been accepted into a prestigious doctoral program in science and technology at Stanford. Talk about a proud mother.

Catherine suggested that we should have Father Dolan, the priest who married us, come over once a week and talk with Mia. Like me, Catherine had noticed at our wedding how easily Mia and the priest seemed to communicate with each other. Catherine told Father Dolan all about Mia and the town of Salvation. Mr. Baker and I thought it was a good idea as long as both of us were present during the meetings. Father Dolan agreed, and their first three meetings went very smoothly. The good Father did not preach. Instead he spoke about Jesus as a historical figure who taught his followers to love and not hate, to forgive and not punish. The only thing he suggested Mia read was the Sermon on the Mount. He gave her a photocopy of the sermon so she wouldn't have to hold a Bible in her hands yet, and he never brought a copy of the Bible with him. He stressed that it was solely her decision whether she wanted to learn more about Christ, and he always kept open the possibility that she might want to learn other religions. The choice was Mia's to make, and there were no right or wrong answers. He kept the meetings very short.

The house staff were all Catholic, and several of the ladies wore crucifixes prominently around their necks, and yet Mia did not seem bothered by these reminders of religion. It was not that long ago that any symbols of Christianity would send her running in the other direction. Since viewing my parents' wedding pictures, she seemed to be able to draw a distinction between the fanatical interpretation of Christianity and the conventional version of religion. At least, that was what I was hoping for, but I still had lingering doubts. In fact, I had a sense that deep down she still felt insecure and worried about her safety and her place in the world that Catherine and I occupied. I imagine there was a time when her biological parents, before entering the world of the *Twilight Zone*, loved and adored their baby girl and would have done anything to protect her. But they lost their way when they joined that cult, and they came very close to pulling Mia down with them. A child abandoned by her parents would feel the pain of that loss forever. I could only hope that Mia would continue to heal at her own pace, and that I would have the wisdom to know when it was the right time for her to receive actual therapy.

During rare moments when Mia seemed uncomfortable, she literally clung to me, wrapping her arms around my waist and resting her head against my stomach. I would usually suggest that we go for a walk and she would nod eagerly, and I would take her by the hand and off we would go. I would ask her a question about the universe or Shoeless Joe or her new computer and she would expound endlessly, and the initial anxiety that sparked the walk would dissipate. It was during one of those walks that I decided that I would definitely be the tutor who would homeschool my little Leonardo. It was bizarre, considering that I had no doubt the child was smarter than me.

I told Catherine about my plan and she asked, "I thought we had agreed to hire a professional tutor?"

"We did, but I want a shot at it first, and if it doesn't work out you know I will step aside and bring in the professional."

"Okay, if that's what you want," she remarked with little enthusiasm. I knew that Catherine saw me as a baseball man, and I imagined that sooner or later she expected me to go back to the game, either as GM of my former team or hopefully as GM of her father's team. It was hard for me to get upset with her because deep down I knew her heart was in the right place. She wanted what was best for Mia. It didn't take a genius to see the potential that this child possessed, and she wanted to harness all that potential in a most constructive, wise and orderly manner.

Mr. Baker happened to be walking by when we were having this conversation, and he overheard my proposal to become Mia's tutor. He brightened up immediately and not only gave his assent but offered to help. "I think that is a wonderful idea, Joe. Would it be too much trouble if I pitched in with tutoring the budding genius?"

"That would be great," I replied as he turned to Catherine.

"Would that be okay with you, sweetheart?"

"Of course, Daddy. I learned more from you than all my teachers combined."

"You know, that child has already beaten me in a game of chess … straight up, no holding back on my part. I don't even know how it could be possible. I've been playing the game for fifty years while the child just learned how to play a month ago."

"She's been studying all the strategies, every night, on her computer."

"And is that supposed to make me feel better? I have been studying the same strategies and have read at least two dozen books on the game over the last half century."

"That's why we call her our little Leonardo," Catherine remarked.

"Da Vinci?" Mr. Baker asked.

"The very same," Catherine said.

"Ha! That's good," her father said. "She really does seem to have it all … spatial-thinking skills, curiosity and a knack for combining ideas in new ways … I'm so impressed with that kid."

"Your new granddaughter is a winner," Catherine said, smiling.

Suddenly, Mr. Baker reached out and squeezed Catherine's shoulders and looked into her eyes. "You know, I've always felt the same way about you. You were and are so very bright," he said. Catherine beamed and hugged her father and mumbled her modest thanks.

I feared that once we moved in that Mr. Baker and I would be talking baseball all the time, but never once did he bring up the subject, even during the winter meetings. It was like the two of us were going through the same phase in our lives, putting aside the game we loved and concentrating our energies on different matters, such as the education of Mia and the wonderment and joy that she brought into all our lives.

***

Mia and I continued our early morning runs. After getting up and putting on my running gear, I would look over one last time at the beautiful woman sleeping in my bed and shake my head in disbelief. I would then walk over to Mia's room, which was the next room over from our bedroom, and knock on the door that she kept half open. She would be sitting at her enormous desk, in front of her state-of-the-art computer, with Mr. Rex beside her.

We would walk down the stairs and at the front door I would reach down and retie her loosely laced sneakers and zip up the front part of her hoodie. It was early December and it was quite cool outside, especially by the beach. Walking down the steep hill from the mansion, in the dark, seemed a bit treacherous, so since moving into the mansion, we decided to take my car and drive to the hotel that we stayed at for over a month, park in their garage and walk down to the beach from there. I was fairly certain that continuing this ritual made Mia happy, and since we were familiar with this area of the beach, it also felt like the safest place to run.

Before meeting Mia, my typical run was seven to eight miles, but now it had increased to ten or eleven miles per day. If Mr. Baker was shocked at Mia's chess acumen, I was just as shocked at her endurance. For a child her age to run this far, with such ease and grace, and at a really good pace, was astonishing.

After we finished, we would drive back to the mansion just in time for the house staff to file out of their home and into the mansion. Mia would run up to her bedroom and jump straight into the shower, and by the time I had finished greeting the staff and climbing the stairs at a leisurely pace, I would hear her pronounce, "I'm all clean." I would then take my shower, get dressed, and Mia and I would walk down to the gym and visit Mom, who would be running on one of the ten treadmills as she watched the morning news on a TV monitor.

Mia and I would then go eat breakfast in the kitchen with María and a few other members of the staff. We all sat at the same large table where we were treated to fresh fruit, bagels, hot buttered rolls and biscuits, pancakes, scrambled eggs and at least three different types of juice. Mia was the only one to have a special meal prepared for her, if one wanted to call it special anymore: chocolate chocolate-chip pancakes and, on rare occasions, cereal with extra chocolate syrup poured into the milk. Catherine tried repeatedly to get Mia in the habit of eating fruit and eggs, but unless they were placed directly in front of her, Mia wasn't interested. To the child's credit, whenever Catherine did manage to corner her with healthy food, Mia would eat every last bite.

Occasionally, Mr. Baker would join us for breakfast, but he would eat lightly, usually taking in just a little fruit and a buttered biscuit with a glass of juice. He would then go for a long walk, during which he would converse with the gardener and some of the other groundkeepers. Then he would pause for a long time before beautifully trimmed bushes of white roses that were his wife's favorite.

Catherine would often look out the window at him as he stopped to visit the flowers, and by the time she turned back around, it was apparent she had been crying.

CHAPTER FORTY

Christmas was just a couple of weeks away when I got a call from my lawyer. He told me that the adoption was moving along steadily and that a social worker had already visited the town of Salvation, collected the information she needed and hightailed it out of there. In her own words, she had said that she "couldn't get out of that place quick enough," and that she'd felt her life was "in danger from the very people preaching the word of God."

The documents that Mia had provided matched everything the social worker collected. Her parents were both dead, and an exhaustive search had turned up no living relatives. Mia had no siblings and had "lived in a dilapidated building not fit for the rats that lived there. She had survived on scraps of food from a nearby restaurant where she cleaned the windows."

The lawyer told me that a social worker who was employed by the Los Angeles court system and who lived in Studio City read the report and agreed to meet with Mia, Catherine and me in two days at my house. I told my lawyer that we would be there, and he told me it would be wise to prepare the child and make her aware of everything that was going on and why.

I hung up and took advantage of the fact that Mia was in the kitchen with María practicing her Spanish. I walked over to Mr. Baker's study and knocked on the open door. When I saw that Catherine was inside talking with her father, I joined them in the study and closed the door behind me. I sat down beside Catherine and told them everything the lawyer had just told me. They were very excited, and Mr. Baker asked if it would be okay if he came along with us. Before I had a chance to say yes, my lovely wife jumped in and replied, "Of course, Daddy, you being there could only help our case."

Later that day, Catherine and I talked to Mia alone in her room. We explained everything that was going on with the adoption and how meeting with the social worker was a routine step in the process. We prepared her for the fact that she would have to talk to the social worker without us, and we reassured her that Mr. Baker and the two of us would be in the next room the whole time. We told her that all she needed to do was to be honest and truthful and that everything would turn out wonderfully. The look of unblinking trepidation in her eyes brought me back to reality; I was reminded that the beautiful and precocious child in front of me was only ten years old, that she had suffered a terrible trauma and that her mental state was still fragile. It would be unrealistic to expect a simple talk like this to alleviate the terrible fear that she could once again be abandoned.

With her face taut and her eyes cast downward, she replied to all of our queries by saying, "Yes, I understand," but her voice had dropped to a mere whisper, and she seemed to be shrinking in front of our eyes. Catherine stopped speaking and looked closely at Mia's downturned face for a long minute, until Mia finally looked up. Catherine wrapped her in a big hug and assured her that there was absolutely nothing to worry about. Mia looked across at me and I winked at her confidently, and a flicker of a smile cut across her face.

The whole scene reminded me of some of the young ballplayers I'd recruited from Central and South America. The hardest part for any seventeen- or eighteen-year-old prospect who was on the verge of joining our minor league system in the US came when it was time to leave their family, village or town behind. Up to that point, they had concentrated so much on the game of baseball and on making it into our system that they rarely thought about what it would be like to actually leave home. When that magical moment came and they signed a contract and were about to board a flight to the States, they often cried like children, surprising themselves and their proud but equally worried and emotional parents. Some of them simply froze. For the first time in their lives they would be leaving behind their families, friends and loved ones, and this almost always sent them into a mild form of shock that could last weeks or months.

The transition was so stressful that I had our team of lawyers arrange for at least two visas for family members to travel with the kids and live with them for at least the first six months, and once they made it to the big leagues, we would start on the process of relocating family members to the States on a permanent basis. It was especially difficult because many of these prospects spoke Spanish and understood very little English … further alienating them.

Later that evening, I bundled Mia up, took her hand and we went for a walk around the property. It was very chilly and the wind was whipping around, and for most of the walk we didn't say much. We sat down on a bench, which was enclosed on three sides like a bus stop, and looked out over the ocean. I asked, "Do you know who the most important person in the whole world is to me?"

She hesitated and then replied, "Catherine."

"No, she's the second most important. You're the most important and I could not imagine living without you." She cuddled up next to me and put her head up against my shoulder. I told her, "At times, when I am alone, I talk to my mommy. You see, I still believe that her spirit is out there, and I tell her all about you. I tell her how wonderful you are and how very happy you have made me, and that the only regret I have is that she and my daddy are not alive to spoil you like they spoiled me. Italian parents, even when they don't have much money, love to spoil their children and grandchildren, and they would love to have spoiled you."

I looked out over the ocean and quite clearly in my mind I could see my lovely mother's face and hear her consoling and supporting voice in the whirling wind. It was the voice of a woman of unparalleled patience and sympathy, a mother who could make her suffering child feel like Mickey Mantle after he'd gone '0 for four' and made three errors in a little league game.

"It was my mother's voice that told me to take you away from that terrible town and to forever protect and love you like she loved me. I promised I would, and I would never break a promise I made to my mom." I looked down at Mia and for the first time, mingling with the tears that were just starting to escape from her eyes, I saw a look of complete faith. In that moment, I knew she understood that I would always be there for her and would never abandon her.

CHAPTER FORTY-ONE

The next morning, we got ready to leave for Los Angeles and my house in Studio City. Catherine announced her intention to drive us all there in her super-size SUV, which was more like a small house in the Bronx. I offered to drive, but my lovely wife wisecracked that drivers like me were the reason chauffeurs and cab drivers would always be employed.

I asked, "And what makes you say that?"

"Because you drive like an old lady," she replied with a laugh.

"Oh, I see," I said. "You're making fun of my driving because I'm careful on the road."

"No," she shot back. "Being careful on the road is a good thing … driving fifteen miles below the speed limit is infuriating. If I let you drive, we'll get to LA in five hours, whereas I think I can get us there in a little over two."

Mr. Baker, who was busy in the backseat putting on Mia's seat belt, said, "That's because he's from the Bronx, sweetheart. Did your parents even own a car, Joe?"

"Not until I was a teenager," I said.

"So that's your excuse?" Catherine said as we both piled into the front seat. Before I could answer, she leaned over, kissed me on the lips and said, "You know I love you, right?" She then turned around and pointed at her father and Mia and said, "And you, Daddy. And you, my sweet, beautiful child. I love you too." They beamed at her from behind dark sunglasses, purchased specially by Mr. Baker for the road trip, and blew her two-handed kisses from the backseat.

"We love you too, honey," Mr. Baker said. "Now pass the trail mix, please."

"Yes, we love you too," Mia said, pushing her Ray-Ban shades slightly farther up her nose. "And the trail mix," she said, smiling.

"Oh! I see how it is!" Catherine said, feigning indignation. "Joe, give them the trail mix, please."

I realized in that moment that Mia had finally relaxed enough to make a joke. This felt like such a big breakthrough that I was in danger of making a big deal out of it and making her self-conscious. I stopped myself just in time and reveled silently in this small but unmistakable step forward in our ability to communicate as a family. I knew from my own upbringing that a family that could poke gentle fun at each other had a fighting chance of staying together forever. I reached into an open bag in the front seat and pulled out a couple of sealed Ziploc bags of snacks that one of the kitchen staff had prepared for our trip: a homemade mixture of pistachios, almonds and chocolate chips. At Catherine's request, Mia had been given twice as many chocolate chips as the rest of us.

"Mind you eat the nuts too," Catherine said, eyeing Mia with mock sternness in the rearview. "Don't just pick out the chocolate."

"I won't," Mia said, and she did as she promised, eating one pistachio or almond for every chocolate chip she popped into her mouth.

Catherine started up the car and we drove down the driveway and turned onto the highway. After the kiss, I totally forgot what I was going to say. I was still trying to wrap my head around the idea that I was married to this stunning young woman. It was all like a dream ... Mia, Catherine and her father ... a perfect dream.

It took my lovely wife about two hours to get to the city limits of Los Angeles, and then another hour to go the three miles to my house. She was huffing and puffing and asking the whole way, "How does anyone live in this congestion? I would go insane if I had to deal with this every day."

"Patience, sweetheart," I said, calmly enjoying my greater tolerance for the big city. "It's a virtue."

She looked at me with disdain and replied, "When I pee all over you, then you can talk to me about patience, sweetheart."

I looked at Mia, who had taken off her sunglasses and was staring wide-eyed at the bumper-to-bumper traffic. I doubt she had ever seen so many cars in her life. I asked, "Are you okay?"

"Yes," she said and continued, "I don't have to pee."

Catherine laughed and then suddenly became serious. I asked, "You didn't, did you?"

"No, but almost."

We finally arrived at my exit and she turned off the highway and drove straight to my house. She parked in the front driveway and I quickly opened the front door to the house, pointed to the bathroom, and like the Flash, she was off and out of sight.

Mr. Baker and Mia walked into the house and he remarked, "Just like her mommy."

I closed the door behind me and said, "Welcome to my abode ... though I can't help thinking that this must look like a prison cell compared to your mansion by the sea."

"Before you were born, Joe, I was sleeping in a trench ... just south of the thirty-eighth parallel, in Korea. After I was discharged and started my business, I slept in more hole-in-the-wall motels than I can recall. It wasn't the best of times, but it taught me valuable lessons about what is important and what is superficial. Living in that mansion by the sea is great, but without my family and my wonderful staff, whom I consider family, it would just be a cumbersome piece of property that blocks out the sun."

I looked down at Mia, who was standing right beside Mr. Baker. He bent down and gently ran his hands through her soft curls and said, "And you, my lovely little genius ... you are one of the main reasons why the sun has been shining so brightly over that mansion by the sea."

Mia hugged Mr. Baker, and though I did not turn around, I could feel my wife standing behind me, and then I could hear her footsteps as she quickly walked away and back down the hallway. I excused myself and walked after her. She was standing in the parlor, beside the sliding glass door that looked out on the pool. I stood behind her and handed her a couple of tissues.

"Just a little nervous about tomorrow," she remarked as she wiped the tears from her eyes.

"That's understandable. Would it help if I said I had no doubt that tomorrow is going to go great ... and that after tomorrow we will be one major step closer to our goal of legally adopting our little Leonardo?"

"It helps, but I'll still be a little nervous."

I wrapped my arms around Catherine. I had no doubt that there was much more on my wife's mind than the meeting with the social worker. She said, "This house is so much like you, Joe. Granted I have only seen a little bit of it, but from what I have seen, it is unpretentious, modest — the type of house you could see a loving family of four or five living in."

"Well for the twenty years I have owned it, I can guarantee you that only I have lived in it, and my parents have been the only visitors to stay for any length of time."

"Do you have a trophy room where all of your awards and championship memorabilia are displayed?"

"No!"

"Do you keep your championship rings in a bank vault?"

"No; one is buried with my father and one is buried with my mom."

"That is a lot of gold to have buried."

"It doesn't add up to a half percent of what my parents gave to me."

"Unconditional love and support."

"Exactly!"

"And the third championship ring ... where do you keep that?"

"In a box in my bedroom closet."

She laughed and then asked, "If you die before me, would you like me to bury it with you?"

"That is the last thing I want you to do with it, and I will make that crystal clear in my revised last will and testament."

"Then what would you like me to do with it?"

"Whatever you want, as long as you don't bury it with me."

She continued to stare out at the pool as I relaxed my grip around her. She was tense.

"Before meeting me, what did you picture your ideal family would look like? A wife with two children, or three or four children like my brother and sister's families?"

"Before falling in love with you, I never thought about what an ideal family might look like. Now I never have to wonder about what an ideal family might look or behave like because I have the ideal family … you, Mia, your dad and the wonderful staff at the mansion. It's like living a dream that I never want to wake up from."

I put my hands on her shoulders and started to lightly massage them. I asked, "What's wrong, Catherine?"

She shook her head and replied, "Nothing."

"Don't give me that. What is it?"

She turned and looked at me and said, "I just wondered if you ever thought about having our own children?"

"If that is what you want, that would be absolutely great with me."

"It might be what I want, but I will not be able to deliver. A childhood illness left me as sterile as a corpse. I am so sorry. It was my responsibility to tell you before we got married, and I told my dad that I did, but then I got scared that you might call off the wedding."

"Catherine…"

"I know. I feel terrible. I'm so sorry—"

"Sorry for what?" I asked. "Being nervous? Wanting to please me? You don't have to be sorry for those things … or for anything."

"A lot of men would have been furious to find this out after the fact," she said, nervously searching my eyes for evidence that I really didn't care.

"Well I'm not a lot of men."

"Don't I know it," she said, relaxing a little. "And aren't I lucky."

"You think *you're* lucky? That's hilarious, and incredibly sweet," I said, "but try this on: I still can't wrap my head around the idea that I get to be married to you … a woman so far out of my league, so beautiful, intelligent and caring."

Catherine's lip was starting to quiver as she stared at me, listening closely and with obvious gratitude and relief.

"No, I'm serious," I said. "The only thing that could make this dream that I am now living any better is if my parents were alive to meet you and Mia and your daddy. In all honesty, I never even thought about having our own children ... everything is so perfect that I don't want anything to change."

She threw her arms around me and we kissed passionately and for a very long time, and all I could think of was that this was the best dream I could ever have imagined.

CHAPTER FORTY-TWO

My wife opened the refrigerator, looked up and down, looked across at me and said, "Apparently, man only needs Budweiser to survive." I looked into the gleaming interior of my barely used refrigerator and saw one item: a case of Budweiser beer. I looked at the newly minted expiration dates, which they started putting on the beers about five years back, and replied, "And wouldn't you know it, they're expired."

She laughed and said, "Well I guess we'll need to go in search of food, like the hunters of old."

After unloading our few bits of luggage, all four of us piled back into her SUV and drove to Monte Carlo Italian Deli and Restaurant in nearby Burbank. They had some of the best Italian food in all of Los Angeles, and a deli section that would make an Italian deli owner in the Bronx proud.

We sat at a table, and a waiter quickly greeted us, handing out menus and running through the specials. He then took our drink orders as we looked over the menu that was a mile long. As I was talking up the chicken parmigiana, I looked over at Mia, who was sitting between Catherine and me, and I noticed her eyes looking at the Italian pastries. "You know, they have wonderful cannoli here," I said. "Possibly even better than the Italian restaurant we ate at back home."

Mia looked up at me with her big blue eyes and I continued, "I just don't know if your mommy will let you have them for dinner."

"No, her mommy will not let her have them for dinner."

"Maybe just one as an appetizer?" Mr. Baker asked and continued, "They're not very big."

Catherine looked at her father and shook her head in good-natured defeat. "Okay, one as an appetizer and then a bowl of pasta with a little butter and pieces of broccoli."

"Seriously, Catherine, broccoli?" I asked.

"And what would you recommend … chocolate chips?"

"I believe she would probably love that. And I have it on good authority that she ate all the pistachios and almonds in the trail mix, so she's got you there."

Here I looked at Mr. Baker, who said, "She did, and she's got you there."

Mia looked shyly up at Catherine, who said, "You people are all in league with each other. But okay, forget it; the broccoli can go and we will add a little cheese." Mia had a cannoli for an appetizer and the three adults had garden salads. Mr. Baker and I had the chicken parmigiana and Catherine had spaghetti with meatballs. Poor little Mia had just plain pasta with a drip of butter and cheese, and three more cannoli for dessert.

Catherine took Mia by the hand and they walked across the street to a Whole Foods market and bought some essentials to take back to the house. I told her not to forget some Budweiser because the beer in the refrigerator had expired. She looked at me and said, "You really are looking to have our first fight as a married couple, aren't you?"

"Now why would I want to do that, especially since I know for a fact I would lose?"

"You're right about that, isn't he, Daddy?"

"She's tough, Joe," he said. "This may not have come up before, but she was the captain of her high school *and* college debating teams, so … good luck to you."

"That I have no doubt believing," I said and laughed.

Mr. Baker and I ordered a couple of Sandeman Founder's Reserve ports as we waited for the ladies to shop for groceries.

Catherine's dad toasted me and said, "Here's to family."

"To family," I echoed happily.

"I was thinking," he said, "that it must seem like you are living in an alternate universe, after being a bachelor for so long and on the road most of the off-season."

"It's like I am living the perfect dream, married to the most wonderful girl in the world, adopting a precious and precocious jewel of a daughter and having the perfect father-in-law. I was just telling Catherine that the only thing that could make this dream better is if my parents were still alive. They would have loved all of you so much."

"I wish I had known them. To raise a son like you, they had to be special."

I lowered my eyes and looked into the glass of port. I picked it up and took a small sip and said, "I wasn't there for them when they needed me most."

"You were doing your job, and I think that's what they would have wanted you to be doing."

"That's no excuse, and I am certain that no one knows that better than you. Did you ever put your job before your family?"

He didn't answer as he swirled the port gently round his glass. "Is this why you quit?"

"Yes!" I said, practically exploding. "I should have stayed with my mom for at least six months after my dad passed away. If I had done that, I'm fairly certain she would still be alive. I should have just told her that she was going to have to move out to California to live with me, and made it happen. I could have taken care of her like she took care of me my entire life. It's not like I had to worry about losing my job."

"Is that what she would have wanted?"

"She never would have admitted it, but I knew deep down that was the responsible and loving thing to do. A neighbor found her dead on the kitchen floor. She died alone, and if nothing else, she did not deserve to die alone."

I shot down the remaining port in my glass and ordered two more. I continued, "That was the overriding reason, but it wasn't the only reason.

I was burned out. I could not take spending another six months down in Central and South America, and occasionally skipping off to Japan and South Korea to look at prospects."

"You could have stopped doing that years ago, Joe. Your scouts could have easily sent you all the footage you needed."

"That's what a lot of people have told me, but that's not the way I did my job. It was important for me to be there, not just to get a first-hand, ground-level look at the kids but to understand their relationships to their families and friends. I had great scouts, and there were very few decisions over the years that were made by me alone. It was very much a collective effort. They were invaluable."

The waiter set two more glasses of port in front of Mr. Baker and me, and I ordered six cannoli to go but told the waiter not to bring them out until we were ready to leave the restaurant.

"Don't think my lovely daughter will approve?"

"Probably not, even though I'm quite certain she would have ordered at least three cannoli to go. Mia might not have my lovely wife as tightly wrapped around her little finger as she does me, but it's close. Besides, I want to keep the little genius as sharp and happy as possible for tomorrow's meeting with the social worker."

"She's frightened?" Mr. Baker asked as he took a sip of port.

"Let's say, she has her suspicions. You don't go through what she has gone through without learning to second-guess the motives of every adult in your orbit."

"Is that what those little strolls that you and she take in the evening are all about — alleviating her anxiety and fears?"

"That, and simple bonding. We've come a long way in a short time just by walking and running together. She's quite the natural athlete."

"I can see that," Mr. Baker said, then paused for a moment. "You do know, I hope, that Catherine is not going to be anything like the GM that you were? I would never allow it."

"And I never would have married her if I thought she was. Catherine and I talked about this before we got married. As much as

I love her, I told her I did not want a part-time wife and mother ... going out of town with the team, unless totally necessary, and especially not going to foreign countries to scout prospects."

"I could have assured you of that. She is 'new school' — more inclined to look at a computer printout of players and how they perform against lefties and righties than to actually get down on the field and watching the movement and agility of the players."

"I don't agree with that approach, but if it keeps her at home at night, I have no complaints." I took a sip of port and continued, "I used to tell the younger scouts in our organization that if there was a computer program out there that assured you of winning seventy percent of your games and winning the championship every year, the Yankees would have stolen it years ago and kept it under lock and key."

Mr. Baker laughed as I continued, "Baseball is a game, not a science. A computer printout of how a player has done against a certain pitcher can come in handy, but what that printout can't tell you is whether that pitcher, on that day, is suffering from a fever, a sore arm or marital problems. A good manager, coaching staff and observant players can pick up on such things from the moment many pitchers take the mound." I looked up and realized that I'd been lecturing a man who I considered a mentor, and I was suddenly embarrassed. "Listen to me, talking to you like you don't already know all of this and more."

"Oh, not at all — I love a good dissection of baseball management. Do you know how rare it is to be able to talk to someone about our work at this level? Please, go on."

"I appreciate that, and I do know what you mean," I said, smiling at my gracious father-in-law. "I was just going to say that a manager who has a red-hot batter, who has previously done very poorly against a pitcher and who the manager might usually sit down or pinch-hit for under normal circumstances, might, under these slightly different conditions, decide to go with the hot batter against the dominant pitcher. Regardless of the outcome, it is the manager and the coaches who see the complete picture and take into account everything that I want working for me. Catherine is fortunate because she has such a manager and coaches. They trust their instincts, they notice the small stuff and they know how to adapt to subtle changes. They don't discard the computer's analysis but neither do they give it total weight. They treat it as one piece of information in a bigger picture."

"What did you see in our former MVP that you were so keen on getting rid of him?"

"His market value. You can't offer peanuts when you're looking to trade for two highly ranked pitching prospects."

"And that was all?"

I looked down at my glass of port. This was the first time Mr. Baker and I had talked baseball. I knew he had misgivings about Catherine's ability to run the team, and he was around the game far too long for me to be anything but honest … but—

"All his drug tests came back negative, and he passed the physical that St. Louis put him through. What else is there?" I replied as I took a sip of my port.

"His swing. Did you see anything unusual?"

"The exit velocity that he hit off-speed pitches out of the park was unusually high. He hit eighty-mile-an-hour pitches for long home runs with the exit velocity that you would expect from a player his size and using a similar bat hitting a hundred-and-one-mile fastball off of Randy Johnson with the meat of the bat. A lot of baseball people don't give much credence to bat speed and exit velocity, but I do."

"And did my daughter agree with your assessment?"

"Yes."

Mr. Baker laughed. "It's a great comfort to me, Joe, knowing how much you love my daughter."

"She's very smart, and people would be very foolish to underestimate her."

"I couldn't agree more, but that doesn't make her a Joe Ciotola or a Dusty Baker or a Joe Torre or a Gene Michaels."

"She doesn't need to be any of those people to be successful. She needs to be simply herself and to listen to the baseball people around her."

Mr. Baker ordered two more ports as he seemed to look past me for a moment, and then he placed his hands under his chin and looked directly at me and said, "Your lovely wife has it in her head that winning a championship would be some kind of crowning achievement for me, but it wouldn't. It would be great for our fans and the city, but a crowning achievement ... no, not at all. When I look at Catherine and see the type of wonderful, caring and loving young lady she has blossomed into, that's a crowning achievement for me. When I go down to the hospital and we have a celebration for a child who has been diagnosed with cancer, had surgery, chemo and radiation, and is finally allowed to go home after being declared cancer-free by the doctors, that's a crowning achievement. Baseball is simply a game that I have greatly enjoyed, but never will a championship bring me the joy I feel every time I look at my daughter, at children brave enough to beat the dastardly disease that has tried to ravage their bodies, or every time I look at Mia and the promise she represents."

The waiter placed the ports down and we both thanked him at the same time. Mr. Baker continued, saying, "I wanted to sell the team after this season, but my daughter begged me to give it one more year, two at the most. I couldn't say no to her after everything she has done. I've lost interest in the game. Last year I don't think I went to the ballpark more than five times. I stayed at home and watched the games on TV, and usually by the second or third inning I fell asleep."

We both took a sip of port, and after a pause, Mr. Baker said, "You know, I never took a penny's profit from the team, never drew a salary. Whatever profit we made went right back into the team and the farm system. Sure, I could have spent money like Steinbrenner or the Red Sox or the Cubs, but I had more important concerns. A winning legacy and championship trophies might have got me more headlines, maybe a plaque in the Hall of Fame, but helping the less fortunate, being part of organizations that are desperately searching for cures against so many types of cancer, cystic fibrosis and MS ... that is a legacy that I can proudly take to the grave. The money I saved by not going after high-priced free agents allowed Catherine and me to build two additional wings on the hospital, and when the team is sold, the vast bulk of that money will go into building another wing. The plans are already drawn up."

I looked out the window and watched as Catherine and Mia crossed the street, holding a number of shopping bags. They entered the restaurant and sat down at the table. "So are we all ready to go home?" Catherine asked.

I asked the waiter for the check and handed him my credit card. Catherine asked him if he could pack three cannoli to go. He looked at me and I nodded and said, "Yes, please do."

Catherine then looked at me and asked, "What was that all about?"

"Nothing, sweetheart."

"Daddy?"

"Nothing."

The waiter gave me my credit card and got my signature. Then he placed a shopping bag with the to-go orders beside my chair. My wife quickly grabbed the bag and opened the two containers with the nine cannoli.

"You got to be kidding me?" she remarked.

"No one said they were all for her," I replied as we all started laughing.

CHAPTER FORTY-THREE

I walked out of the en suite bathroom after brushing my teeth and looked across at Catherine, who was lying in the bed in her pajamas, scrolling through texts on her phone. She looked at me, put her phone aside and smiled.

"So what do you think … half the size of the bed that we sleep in at the mansion?"

"More like a third the size," she replied with a laugh as I sat down on my side of the bed. She continued, "So what I want to know is, how many other women have slept in this bed besides me?"

"In all honesty, you're the first," I replied.

"Really, Joe, you can do better than that."

"Really, Catherine, I am telling you the truth. I have had this house for twenty years, and more than half the time I have been out of town, and at least half the time I have been here, I fell asleep on the couch in the living room looking at ESPN." I lay down next to Catherine.

She asked, "So what did you and my daddy talk about when we were off shopping?"

"We talked about you and Mia and how lucky we were to be living with two such beautiful and intelligent young ladies. What else would we be talking about?"

She sat up and looked down at me and replied, "You are a terrible liar. Has anyone ever told you that?"

"No, you're the first," I replied as she lay back down and turned on her side away from me. I reached over and gently touched her shoulder and asked, "Can I ask you a personal question?"

"I don't see why not. You are my husband ... a lying husband, but still my husband."

"Is there a reason why neither you nor your father talk much about your brother and sister? Family seems so important to the both of you. I just find it kind of unusual."

Catherine sighed and remained silent for a long time. Just as I was getting the uncomfortable feeling that I had wandered into forbidden territory, she said, "Both my brother and sister and their families lived with us right up to the time my mom passed away. They both married into families almost as rich as ours. Once my mom passed, I guess they figured they had done enough helping to care for her and that it was time to concentrate on their own families. They didn't want anything to do with the family's charities. I had the feeling they thought it was a waste of time to help other people with their problems."

"They sound very different from you and your dad," I said, trying to avoid sounding too judgmental. "I'm sorry to have brought this up. It feels like I hit a sore spot."

"That's true, but I'm glad you asked. I've been trying to think of a way to talk to you about them. It just seems so odd that you haven't met either of my siblings yet. Can you imagine allowing that to happen if the shoe were on the other foot? Or if your parents were still alive?"

"I can't."

By now Catherine was in a mood to talk about it, so I sat back and listened.

"Since I was just a child younger than Mia, I always remember my father taking my brother and sister and me aside on our birthdays and on Christmas Eve and reciting a speech that President Theodore Roosevelt gave to a college preparatory group of rich, privileged boys attending the Groton School in Massachusetts. He recited the speech to us so many times that I can quote parts of it from memory."

I looked at her, dubious, and said, "Really?"

"I think so. Give or take a few lines. He told them to be 'practical as well as generous' in their ideals and said to 'keep your eyes on the stars, but remember to keep your feet on the ground.'"

"I've heard that one," I said, not realizing where the line was from until that moment.

"Yes, that must have resonated with a lot of people because it has become a well-known saying. It's wonderful advice."

"Is that it?"

"What?"

"I seem to recall a boast about memorizing the whole speech. Let's have it."

"Hmm," Catherine said, sitting up straight and concentrating.

"Wait, let me call it up on my phone so I can check you for accuracy."

"What? You don't trust me? What good is a marriage without trust?"

"I trust you as far as I can throw you, my sweet."

"Now you're calling me fat."

"Hardly. Come on, now. Recite the text."

Catherine shot me a look, cleared her throat, and held forth, complete with hand gestures: "I want to speak to you first of all as regards your duties as boys; and in the next place as regards your duties as men; and the two things hang together."

She interrupted herself to point out that her father, being a progressive person, always mentioned that the speech applied equally to boys, girls, men and women; that it was, in fact, a guide for everyone.

She continued quoting Roosevelt: "The same qualities that make a decent boy make a decent man. They have different manifestations, but fundamentally they are the same. If a boy [or a girl] has not got pluck and honesty and common sense he is a pretty poor creature; and he is a worse creature if he is a man [or if she is a woman] and lacks any one of those three traits."

I made sure to urge her on with my eyes, registering appropriate amounts of awe at her memorization skills.

"Because much has been given to you, therefore we have a right to expect much from you; and we have a right to expect that you shall begin to give that much just as soon as you leave school and go to college, so that you shall count when you are there.

"Of course, the worst of all lives is the vicious life; the life of a man who becomes a positive addition to the forces of evil in a community. Next to that and when I am speaking to people who, by birth and training and standing, ought to amount to a great deal, I have a right to say only second to it in criminality comes the life of mere vapid ease, the ignoble life of a man who desires nothing from his years but that they shall be led with the least effort, the least trouble, the greatest amount of physical enjoyment or intellectual enjoyment of a mere dilettante type…"

When she paused, I began clapping. It seemed the only response, and I was genuinely impressed.

"Thank you. Thank you," Catherine said, bowing from the waist down and sliding back down the mattress until her head was on the pillow again. "My daddy is not a very political man, but he loves President Theodore Roosevelt. The actual speech is much longer than that, and my father gave us all copies of the speech. It is one of the most cherished things I own. This is what my father expected from all of us. It is the code that he lives by, and my two siblings simply tossed it aside and are happy living 'a mere dilettante type of life.'"

"Do your brother and sister visit with the grandchildren?"

"Occasionally, but not during the holidays. God forbid they should have to ruin their holidays by trailing along with us to the hospital to help give out gifts to the children. We do it both Christmas Eve and Christmas Day, so please don't make other plans. And you might want to start thinking now about which costume you want to wear. Mr. Claus is already taken, and naturally Mia and I will be playing elves. I think you might make a good dancing snowman."

"Really?"

"Yes. After María has had a few eggnogs with rum, she takes over the dance floor and can make an amateur like you look like Grace Kelly. Maybe she can give you a few lessons before the festivities start."

"It must really hurt your father that he doesn't get to see the grandchildren very much."

"It kills him, but now he has Mia to help fill that gap. He loves that child so much. She and you have been a godsend to both of us and to the staff."

"He sees you when he looks at Mia, and you are his proudest achievement. That is exactly what we talked about when you girls were off shopping."

Catherine started to cry, and I gently rubbed her shoulders. She tried to stifle her sobs as she said, "I doubt I would even be able to shed a tear if anything happened to my brother and sister. I can hardly believe it has come to that."

I wrapped my arms around my wife's quivering body and kissed her good night.

At three o'clock I woke up and slid my hand over to where I expected Catherine to be but found her half of the bed empty. I looked around in the darkness but couldn't see anything, so I got up and checked the bathroom. She wasn't in there either. I could smell her perfume, or at least I thought I could. I shivered at the half-coherent thought that everything I had experienced since leaving the team — my wedding to Catherine and my impending adoption of Mia, even the events in Salvation — had all been an elaborate dream. I stood in the hallway and listened. The house was completely silent, just as it had always been for the last twenty years whenever I had slept here. I remembered a line from Joseph Conrad's *Heart of Darkness*: "We live as we dream — alone."

I walked a few steps to the room that Mia should be sleeping in and shut my eyes as I opened the door. I was afraid to open them, but open them I did, and there in the bed was my wife, asleep, with her arms wrapped around our sleeping child. I closed the door and stood for a long moment in the hallway, with my head bowed. I was not alone.

I walked back into my bedroom and climbed into bed. The scent of my wife's perfume was like an elixir. I kept hearing the same silent mantra in my head: *It is not a dream; I am not alone.* I closed my eyes and tried to sleep but couldn't. The image of Catherine, asleep, hugging Mia, kept running through my mind. Then with the insight afforded to me by being in a semi-conscious state, I suddenly realized that Mia was Catherine's gift to her father. She couldn't get pregnant, and her siblings' children, her father's grandchildren, had been taken away from him. Mia, not baseball, was the one constant that united all of us and made us a *family.*

CHAPTER FORTY-FOUR

I got out of bed at my usual time, put on my running gear and walked into the living room where Mia was waiting for me. I asked her if Mommy was still asleep and she nodded and smiled. I zipped up her hoodie, retied her loose sneaker laces and warned her that she had to remain close to the curb because running on the streets was more dangerous than running on the beach. I wanted her to be on higher alert, even though in reality, Studio City had very little traffic, especially at this time in the morning.

We left the house and walked a few blocks. The air was a lot warmer here than it had been by the beach. We started running and she followed my instructions by hugging the curb. The only problem was that she continued running way past any previous distance we had run, and by the time I put out my hand to stop her, I was about ready to drop. It took me a couple of blocks to fully catch my breath, and then we casually walked around the community as I pointed out the different styles of homes, and the neighborhood feeling that one senses in an area like this one, in contrast to the beach.

She asked, "Is this like the neighborhood that you lived in with your parents?"

"Except for the size of the homes and the distance between the homes, it's sort of similar. The homes in the area of the Bronx I come from are very close together, but everyone on our block knew each other and our neighbors were always there if you needed help. I loved growing up there."

"Was your mommy the most beautiful mom in the whole neighborhood?"

I laughed and then replied, "I think she was, and I know my father thought she was, but I'm sure my friends also thought their moms were the most beautiful."

"I think your mommy is the most beautiful mom I have ever seen."

"Thank you, Mia." She put out her hand and I took it and we kept walking.

Back at the house, Catherine was in a bit of a state, trying to decide which outfit Mia should wear when she met with the social worker. Mia slipped past her to get to the shower, and Catherine didn't even notice; she was too busy weighing the merits of ten different outfits. Most of them were tailored dresses that seemed like they would be totally uncomfortable. One after another, she was showing them to her father, who was trying to be as helpful as possible, but gradually running out of patience.

I took my wife by the hand and said, "I have an idea. Why not let Mia wear whatever she feels most comfortable wearing?"

"Because she'll just choose shorts and a T-shirt and her dirty sneakers!"

"Exactly, and she'll look and feel a lot less self-conscious."

Catherine didn't look convinced, but she was at least considering the idea. "What do you think, Daddy?"

"I think Joe is one hundred percent right," Mr. Baker replied.

Just then, Mia stepped out of her bedroom wearing shorts, a T-shirt and her dirty sneakers.

"I'm all clean!" she announced. And with that, all was settled.

CHAPTER FORTY-FIVE

Theresa Greco, the social worker, knocked on the front door at exactly two o'clock. Ms. Greco was handsomely dressed and carried a brown leather briefcase. She was young and attractive with wavy dark hair, brown eyes and olive skin. She could easily have been the model on the front cover of a magazine exclusively devoted to the Bronx, and when she opened her mouth to speak, there was no doubt she was from New York. In fact, this young lady looked like my mom in her wedding photos, and when I looked at Mia, I was quite certain she saw the resemblance.

The young woman introduced herself, and when I asked her what part of the Bronx she was from, she replied with a laugh, "Less than a mile from where you grew up, Mr. Ciotola, but I will always be a die-hard Yankee fan no matter how long I live out here. I can't tell you how heartbroken I was when Derek Jeter got married. I have been in love with him since I was a little girl."

"I'm certain the perfect man is somewhere out there waiting to meet you."

"But will he be playing shortstop for the Yankees?"

I laughed and replied, "Maybe not for the Yankees but maybe for the Dodgers."

"That won't do; I can't stand that team. Is there any truth to the rumor that you might be going to the Yankees?"

"I'll let you in on a secret: There is not a chance in the world. If I ever get back into game, it will be with the team that I have been with my whole career."

"How about your wife's team?"

Catherine wrapped her arms around me and remarked, "I've already been turned down, and I was certain I had the inside track."

Theresa bent down and looked at Mia and remarked, "You are so beautiful, Mia, and your hair is stunning. It takes me hours just to get a wave in my hair."

Theresa gently rubbed her hand down along Mia's arm and asked, "And do you have a favorite baseball team?"

"Yes, my mommy's team."

"Not your daddy's?"

"No, just my mommy's. Since my daddy resigned from his team, it's just my mommy's."

"And do you have a favorite baseball player?"

"Yes, Charlie Brown and Snoopy," she said. Theresa laughed along with the rest of us.

"Wonderful choices, sweetheart."

We all gathered in the living room and Theresa handed out brochures and pamphlets on adoption. Catherine and I signed a number of forms agreeing to the terms and conditions set down by the state of California concerning adoption. It was apparent that Theresa had done her homework. She knew the whole backstory concerning Mia. She had copies of her medical records, which were provided by my wife, who had the foresight to have Mia thoroughly examined by doctors just a few days after meeting her. Theresa looked down at our financial statements, shook her head and simply remarked, "No problem there."

She smiled at Mia, who was sitting between us on the couch, and asked, "How about you and I have a little talk about Charlie Brown, Snoopy, and how it is that you learned how to play chess in one day and suddenly became a master?"

Theresa stood up and reached for Mia's hand, but first Mia hugged and kissed Catherine, Mr. Baker and me. I then walked the ladies to the parlor and closed the door. I walked back into the living room and found my wife crying. I sat down beside her and remarked, "Everything went great, sweetheart."

"I know. She's so sweet. Just the idea that the state could possibly take her away from us makes me nervous."

Mr. Baker stood up and walked over to his daughter and harshly remarked, "Stop it, Catherine! The idea that I would allow anyone to take that child away from us is insane."

Mr. Baker walked into the kitchen and poured himself a glass of water. He sat back down and looked across at his daughter, who had stopped crying. It was the first time I heard him speak harshly to his daughter, never mind openly reprimand her.

"I'm sorry, Daddy."

Mr. Baker simply nodded and then looked at me and remarked, "Theresa seems like a lovely young lady."

"Yes, she does," I said, taking Catherine's hand, which was shaking, and holding on to it firmly. "Even if she is a Yankee fan."

"Ugh!" Catherine exclaimed.

I felt helpless. I felt like I should have stood up for my wife when her father spoke to her in that tone of voice. The problem was that he was right. Catherine really seemed on edge, whereas Mr. Baker and I understood that everything was going smoothly. When one gets married or has been dating another person for a long time, it is only natural that each other's vulnerabilities become noticeable. I'm sure that my parents, who in my eyes were perfect, masked their vulnerabilities in front of me and smoothed over any weaknesses they each might have had, helping each other during those rough times.

The Catherine that walked into the hotel suite that first day to meet Mia was perfect, but that was for a moment in time. It was Catherine's frailties that made her human, that made me want to help, and it was those imperfections that made me love her even more.

About forty-five minutes later, Theresa and Mia walked out of the parlor, still laughing and talking about something to do with the solar system. Theresa's expression said it all. She was in awe of this little girl, who only a few months ago was living under conditions that no one should have to endure. Theresa remarked, "*Your child* is definitely MIT-bound in not so many years."

"Oh, Theresa, please don't say that," I said. "We were thinking more like Caltech or Stanford. We could never bear living that far away from her if she went to MIT."

"Don't be silly, Joe, if she went to MIT we would just have to pack up and go live in Massachusetts until she graduated."

Theresa laughed. "She told me you call her your little Leonardo."

"Yes, we do," I replied.

"Well I think Mr. da Vinci would have been honored to have her as one of his students."

Mia stayed in the living room as the rest of us went into the parlor to discuss what further steps would be needed to make the adoption legal.

Theresa said that she had everything she needed, that it was situations like this that made her job so fulfilling and that she would get all the paperwork down to the courthouse today and into the hands of the judge who was handling the case. With any luck, Mia might be legally ours by Christmas, even though there was usually a probation period of six months to a year where a social worker (probably her) would schedule visits to verify that everything was going well. She handed all of us her card and told us to call if we had any questions.

As she stood up, she touched the crucifix around her neck and said, "You know, I went to Catholic schools nearly my entire life and still try to make Sunday Mass as often as possible, and yet it really gives you a moment to pause and reflect, after seeing what this beautiful child has lived through, to understand how dangerous any religion can become when it goes so far off the beaten path and becomes so radicalized."

After Mia was invited to join us, all four of us walked Theresa to the door and thanked her profusely for her kindness. Mia went in for a big hug and Theresa bent down and kissed the top of her head. She then looked up at me, smiled and said, "You might not have got the Yankees job, but you did so much better." She glanced at Catherine and Mr. Baker and stood up and put out her hand to me, and I gently shook it. "It's been a pleasure, Mr. Ciotola. Merry Christmas and Happy New Year!"

I watched her as she walked down the driveway. It was like I had been given a second chance to say good-bye to my mother. Catherine put her arm around me and asked, "What's wrong, Joe?"

I shook my head and said, "Theresa looks just like my mother … just like her." I fought back tears as Mia handed Catherine her phone with the picture of my mother on her wedding day. Catherine looked at the picture and said, "Oh my God! She's the spitting image of her."

"It's why I knew everything was going to turn out perfect," Mia said in her soft, melodic voice as I closed the door.

I walked into the kitchen, opened the refrigerator and took out the box with the three cannoli. I put them on a plate and poured a glass of chocolate milk. I took Mia by the hand, sat her down at the table and put the plate and glass of chocolate milk in front of her.

I turned and looked at Catherine hugging her father, and I smiled.

CHAPTER FORTY-SIX

While Catherine was walking back and forth throughout the house talking to executives and scouts from the team and also talking to hospital personnel about the upcoming Christmas festivities for the children, and while Mia and Mr. Baker were playing chess, I walked into my little office and sat down at my desk. I dialed the number for Du-par's restaurant and asked for Martha, the waitress with the little nine-year-old boy, Stephen, who was a fan of my former team and who had been sick the time I last ate there, before I went on the trip that would change my life.

The receptionist who answered told me Martha was away on family leave and that she was not certain when she was coming back to work. I asked her if everything was okay with her little boy and there was dead air on the other end of the line.

"May I ask who is calling?" the receptionist finally asked.

"Yes, this is Joe Ciotola. I ate there a few months back and Martha told me about her little boy, Stephen."

"You're the baseball guy?"

"Yes," I replied.

"Little Stephen passed away two weeks ago. He was doing so well; the cancer went into remission, and all he could talk about was the upcoming little league season and the letter he received from the famous baseball GM, Joe Ciotola."

The receptionist, Maggie, started to cry and so did I. She continued, "The cancer came back and spread rapidly. Martha was devastated. Stephen was buried in his baseball uniform and with the letter you sent him."

I asked her if I could drop off a little something for Martha tomorrow morning, and she said yes, that she would be there all day and would make sure Martha got it. I thanked her and hung up.

I dried my eyes with a tissue and opened the top drawer of my desk and took out a stack of old baseball cards I had collected when I was about Stephen's age. I looked through the stack, remembering the many heroes I had back then and the future I had hoped someday to have. I had a Willie Mays, a Frank Robinson, a Mickey Mantle, a Reggie Jackson, a Graig Nettles, a Ron Guidry, a Roberto Clemente, a Yogi Berra…

During a break between calls, Catherine wandered into my office and saw me sitting at my desk.

"What are you doing in here?" she asked sweetly.

Her voice startled me, and I swung around, hoping she wouldn't be able to tell that I'd been crying. I fanned the stack of baseball cards in front of her and said, "Just looking at my old dream team."

Catherine came over and sat down on my lap and put her arms around my neck. I asked her if I had been an especially good boy today because I wasn't used to beautiful ladies sitting on my lap. She laughed and replied, "You have been a perfect boy, a perfect husband and a perfect daddy."

I laid the cards on my desk and wrapped my arms around her waist. She kissed me, and as she pulled away and gazed at my face, I looked into her dark-blue eyes and wondered, for at least the third time that day, how I had managed to get so lucky. I put the cards back together and tied the rubber band around them and handed them to Catherine. "Give them to the kids at the hospital. There is at least one in there that could probably pay for a college education."

"No Joe, those cards are part of who you are, but thank you."

She handed me back the cards and I remarked, "I really would like you to give them to the kids."

She took the cards, opened the top drawer of the desk, put the cards back inside and closed the drawer. She reached over and kissed me again and said, "I love you so much." Her phone rang; she excused herself, got up off my lap and answered the phone on her way out of the office.

I sat there for a long time and thought about a child I never met. A nine-year-old who would not get to play little league ever again or watch a baseball game with his loving mother or look at the box scores first thing every morning. I remembered not too long ago watching an animated "sun" rise — it was shaped like a baseball with the stitched imprint — and Charlie Brown waking up and smiling as he looked outside at the glowing baseball in the sky.

I remembered when the promise of baseball made waking up every day wondrous and exciting — filled with the possibility of making a diving, game-saving catch or getting the game-winning hit. *Yes*, I thought, *I remember…*

***

It could have been fifteen minutes later or an hour. I didn't know. I turned my head and looked outside to see Mia walking along the edge of the pool. Catherine was watching her from a beach chair, while still talking on her phone. I walked out of my office and joined them by the pool.

"Mia," I said, extending my hand and catching Catherine's eye so she would know that I was taking over.

With Mia's hand in mine, I led her to a nearby shed that I had built to hold all my baseball equipment that I had accumulated over the years. On the top shelf was a row of baseball gloves in all sizes. I looked at Mia's hand and smiled as I took out my baseball glove from when I was just a child, younger than Mia. The glove fit her little hand perfectly. My lovely wife walked over and grabbed herself a glove that had fit me during my teen years, and I put on the last glove that I'd used in my short-lived career as a player.

Moving to a big grassy area at the back of the property, we formed a triangle with about fifty feet between us and started tossing the ball. I tossed the first one to Mia very softly, and she fumbled the ball, but after a few more tosses, and with a little help from her mommy, she got the hang of it. Her mom instructed her not to aim the ball or to throw it too hard but to simply lob the ball in my direction. After a few failed attempts in which she threw the ball over my head or woefully short, she started to hit her mark. Under the hot California sun, the three of us — mom, dad and daughter — tossed the ball back and forth for a long and wonderful time.

CHAPTER FORTY-SEVEN

The next morning, Mia and I went for our run. Without planning to, we ended up running a little longer than the day before, when we'd broken our previous record. It was like she was training us to run a marathon. This was something I had no interest in doing, but I also realized that if Mia wanted us to run a marathon, we would probably end up doing just that. She could be quite convincing, in a Mia sort of way.

After our run we walked down to Du-par's restaurant. I had written a letter and put a check in an envelope for Martha. The letter was difficult to write. In *The Sun Also Rises*, Hemingway wrote, "The only thing a person takes with him when he dies, is what he left behind," but I don't think Mr. Hemingway was thinking about a nine-year-old boy when he wrote those words of wisdom. Even so, I was quite certain that little Stephen left behind many wonderful and courageous memories that would live forever with his mother and friends.

I held Mia's hand as we walked through the lovely streets of Studio City. It was a little past seven in the morning and it had always been my favorite time of the day. The sun, low in the sky, cast its tranquil shadows across the Earth, and as I looked down at Mia, I couldn't help but think that she was the greatest gift I had ever received.

We stopped at a little bridge across from CBS Studios and looked down at the creek that ran underneath it. It was dry, apart from a trickle of water that was struggling to make it to the Los Angeles River. "Is it because it doesn't rain here much that there is so little water?" Mia asked.

"Exactly," I said. "The state of California has been in a continuous state of drought for the thirty years I have lived here, but when it does rain it tends to rain for weeks. In all the years I worked for my former team, we never had a home game rained out. That might actually be some type of record."

She pointed at the CBS Studio Center and asked, "Is that where they make movies?"

"It's more like a place where they shoot TV shows, but I imagine they shot a lot of movies there back in the 1950s and before. For a short time, it was named the MTM-CBS Studio. MTM stands for Mary Tyler Moore. She was a famous actress who starred in two famous TV shows. She and her husband were partners in the studio. She was very beautiful and when I was just a kid, I had such a crush on her."

We walked into Du-par's, which was already crowded with breakfast customers. I asked a waitress if I could speak to Maggie, and she was good enough to take Mia and me to a back office where Maggie was sitting in a chair behind a desk. She stood up to greet us and asked if Mia was my daughter.

"Yes," I replied as Maggie affectionately touched Mia's hair.

"You're very beautiful, Mia."

"Thank you," she replied in her typical soft and melodic voice. I looked across at a picture on the desk of a smiling little boy wearing a little league uniform and holding a bat. Noticing my interest in it, Maggie picked up the picture and handed it to me. "That's Stephen," she said. "He was a real cutie."

I looked closely at the picture, and for a long moment, it was like I was staring at an amalgam of every little league kid I had ever played with, every young kid I had ever scouted from Cuba, Central America or Japan. At the same time, I remembered every grieving mom and dad waving good-bye to their son at the airport. Most of them never made it to the big leagues, but at least each one had a chance to chase their dream. I started to hand the picture back to Maggie when Mia reached over and gently took it from me. She looked at it closely, as though she was seeing something in it that I had missed.

She asked, "What position does he play?"

Maggie looked at me as though she was ready to burst into tears, and then managed to say, "He plays shortstop."

"Like Derek Jeter?" Mia asked.

"Yes, he plays shortstop like Derek Jeter," I replied as Mia handed me the picture and I gave it back to Maggie. I handed the envelope with the letter and check to Maggie and she remarked, "You're a really good guy, Mr. Ciotola."

"It's just Joe. It's always been just Joe." We hugged and I whispered into her ear that if Martha needed anything, she could just call me, that I had put my phone number in the letter.

Mia also hugged Maggie, and then we walked out of the restaurant and I took Mia's hand and we started walking back to the house.

"Is everything okay with the little boy?" Mia asked and I pretended not to hear her.

"Daddy," she screamed, "is everything okay with the little boy?"

I looked into her troubled face and said, "He died a couple of weeks ago from a terrible disease."

Her face turned pale, and she turned and ran to the side of a building and started to violently vomit. I felt helpless as the tranquil shadow of a new day turned into a shadow of death.

She stopped vomiting as I walked closer to her. She kept her head down and she was heaving and crying. She had spewed vomit all over herself, and it was dripping from her mouth. I took some tissues from my pocket and guided her to stand up straight so I could wipe her mouth. This went well enough, but it was useless trying to clean her clothes. I put my hand behind her head and gently pulled her into a hug. She was still sobbing, and I could feel her tears trickling through my shirt. I realized suddenly that I should never have brought her on this errand with me, and that I had fooled myself into believing that she could handle anything. After witnessing what she had lived through in the town of Salvation, I thought she was tougher than she really was. Now I could see that she was just a child — a beautiful, sensitive, curious, intelligent child, but one who was still vulnerable and who still needed to be protected from so many things.

I called Catherine and asked her to pick us up and said I would explain everything after we got home. She was there in less than five minutes and both Mia and I got into the backseat. Mia was tucked up against my body and Catherine looked at us with horror as I put my finger to my mouth and shook my head, and she didn't say a thing and just drove back to the house.

Mia immediately jumped out of the car as Catherine parked in the driveway. She ran into the house and into her bathroom. Once I was certain she was in the shower, I went into the bathroom and put her soiled clothes into a garbage bag and dumped the bag into a garbage can that I kept outside. Then I went back in to see Mr. Baker and Catherine, and I explained what happened.

Catherine waited until she heard the shower turn off in Mia's bathroom, then got up and walked into Mia's bedroom and closed the door. Mr. Baker looked at me and said, "That child is truly remarkable. In so many ways, she reminds me of Catherine. When we first started taking Catherine to the hospital to visit the children, she would get so upset when she heard that a child she had visited with for only a few minutes had passed away. We would find her crying hysterically in her room. It got so bad that my wife wanted to stop taking her."

He suddenly stopped talking, as he seemed to drift off. It was a habit of Mr. Baker's to drift off whenever he spoke about his wife. He continued, "I told her that I was never prouder of our daughter than when she displayed so much emotion for a child she hardly knew. It showed sensitivity to those less fortunate than us that I never wanted her to lose. She was about Mia's age when she first started visiting the hospital. My wife asked her if she would prefer not to go, and told her we would understand and not be mad. My daughter was shocked by this offer and replied with an emphatic no, saying she would never stop going to the hospital until they found a cure. True to her word, she has never stopped visiting the hospital and doing as much as possible to help out. Thankfully, the survival rate has increased to over eighty percent, but for every child who doesn't make it, like little Stephen, it makes it even more difficult to accept."

I lowered my eyes and looked across at the chessboard that Mia and Mr. Baker had been playing on. It was an old-fashioned chess set, without any elaborately carved pieces. It was the type I learned to play on when I was still a youngster.

Mr. Baker continued, "You and Catherine are very lucky to have Mia."

"We are all very lucky, Mr. Baker. Just like you and I and Mia are lucky to have Catherine."

"Yes, no one is luckier than me."

Just then, Catherine walked out of the bedroom holding Mia's hand. Mia was all clean and snug in her Charlie Brown and Snoopy pajamas. She looked very tired, but that didn't stop her from running over to Mr. Baker and me and hugging us. Catherine then took her back into her bedroom and tucked her into bed. She then walked back out to the living room and said, "The little angel is tired. She told me that little Stephen looked so happy in the picture that it made her so sad when she found out that he had died, that it made her sick."

"And what did you tell her?" I asked.

"I told her how proud I was of her," she replied as she looked at her father. "She's even more special than even I could ever imagine."

"And do you know who is just as special?" I asked.

"No, who is just as special?"

"You, Catherine; you are more special than even I could ever imagine."

She started to cry, but before she had a chance to run off to our bedroom, I grabbed her by her hand. I wiped the tears away with my hands and said, "To quote one those hated Yankees, 'I feel like the luckiest man on the face of the Earth.'"

She laughed and replied, "I never said I hated all the Yankees. There are a few I admire, like Mr. Gehrig." I kissed her and we hugged; and though the early morning tranquility had dissipated, my heart glowed with appreciation.

CHAPTER FORTY-EIGHT

After a few hours had passed, I walked into Mia's room and looked down at the sleeping child, who was holding Mr. Rex. Yes, Rex had made the trip with us. I noticed her eyes open, and I sat down on the bed beside her and ran my hand through her hair. She didn't feel warm, which made me feel better knowing that she wasn't running a fever. Yes, I had turned into my parents and I couldn't feel happier about it.

"How are you feeling?"

"Better," she replied as she tugged at Rex and continued, "I'm sorry I got sick."

"You don't apologize for getting sick, and you never need to apologize for caring so much about less fortunate people."

She lowered her eyes and softly replied, "Thank you."

"It just occurred to me that we need to visit the other Rex living at SeaWorld. After the holidays are over, how about we make an appointment to see him?"

Her eyes opened wide with anticipation, and for a moment the despair of the morning had dissipated.

Later that day, still dressed in her pajamas, Mia was playing chess with Mr. Baker. Catherine and I took the opportunity to jump in her car and drive to Monte Carlo Italian Deli and Restaurant to pick up dinner for the family and dessert for the child.

"So how many cannoli does she get to have?" I jokingly asked Catherine.

"Why don't you decide on that? After all, you had as much of her vomit on you as she had on herself, and not to be too gross, but I'm sure some of the content of that vomit included the five cannoli she ate yesterday."

"How about twenty? I mean, they're really not that big. In fact, they're tiny compared to the cannoli I used to get at Leonard's in the Bronx."

"*She's* tiny, Joe, or have you not noticed that?"

"That's because she runs every morning with her daddy."

"Oh, is that it?" she laughingly asked.

"Okay wiseass, how many do you want to get her?"

"Eighteen. After all, we are going to be here for another day and a half, and the poor baby was sick."

"Eighteen. I could live with that," I remarked as she lovingly punched me in the arm.

"I have a favor to ask of you," she said.

"Okay, and what might that be?"

"I want you to pack up all the awards, citations, the last of your championship rings and everything that has to do with your parents and take them back to the mansion with us when we leave."

"What about the baseball cards?" I asked.

"Don't be such an ass. Especially the baseball cards."

"If it means that much to you, I will gladly allow you to go through all my stuff and pack up whatever you like. It's all in the closet I told you about in my office, except for the cards, which are in my desk. All documents and papers concerning my parents are in a bank vault, so you don't have to worry about any of that."

"You're giving me permission to go through all your stuff?"

"Yes, my lovely wife, I am giving you permission to go through all my stuff. I have nothing to hide from you."

"It had to mean something to you, once upon a time?"

"Of course it did, once upon a time."

"Doesn't your legacy mean anything to you?"

I looked out the passenger's-side window as we passed the Starlight bar, where Lauren used to work. "I would hate to think that my legacy consisted of only my baseball accomplishments."

"I have never heard a bad word said about you, Joe."

"My parents deserve the credit for that. Like you, I was taught to treat everyone with respect and kindness." I looked across at my lovely wife and asked, "Why does it matter so much to you?"

"Because I want our daughter to always have a record of her daddy's accomplishments on and off the field."

"She's already done a comprehensive search of her father on the internet. She reminded me of things I had long ago forgotten about."

"It's not the same, and no one knows that more than you. Look at the effect your parents' wedding pictures had on her. She didn't find those pictures on the internet."

"No, she didn't," I replied as the image of my mother lying dead on the floor of her kitchen, alone, stabbed at my conscience like a knife through my heart. "I don't need to worry about my legacy now that I have Mia and you."

Catherine parked in the parking lot of the restaurant and we walked in and gave our large take-out order to the gentleman at the counter. Catherine and I sat down at a table and had a drink as we waited.

"Do you know what I love most about this place?" I asked.

"That it smells like an Italian deli back in the Bronx," she replied.

"Exactly! You're not only beautiful and intelligent but a mind reader."

She laughed and said, "Joe Ciotola, you could live in California … or for that matter on another planet … for another fifty years and you'll never be mistaken for anything other than a kid from the Bronx."

"And is that such a bad thing?"

"No! It's an absolutely wonderful thing," she said as she reached over and we kissed. The gentleman at the counter called our order and we walked up to the counter where three shopping bags were waiting for us. The gentleman took the cannoli from a display below the counter and put them into two separate boxes, which he put into a fourth shopping bag. He said, "We put two extra cannoli in so you have an even twenty."

Catherine and I started laughing and he asked, "Is everything okay?"

"Yes, everything is wonderful and thank you so much." I paid the bill, left a big tip and we grabbed two bags each and walked out of the restaurant and drove back to the house.

Mia and Mr. Baker were still playing chess when we entered the house with the food and cannoli. I walked over to them while Catherine went into the kitchen with the food. I asked, "Is this the same game you were playing when we left?"

Mia nodded, and Mr. Baker said, "She's quite the competitor."

Whatever suspicions I had about Mr. Baker going easy on Mia were erased as I looked at his contemplative expression. He was a man bent on whipping his opponent, and my little Leonardo wasn't giving an inch. I knew it would take a bit of magic to break their concentration and put the game on hold. I said, "Well if you're hungry we have plenty of food, so you might want to get it while it is hot." That had little to no effect on either of them, but when I mentioned the magic word, *cannoli*, my little Leonardo, who looked extra adorable in her Charlie Brown and Snoopy pajamas, perked up right away. She looked up from the chessboard as her concentration shifted from rooks and kings to a box full of tube-shaped shells piped full of creamy ricotta cheese and smothered in chocolate chips.

Mr. Baker laughed, and not being the type to take advantage of a weakened opponent, he agreed to put the game on hold until after dinner. We walked into the kitchen and my lovely wife had all our dinners laid out for us on the kitchen table. Mia sat down to a bowl of pasta with butter and a side dish of steamed broccoli.

Catherine, quick to notice her child's anxiety, opened a box of cannoli and said, "Eat all your pasta and broccoli, and I'm fairly sure you will be richly rewarded." Sure, it was cruel and unusual punishment, but one cannot live on chocolate alone … or can one?

Mia ate every morsel of her pasta and broccoli and was rewarded with three cannoli, but when my wife turned away, I reached into the box and put two more cannoli on Mia's plate.

"I saw that," my wife remarked.

"Of course you did," I replied.

Catherine looked at Mia and Mia looked at both of us, then at Mr. Baker. Without a word, Mia picked up the two extra cannoli and put them back in the box.

"But they're so small," I said in what must have been a whiny voice, since my wife looked at me like she was going to stuff a cannoli in my mouth just to shut me up. She then reached back into the box and put the two cannoli back on Mia's plate.

"Thank you," Mia said in her softest and most melodic voice.

Catherine shook her head and walked over to the sink as I said to Mia, "Your mommy is a real softie."

Catherine turned to Mr. Baker. "Did you hear that, Daddy? I'm a real softie, according to my husband."

"I wouldn't go there, Joe," Mr. Baker cautioned. "Pretty soon she'll be stopping you from having a cold beer and putting the fear of God in you if you even go near the refrigerator."

"You would stop your loving husband from having a beer?"

"It's not the only thing I will stop you from having if you keep it up."

I stood up and walked over to her and put my arms around her waist and asked, "Did I tell you how very much I love you, today?"

"Yes, you did, on numerous occasions. You even told me that you felt like the luckiest man on Earth to have me."

"Well doesn't that count for something?" I asked as I put my hand on the refrigerator door and she immediately slapped my hand away.

"Wow, that hurt!" I exclaimed as she started to laugh, and I pulled her toward me and we kissed. When my lips were my own again, I quoted Mr. Gehrig's farewell speech from July 4, 1939 ... the most famous speech in baseball history: "Yes, I feel like the luckiest man on the face of the Earth." And we kissed again, and Mia clapped.

***

Catherine and I were left doing the dishes and cleaning up the kitchen. We allowed Mr. Baker and Mia to resume their chess game. After we were finished, we sat down at the kitchen table and I poured Catherine a large glass of white wine and I had a nice ice-cold beer.

From the living room, I heard the whisper of "checkmate," and I asked Catherine, "Did you hear that?"

"No!"

"I think our daughter just beat your daddy."

Catherine started to laugh and said, "Poor Daddy; he takes his chess matches so seriously."

We walked into the living room and I put a beer down in front of Mr. Baker with a frosted mug. "It helps," I assured him as I handed the champion a cannoli on a paper plate.

Later that evening, we all sat on the couch in the living room and looked at *A Charlie Brown Christmas*. All during Linus's speech on the meaning of Christmas, I watched Mia closely. The religious references did not seem to bother her at all as she rested her head comfortably on Catherine's lap. In fact, both my wife and Mia seemed totally engrossed in the show while Mr. Baker looked slightly preoccupied with some other issue … most probably the fact that he was just beaten by a ten-year-old who just learned how to play the game of chess a month ago. He would never admit it, any more than an all-star player striking out against a rookie knuckleball pitcher would ever admit that he was embarrassed.

I had always been a big fan of Chuck, Linus, Snoopy and Schroeder, and I could watch all the shows over and over again and always found myself reading the old comic strips. It's amazing how much we can learn from eight-year-olds.

A few hours later, I checked on Mia, who was asleep in her bed, holding Mr. Rex, and then I walked into my bedroom where my wife was already tucked in, checking her texts and emails. I got into bed, and she put aside her phone. "It didn't turn out to be such a bad day, did it?"

"No! It might have started off rough, but your maternal instincts took over and you made it into a wonderful day."

She turned on her side and I said, "But I have a big problem."

"What's that?" she said, looking alarmed.

"I don't know what to get you for Christmas. Can you give me any ideas?"

"Oh my gosh — don't scare me like that," she said. "Besides, I have everything I could possibly want — a loving husband, a beautiful child and a daddy who seems happier than I have seen him in many years. Have any idea what I might get you?"

"No! Like you, I have everything I want and need. In fact, I have much more than I thought imaginable. I left this house three months ago, got into my car and didn't plan on coming back for a long time, if ever. A few hundred miles into my impromptu trip I stopped off in a town that any reasonable person would have kept on driving past. I picked up a dirty, emaciated child whose age and sex I wasn't even sure of. We stopped in San Diego and checked into a suite at the hotel where I ran into a beautiful, compassionate young lady…"

Catherine was propped up on one elbow, smiling at me and listening.

I stopped suddenly and said, "Well I guess you know the rest of the story. I must have been a really good boy this year because Mr. Claus has filled my stocking with far too many blessings. What are we going to get your dad?"

"Like us, Christmas arrived early for him, even though he might appreciate a book on chess and whatever new strategies they might have come up with recently."

"I guess that leaves Mia and the staff."

"The staff I have already taken care of, little knickknacks from back home and a lot of cash. They're really wonderful."

"And will María's two children come down?"

"Of course, and they will come down to the hospital with us and spend as much time with the children as any of us. They're nothing like my brother and sister, and they're as American as you and me, and really smart."

"I gathered that. MIT and Stanford ... even a dumb jock like me knows those two universities are like the Hall of Fame of higher education."

Catherine laughed and just as quickly became deadly serious and said, "The day will come when my selfish brother and sister will pay dearly. That I will guarantee you. They will pay!"

She sounded like a Mafia hit man. It was a side of Catherine I had never seen before and I knew I had to quickly change the subject before the poisonous venom boiling inside her spilled out any further.

"And I guess that leaves Mia. What are we going to get our little Leonardo?"

"Oh, that's an easy one. A thousand cannoli and other assorted chocolate cakes, pastries and candy ought to do it."

"No broccoli?"

"Oh, there's going to be plenty of broccoli and other vegetables in our lovely child's future, but that can wait until the New Year. Don't want to spoil her first real Christmas."

"That's very sweet of you," I joked.

"Well someone is going to have to be the disciplinarian when it comes to raising our child and it certainly isn't going to be you ... nor my daddy, nor for that matter, María. That little girl has the three of you under her thumb."

"But not you ... not the mother who bought her the most expensive computer, the most expensive cell phone and a wardrobe worth more than the average family spends on food in a year."

"All things that our little Leonardo will need. I expect in a year or two she will be writing her own computer programs and I don't want her working on inferior machines."

"Look out, Bill Gates..."

"That's right, look out Mr. Gates and the rest of you computer nerds."

CHAPTER FORTY-NINE

I woke up at my usual time, put on my running gear and looked across at my beautiful wife. The idea that I was sharing a bed with her still had not sunk in yet, let alone the idea that we were married.

I walked out into the living room and there was Mia with Mr. Rex, sitting on the couch with her laptop open. I looked over her shoulder and saw that she was reading about cancer. I did not bring up the subject of the disease that killed little Stephen. I simply asked, "Are you ready to go running?"

She nodded and got up from the couch, kissed Rex and walked over to me. I zipped up her hoodie and reached down and retied her laces. As I did so, I marveled at the fact that this simple act each morning brought me so much happiness. I held on to the happiness consciously, storing it up for a time later when she wouldn't need my help.

We walked outside and started running. I was no longer setting the pace — she was — and each day we seemed to be running a little faster and a little farther.

After we were finished running, we walked for a few miles. It was another beautiful sunny Southern California morning. We stopped for a moment and she looked up at me and said, "I know one thing I want do when I get a little older. I want to help find a cure for at least one of the many cancers that kill people. That would make me so happy."

I bent down, ran my hand through her lovely hair and said, "Nothing, nothing would make me prouder." I kissed her on her head, and we continued our walk.

CHAPTER FIFTY

I was unceremoniously removed from my office by my wife, who came into the room with a bunch of empty boxes, followed by her assistant, Mia. She threw the closet door wide open and said, "Time to get your daddy's glorious legacy in order and safely stored in a vault." She waved good-bye to me and I wished them both good luck.

I walked out into the living room and asked Mr. Baker if he would like to go for a walk. He eagerly agreed and off we went.

"Don't worry, Joe, your wife has been getting my legacy in order ever since she was a teenager."

"If it makes her happy, she can go through every aspect of my life."

"It's important to her. I often joke with her and tell her she would make a wonderful historian or archivist."

"I imagine some of it has to do with her growing up around baseball people."

"I suppose so," Mr. Baker said reflectively. We walked on for a while without saying a word, and then I asked, "Will your other daughter and son be coming down with their families for Christmas?" I already knew the answer, but I felt compelled to get his side of the story. It all seemed so out of character for a man who cherished family.

"No," he said. After a moment, he continued, "They have their own families and in-laws to deal with. I'll be lucky to speak to my grandchildren on Christmas. In fact, I consider Mia more of a grandchild than my own blood."

"Was there some kind of falling out, if you don't mind me asking?"

"I don't mind one bit, Joe. You're part of our family and there is no reason you shouldn't know. Growing up dirt poor in a rural part of Texas with my parents and two sisters, in what wasn't much bigger than a shack, I always remember the kindness and caring of our neighbors. Whatever food they had, they shared with us. When my father had a heart attack, our neighbor drove over a hundred miles to take him to the nearest hospital. He stayed with him and my mother for a week, and then my father had a second heart attack and died. Our neighbor then drove my mom and her deceased husband back to our home so he could be buried in the backyard. The townspeople collected enough money to buy him a nice coffin. The service in our backyard was attended by at least two hundred people. That was nearly everyone in the town, and all of them brought food — enough to feed my mom, two sisters and me for at least three months."

He stopped speaking for a while as he wiped tears from his eyes. He then continued, "I raised my three children to care for the less fortunate and the sick. I preached it to them and reminded them that they had been born into privilege, and that they had a solemn, lifelong responsibility to help those less fortunate than themselves. My daughter and son didn't understand why they had to spend Christmas Eve and Christmas Day at a hospital, especially when they had their own children, who they felt deserved wonderful memories of the holidays ... not the sight of sick and dying children. They said that they would write the hospital generous checks but weren't going there anymore, especially around the holidays. I reminded them of something President Theodore Roosevelt once said: People don't care how much you know, or how much money you have, until they see through your actions how much you care — I added a few of my own words to the quote but I don't think Mr. Roosevelt would care about that too much.

"The quote fell upon deaf ears and, in turn, I became deaf to their logic and I told them how sad this would make their mother if she was still alive. Since then, I have only spoken to them and my grandchildren on the phone. I don't know if Catherine communicates much with them. I've told her that, regardless of what I might think, she had to remember that they are her siblings and that one day they may need each other. Catherine is very strong-willed, and she doesn't forget or forgive very easily. The situation created a rift in our family and I don't know if it will ever be repaired. Catherine feels like her brother and sister have betrayed everything our family stands for ... that they're selfish, self-centered and uncaring. Like you, Joe, I cannot forget where I came from or the dire circumstances we lived under, and if it wasn't for the caring and generosity of our neighbors and friends, most of whom had little more than we did, I don't know if we would have survived, especially after my father died."

We continued walking. It was a lovely late autumn day, and some of the trees had actually started changing color and shedding their leaves ... a less common sight in Southern California, where the mild temperatures during autumn and winter resembled late spring in most parts of the country. The crunching of leaves under our feet was like music to my ears.

Mr. Baker started to speak again, "In the contracts of all our ballplayers, coaches and executives, we added an appendix that stressed the importance that our family put on getting involved with the community ... visiting hospitals, schools and shelters. Seeing so many of our ballplayers visiting the hospital during the holidays meant more to me than any donation they might make. A child doesn't necessarily understand the importance of donations, but seeing one of their heroes walking through the door of their hospital room and talking to them and signing autographs puts a smile on their little faces that is worth all the money in the world."

I had my suspicions at first about Catherine's real reasons for wanting to help with Mia at the beginning. She was so polished and cultured, always spoke with correct grammar and wore thousand-dollar outfits. I remember doubting whether she'd worked a real day in her life, or ever got her hands dirty with a grueling job. My suspicions quickly faded as I got to know her, and hearing Mr. Baker speak sealed tightly the image I had of my wife as a divine, selfless person. I could not have been prouder to call her my wife and Mia's mom.

The mansion by the sea was a parody, a disguise, and spoke nothing of the owner or his deceased wife, or of Catherine, or María and the rest of the staff. The contents, indeed the soul, of the mansion — the people who lived inside it — were as generous and loving as any people I had ever met.

I would later learn that Mr. Baker bought the mansion and the surrounding property after he heard that the original owner was planning on demolishing the structure before the city council declared it a historic landmark. It was in terrible shape, and the owner did not have the capital to fix it up, and he felt the property, minus the deteriorating mansion, and the removal of restrictions imposed by the city council, was worth more to investors, developers and hotel chains if they could maximize the area and increase the potential market.

Mr. Baker paid a hefty price, and the original owner was more than happy to sell it to him as it stood rather than risk unforeseen problems that could arise at any time with a real estate deal of that size. The sale went through without a problem and Mr. Baker and his wife supervised the renovations without damaging or changing the exterior of the structure. It was declared a historic landmark shortly thereafter with Mr. Baker's blessings.

Upon Mr. Baker's death, the mansion would go to Catherine. It was clearly written in his last will and testament. The tiny mansion that the staff lived in and owned was a gift to them, and the only stipulation was that if they ever decided to sell their property, it would be sold back, at market value, to Catherine.

Mr. Baker might have paid a hefty price for the mansion more than thirty years ago, but that price in today's market would be considered peanuts. The mansion and all that property, easily larger than the new Yankee Stadium, was worth billions.

CHAPTER FIFTY-ONE

After our walk, Mr. Baker and I entered the house and immediately came upon a bunch of boxes that had been piled next to the front door. Each one was labeled "Joe's legacy" and assigned a number. The boxes were sequenced over five-year periods, starting in 1988, when I signed my first minor league contract. That box, clearly visible, was labeled 1988–1993, with the added remark "the dumb-ass jock's beginning."

I looked at my wife and daughter, who greeted us at the door. I pointed to the box with the insulting description and remarked, "I can't imagine our daughter writing such profanity, so I guess that leaves only you."

"Wow! Your intellect has vastly improved since your dumb-ass-jock days. I'm impressed." She laughed as she kissed me and then hugged her father and asked, "And did you have a wonderful walk?"

"Yes, it is quite beautiful out."

"And did you talk a whole bunch about me or Mia?"

"A little bit of each. I see you two young ladies have been very busy."

"Well someone has to protect the dumb-ass's legacy ... and I must say, it's quite an impressive legacy for someone who grew up a Yankees fan."

"Wow, someone is in an awfully good mood," I remarked. "You wouldn't have had a glass or two of wine while we were gone?"

"I've finished one glass and I'm currently working on my second. Jealous, are you?"

"No, not at all. If all it takes is a glass or two of wine to get you to do all my filing and sorting, I'll keep your glass filled all the time."

She threw her arms around me and asked, "Do I look like a secretary?"

"No, you look like the most beautiful, loving and caring woman in the world, and how a dumb-ass like me got so lucky to be married to you is beyond my comprehension."

We kissed, and then I looked down at Mia and asked, "And did you have a glass of wine?"

She shook her head and Catherine replied, "No, she had a large glass of chocolate milk and a cannoli."

"Only one cannoli?"

"Two. Or was it three, Mia?"

Mia put up three fingers and her mommy remarked, "She worked very hard and deserved it … after all, they are tiny." I laughed.

I walked down the hall and into the bedroom and took off my sneakers as I sat on the bed. A moment later, my wife walked into the room holding her second glass of wine. She sat down on the bed beside me and remarked, "We couldn't find any records, awards, citations, trophies or documents for the last five years, except for your World Series ring from three years back. Did you put that part of your legacy somewhere else?"

"I don't know … maybe there wasn't much to hold on to?"

"Seriously Joe, you made the playoffs all five years, going to the World Series twice and winning once, and nothing to show for it but a ring."

"And an enlarged bank account." She glared at me as I took her glass and took a sip of her wine. "I don't know what you want me to tell you."

"The truth, if it doesn't hurt too much."

"I'm fairly certain you know the truth, Catherine."

Catherine looked straight at me and smiled faintly. She took a sip of wine and said, "Because every reward, every citation and every article written about your brilliance was a nightmarish reminder that you weren't there for your mom … or your father."

"That's right. Besides the ring, I discarded it all and I would be extremely thankful if you did not try to dig any of it up."

"If that's your wish … but…"

"I know, sweetheart, my parents would never think of it that way and would be proud of me, but that rationale doesn't work for me anymore. I knew my responsibility at the time was not to baseball but to my parents. The two people who loved me unconditionally and sacrificed so much for me, and I was not there for them at their most vulnerable and worst of times. That's a sin, and no amount of penance is going to make it any different."

"How did you manage to get through these last five years and be so successful with the type of guilt you've been carrying around?"

"I had really good, knowledgeable baseball people working for me. It was my trust in them that allowed our team to be so successful."

"You never did plan on going back?"

"When I first resigned, I thought that I just needed time away from the game, a year or so, to figure everything out. But after all that has happened in my life over the last three months, I really can't imagine ever going back. Mia, you, your dad, María and even Rex at SeaWorld have all allowed me to refocus on what is really important in life … and all of you have contributed to a joy and comfort I have not felt since I was a kid sitting on the couch in my parents' living room, squeezed between my mom and dad and looking at TV … a joy, comfort and intimacy that fifty thousand cheering fans could never give me, that all the accolades in the world could never replace."

Catherine sat silently as she gently reached over and rubbed my neck. I continued, "Instead of thinking about spring training, I am excited, along with your dad, to be tutoring and homeschooling Mia."

"And I'm sure you'll be just as brilliant and dedicated as a teacher as you were at arranging winning baseball teams."

I laughed. "Hopefully, at least until the student becomes the teacher."

"She might be a smart little whippersnapper, but she can learn more from you and Daddy than any schoolteacher could ever teach her."

"Especially if we dangle cannoli and chocolate cake in front of her."

Catherine laughed as she reached over and kissed me passionately on the lips and said, "I love you so much, Joe Ciotola." She got up to leave and I called after her, saying, "Hey, just because I don't want to be employed by any team doesn't mean that I won't be watching every one of your team's games and rooting harder than I did for the Yankees when I was a kid. And never hesitate to ask me anything, because I will be watching carefully."

She smiled and asked, "If you had one word of advice to give to a first-time GM like me, what would it be?"

"Patience," I replied.

"And if I don't have the luxury to be patient?"

"The baseball season is very long. You will have quite a few opportunities to practice patience."

"How about one other word of advice?"

"Trust," I replied.

"How about I go get you an ice-cold beer?"

"Haven't you already done enough for me today?"

"No, going through all your stuff was like going through a treasure chest ... a roadmap on how to be successful and retain every bit of the humanity you were raised to exhibit by your parents." She started to walk toward the door, stopped and turned around and said, "Our daughter could not restrain her curiosity and read a number of letters that you exchanged with your parents. She cried, and so did I."

"I don't remember them being so sad," I remarked.

"They weren't, but the love and tenderness that the three of you showed toward one another was so palpable that it was as though they, and you, were in the room with us."

Catherine walked out of the room.

Later that evening, we all sat on the couch in the living room and once again watched A Charlie Brown Christmas. The only difference was that Mia rested her head on my lap, and during Linus's speech on the meaning of Christmas, I didn't have to look anxiously at her, because after knowing that she read some of the letters exchanged between my parents and me, she had to realize that our God was kind and loving and against all kinds of cruelty. The letters exchanged between my parents and me always included beautiful passages from the Bible and always mentioned the goodness and love we placed in Jesus.

In the morning, Mia and I went for our run, with her pushing me farther still. Back at the house we cleaned up and packed my "legacy" into the car. Catherine pulled out of the driveway, turned onto Moorpark and drove past the Starlight bar and onto the highway.

After about an hour of bumper-to-bumper traffic, the roads finally cleared and we made it back to San Diego in a little over four hours, just as it was getting dark out. Mia had been sleeping in the backseat, with her head resting against Mr. Baker's arm, and as we approached the mansion, Catherine asked her father to gently wake her up. When I asked her why, she said, cryptically, "You'll see."

As we approached the driveway to the estate, I could see a glow through the trees. Mia was rubbing the sleep out of her eyes when we climbed to the top of the driveway and emerged into a winter wonderland the likes of which I had never seen.

Mia and I gaped out of the windows, unsure where to look first. The entire grounds had been transformed into a celebration of Christmas. Both sides of the driveway were blanketed in rolling mounds of fake snow that was as close to the real stuff as I had ever seen. Dancing animatronic snowmen, handsomely dressed, greeted us with wide grins and long carrot noses. Catherine shut the radio off, and Christmas music blaring from hidden speakers filled our ears with the joyous sounds of the season.

The car crawled along at a snail's pace as we took in the scenes of Christmas villages as wide as city streets, populated with life-size mechanical dolls — little girls dressed in ruffled red petticoats and little boys in festival waistcoats — skating across frozen ponds. Then we looked way up to the top of the house and saw the most dazzling sight: On the roof of the mansion, Santa and his eight loyal reindeer were flying through the air in a figure-eight pattern, their sleigh attached to the rails of an electric railroad track.

I turned around and looked at Mia. Her mouth hung open and her mesmerized expression reflected the dormant younger child still very much alive in her ten-year-old body.

"Beautiful, isn't it?" Catherine asked. She was smiling and looking from my face to Mia's face and back, enjoying our amazement.

"Magical," I said, as the child buried inside my fifty-year-old body was exhumed.

"María has been one busy lady. She and her ingenious children were the original architects of this whole magnificent display. The expression on the children's faces when they see it is priceless."

Catherine parked the car in front of the house, where animatronic dogs and cats dressed in Christmas scarfs barked and meowed, "Merry Christmas and Happy New Year!" Henry opened the front door and greeted us, and from the smell of brandy on his breath, it was apparent he had already started celebrating.

María ran out from the kitchen and hugged and kissed Catherine, who immediately started praising her and apologizing. "You did a wonderful job. I'm sorry I wasn't here to help."

"The workers did everything. I just supervised," María said as she bent down and hugged and kissed Mia and asked Mia in Spanish, "Y cómo está mi bebé?"

"Soy maravillosa, María. Te extrañe mucho," Mia replied.

"And I missed you so much, my beautiful child."

The interior of the house was just as elaborately decorated as the outside, with a giant Christmas tree in the grand foyer, hundreds of gifts beneath the tree, and an assortment of animatronic humans, pets, cows, sheep and reindeer scattered all around. Of course, Mr. and Mrs. Claus were there too, at the center of the action.

After we stood there for a while, gaping at the scene and trying to take it all in, Mia and I thought we would carry our luggage upstairs. We walked down the long hallway and I noticed how many of the doors to the unused bedrooms were open. They were all beautifully decorated with Christmas ornaments and figurines, and beside each bed was an IV pole that one would usually see only in hospitals, fitted with bags of fluids and medications. In an instant, it finally became clear to me that the "children with the priceless expressions" that Catherine had just referenced were the children from the pediatric oncology unit of the hospital. The Bakers weren't just rich donors. They were fully involved participants in the lives of these children ... providing not only the real chance at being cured and living long lives but stimulating their imaginations and dreams. The Bakers were putting into action that phrase by the famously good-hearted Cubs shortstop Ernie Banks, who was fond of saying, "When one stops dreaming, one stops living." Catherine and Mr. Baker were not about to let any of the children at the hospital stop living for lack of a dream. If they could not be saved for medical reasons, then that couldn't be prevented, but they would not be left to languish without hope.

We first stopped in Mia's bedroom and I laid down her luggage. She was unusually quiet and I asked, "Is there something wrong, sweetheart?"

She was anxious and her eyes were cast downward. I took her by the hand, and we sat down on the bed. "What is it, angel?"

"I don't have any money to buy gifts," she replied.

"Well it's interesting that you mention that because I was going to ask you if you wanted to go Christmas shopping tomorrow. I figured we would put both our names on all the gifts we buy."

"I still don't have any money to help pay for the gifts."

"But I have plenty of money, and since you and I are a team, I don't see why it matters if you don't have any money."

She looked up at me and threw her arms around me and hugged me tightly. The idea that I'd held until recently — that I would never be a father — had completely dissipated. Not only was I a father but I was the luckiest and the most grateful of all daddies.

Later that evening, Catherine and I placed all of my so-called legacy boxes, which she and Mia had packed, into a vault that was as big as any bank vault. It was fireproof and contained the latest security and alarm systems. I asked her if she could give me the code to the vault in case I needed to retrieve a document, and she started to laugh.

"What's so funny?" I asked.

"There are only two people privy to the code and that's my daddy and me. If you need to retrieve a document, just let one of us know and we will open the vault for you."

"And if neither of you are available?"

"Well then, I guess you're out of luck," she replied.

"Since you won't give me the code, can I at least get a kiss?"

"You can get all the kisses you want, and if you say please, I can close the door and we can get really naughty. Ever do it inside a vault before?"

"No, have you?"

"No, but I'm game if you are, and we can be as noisy as we want because it's soundproof." We started to kiss passionately and just as we started to rip our clothes off, I noticed all the cameras recording us, at every possible angle.

"Stop!" I exclaimed and quickly started to cover her up.

"What is it? Have I become that undesirable already?"

"No, but I prefer not to have our sex life recorded."

She looked at the cameras and started to laugh and remarked, "Wow! I never even thought about that."

We walked out of the vault, and she locked the door and said, "That sucks; that would have been really fun."

"It's not like we can't pick up where we left off in our bedroom."

"But we can't be as noisy," she dejectedly remarked.

Mr. Baker stepped out of his study as Catherine and I were making our way to the bedroom. He called after her, "Catherine, we need to talk and go over our plans so the hospital can make the necessary arrangements with their staff and with the children's parents."

Catherine looked at me and whispered, "Rain check."

"Rain check," I repeated as I kissed her. She turned and walked toward her father. As I walked up the stairs toward our bedroom, I could hear Mr. Baker ask, "I wasn't interrupting anything, I hope?"

"No, Daddy, of course not," I heard my lovely wife reply.

***

I knocked on Mia's bedroom door, which was open, and walked in. She was sitting at her desk with Rex next to her, reading about the many different types of cancers.

"I was hoping I might interest you in taking a walk and looking at all the beautiful decorations?"

She looked up at me with wide eyes and said, "Yes, I would love that." She saved the material she was reading and put on a jacket that I helped her zip up, and then I bent down and retied her loose sneaker laces.

We walked out the front door and were greeted by the mechanical dogs and cats wishing us a Merry Christmas and a Happy New Year. Naturally, Mia petted each one and giggled, her face aglow with a twinkle in her eyes. With her locks of hair perfectly framing her lovely face, she could easily have been mistaken for one of the Christmas dolls.

I took her hand and we walked through the Christmas villages, and for the first time in years, I could say that I honestly felt the joy of the season ... through the eyes of a child.

Afterward, we sat down on our favorite bench that looked out over the ocean, and whereas I had never equated the beach with Christmas, that would forever change from this day forward. I guess there was a certain truth to the saying that you could carry the spirit of Christmas wherever you might be if you so desired. The sky above was eclipsed with what seemed to be a billion stars and a crescent moon, or as my little Leonardo informed me, what astronomers called a *waning moon* ... the final phase in the twenty-nine-day lunar cycle, in which the moon got smaller and smaller, and less visible in the sky.

María suddenly surprised us as she sat down on the bench next to Mia and ran her hand lovingly through Mia's hair and remarked, "Te he estado buscando, mi hermoso ángel. Tengo una sorpresa esperándote en la cocina."

"Gracias, María," Mia replied as she hugged María and kept her head nestled against her breast.

María looked at me and said, "A chocolate soufflé for your beautiful daughter."

"Thank you, María." I understood Spanish quite well after spending so many years down in Central America, but I still wasn't confident when it came to speaking the language.

Mia's intellect greatly surprised me, and her beauty was staggering. But the most shocking thing about this precocious child was the affection she showed toward others and which she enjoyed in return. I would have thought that, having lived under the conditions in which I found her, she would have been suspicious of everyone ... distant and guarded like a soldier fighting a tense war in an impenetrable jungle.

It was as though she had an animal instinct that allowed her to distinguish between good and threatening individuals. María wore a crucifix around her neck that lay against her chest and was quite visible. Mia's head was buried just below the crucifix and it did not seem to upset her at all.

"Your daughter and son will be here soon?"

"Sí, señor Joe. Estoy muy emocionado!"

"Debes de estar orgulloso," I remarked.

"Si, muy orgulloso!"

Mia turned and looked at me and asked in Spanish, "Tú hablas español?"

"Yes, sweetheart, your stupid father speaks some Spanish. I did spend a very long time in Spanish-speaking countries."

"No, no le hagas caso a tu papi. Él no es estúpido, es brillante."

"Si, muy brillante," Mia agreed.

"Me siento muy bendecida por el trato maravilloso del Sr. Baker y su familia conmigo," María remarked as she kissed the crucifix.

"And they have been very blessed to have you and your family," I said. "And Mia and I feel very blessed to have you as part of our family."

"Muchas gracias."

María stood up and kissed Mia all over, on her head, forehead and face. She then started to leave as Mia said, "Te quiero mucho, María."

"And I love you mucho, mi pequeña angel."

María turned and walked toward her house as Mia remarked, "Ella es tan dulce."

"Yes, she is very sweet, my little angel."

I took her by the hand and we walked back into the house. Catherine and Mr. Baker were still in the study as we started to quietly walk up the stairs. Mia suddenly stopped and asked if we could go to the kitchen first. The idea that she could forget about the chocolate delight that María left for her would be unthinkable. We walked back into the kitchen and we both sat down as I watched her eat the chocolate soufflé with a glass of chocolate milk. I took a bite of the soufflé and it was simply delicious.

Mia, after eating every last morsel of the dessert, walked over to the sink, washed and dried the plate and put it back into the cabinet beside the sink. She then found a pen and pad on the counter and sat down to write María a thank-you note, in Spanish, which she then left on the table.

We walked out of the kitchen and quietly made our way past the study and up the staircase to our bedrooms. I waited for Mia to put on her pajamas and brush her teeth, and then I tucked her and Rex into bed.

I walked into my bedroom, changed into my sleeping clothes, brushed my teeth and lay down on the bed. I was exhausted. I closed my eyes and quickly fell asleep, and before I knew it, I was back in the batter's box, looking down at Mr. Koufax. I tightened my grip on my bat as I felt beads of sweat running down my face. I thought to myself, *I've been here before and I better get ready to duck or get killed.*

Sandy went into his famous high-kicking windup and long forward stretch and released a pitch that I wasn't even sure I saw, and before I could react, I could hear the pop of the ball in the catcher's mitt and the home-plate umpire calling me out. I walked back to the dugout with my head held high. After all, striking out against Mr. Koufax was as natural as breathing and it sure as hell beat getting beaned in the head.

I woke up at my usual time, and whereas facing Mr. Koufax could be nightmarish, waking up next to my wife was heavenly. I put on my running gear and walked down to the kitchen where Mia was talking to María. I zipped up her hoodie, retied her loose laces and off we went for our run.

After returning to the mansion, we went to visit the mommy in the gym. She was running on a treadmill while listening to music on her iPod. She removed her earphones and asked, "And did my two marathoners have a good run?"

"Yes, quite chilly outside but after a few miles we warmed up."

"Maybe you should try running on the treadmills."

"I don't think so," I replied as I looked down at Mia who shook her head.

"After breakfast, we'll be going Christmas shopping," I said.

"Am I invited, or is this just another daddy and daughter thing?"

"Well we were possibly thinking of buying you a gift or two. After all, you've been pretty good."

"I told you, I don't want anything. I already got the two best Christmas gifts I could ever want and I'm looking at both of them right now. Besides, you don't have a clue what to buy for a girl. Surely, you haven't forgotten our first shopping trip?"

"How could I? I kind of consider it our first date."

"Yes, and your contribution was a pair of Charlie Brown and Snoopy pajamas."

"And she is still wearing them," I remarked as I winked at Mia.

"Okay, I'll give you that one, but just for the record, do you even have a clue what you might buy me?"

"Well I was thinking of an oversize sweatshirt. The type you like wearing around the house … with a large New York Yankees logo across the front and back."

She started to laugh and asked, "Surely, you're joking?"

"You mean you wouldn't wear it if I, your husband, gave it to you?"

"I would rather wear a soiled diaper," she replied.

"Wow! That's nasty."

"How about if I get you an oversize sweatshirt with the words *dumb-ass jock* printed across it?"

"I'll wear it, especially if it was from you ... with love."

She shook her head and got off the treadmill and I whispered in her ear, "By the way, is there an expiration date on that rain check?"

She laughed. "Keep it up and I'll have you wishing you never noticed those cameras in the vault. At least that way you would have a recording of the last time we were ever intimate."

"That's cruel," I replied.

"Well I can be quite cruel if the circumstances call for it. Just ask my daddy."

I decided against asking her father, and kept my fingers crossed that the "cruel gene" did not manifest itself too much during the upcoming baseball season.

Catherine came along on our shopping trip, and thank goodness she did because I was totally lost. I told her about Mia's concern about having no money and she handled the whole situation as though she knew about it in advance. She asked me for my credit card and handed it to Mia and told her to hold on to it since she was certain that she and her daddy would be giving out their gifts as daddy and daughter, the same way Catherine and her daddy did.

They grabbed a shopping cart and went off on their own as I sat down in a chair and watched all the Christmas shoppers pass by. About an hour later, the two girls pulled up beside me with a cart filled to the top with gifts. "Wow! That didn't take long. What did you do, just grab everything you came across?"

"No, but I imagine that's what you would have done after a couple of hours of not being able to decide on anything." I started to stand up and Catherine playfully pushed me back into the chair and remarked, "You're a lot more useful just sitting there."

"If you insist."

"I insist," my loving and beautiful wife replied as she and Mia walked over to a cash register to check out. I kept a close eye on both of them, and when it came time to pay, Catherine looked at Mia and said, "You're paying; you have the card."

Mia pulled out my credit card and slid it into the machine like a real professional and then was instructed by her mom to forge my name, which she did. Mia put the receipt and the card back in her pocket as my wife called me over and said, "Don't be totally useless; come over here and grab the bags."

I did as I was instructed and was more than happy to do so.

CHAPTER FIFTY-TWO

The Christmas party for the children at the mansion was scheduled for December 22, but the days leading up to the party were hectic. Pediatric Oncology had its own set of rules, and it was very important to Mr. Baker and Catherine that every child be made to feel special and unique. It was not only the children currently undergoing treatment at the hospital — the inpatient children — but also all the outpatient children who were invited, including all those from the last three years who had been declared cancer-free and who were now back at home, living normal lives. Getting all of this together required consent forms signed by the parents of all the children, and if a child wanted to stay overnight, with or without their parent, as everyone was invited to do, the parent had to agree and sign other forms.

The outpatient children and those who were cancer-free and living normal lives usually went back home once the party was over. The inpatient children were the ones who usually stayed overnight. Catherine told me it made her very happy that those children stayed over instead of going back to the hospital because no matter how cheerful they tried to make the hospital for the children, it was still a hospital. The mansion was more like Disneyland. Nurses and two doctors from the hospital volunteered to monitor the children throughout the party and most of the nurses and one doctor would be staying overnight to keep an eye on their patients. Two ambulances would be parked right outside the mansion, and the paramedics were welcome to join the celebration.

Henry was going to play Santa Claus, and Catherine warned him that she had better not smell alcohol on his breath. Exactly what she planned on doing if she did smell booze was hard to say. It was the only time I ever saw Catherine come down hard on any of the staff. After living at the mansion for nearly three months I still wasn't sure what Henry did, besides occasionally opening the front door, drinking Mr. Baker's hundred-year-old cognac, and playing chess with Mr. Baker when Mia wasn't available. Mr. Baker and Henry had been friends for nearly fifty years, and if nothing else, Mr. Baker was very loyal. I once asked María if she knew what Henry's responsibilities were and she simply rolled her eyes and remarked, "La mascota — el perro de la familia. The family dog, señor Joe."

María's two children arrived on December 20 and everyone joyfully greeted them. Her daughter, Victoria, was gorgeous and as polished and refined as Catherine. She spoke with a distinctly Southern California dialect, as did her brother, Alberto. They were both born in America, and yet in a strange way they highlighted, for me, the contrast between the many Latino ballplayers playing in the major leagues — athletes who came to the United States with little education and less money but who excelled in the sport and made millions of dollars and were idolized by millions of fans — and the well-educated Latinos who would go on to become college professors, scientists, artists and politicians.

I watched as Victoria hugged Mia and spoke to her like they were going to be best friends, if they weren't already.

"And so, you are the beautiful angel my mama can't stop talking about," Victoria said. "I've tried to tell her that angels can only be found in Heaven, but now I see that I'm wrong. You're simply adorable."

Mia blushed and smiled up at Victoria, who was still holding on to her and beaming at her warmly.

"You know," Victoria continued, "my mama told me something else too. She said you want to find a cure for at least one of the many different types of cancer. Well that's also what I want to do, and I think if we work together, we might just find a cure for all the cancers. Would you like to work with me and make that dream come true?"

Mia's face lit up and she replied, "I would love that, Victoria."

"And together we will show the world what two dedicated women can do to make it a happier place for everyone." Victoria raised her palm and a smiling, excited Mia reached up and gave her a solid high five.

Alberto had been watching from a couple of feet away and moved closer now. "Hey, what's going on here?" he teased. "Mama promised me that she was going to help me write computer programs and you're already trying to steal her away. Wow! Talk about backstabbing."

"Don't listen to my brother, Mia. He's what we affectionately call a computer geek ... a little too much gaming has severely compromised his ability to think rationally."

Alberto looked at his sister and laughingly remarked, "This here geek can still kick your butt any day on a basketball court."

"Yeah, on a basketball court set up on your computer, but not out there in the real world."

Catherine interrupted and remarked, "You should know better than to get into a debate with your sister, Alberto."

"You're right, but it's occasionally worth a try."

Catherine moved in to break up the mock fight and wrapped her arms around Alberto for a big hug. "Welcome home, computer geek. We've missed you."

"I missed you too," Alberto replied.

As I watched this loving scene unfold, I couldn't help thinking that Victoria and Alberto were like living emblems of the American Dream. I had heard from Catherine and María that they were proud of their heritage, but at the same time they were clearly on a path to contribute mightily to American society and to benefit all mankind. They were the examples I wished the Latino ballplayers would tell their children to admire and emulate. Great ballplayers are not like racehorses, and their offspring are seldom, if ever, born with the great instincts and athletic abilities of their parents. Providing and encouraging your children to continue their education opens the door to a world of possibilities and realistic opportunities that a baseball field or a basketball court or a football field can never provide. For every minor league player who makes it to the majors, there are a thousand talented and hardworking players who don't.

As I thought about all of this, I realized that I would never discourage children from playing sports. In fact, athletics were very important for teaching kids about teamwork, helping them forge lifelong friendships and learn how to trust in each other, and getting them working as a unit toward a common goal. In that sense, sport mirrored life. Scientific, medical and technological advances and discoveries were usually the by-products of collaboration and teamwork. Even the great Leonardo da Vinci embraced the concept of collaboration and teamwork both in his artistic endeavors and in his scientific discoveries.

For many children, especially youngsters from the inner cities and first-generation immigrants, sports were a way out. They walked onto a basketball court and they dreamed of being the next Michael Jordan or LeBron James, but for ninety-nine percent of those kids, that was exactly where their dream ended ... on a concrete outdoor basketball court in the inner city with one overhead streetlight providing enough light to play well into the night.

I was no different, and my parents were my biggest cheerleaders, yet the refrain I heard the most from my parents was how important an education was, and when I received a college scholarship to play baseball, the choice was made for me. The offer to sign a minor league contract straight out of high school was immediately rejected by my parents, and to be totally honest, I was not thrilled at the time with their decision, but as my father said, "If you're good enough to play in the major leagues, the scouts will notice you just as quickly playing on your college team, and at the same time you will have a college degree to fall back on."

They were right, and after graduating from college I signed a better offer than the one originally offered to me straight out of high school, with a minor league team affiliated with a big league team. When my major league career fizzled out rather quickly, instead of going back down to the minor leagues, I got a job in the front office. That was mainly thanks to my college degree. As I watched Victoria's and Alberto's polished interactions with everyone at the house, my mind was overtaken by a jumble of memories. I thought about my parents' loving attempts to guide my own career, about the many ballplayers that I had recruited over the years and their children. I hoped that the ballplayers that I had brought to this country took full advantage of their time here, and that any children they had in this country were being guided to get the best education that their families could afford.

***

Just as it was getting dark outside, the bus carrying the children, their parents, nurses, and doctors from the hospital pulled into the driveway of the mansion. The driver slowed to a crawl as he made his way along the driveway to the house to give the passengers a good look at all the decorations, displays and magic of the season. I stood at the front door and watched as my wife and Victoria, dressed as elves, and Mia, dressed as a fairy, greeted the children as they disembarked from the bus. It was like my wife said: The expressions on their faces were wondrous and joyous — masking, and at times even erasing, if only temporarily, the pain and suffering that so unjustly afflicted them. I turned and walked along the front porch to see the kids arriving, and without warning, as I looked at their faces, tears began streaming down my own. Many of the children were bald from chemotherapy and radiation treatments, while others looked as gaunt and unwell as Mia had looked during those first few weeks after our escape from the town of Salvation. Still others reminded me of little Stephen as they walked or rode wheelchairs up to the house wearing baseball hats and sweatshirts printed with Catherine's team logo.

Suddenly María was there. She touched me on the shoulder and asked, "What's wrong, Mr. Joe?"

I struggled to get control, looking up at the ever-expanding universe and outward at the mysterious, riddled ocean, and shook my head and replied, "At times, life just seems so unfair."

"Si, and that is why God gives us men like Mr. Baker and his family so that they can ease the pain and make it less unjust."

"You're right," I said. "Thank you. I am better now. This is no time for tears. These kids are here to have a wonderful time."

María and I followed the children into the house, and she took me by the hand and led me into the kitchen. She opened the refrigerator and took out an ice-cold beer, which she poured into a chilled mug for me. The Christmas music was blasting and yet we were still able to hear the laugher of the children, the parents and the nurses.

"Have you ever heard such wonderful sounds, Mr. Joe?"

I looked at María, who picked up a video camera, and I replied, "No, señorita María. La risa de los niños es el más bello sonido."

"Si, the laughter takes away the pain and helps with the healing."

We walked out of the kitchen and into the joyous celebration. María was in charge of videotaping and I watched as she pointed her camera directly across at Mr. Baker, whose expression was one of true joy. Just then, I remembered what he said in response to a reporter's question about why he didn't increase his payroll and go after high-priced free agents. He replied that he would rather spend his money helping and hopefully curing cancer so that all children would one day have a chance to play baseball.

***

The two elves, Catherine and Victoria, handed Santa Claus three gifts personally addressed to each child. The beautiful fairy, Mia, helped each child set up their new iPad tablets. After all, what child should go without some sort of computer device? That would be cruel and unusual punishment. The other two gifts consisted of a combination of sports attire, computer games, beautiful electronic dolls, music boxes, stuffed animals and cool-looking sneakers.

The children rushed to open their gifts, and in no time the place was covered in a sea of discarded wrapping paper. María moved deftly around the children with her camera, capturing the joy and magic of the moment. I must admit Henry played a good Santa and the children really enjoyed his "Ho Ho Ho!" When I mentioned to María how well Henry did playing Mr. Claus, she replied, "That's because he had the wolf breathing down his neck." The "wolf" in question was currently dressed as an elf and had the name Catherine.

The party disbanded around nine o'clock when the outpatient and cancer-free patients boarded the bus with their parents, most of the nurses and one of the doctors. They were driven back to the hospital where most of them had left their cars.

Ten children, each with at least one parent, and a couple of nurses and one doctor stayed overnight. Thankfully, there were no complications, and long past midnight I could hear the children playing with their gifts, and the melodic, soft voice of my little Leonardo patiently helping the children with their new devices and at the same time playing with them.

I found Catherine in our bedroom taking off her elf outfit and I asked, "Seriously Catherine, you're taking off your outfit without asking permission from me?"

She looked at me and with a wicked smile replied, "I never would have thought you were into elves."

"I'm usually not, unless they go by the name of Catherine Baker. The most beautiful wife ... slash ... elf in the world."

I walked up to her and put my arms around her waist and said, "You were wonderful tonight."

"Thank you, sir, and you weren't so bad yourself."

"I didn't do too much, except pick up wrapping paper."

"It was your first time."

"It was Mia's first time and she's still going strong."

"That's because she's young and energetic and powered by enough chocolate and sugar to run two marathons."

"And is that your excuse?"

"You don't see me still out there," she replied.

"But you're young and energetic and powered by a source that only a goddess possesses."

She laughed hysterically and then replied, "Wow! You really are trying to cash in on that rain check."

"Do you blame me? It's only once a year that I'm going to catch you in that elf's outfit."

"There's Christmas Eve and Christmas at the hospital. I'll be wearing the same outfit. Should I expect the baseball wizard to turn into a stud? After all, there's only so much a goddess's body can handle."

"Oh, I'm sure the goddess could handle an old stud like me."

"I'm not so sure. I've seen that old stud in action and there seems to be plenty of kick still left in him."

"Really? Are you sure you haven't been cheating on me with some other stud?"

"I'm fairly certain," she replied with a laugh and then pushed me onto the bed and crawled on top with only her cute little elf hat on.

CHAPTER FIFTY-THREE

The following morning, I got up at my usual time, looked at my beautiful wife, who was still asleep, and put on my running gear. I went out into the hallway and found it relatively quiet, with the bedroom doors partially opened where the children and their parents were sleeping. I walked over to Mia's room and naturally she was at her computer, with Rex beside her.

I asked, "Sweetheart, have you been asleep?"

"Yes," she replied as she kept reading an article on childhood cancers.

"Well why don't you skip running today?"

"No, I'm fine, Daddy." She turned around and I bent down and retied her laces and pulled up the zipper on her hoodie. We walked down the staircase, and standing beside the tree was María, talking to a nurse in Spanish. We waved at them and headed toward the front door. I was starting to believe that both María and Mia were powered by chocolate and sugar, and that neither of them needed sleep.

We walked outside and were greeted by the dogs and cats wishing us a Merry Christmas and a Happy New Year. Mia bent down and petted a few of them and looked up at me and smiled. We walked past two ambulances parked just outside the front of the house and Mia looked intently at them. We then continued walking down toward the beach and she suddenly remarked, "I am going to work hard at finding a cure for cancer … really hard."

I looked down at her and not for a moment did I doubt her sincerity. Nor did I doubt that if anyone was going to find a cure it might very well be her.

After we finished our run, which was getting longer every day, we cleaned up and went down to the dining area where a big table was set up, and where the children, their parents, the nurses, the doctor, Catherine, Victoria, Alberto, Mr. Baker and the entire staff were sitting eating breakfast, which was catered by a local company that Mr. Baker had hired. Mia and I sat down next to Catherine and placed our orders.

A few hours later, the children, carrying all their presents, got onto the bus that the hospital had sent back. But they were not allowed to leave until Mia had hugged every last child, being very careful not to dislodge any of the implanted ports that were placed in the children and through which the chemotherapy was administrated into their little bodies.

The bus drove off and we all waved good-bye, and then Mia turned and hugged me and wouldn't let go as I felt her tears pass through my shirt and anoint my skin.

CHAPTER FIFTY-FOUR

That evening the family and the entire staff gathered in the dining room for what would be our Christmas dinner. Since we would be spending most of Christmas Eve and Christmas Day at the hospital and visiting shelters, December 23 was in a sense the day we celebrated Christmas. Altogether there were nearly twenty of us and we sat around one big table, like at breakfast, and the same local company that had catered breakfast also catered dinner. Just as we sat down, my cell phone, which I had placed on vibrate, went off and as I glanced down at the display, I saw the call was from Theresa, the social worker.

I took Catherine by the hand, excused us and walked out of the dining room. I answered the call and Theresa said, "I have wonderful news." I told her that I was going to put her on speaker so that Catherine could hear. I turned the phone on speaker, and Theresa continued, "Like I was just telling your husband, I have wonderful news. The judge, just before leaving for Christmas recess, approved your adoption request. Mia is officially yours, and your lawyer and my office will be sending you official copies of the approved adoption. Congratulations!"

Catherine's mouth was hanging open and she looked from me to the phone and back to me, unable to speak. She started to cry as she threw her arms around me, then she finally spoke into the phone, saying, "That is the best Christmas gift we could ever have hoped to receive. I don't know how to thank you enough, Theresa."

"Yes, Theresa, I'm all choked up but thank you so very much. Thank you."

"I am so very happy for all of you … so very happy," Theresa remarked as I could hear her choking up a little over the phone.

"Theresa," I said, "Can you do one more thing for us? If I keep you on speaker, can you tell the rest of the family and Mia the great news? Everyone is gathered around the dining room table now, and it would be perfect."

"I would love to," she replied.

Catherine and I walked back into the dining room and I said, "If you can all give us your attention for a moment, a very dear and loving friend has some great news to share with all of you." I placed the phone on the table and put the volume on high. "Go right ahead, Theresa."

"Hello, everyone. Merry Christmas and Happy New Year. Like I just told Catherine and Joe, the judge overseeing Mia's case just approved the adoption. She is officially part of your family. Congratulations!"

There was a collective sigh and then clapping as a great cheer went up. My wife hugged her dad and they were both crying. I picked up the phone, turned it off speaker, took Mia by the hand and walked out of the dining room. "Theresa, I have a beautiful little girl who wants to say a few words to you."

I handed the phone to Mia and she said, "Hello, Theresa…"

For the next fifteen minutes Mia told her all that she had been doing — helping the children suffering from cancer, learning how to play chess and speak Spanish — and how one day she was going to help find a cure for cancer so that no children would ever have to suffer from it again. After she was finished, she handed the phone back to me and I asked, "Are you going back to the Bronx to spend the holidays with your family?"

"I'm afraid not. It's just not in my budget. They understand."

"That's what my parents used to tell me every time I couldn't make it home for a special occasion. Are you working during the holidays?"

"No, I'm off until after the new year. Time to catch up on some paperwork."

"Is it okay if I call you back in fifteen minutes?"

"Of course," she replied.

"In the meantime, why don't you start packing?" I hung up and called the airlines and got her a round-trip first-class ticket to New

York. I then called up a limousine service I'd used many times and gave them her address and all the information they needed and asked my favorite driver to pick her up in an hour. Finally, I transferred five thousand dollars into a PayPal account under her name.

As soon as the arrangements were made, I called her back and told her that there was a round-trip first-class ticket waiting for her at Delta airlines, leaving at ten tonight and flying into LaGuardia, which was the closest airport to the Bronx, and that there would be a limo outside her apartment in approximately one hour and there was five thousand dollars in her PayPal account to use as she pleased.

She immediately refused and said, "I'm not allowed to accept gifts like that from you."

"Who said they were from me or my wife or her family? I told this rich little girl about your situation and she insisted on doing all this, and there was no way I could talk her out of it. She's an insistent little thing."

"I don't know what to say."

"There's nothing to say, Theresa. Once upon a time, like I told you before, my parents would always say they understood when I couldn't make it home for the holidays or big occasions. Now that they have both passed away, there's not a day that goes by that I don't regret not making it home. I don't want you ever to carry that kind of guilt around with you. Merry Christmas and Happy New Year and thank you so much." I handed the phone back to Mia and she said, "I love you so much, Theresa. Merry Christmas to you and your mommy and daddy."

Mia handed me the phone and we walked back into the dining room and sat down with the rest of the family. Mr. Baker asked, "Would anyone like to say grace and give thanks to God for all that we have?"

Mia raised her hand and replied, "I would, Mr. Baker." She bowed her head and made the sign of the cross and in Spanish said, "Bendícenos, Señor, y estos, tus dones, que estamos a punto de recibir de tu generosidad. Por Cristo, nuestro Señor, amén. Gracias."

I reached over and kissed my little Leonardo on the head and then her mother hugged and kissed her more times than I could count. Everyone else seated at the table looked across at the child; a few, like María, had tears rolling down their cheeks, but most had expressions of pure joy and happiness. Mr. Baker raised his wineglass and exclaimed, "Feliz Navidad! Merry Christmas!" And with that, everyone dug in and enjoyed the feast.

Christmas Eve and Christmas were spent at the hospital, homeless shelters, and homes for battered women and their children. Mr. Baker played Mr. Claus both days, with Catherine and Victoria playing elves, and Mia playing the helpful fairy.

On Christmas Eve, I called Lauren up to wish her Merry Christmas and she sounded so happy, and I could hear her children playing and laughing in the background. She sounded like the Lauren I had met years ago, before she married her ex-husband. I asked her what she had planned for Christmas and she said that Rick, my lawyer, was coming over for dinner. Apparently, she and Rick had been seeing each other since shortly after her divorce, a little fact that he forgot to tell me when I called him up to thank him for everything he did to get the adoption on the fast track and quickly finalized. That was truly wonderful news because, if nothing else, I knew he was handsomely employed and a really good guy.

CHAPTER FIFTY-FIVE

The day after Christmas, the staff and the entire family went to SeaWorld to visit the one and only Rex. We all took the backstage tour, and Mr. Rex greeted his fan club with a festive cry that had me believing that he knew what day it was and exactly who was there to see him. Mia, Catherine, Victoria and María were all over the handsome little guy, taking turns hugging and kissing the star. I felt a little jealous. He had two beautiful girls on each wing, which he occasionally flapped, spraying everyone with water. I doubt George Clooney was ever draped in so many beautiful girls all at once.

After the first tour was over, Mr. Baker and the rest of the staff took a stroll around the park to look at other exhibits. The four beautiful girls and I went on the second backstage tour to visit the one and only Rex once again. He was definitively a chick magnet. There was no denying that.

We left the park just as it was closing and we all climbed into Catherine's SUV, which accommodated us easily. The smell of fish was heavy in the air and we drove with the windows half down, even though it was quite chilly outside. Catherine parked in the driveway of the Italian restaurant she had introduced Mia and I to after our first family visit to see Rex.

We walked into the restaurant, fifteen of us in all, and the manager put together four tables so we could all sit together. We ordered five pizza pies, garlic rolls and four bottles of Chianti. Mia had her usual — noodles with butter — and her mother thankfully did not force any broccoli on her. Afterward, we ordered a variety of desserts, including tiramisu, cannoli, zeppole and cassata. Naturally,

Mia got four cannoli for herself and a glass of chocolate milk, and Catherine ordered two dozen cannoli to go. I whispered into her ear, "I see you're still carrying that Christmas spirit around."

"They're small and she deserves it. Surely, you don't think I am going to let you do all the spoiling. And for the record, I try to carry the spirit of Christmas with me all year long."

"Does that mean you're not putting the elf outfit away?"

She kicked me under the table and asked, "Does that answer your question?" I looked at her and nodded, and she laughed.

CHAPTER FIFTY-SIX

I lay sideways on the bed, looking up at the ceiling, as Catherine walked out of the bathroom after just having taken a shower. She sat down on the edge of the bed next to me and asked, "A penny for your thoughts."

"That's kind of cheap. Is that all my thoughts and ideas are worth?" I jokingly asked.

"For the most part, yeah," she replied with a laugh as she lay down beside me.

"I was just thinking what a wonderful, productive time I have had this Christmas, even if my lovely wife discarded my gift."

"I still can't believe you went out and bought me that Yankees sweatshirt after everything I told you."

"Hey, it's not like you are the easiest girl in the world to shop for. Did you really throw it out?"

"No! I hung it up in the very back of my closet. After all, it was our first Christmas together and even though it was a terrible gift it did come from the best husband in the world. Besides, the other gift you gave me was the best gift of all."

"And what was that?"

"Mia, you dumb-ass."

"I didn't realize that Mia was a gift from me to you. I thought she was a gift to both of us."

"But if it wasn't for you, there would be no Mia in my life."

"And I would probably still be trying to figure out what to buy for a ten-year-old girl."

"You were like a fish out of water that first day we went shopping, but then…" She suddenly stopped talking and took my hand. "You saved a little girl, a precious, loving, caring little girl, and for that you can give me all the Yankees sweatshirts you want, and whereas I won't wear them, I will always keep them."

"Hanging in the back of your closet?" I asked.

"In the very, very back of my closet," she replied with a laugh.

"Taking our lovely daughter away from that town was simply the right thing to do. It's what you would have done, and your father and mommy, María and Victoria and probably even Henry."

"Okay, Henry? That is really pushing the envelope."

I laughed as I squeezed her hand a little tighter and remarked, "On Christmas Eve, at the hospital, I talked to Mr. Castello, the pitching coach in charge of the two prospects."

"Yes, I saw you. It was very nice of him to come."

"He told me that he has already started working with the kids and is quite impressed. I had no idea they were even down here."

"We arranged for them to come down here shortly after the trade was made. We put them up in a hotel next to the ballpark, and Mr. Castello has had a few training sessions with them a few times each week ... nothing too strenuous. Why do you seem so surprised?"

"I'm not. I was just a little surprised that you didn't mention it to me ... that's all."

"I'm simply respecting your wishes. I know, especially after our talk in your home back in Studio City, that you want as little to do with baseball as possible."

"That's true, but you're my wife, and my grievances with baseball and the poor personal decisions I have made are two different things. I want you to succeed more than anything and I will do anything in my power to help you be successful."

"I know that, Joe, but I'm not going to bother you with simple decisions like bringing those two kids down here early and not waiting for spring training. I'm fairly certain that if the situation was reversed you would have done the same thing."

"You're right, and it really has nothing to do with the kids or with your team. It really has to do with the conversation I had with Mr. Castello about growing up in the Bronx."

"I didn't realize he was also from the Bronx," Catherine said.

"From the Sound View area of the Bronx, about six or seven miles from where I grew up. He went to James Monroe High School, the same school as the Mets' first baseman and great pinch hitter, Ed Kranepool. You're way too young to remember him."

"He was part of the 1969 Miracle Mets team that won the World Series in five games against the heavily favored Baltimore Orioles."

I looked at her and remarked, "You know, nobody likes a show-off."

"So it's showing off when I display my knowledge about the history of the game, but not when you do it? Wow! I never thought of you as a sexist. I might seriously have to think about you homeschooling our little Leonardo. You might decide she'd be better off if she learned how to knit and sew and attend to her husband's every need and desire."

"Have you ever been spanked?" I asked.

"No! Why? Are you into that?"

"No, I'm not into that. Where I come from any guy who hits a woman is considered a real coward, but in your case that might not be so true." I playfully slapped her across the side of her butt.

"Wow! Now I'm really turned on," she jokingly remarked as I looked down at her smiling, beautiful face.

"Okay, back to my story. Mr. Castello told me that when he was just a child he remembers sitting in the living room in their small Bronx apartment and listening to his parents, aunts and uncles tell stories about the great Joe DiMaggio. Back then, as a child, the game of baseball was magical to him, and one day he wanted to grow up to be just like the great Joe D."

Without missing a beat, Catherine quoted from Hemingway's classic novel, *The Old Man and the Sea*: "'I would like to take the great DiMaggio fishing,' the old man said. 'They say his father was a fisherman. Maybe he was as poor as we are and would understand.'"

"Marvelous," I said, really impressed now.

"It's one of the few quotes about a Yankee that doesn't make me sick," Catherine said.

"Well I'll take it," I said. "And I told Mr. Castello that my parents used to talk about Mickey Mantle like that when I was a child, and that one day I wanted to grow up to be just like him. That's when waking up in the morning and opening the newspaper and looking down at the box scores and seeing that my favorite player hit a home run or went three for four would make my day. No amount of World Series rings or playoff appearances or being on the cover of *Sports Illustrated* could replace that magic. The media has gotten so big, highlighting every fault on and off the field, and players' egos ... and agents' greed ... are so out of proportion to the daily struggle of working-class families, that I wonder if the children of today could ever feel the same magic for the game that Mr. Castello and I felt growing up."

Catherine was silent for a long time and then asked, "If our daughter decided that she wanted to follow in her parents' footsteps and enter the world of baseball, would that greatly disappoint you? Would you try to stop her?"

"How could I in good conscience stop her? Three of the four people that have had a major and positive impact on her life since I took her away from that town have been heavily involved in the game, at the highest level. I don't think she associates anything negative with the game, at least not yet. It's still Charlie Brown and Snoopy to her."

"But you would be disappointed?" she asked as I looked straight up at the ceiling and shook my head. We heard a knock on the open bedroom door. Catherine and I immediately sat up and saw Mia dressed in her Peanuts pajamas.

"What is it, sweetheart?"

Mia walked slowly toward us, holding a folder with a stack of pages printed off the computer. She said, "I have categorized all the different types of cancer and many of the causes, but I need to read a number of very important books that could help me understand much more about the disease. Do you think I could use the money I got for Christmas to buy the books?"

"Of course, angel. We can buy them online or drive downtown to the bookstore and see if they have them."

"I think I would rather go down to the bookstore and see if they have them. I like the smell of all the books."

I reached over and took the folder from her. The title of her project was *The Stephen Assignment.* I flipped through the many pages that had numerous notes written in the margins, like one might expect from a professor or researcher.

"Who gave you money for Christmas?" Catherine asked.

"Daddy," she replied in her soft, melodic voice.

"Wow! Your daddy really goes out of the way when it comes to gifts."

"It's what I asked for, Mommy."

Catherine picked her up and sat her between the two of us and asked, "Did you have a good time visiting Rex?"

"Yes, I love Rex. I wish I could take him home with us, but that wouldn't be very nice because penguins are like us. He would miss his family."

"Yes, he would, but we will make a point to go and see him every month or so."

Mia hugged her mother and stayed cuddled up against her. She could never pass for my biological child but, my God, she could easily pass for Catherine's biological child. I came to the last page in the folder and it was a compilation of Shoeless Joe Jackson's career statistics and his World Series numbers. I simply closed the folder and looked down at the title once again, and below the title, her name — Mia ... no last name.

I tickled her stomach and Mia looked across at me and I said, "You know, you are not just *Mia* anymore. You're Mia Baker Ciotola." She took the folder and ran back into her room and a few moments later re-appeared with a revision and her full legal name: *Mia Baker Ciotola.*

She wrapped her arms around me and wouldn't let go as I handed the folder to Catherine. "You are my greatest discovery, and your mom and I could not be any prouder of you."

Catherine, never one to miss out on a good hug, threw her arms around the both of us, and we remained like that … a united, loving family … for an endless amount of time.

***

I tucked Mia into bed as Catherine took a shower. "I see you are still studying up on Shoeless Joe Jackson."

"Yes, I want to write a letter to the Hall of Fame Committee and put down all the reasons why he should be in the Hall of Fame and why the lifetime ban should be lifted. Will you help me?"

"I would love to help you, sweetheart."

"Thank you," she said as she hugged Mr. Rex. I reached down and kissed her on her head and said, "I love you so much."

I walked out of her room, leaving the bedroom door open, and walked toward the staircase, past the numerous bedrooms that were still decorated, with only the IV poles removed, and the lingering laughter and joy of the children forever etched into my brain like a favorite song.

I leaned over the top of the staircase baluster and looked down on all the Christmas decorations that would remain up until the day after New Year's. There had been thousands of petitions signed by fans and ballplayers and sent to the Hall of Fame committee and the commissioner of baseball asking to have the case against the great Shoeless Joe Jackson re-examined and the ban lifted, but to no avail. The man has had neighborhood ballparks named after him, and statutes erected, and after a hundred years he still has the third-highest career batting average in all of major league baseball. Ty Cobb, a known bigot and nasty human being, has the highest average, and he is revered by the baseball hierarchy, and hitting awards named after him are given out to professional ballplayers.

Cobb and Jackson played at the same time. A jury acquitted Jackson, and until this very day there is no concrete evidence that he bet on the World Series, but the wheels of baseball move slowly, and justice and truth do not always prevail. Maybe a letter from a little girl with the last names Baker and Ciotola would work a miracle. After all, *one should never stop dreaming, because when you stop dreaming you stop living.*

I walked back into our bedroom to find Catherine sitting up in bed. I changed my clothes and got into bed beside my wife. I kissed her good night as we both cuddled up under the blankets.

"I have never met a child as special, intelligent or caring as Mia," Catherine remarked.

"Sure you have," I replied.

"I have? Who?"

I turned over in the bed and looked down at my wife.

"You, Catherine Baker. You were as special, intelligent and caring at her age and still are," I replied and put a finger across her mouth before she would try to deny it. "In my former profession, many of my colleagues believed I was a great scout and could spot talent and character a mile away. I don't know if that is true, but for the moment, let me bask in some undeserved glory and please don't argue with me."

I wiped away the tears that were rolling down her lovely face and again kissed her good night.

"I don't ever want her to leave us, Joe."

"What would make you think she might be leaving us?" I asked.

"I mean, like when she goes off to college."

"That's still a long time off."

"I don't know, for all we know it could be in six months."

"I would never allow it to happen, and I would hope you would stand by that decision."

"Of course I would, but would that be selfish on our part?"

"No! You and I know what that child has been through. She needs a loving family and friends around her, not for six more months or six years, but forever. I don't care if I have to build her a lab and hire research assistants. She will always be near you and me and María and your father."

Catherine rubbed my arm. The idea of Mia not being in our lives was something I could not accept, at least not now. Suddenly, Catherine started to laugh, and I asked, "What's so funny?"

"You and me, that's what's so funny … it didn't take us too long to become overprotective parents."

"I like to think of it as loving parents."

"Okay, if you say so, but how are we going to behave when a boy asks her out on a date, and she insists on going?"

"She can go, with the two of us as chaperones."

"Chaperones?"

"Yes, Catherine, chaperones. It's not a novel idea. It's been used as a deterrent for the last thousand years."

She started to laugh uncontrollably as I picked up a pillow and hit her across her stomach. "This is all your fault. You're the one that started me on this train of thought." She continued to laugh … a laugh as infectious and lovely as she was beautiful.

CHAPTER FIFTY-SEVEN

The next morning, Catherine, Mia and I drove downtown to the bookstore. I had given Mia two hundred dollars for Christmas, which she carried in her pocket, along with her cell phone that she was not allowed to leave home without. She had a list of books that one might expect a first-year college student to be buying: *Introduction to Biology*, *Introduction to Medicine*, *Genetics*, *Childhood Cancers*, etc.

She was intent on spending her own money, and after purchasing all her books she was left with a grand total of $2.56. And now it was up to me to figure out a way to put more money into her piggy bank. She was fiercely independent when it came to having her own money.

Back at the mansion, Mr. Baker and I immediately started pulling together all the paperwork necessary to qualify for a homeschooling license to tutor Mia. California law made it relatively easy to offer your child the homeschooling option as an alternative to the traditional classroom setting with other students your age and a certified teacher in charge.

Mr. Baker's lawyer suggested that we establish a private school right in the mansion, which was quite easy to do, and then file a private-school affidavit form. A teaching certificate was not required, and since Mr. Baker and I had both graduated college and were well-respected members of society, all of that went quite smoothly.

Since the only student registered in our private school was Mia, there were very few regulations to follow. As we learned from the application process, we had to do two main things: maintain attendance records showing the days our school was in session and noting the days our student was absent, and prepare a list of the courses of study based on the statutory requirements set forth in the Education Code. That didn't seem so hard.

As we looked over the statutory requirements in the Education Code, we realized that we needed to put together an elementary course of study that included English, mathematics, social science, science, visual and performing arts, health and physical education. That covered grades one through six. Then for grades seven through twelve, we were required to offer Mia courses in English, social sciences, foreign languages, physical education, science and mathematics.

The most difficult choice Mr. Baker and I faced was whether to start Mia at third, sixth, tenth or twelfth grade, or to simply have her take the California High School Proficiency Exam and move right on to college. Of course, that was not an option, and so we decided to experiment and see exactly where we needed to start with each individual subject. Despite my little Leonardo's genius, there was no way she could know everything she should know about American and world history, classic literature and music, science or mathematics ... unless of course, in the short time she was a member of our family, she had memorized the entire internet, which was a frightening possibility.

The deadline for applying for a homeschool license was October 15, and we were already well past that date. We applied for an exception, and with the help of Mr. Baker's lawyer and on Theresa's recommendation and case study, our request was granted. Mia would begin on January 31.

CHAPTER FIFTY-EIGHT

The baseball season is very long. No sooner was the World Series over than it seemed like pitchers and catchers were reporting for spring training in the middle of February. Spring training exhibition games started in early March and lasted for about a month. The regular season began in early April and ended the first few days into October. The playoffs and World Series lasted the entire month of October.

The regular season was 162 games, double the number of games played in basketball and hockey. Seldom, if ever, would your roster remain the same throughout the entire regular season. Injuries and players going into prolonged slumps would often create a carousel of players going back and forth between the majors and the minors, and GMs were always looking into trades to bolster their teams, or if their team wasn't going anywhere, they would often try to unload big-salary players and start rebuilding for the future ... more or less giving up on the current season.

Losing a star pitcher could devastate a team. Losing your number 1 and number 2 starting pitchers could see a team picked to go to the World Series tumble into last place. It is a baseball cliché that pitching is ninety percent of the game, and like most clichés, it was more or less true, although some would argue that number down to seventy-five percent. All I knew was that in all my years in the game, at every level, I never saw a team win a championship without great pitching.

Mr. Baker accompanied Catherine down to their spring-training facility in Scottsdale, Arizona. For Mr. Baker, it was a chance to talk to the coaches, team attendants and some of the ballplayers who had been with the team for many years. He did not intend on going to any of the games during the regular season, and this would most likely be his one chance to converse with all members of the organization. It was, in a sense, his farewell tour. He owned a hundred percent of the team, and so there were no shareholders he was beholden to, and the only board member he had to deal with was Catherine.

If, God forbid, anything should happen to Mr. Baker, Catherine inherited the team as well as the mansion, along with a fortune that I estimated must have been worth hundreds of millions of dollars. Exactly what his other daughter and son and grandchildren were set to inherit, I had no idea. Mr. Baker told me that once the team was sold, he planned on taking as much money as needed from the sale to build a new wing on the hospital. Now that the one grandchild he adored, Mia, was intent on growing up to be a researcher and finding a cure for cancer, he might be building a research facility as well.

Mr. Baker saw Catherine in Mia ... and to a lesser degree, he saw Catherine in Victoria. During the Christmas holidays, Catherine and Mr. Baker, on several occasions, took Victoria aside and met with her behind closed doors in the study. Victoria, who was getting ready to graduate from MIT and begin doctoral work in Stanford's prestigious Science and Technology program, would be the ideal individual to run a research branch of the hospital, especially one dedicated to studying and eradicating cancer. She would have at her disposal funds that she would otherwise have to beg for from the government or pharmaceutical companies, and I'm sure she would receive a very hefty salary. Having all of that, while also being close to her mother and perhaps living at the mansion, getting married and raising a family in that environment, would be like a dream.

I never asked Catherine about the meetings with Victoria, and she never brought them up, but the whole time she was visiting, Victoria and my wife were inseparable. They even went on the behind-the-scenes tour to visit Rex for a second time in less than an hour.

Mr. Baker made it clear to me that he did not want Catherine to waste her life and talents running a baseball team. His intention had always been to sell the team when he stepped down, but he felt obligated to give Catherine one more go at winning a championship that she had convinced herself would mean the world to her father, even though that didn't seem to be the case.

Mr. Baker's love for the game had diminished, and the direction the sport was going in was less and less to his liking. He was a man of integrity and honor, and when steroids and performance-enhancing drugs overwhelmed the game in the '90s and early 2000s, he was the only owner to publicly lay blame on the owners and the commissioner for looking the other way as attendance rocketed and performance records that had held up for decades were smashed into oblivion with the help of drugs. I remembered clearly the courage he showed in the early 2000s when he spoke publicly about the two "great stains" on the game of baseball: segregation and steroids. No one else had spoken out about these twin scourges to the press, and I admired him for it.

***

While Catherine and Mr. Baker were in Arizona, Mia and I took María out for dinner at her favorite Mexican restaurant, La Puerta. One of the many great things about living in Southern California was the Mexican food. It was the best Mexican food I had anywhere in the world, including Mexico. Well in all honesty, María made the best Mexican food I had ever eaten … so good that even the picky, chocolate-addicted Mia loved it. I also had a theory that I would never tell my wife, that María sprinkled all Mia's dishes with chocolate.

Mia got along with everyone, but she had a special bond with María. María, though only forty-five years old and quite beautiful, was like a grandmother to Mia. She was very Catholic and wore a crucifix around her neck, like my mother and like most of the staff at the mansion, but she never preached. She, along with Father Dolan, helped probably more than anyone to gently encourage Mia's acceptance that God was good and that religion could help people rather than hurting them. She taught Mia prayers in Spanish, and whenever Mia prayed, such as at Christmas dinner, she spoke in Spanish.

At the restaurant, we were all handed menus, and with a little help from María, my daughter ordered her own dinner and dessert entirely in Spanish. María had a couple of margaritas with her dinner and she talked about how troubled she was with the way Mexicans and immigrants were being portrayed by the current administration in Washington, DC. She remarked, "Nunca pensé llegar a escuchar que el presidente de los Estados Unidos dijera cosas tan horribles sobre los mexicanos y los inmigrantes."

I replied, "Si, estoy totalmente de acuerdo. Hopefully, the day will come very soon when this disease infesting our politicians will be eradicated. ¡Es vergonzoso!"

"Si, señor Joe."

Mia reached over and grabbed María's hand. I had overheard María telling Mia in the kitchen at the mansion a number of times not to believe what she was hearing on the TV coming out of the mouth of our president about Mexicans and immigrants. Each time it made me cringe, that in this day and age, in our country of all countries, this type of hatred was coming out of the mouths of our leaders. Ignorance is bliss, and if left unchecked it could spread like wildfire. Hopefully, the direction of the wind would change, and the fire would turn on its perpetrators.

CHAPTER FIFTY-NINE

T.S. Eliot famously designated April as "the cruelest month," and Catherine's team seemed to be trying to prove his point. Her team finished the month with five wins and sixteen losses and a solid hold on last place. The two pitching phenoms, for whom she traded her MVP, started a total of six games, never lasting past the third inning, with a combined Earned Run Average of nearly seven runs per nine innings. On the plus side, they were averaging one strikeout per inning.

May was not much better. Still following Mr. Eliot's depressive template, still doing not much more than "breeding lilacs out of the dead land," my poor wife's team went nine and seventeen, and maintained its firm hold on last place. But the two phenoms did make it into the fourth inning twice, and their combined ERAs dropped a bit below seven runs per nine innings, and they were still averaging a strikeout an inning.

No one doubted that the two young pitchers had plenty of talent; their fastballs approached a hundred miles an hour, and their curveballs hovered at around ninety miles an hour. They were quite simply nervous, giving the hitters every opportunity to steal signs and take advantage of their uneasiness. Unless you were Mariano Rivera, who could get hitters out consistently while breaking their bats with literally one pitch — delivering the *cut fastball* that every hitter and fan in the stadium knew was coming — there were very few, if any, pitchers who could go on to have successful careers with only one pitch in their arsenal.

I could see with my own eyes what was happening. The two phenoms were telecasting to the hitters the position and type of pitch they were going to throw before ever letting go of the ball. Their body language was giving them away. With that type of information, major league hitters would take you to the cleaners nine out of ten times. It was like throwing red meat to a hungry tiger. They were going to chew you up and spit you out.

I knew the manager and coaches were quite aware of this, and I also knew that it wasn't something that they could fix overnight. It took time and patience to eradicate 'tells' and other bad habits. Hopefully, with more and more innings under their belts, they would learn to hide the type and location of their pitches, and their performance would improve alongside their confidence.

June arrived, and just as we had during the previous two months, we gathered in the TV room, which was more like a movie theater, with a giant screen and customized leather theater seating, and watched Catherine's team play.

Mr. Baker sat in the very back row, and Catherine, Mia, María and I all sat one row forward. The rest of the staff was scattered all over the theater. Mia sat next to me with her arms intertwined in mine and her head resting against my shoulder. María sat to Mia's right, and Catherine sat to my left. It was the top of the seventh inning and Catherine's team was comfortably ahead 7 to 3. I leaned over and gently massaged my wife's neck. The first two players got on base, and the next batter hit a sharp ground ball deep in the hole. The shortstop grabbed it and flipped it to second for one out, but the batter beat the throw to first, avoiding a double play. The next batter stepped up to the plate, and on the first pitch, sent a ball deep over the right-field wall for a three-run homer. Mia's grip around my arms tightened and Catherine's whole body seemed to go stiff.

The starting pitcher was removed, and their overworked bullpen ace was brought in to stop the bleeding. The first two men he faced got on with walks, and the third batter hit a wicked line drive between the center fielder and right fielder that went all the way to the wall. The two men on base scored easily and the batter ended up on third base, and suddenly Catherine's team was losing 8 to 7, and just as suddenly, Catherine jumped up from her seat and screamed at me, "Any new ideas, genius? Please, just please bestow some of your wisdom on me. Surely, the great one can figure out this mess of a team he helped to assemble?" She violently kicked the seat in front of her and continued, "What, nothing from the great one? Not one bit of wisdom?"

Mr. Baker stood up, and in a tone as harsh as a drill sergeant, he yelled at his daughter, "Catherine! Catherine, get your ass the hell out of this room. Now! Now!"

Catherine bowed her head, and like a frightened, hurt child, she walked out of the room. Mr. Baker remarked, "I apologize for my daughter's behavior. It will not be happening again." He sat back down. No one moved, and we all went back to watching the game, which Catherine's team eventually lost 11 to 9.

Mr. Baker left the TV room just after the last out was made, and a few minutes later, I walked out with Mia and María. María took Mia into the kitchen where she had a late-night snack waiting for her. I walked up to the bedroom where I found my wife in bed, under the blankets, tightly grasping a pillow and crying. I could not help thinking at that moment of a quote from a movie with Tom Hanks, the manager of an all-American professional female baseball team, telling a crying player on the team, "There's no crying in baseball."

Of course, there was plenty of crying in baseball, and ninety-nine percent of it was done by male players, but when success was linked to the irrational goal of winning a championship for your father, failure was especially difficult. At no moment during or after my wife's blow-up did I feel angry with her. In fact, I suspected it would happen, but what made me especially sad was that I knew that my wife was one of the kindest and most caring and loving individuals I had ever known, and to see her hurting so much made me extremely upset.

After standing next to the bed for a moment, I sat down beside her, gently brushed her hair away from her face and simply said, "Hey."

"Hey," she replied as she tried desperately to hold the tears back. "I'm sorry."

"It's okay. If you think a little outburst is going to send me packing, well then, you're crazy. I love you so much, Catherine." I kissed her on her forehead and repeated, "I love you so much."

"And I love you so much," she replied. "There won't be any more outbursts, I promise. I'm finished."

"You're quitting," I remarked with disbelief.

"No, but I'm certain that by tomorrow I will be fired. My father made it perfectly clear from the beginning that if I ever blamed anyone besides myself for the team doing poorly, that I would be gone."

"And so that's it? You're just giving up without even a little fight? I think that would hurt your father even more. I know he's a man of his word, but I also know he can be quite forgiving if you give him a good enough reason to give you a second chance. He's downstairs in his study right now. I think it would be the perfect time to make a strong case for why he shouldn't fire you."

I watched as my beautiful wife put on her robe, washed her face, put on her slippers and walked out of the bedroom and down to the study to talk to her father. I pulled off my shoes and lay down on the bed. I waited for about an hour before falling asleep. When I awoke it was three in the morning, the lights were out and there was no wife sleeping beside me. I turned on a light and picked up a note she'd left for me on her pillow. "Hey, there. My father forgave me, and I still have my job. I'm in Mia's room if you want to come and visit. Love you more than anything, and thank you for forgiving me and for your advice about my daddy."

I got up off the bed and walked out of the bedroom and stopped at Mia's room. The door was open and my extra-special wife was asleep on the bed hugging our extra-special sleeping daughter.

CHAPTER SIXTY

The St. Louis Cardinals came to town on June 5 for a four-game series. They were in first place, with a hefty lead in their division, and the reigning MVP was having another MVP year. The local sports shows were all over the one-sided trade and making fun of the lady GM of the team that gave away the MVP for two overrated prospects. As fate would have it, the two overrated pitchers would be pitching the first two games of the series.

That night, we all gathered in the TV room to watch the game. Mr. Baker sat in the last row, and Catherine, Mia, María and I sat directly below him, and the rest of the staff was scattered all over.

The first overrated pitcher took the mound, and immediately I could see a change in his demeanor before he even threw a pitch. He looked like the kid I had first noticed in the minor leagues and wished back then that he was in my organization. The first three Cardinal hitters struck out on a total of eleven pitches. In the bottom of the first, Catherine's team put up four runs on a grand-slam home run by the center fielder who she traded for and who was only supposed to be able to hit lefties. That night, his first grand slam of his career came off a righty, and Mia stood up and started clapping, and then so did I and everyone else in the room. Baseball people are very superstitious, but when an adorable ten-year-old child wearing her mother's team cap starts clapping, everyone follows her lead.

In the top of the second, the reigning MVP stepped up to the plate to a standing ovation from the crowd in appreciation for what he had done for his former team. On three straight ninety-mile-an-hour wicked curveballs, he went down on strikes; the first of his three strikeouts of the night. The overrated pitcher threw a two-hit, fourteen-strikeout complete game, and Catherine's team won 11 to 0. Mia clapped and clapped, and we all followed suit.

The very next night, the second overrated pitcher took the mound and struck out sixteen, pitching a three-hit complete game shutout, and Catherine's team won 7 to 0. Missing from the starting line-up for the Cardinals was the reigning MVP, and he was not even on the bench.

The day after that, we all found out why the MVP was MIA. The league office suspended him for sixty days for failing his second drug test of the young season. Ballplayers could come up with all the excuses in the world for using steroids and performance-enhancing drugs, but from me they got no sympathy. They were cheaters, plain and simple.

Catherine asked me how I was so sure that he was using steroids, and I simply told her to ask her daddy.

Catherine's team swept the four-game series against the Cardinals and so began what I used to call the slow crawl into first place. By the All-Star game, the second Tuesday in July, they were only five games out of first place. By late August, they were running away with the division. By mid-September, they were the first team to clinch a playoff spot. By the end of the regular season, the two overrated pitchers were being called the Koufax and Drysdale of their generation … finishing the last four months of the regular season with a combined twenty-five and two record, ERAs below two runs a game, and each with over two hundred strikeouts.

Time and patience! Time and patience! The baseball season is very long, giving teams a chance to bounce back and other teams a chance to take a dive.

CHAPTER SIXTY-ONE

Catherine's team finished with the best record in the National League, which gave them home-field advantage throughout the playoffs. The Yankees had the best record in the American League and if they made it to the World Series, they would also have home-field advantage.

Catherine's team had a bye in the first round of the playoffs. It gave her team a couple of extra days to rest, which was a good thing.

Their first playoff series was the best of five against the team that was picked at the beginning of the year to win the National League title and make it to the World Series, the St. Louis Cardinals. The experts were expecting a tough series, with St. Louis winning in five. Once again, they were wrong, and Catherine's team swept the Cardinals. The two phenoms and their third starter gave up a total of four runs, striking out an astonishing forty-five batters ... the most in a series that went only three games. Catherine's team scored twenty-eight runs against a team that many believed had the best pitching staff in the National League. The reigning MVP limped through the series going one for ten, his only hit a broken bat single that went barely over the outstretched glove of the second baseman.

The Yankees took care of business just as quickly in their playoff series.

Catherine's team faced the Atlanta Braves in the next series, a best-of-seven series in which the winner went on to the World Series. The experts gave the edge to the Braves, picking them to eliminate Catherine's team in six. Instead, Catherine's team eliminated them in four straight games. The two phenoms and the number 3 and 4 pitchers gave up a total of ten runs, striking out a record fifty-three batters and scoring a respectable twenty-two runs.

In the other league, the Yankees took six games to win their series and go to the World Series for something like the forty-fifth time. The Yankees had the best hitting and the best bullpen in all of baseball and a very good starting rotation. The Vegas odds on the series were two to one in favor of the Yankees. In short, if you picked the Yankees, you had to put up a thousand dollars to win five hundred. If you bet on Catherine's team, you had to put up five hundred to win a thousand.

The first game was at the new Yankee Stadium with nearly sixty thousand fans screaming and yelling. It was, in my opinion, the most intimidating place to play a game in the World Series. The day before the first game, my wife asked me, "And so who are you rooting for?"

"I only root for one team and that's your team. Just for the record, what would you have done if I said I was rooting for my favorite childhood team, the Yankees?"

"I would have kicked your ass right out the front door," she replied with a laugh.

We watched the World Series in the same TV room we watched all the games throughout the year. Phenom number 1 pitched the first game, and he didn't make it out of the fourth inning. It was his worse start in over four months. The Yankees won convincingly 8 to 1.

Phenom number 2, referred to as Drysdale, started the second game, and if the rowdy crowd of sixty thousand expected a repeat of game one, they were greatly disappointed. In one of the most dominant performances I have ever witnessed in a World Series game, Drysdale pitched a complete game shutout, allowing two hits and striking out sixteen. Catherine's team won 4 to 0.

The series turned to San Diego, and games 3 and 4 were hard-fought matches, which were won by Catherine's team. The number 3 and 4 pitchers from last year's team pitched just well enough to win … their performances were nothing short of gritty. They kept the games close, and with some clutch hitting, they were able to pull out the games and give their team a commanding lead.

Phenom number 1, who was now being referred to by his nickname, Koufax, started Game 5. He took the mound, and before he threw his first pitch, I knew I was looking at a very special moment. In a performance reminiscent of the real Sandy Koufax pitching Game 4 of the 1963 World Series against the mighty Yankees, phenom number 1 struck out nineteen Yankees, allowing one hit and no runs, and Mr. Baker's team won 7 to 0. Mr. Baker's team won the World Series, and Mia clapped and clapped and jumped around joyously as I walked over to Mr. Baker and shook his hand and exclaimed, "Congratulations!"

He replied with tears in his eyes, "Thank you, Joseph. Thank you for loving my daughter so much. Thank you."

Catherine left for the ballpark after the seventh inning. Mr. Baker thought it was important to have a family member present when the last pitch was thrown and the team was crowned World Champions. Mr. Baker had a stretch limo waiting outside, and he and the staff crowded in, along with Mia, to head to the ballpark.

I went back into the TV room alone and watched the celebration. A few minutes later I heard the door to the room open. Mia ran toward me and hugged me.

"Why didn't you go to the park? It would have been a lot of fun."

"No, I told Mr. Baker that I needed to be with my daddy, and he said he totally understood." Tears rolled down my face as we tightly hugged each other. We watched as Catherine and Mr. Baker were handed the championship trophy, and they held the trophy up high and said, "This belongs to the city of San Diego. Thank you."

"Mommy looks so pretty and happy. I am so proud of her," I remarked as Mia looked up at me and replied, "I am so proud of you, Daddy. I love you more than anything in this world. I know your mommy and daddy are so proud of you." I leaned over and kissed my lovely daughter on the head as tears rolled down my face and onto the head of the greatest prospect I ever discovered. In the background, Queen's classic, "We Are the Champions" kept the mood of excitement humming along.

After looking at the celebration for another hour, I turned on the movie, *A Field of Dreams*. Mia and I watched it together, and whereas I might not live to see Shoeless Joe Jackson inducted into the Hall of Fame, it warmed my heart to think that Mia just might. And whereas, I would never play catch with my mommy and daddy again, I could still play catch with my daughter and my wife.

CHAPTER SIXTY-TWO

The celebration went on for days, culminating in a parade to City Hall where the players, coaches, managers, Catherine and Mr. Baker made speeches.

A couple of days later, while I was in our bedroom, Catherine came in and closed the door. She looked at me and said, "My daddy and I have decided to sell the team, but before we finalize any deal, we think you deserve a chance at running the team as the GM if you want. In that case, we will keep the team."

"That is very generous of both of you, sweetheart, but my baseball days are over. Sell the team and build that wing on the hospital. That would make me very happy."

"I have decided to take a job with the Red Cross down here in San Diego where I think I can really make a difference."

"I think that is wonderful. You wouldn't happen to know of any other jobs with the Red Cross that might be open for a former GM and dumb-ass jock, would you?"

"Actually, I do, if you don't mind working for a lady."

"No, especially if the lady is married to an out-of-work former GM."

"That's exactly who it is," she replied as she threw her arms around me and we kissed. "Thank you, Joe, for everything. Thank you, thank you."

"Thank you for making me the happiest husband in the world and for being a wonderful mom to Mia."

"Oh, and the best news of all is that Mia will be working part time with us. She's such a natural."

"And how much will our lovely little Leonardo be making?"

"The same as if she had her own paper route — about four dollars and fifty cents an hour."

"Sounds fair," I replied with a laugh.

"And do I have a title?"

"Of course — assistant to me."

"And Mia?"

"President. Surely, you didn't expect a lesser title for such a valuable member of the team."

"Surely not," I said as I walked down to Mr. Baker's study with Catherine. Mr. Baker sat at his desk, and Catherine and I took a seat across from him.

"My guess is that you did not accept the job as GM?" Mr. Baker asked.

"No I did not," I said, "but I do appreciate the offer. At the moment I have another important job to do, and so do you. Homeschooling your granddaughter."

"Yes and isn't it a wonderful job?"

"The best I have ever had. I never would have guessed that I could learn so much from an eleven-year-old. They certainly do mature early these days, but then you already knew that."

I looked across at Catherine and Mr. Baker said, "Yes, I have been blessed a million times over."

"And he's taking a second job, Daddy — assistant to me at the Red Cross."

"Be careful, Joe. I heard she can be a really tough, hard-driving, goal-oriented boss."

"I wouldn't expect anything less."

Mr. Baker laughed as he reached over and handed me a piece of paper. I looked down at it and had to look twice. It was a check made out to me for ten million dollars. "That's for helping us achieve a long-sought-after goal for the city and our fans."

"I don't think so. I have plenty of money and in case I run into trouble I have a wife who has more money than I could ever dream of.

Why don't you take that check and put it as a down payment for the research center you plan on building."

"And how do you know about that?"

"Just an educated guess. Your granddaughter wants to find a cure for cancer and naturally she is going to need an all-purpose lab with a talented staff, possibly including someone with credentials like Victoria, and a director of operations who can achieve the impossible, like your daughter."

Mr. Baker smiled as I reached over and held my beautiful wife's hand.

CHAPTER SIXTY-THREE

I still had some unfinished business before I started my new career. I asked Mia if she would like to accompany me to New York, and naturally she couldn't resist. Catherine was sad that we were going, but she understood, as did Mr. Baker.

We left from San Diego Airport at seven in the morning and arrived at LaGuardia airport at two in the afternoon. It was cold in New York and I bundled Mia up in a winter coat and gloves. I rented a car and drove over the Whitestone Bridge and into the Bronx. I drove down Lafayette Avenue and turned into the entrance of Saint Raymond's Cemetery. I stopped before every one of my relatives' graves and told Mia a little story about each … about my Uncle Tony, Aunt Rena, Aunt Carmela, Uncle Al, Aunt Catherine, Uncle Nick, Aunt Louise, Uncle Sonny, Aunt Jeanette, Aunt Philomena, Aunt Rosie, Aunt Mary, Uncle Carlo, Uncle Joey and my grandmother and grandfather.

Finally, we stopped and got out at section eighty-seven, where my mom and dad were buried. We stopped at their grave and I looked down at the headstone with an engraved picture of Saint Joseph holding the baby Jesus, and my parents' names directly below it. I reached over and kissed Saint Joseph and baby Jesus. St. Joe was my mother's favorite saint, and I was named after him.

"Mom, Dad, I want you to meet Mia, your granddaughter. I know you already know about her. I could hear both your voices in my head the whole time. I can only hope you forgive me for not being there for both of you when you so desperately needed me, but please never doubt that I have always loved the both of you more than my own life.

I am trying to make good for all the bad I have done. I am truly trying my hardest. I love the both of you so much." I kissed the headstone once again and bowed my head and said a prayer. Mia kissed the headstone and ran back to the car.

I walked back to the car, opened the door and got into the driver's seat. I looked at Mia, who was crying, and I said, "Please, don't cry sweetheart. My mommy used to get so upset when she used to see me crying when I was your age."

I drove out of the cemetery and parked in the driveway of my parents' home, my home. We walked into the house and it looked so much smaller than I remembered. It had been nearly five years since I had been in the house. I had a maid service come in every two weeks to clean. My mom loved a clean house.

Mia looked at all the pictures on the walls. My mother was so lovely that my father would often joke that his marrying a woman as beautiful as my mom was the most convincing proof that miracles do happen. My mother laughingly agreed.

I gave Mia a tour of the house, and as I entered my room, I could actually visualize my mother sitting beside me on the bed and kissing me good night while tucking me in. All my trophies and awards from my days of playing little league were still on the same shelves my mom originally put them on. My record albums were still there, nearly half of them Beatles LPs, next to an old-style turntable and big speakers.

That night we walked to Leonard's Bakery and I bought Mia a dozen cannoli — large, creamy, full of chocolate chips. I bought myself a couple of slices of pizza and some beer and Mia a quart of chocolate milk. We sat on the couch in my parents' living room and I took out family albums. Mia was fascinated by my mother — from the time she was a little girl wearing a Catholic-school uniform, through high school, her wedding and after I was born. My mother was mesmerizing, but exactly what Mia saw in her I wasn't sure. Back at the hotel in San Diego, when she first saw pictures of my mother on her wedding day, so happy, surrounded by religious symbols, it seemed to have a great, life-altering effect on Mia's understanding of religion. Those pictures by themselves seemed to show Mia that all religion was not like the extreme, cult-like version practiced in the town of Salvation. It also helped that everybody she knew — Catherine, María, Mr. Baker, Father Dolan, Theresa and I — were religious but also kind, caring and loving.

In the morning, we went for our run at Maritime College, originally called Fort Schuyler, along the East River and under the Throgs Neck Bridge. We visited the maritime museum and walked through the stone fortresses built during the War of 1812. It was a beautiful campus, and Mia was quite impressed. We then walked to Patty's on the Bay and ate breakfast.

Back at the house, I walked into the kitchen. I avoided looking down at the floor where they had found my mom, and instead looked at all the notes posted on the refrigerator, reminding my parents of birthdays, doctor appointments and the day I would be coming home to visit ... always with a happy face beside the date. I looked out the kitchen window at the backyard. I could see my mom and dad playing catch with me. My mother had an arm like Nolan Ryan. I could see a collage of my life, with the screams and cheers from the many ballparks and playgrounds I visited muted out, and instead, the consoling, encouraging and loving voice of my mom narrating throughout ... from the bedside chats to the reassuring promise that tomorrow I would play better, that even the great DiMaggio had hitless games ... to the signing of my first big league contract ... to the winning of World Series titles ... to her voice in my head telling me to rescue the little girl from that terrible town ... to opening the front door and looking into the face of Theresa and knowing, right then and there, that the dirty little girl was forever my responsibility, Catherine's responsibility and the path to a brighter and more perfect future.

I took out two baseball gloves and a ball that I brought along with me. I handed Mia her glove and we walked out into the backyard. It was cold, but I was fairly certain that neither of us felt so much as a chill. I tossed the ball to Mia and she tossed it back and we played catch until after dark. From the kitchen window, I could feel my mother and father smiling as they looked at their son playing catch with their lovely granddaughter.

That night Mia took out the family albums I had put away in my parents' bedroom closet and looked at the pictures for hours. "You can take them back with you to San Diego, if you like. I think my mom would love for you to have them." Mia smiled and replied, "Thank you so much. I would love that." She looked up at me as though she was about to ask a question, which was always a distinct possibility, or to enlighten me on a subject or a phenomenon that was right in front of me nearly every day of my life but I had not taken the time or possessed the curiosity to ask about ... like why is the sky blue?

She shyly lowered her head and continued to look at the pictures and then in a barely audible voice asked, "Are you going to sell this house?"

"No! Why would I do that? Where would my parents live? They love this house."

She looked at me, with a glimmer of a smile, and once again lowered her head. I sat down beside her and turned to a page in the album with a picture of the happy couple moving into the house. "You have to promise me, Mia, that you will never sell this house, never let anyone talk you into selling this house. It's their house, and it will always be my home."

"Yes, Daddy, I promise," she replied as tears from her eyes fell onto the page. But before she could wipe them away, I turned the page.

CHAPTER SIXTY-FOUR

We arrived back in San Diego a few days later and my wife and María picked us up at the airport. They were excited to see us, as we were to see them. That night I went to bed early. I was exhausted. I closed my eyes and suddenly I was walking up to the plate and looking across at Sandy Koufax on the mound. I looked toward the first-base seats and noticed my mom and dad, María and Mia, Catherine and Mr. Baker, and Stephen and his mother on their feet clapping.

I stepped into the batter's box and the great Sandy Koufax went into his classic windup and released the ball, and for a moment I closed my eyes, and as I swung, to my surprise, I hit the ball really hard, and as I opened my eyes, I watched the ball land in the left-field stands. I started to run around the bases as I looked at my fan club sitting along the first-base line clapping and screaming. I touched third base and as I was heading home, I quickly glanced back at the first-base side, and the only ones still there were Mia, Catherine, Mr. Baker and María. I touched home plate and paused as I looked up at the dark-blue sky and whispered a little prayer.

I suddenly woke up and looked across at my lovely sleeping wife, and in the next room I could hear Mia getting ready to go for our run, and from downstairs I could smell María's homemade Mexican bread baking in the oven.

I changed into my running gear and went into Mia's room where she and Rex were reading articles on her computer. I reached down and retied her sneakers and zipped up her hoodie. I then took her hand and we walked down the stairs. We opened the front door and went for our run, a little farther than the day before.

ACKNOWLEDGEMENTS

To the great people at Iguana books, especially my editor Lee Parpart, who makes everything I write so much better.

To my lovely wife, Melissa, my mother-in-law, Lou, and my father and mother, who I have made crazy for far too many years rooting for my favorite sport teams.

CPSIA information can be obtained
at www.ICGtesting.com
Printed in the USA
LVHW041256310520
656997LV00002B/67